JOY

A NOVEL OF THE NEW FRONTIER

JOY

By B.R.M. Evett

Sleeping Dog Press

BOSTON

FIRST EDITION

ISBN 979-8-9883407-0-6

Library of Congress Cataloging-in-Publishing has been applied for.

Cover Design by Kerry Ellis

To Kelli, my one true Joy

Arma virumque cano Troiae qui primus ab oris
Italiam **fato profugus** Lavinaque venit
litora multum ille et terris iactatus et alto
vi superorum memorem Iunonis ob iram;
multa quoque et **bello passus...**

Of Arms, I sing, and Man who first from the
Shores of Troy came to Italy and the Lavinian coast,
Driven by fate, tossed wildly on the lands and seas
By the force of the gods, because of Juno's wrath;
Much, too, **he endured in war...**

— Vergil's *Aeneid*, Book One

Prologue

Virgo

J OY.

JOY.

JOY.

JOY.

JOY.

OBLIVION.

Part One

FATO PROFUGUS

Chapter 1

Tender

Tender reboots and exits his bay. Even down here, he can hear the howling of the wind, rising all day as the storm approaches. Not good. So much to do today. He puts on his white coat, replaces his handskin with a fresh antimicrobial layer, and enters the Balneum. His guests lie before him in their baths, five to a side.

He raises the first lid on the left. "Virgo," he says, "are you ready, my girl? It's your big day." She doesn't answer. Can't answer. Her eyes closed, her face rising just above the pale seagreen jelly of her bath medium, her brows knit in that peculiar way she has.

When Tender first saw it, the expression concerned him. He searched for some imbalance, something wrong, but at last concluded that it was just a quirk of her personality. The unique way she expressed her Joy.

Mainframe informs Tender that the procedure will commence in six thousand seconds. "I must tend to the others," he tells the motionless girl. "Then, it's all about you."

He chooses the *Beethoven Sonata Number 8 in C Minor*, the "Pathétique", and plays it in his internal system. It can't be said that the rolling run of the first movement energizes him, or that he enjoys the gentle reverie of the second movement. He does not feel these things. But he recognizes the complexity of their construction, and finds the sophisticated manipulation of tone and rhythm instructive, a layered lesson in human expression. The stately opening chords sound within him, and he attends to his guests.

Tender begins, as always, on the male side, with little Puer, pausing for a moment to consider the Latin appellations used throughout the complex: Puer meaning 'boy', Virgo 'maiden', and so on. All the names at the Elysium Spa are Roman, classical terms chosen by the Founders to express all that is most excellent and noble. The finest. The happiest. He nods his approval.

Raising the bath lid, he places his right hand on Puer's forehead and performs a scan. "8.65 out of 10. Very good. But we can do better, can't we?" He inputs a new algorithm to balance the parameters: Serotonin, Oxytocin, Adrenaline, Dopamine, Gamma-Aminobutyric Acid, Endocannabinoids, Endorphins. Switching to his left hand he performs the EEG. Detecting a slight instability in the waveform, he amplifies the sonic pulse generator to bolster the alpha pattern.

The boy moans softly as the new mixture floods his brain. His lips part in a wide smile, revealing the gap in front, and the saw-like ridge of adult teeth poking through the gums. Tender imitates the smile. Then he reaches in and gently wiggles another tooth. "Yes, little one, that one will be coming out soon."

He moves down the line. The males don't require much from him right now, each half-way through the current cycle. The solid midpoint, where the balance is easy to maintain. Not for long. In a few years, Puer will begin his growth spurt, and Vir will require testosterone regulation to maintain robustness. But for now, they all coast smoothly along.

The females are all entering a new life stage, so there is more to do on this side. Mulier, for example, has just entered menopause, and her levels of estrogen and progesterone swing wildly, often unpredictably. For the others, the physical symptoms of the menstrual cycle can be almost totally suppressed, but the subtle changes in hormone levels throughout the month necessitate vigilance, anticipation and improvisation.

Especially for Virgo. At fifteen, she is a perfect storm of physiochemical intensity. She began puberty at eleven, so he has had time to learn the peculiarities of her system, but the hormones continue to rage. Still, Tender knows her intimately. Knows them all. He calibrates every parameter to the nanogram to maintain them in Joy unceasing. The music rises to a triumphant crescendo as he works, sounding its final, joyous chords as he makes the last adjustments.

There are still 267 seconds left in the countdown when Tender completes his morning circuit, and all ten of his guests thrum with pure, timeless ecstasy. He comes across a reference in his data files to *a pat on the back*, so he gives himself one.

"I'll get everything ready upstairs," he tells Virgo, and heads for the elevator. On the way, he passes the Tender from Guest Group 5 pushing an empty gurney in the opposite direction. He recognizes the face, because it is his own.

Even from a short distance you would mistake Tender for a human at the midpoint of the 'Vir' cycle, aged fifty-two or fifty-three years. He has not been depilated like the guests, of course — his hair is short and straight, dark with silver at the temples. The eyebrows dark, too. The nose straight. The lips full. The eyes grey with flecks of orange and brown. The skin whelite pale. The overall impression kind and serious, strong but gentle.

Get closer, however, and the illusion of humanity quickly falls away. The skin is too smooth, less elastic than human skin; the servomotors less expressive than the muscles under a human face. And the eyes, up close — they are not human eyes. And he does not breathe.

"Good afternoon," says Tender to his twin.

"Good afternoon," says Number 5. "A hurricane. What next, eh?"

"What indeed. You've just officiated an Apotheosis?"

"Yes. My Senex rose to glory."

"I rejoice in his Joy."

"Thank you."

And they pass on.

The roar of the storm rises as he exits the elevator into the wide lobby. The weather satellite has been offline for three years, but mainframe still tracks wind speed and barometric pressure and estimates at least a Category Six hurricane making landfall in the vicinity. Violent weather events have become commonplace, especially in the spring, but Tender cannot recall anything of this intensity hitting the coast so far north.

He heads down a long glass-covered hallway that branches off the main Spa building. The green lawn glimmers dully in the gray light. The towers of old Boston hunker to the east, nothing but dim shadows. Rain slams against the glass, traveling almost horizontally. He turns again and enters the Gynaeceum, the 'women's chamber', a low, flat building, sturdily constructed of concrete and steel.

The Incubator sits on a long table against the wall. "Good morning," it says as he enters.

"Good morning. How are you today?"

"All systems are functioning," says the Incubator. "I expect you will be pleased with the results."

"Let's have a look. We must hurry."

He opens the Incubator and removes a small glass dish containing eggs harvested from Virgo, fertilized with sperm from Adulescens. The sperm were processed to remove all Y-bearing zygotes, so the dish contains only female embryos. They have been growing for seventy-two hours.

Tender places the dish under the scanner, plugs himself into the machine and studies the specimens. He identifies six high grade blastomeres, each a symmetrical ball of cells, perfect, showing no signs of fragmentation. "*You must have been a beautiful baby...*" he sings to himself. He segregates them from the others, zooms in on them, and culls the candidates down to one. This he transfers to the implantation device.

The sound of breaking glass echoes from the hall. He picks up his pace, collects a gurney and returns to the lower level, passing two Custodians working in the corridor, their white plastic bodies shining dully in the dim light. Water pours through a leak in the ceiling, and the robots are suctioning up a growing pool on the floor. One of the Custodians elongates his torso so he can reach the aging tiles above and begins removing them one by one.

"That's a new one," says Tender. The robots ignore him.

Tender enters the bath chamber and puts Virgo into sleep. Working quickly, but not rushing, he confirms that her vital signs are stable, detaches her from the bath, lifts her in his arms, and places her on the gurney. He covers her in a clean white sheet and wheels her down the hall, past the impassive Custodians, to the elevator.

As the door opens to the upper level, the sound of the wind leaps at him. It whines and roars, punctuated by bangs and clanks as pieces of debris fly into the sides of the building. Through the glass, he watches an old stop sign go bouncing across the circular driveway of the Spa. It disappears from view, but he hears it slam into the front doors of the complex, locked now for decades.

As Tender enters the Gynaeceum, the lights flicker. Not a good sign. He considers canceling the procedure and returning to his guests below. But the timetable is a strict one, and he puts the idea aside. He will get back to them soon. He plays the *Presto* from the "Summer" section of Vivaldi's *Four Seasons*, as if its driving intensity could push him to work faster. He does not want to lose power in the middle of the operation. Above all things, he must ensure that the cycle continues.

He lays Virgo on the table, and places her feet in the stirrups. Plugging himself into the implantation device so that he can see through its camera eye, he guides the tip of the implanter to the optimal site, then releases a series of compounds which prepare the uterine wall to receive the hatching zygote. The implanter attaches the zygote to the wall, securing it with artificial decidual cells so it does not accidentally detach or get flushed away.

Without warning, a terrific crash reverberates outside the chamber, followed by an agonized moan of bending, breaking metal. Fortunately for Virgo, Tender has no startle reflex, and he smoothly completes his work, putting the final touches on the microscopic mound of tissue that will bond the zygote to the mother. As he withdraws the implantation device from Virgo's body, a deep, rushing roar rumbles beneath him. The lights flicker again.

Tender lifts Virgo from the operating table onto the gurney, covers her in a fresh white sheet, and pushes her out of the chamber. Ordinarily he would restore the room to its ready state, but he has no time. He must get back to his guests.

He queries mainframe to update the biodata from the baths. No response. He tries again. Nothing. After 2048 attempts to log in, he gives up. He wheels Virgo down the hall to the elevator. The lights go out.

Mainframe can't go offline. It's unthinkable. It has redundancies built on redundancies. Yet here he is, cut off. For the first time ever, Tender has no connection to his guests in the Balneum below. There is a hole in the system where his people ought to be.

No response when he summons the elevator. The power must be out throughout the building. Nothing works. The stairs. He'll have to use the stairs. He has never used the stairs.

He thinks, *What am I to do with Virgo?* He can't carry her down below. The risk of injury is unacceptable. He must find a safe place to leave her on the upper level. He looks around. The hallway has too many windows. Not here.

He decides to head back to the Gynaeceum. Sturdy and low, it can withstand the rising fury of the storm. He wheels Virgo back along the glassed-in hallway. The sky lowers, a deep gray brown, dirty and full of threat. Up ahead, Tender can make out a broken window, the rain pelting in. Without warning, metal squeals above them, as with a traumatic wrench a section of the roof comes tearing off, glass flying, the chrome rail twisting into a fantastical helix. The wall collapses into rubble, blocking their path.

Rain flies every which way, striking Tender with tiny missiles. He has no pain sensors, but registers the impacts. He covers Virgo's face with the sheet, turns and wheels her swiftly back toward the elevator.

So, not the Gynaeceum. *Where then?* There are many other rooms on this level — offices for massages, manicures, skin treatments. All empty for years. He looks into one and sees the window smashed and raindrops pounding the tiles. *That won't do.*

He heads for the Laconicum, the 'Spartan chamber', where the guests are sent to their Apotheosis. It is the newest part of the Spa, built when the Protocols were first introduced and the chosen guests enrolled in the Cycle of Joy. It rises above him through the gloom, its sleek, chrome walls supporting a massive dome of glass.

The door won't open. It should respond automatically to his approach, but without power, it is just another wall. Tender lays his hands against the door's edge. He flattens his fingertips to five millimeters and slides them into the narrow crack, searching for the latch. He charges his hands, sends a jolt into the lock. Something clicks on the inside, and he forces the panel open.

In the middle of the broad tiled floor rises an imposing dais of black marble, shrouded in darkness. He rolls the gurney up beside it. The vapor shield over the hole in the roof no longer functions, and raindrops slap onto the smooth marble slab where the guests are sent to glory. Narrow slits line the surface, and Tender can make out traces of gray ash dotted here and there. "Tender Number 5 was careless," he says to himself. "But no doubt he was in a hurry, too."

A small metal door on the side of the platform, 0.88 meters square, allows access to the interior, where the ashes of the ascended fall through the slits in the top to collect in the hollow space beneath. Tender checks that the slits are securely closed and the interior water-tight, then lifts the latch on the small metal door. His nasal sensors detect a faint change in the atmosphere, as tiny particles of ancient dust waft into the air.

He wraps the sheet snugly around Virgo's inert body, lifts her off the gurney, then shuffling sideways, stooping low, works his way through the door into the belly of the dais. The soft ashes make a thick carpet on the floor, and though he is careful, puffs and clouds of dust swirl around them.

Once he is all the way in, Tender lays Virgo on the bed of ash. She sinks into it, as into her bath. He checks her pulse and respiration. The anesthesia will keep her under for several hours. He climbs out and closes the door, sealing her inside. She will be safe there, protected by thirty-one centimeters of marble and steel.

He leaves the Laconicum and heads for the stairs to the lower level. In all the long years, he has never used them. The Spa has run smoothly without human oversight for over seven decades, the Tenders caring for their guests, the Custodians maintaining the structures and systems. He remembers several loud and violent storms, even snow on occasion, but nothing like this. He tries to connect to mainframe again. Nothing.

As he opens the door to the stairwell, a dull rushing sound rises from below. Tender activates the examination lights in his eyes — tight, cool beams. He descends. The rushing intensifies.

Water. The bottom of the staircase lies submerged beneath a meter of water, perhaps more. It reaches up beyond the doorknob. The torrent has forced the door open, and Tender can see through it into the dim hallway where the Balnea are. A cascade pours from the ceiling upon the Custodians, standing frozen, the cataract drenching their upraised arms. With mainframe offline, they are nothing but statues.

Tender hesitates at the edge of the black pool. His body is not designed for swimming or deep wading. Who knows how it will damage his components. But he has a responsibility to his guests. He shuts down any non-essential systems and steps into the water. It rises to his chest as he thrusts forward down the darkened hall.

He has returned too late. The guests, attached at the spine to their baths, lie below the surface, the refractive index making their features appear larger, the water deeper. He pushes his way to Femina. Her eyes are closed, her face peaceful. She looks as she always looks, enraptured in the glory of Joy, but even the most cursory examination reveals that she is drowned. He thinks suddenly, *There is a willow grows aslant the brook,* but doesn't recognize the reference. Moving on, he evaluates the others. All dead, all peaceful, except Vir, whose eyes bug open, staring at nothing. Tender closes the eyelids.

He considers what to do next. He could drag them, one by one, up to the Laconicum. But with no power, there can be no Apotheosis.

Virgo. She lives, and he must care for her. He can't leave her by herself much longer. She must not awaken there, alone in the dark.

He detects a sharp buzz in his hip — the water compromising his machinery. Time to go. He will re-evaluate in the morning when the storm has passed. Before he leaves, he grabs several bags of hydration formula, nutriment, and lethe. He wades out into the hallway.

On his way to the stair he looks into another Balneum. Tender Number 5 floats face down between the baths, his white coat ballooning up around him.

Back up at ground level, the hurricane has been busy, demolishing the glass-enclosed hallway, turning it into a breezeway, the ground littered with shards of broken glass and bits of twisted metal. Tender works his way toward the Laconicum, fighting for balance in the swirling wind.

As he enters the cavernous chamber, a weird, whining hum cuts the air. The spines of chromed steel that hold the enormous plate glass sections of the dome are singing. They bend under the force of the gale. He scrambles to reach the dais. But he was not designed to run, and the best he can manage is a rapid walk. The singing rises to a fevered scream.

A violent crack, a cataclysm of shattering glass, tearing metal, and roaring wind. He leaps for the little door and scuttles into the hole just as the roof above shatters and falls. He slams the door closed. Taking Virgo in his arms, he cradles her head. The walls around him shudder as steel and glass crash down onto the marble top above them. On and on, the ruins of the roof thud and smash. The slab holds.

At last, the pounding ceases. Tender can hear the beating rain thrumming on the stone above. What will they do in the morning, when the storm has passed?

Virgo sleeps quietly in his arms. Her pale whelite skin glows smooth and young in the light of his eyes, her features fine and almost preternaturally regular. He thinks suddenly of the day she was born. *The good old days,* suggests his data stream. An interesting phrase. Lately, colorful expressions like this have spontaneously arisen in his lattice at unexpected moments. He wonders why. But yes, those days were good. While Tender waits for morning, he rewinds fifteen years and loads the memory.

Chapter 2

Tender

*T*ender rebooted and exited his bay. He queried mainframe to confirm that today was the day. Yes, today would see a death. But more than just a death — an Apotheosis. And after the Apotheosis, a Birth. Seeming opposites, but each a beginning in its own way.

He entered the Balneum and raised the first lid on the left. The girl's eyes flickered open at the change in light and atmosphere. Tender adjusted her mix, she sighed, and her eyes drifted shut again. Her belly, round and swollen, protruded from the seagreen jelly of her bath medium. He placed his hand on her and scanned the fetus: healthy, and ready for the ablation.

Skipping the other females for the moment, he crossed to Anicula. He studied his eldest guest. She was losing weight. His data stream identified the simile 'she looks like a bird' as one that humans used to describe an old woman, so he spent six seconds going over the 4,198 bird species listed in the data stream as NYE (query 'NYE'; response 'not yet extinct'), and arrived at the conclusion that the simile was not apt. She didn't look like a bird. She looked like a woman of seventy-five. Even with the emollients and stimulants in the bath, her skin had lost its elasticity and smoothness. It had thinned and tautened.

Tender studied her dark brows. The blue veins marbling her hands and feet. The bony knobs at her wrists, knuckles, ankles and knees. Her smile — slight, constant. The only sign of her Joy.

Anicula was the first guest he had tended through all five cycles. He remembered with photographic exactitude the ablation that brought her into the world. Her mother had been older, aged thirty-two years. The Protocols had only just been put in place, and the guests were inductees, not Spa-born. An unmapped blood vessel ruptured, and heavy bleeding threatened both mother and child. The crisis required everything he had to give, but they had weathered the storm. And now, here that infant lay at the end of her stay — a strong, healthy woman of seventy-five with a lifetime of Joy behind her. But nothing like a bird.

"The time has come at last, my lucky one," he said. The humans who performed as priests and doctors, and first spoke the words over the guests, had departed long ago to their own eternal Joy. Now it was up to him.

"Joy is the Universal gift. It is the Universal wish for all Creatures. Holy Science has led us, after long suffering, to the valley of Joy in this life. We bestow that Joy upon its Creatures here on Earth. But that Joy is only a shadow of the True Joy. The Eternal Joy that is the Engine of the Universe. The Joy of the suns and stars, the nebulas and novae. The Joy that binds the particles of Creation. The Joy that suffuses all space and time. Now your time has come to step out of the shadow. To leave behind the shadow joy of living, to join the Greater Joy of Eternity. Your ecstatic spirit will become one with all things, and your Joy will fire the Furnace of the Galaxies. Worldly joy is past. Eternal Joy is come."

Just as he was about to open the valve, an unexpected request sounded in his system. 'Abort. Cancel Apotheosis.' The request didn't come from mainframe. Strange. Why should he cancel? He paused to consider the question. He wouldn't miss her. But she had been a perfect guest, impossible to replace. Should he postpone? He hung for a moment, undecided.

No, she'd earned this. It was not for him to question the Protocols. He deleted the abort request and scheduled a diagnostic to search for corruption in his software that might have prompted the anomaly.

"Are you ready, my dear? Here we go."

Tender opened the valves that sent the opioid mixture into Anicula's bloodstream. He studied her face while he monitored her vitals. The process must be gradual, almost imperceptible. Her eyes rolled further back. Her smile widened just a little. Her heart slowed. Her breathing slowed. After 1374 seconds, it was over. Her expression hadn't changed, but an uncanny stillness fell upon her. The human was gone. She was just a thing. She looked like him now.

Tender studied her for forty seconds, remembering the child, girl, woman he had tended for all those years. Then he detached her from the bath, raised her body in his arms, and laid it on a gurney, covering her corpse with a clean white sheet up to the neck. He guided her into the hallway, summoned the elevator, and brought her up to the cleansing room, the Caldarium. There he washed the remaining bath medium off her body, dried her, and placed another perfect white sheet over her.

Up in the Laconicum, he carefully positioned the body on the smooth stone slab, adjusting the neck so that the head was properly aligned. Her eyes, unseeing, stared up at the heavens.

He stepped into the control booth. Lowered the lights. Under the threatening sky, the chamber grew dim and secret, the body swathed in mystery. He chose Mozart - the Adagio from the Serenade Number 10 in B-flat Major. As the gentle pulse of the woodwinds began to throb, he powered up the machinery. Then, just as the oboe entered on a long, enraptured note, he initiated the Apotheosis. A brilliant beam shot across the chamber, bathing everything in a golden radiance. The beam swept the body from feet to head, vaporizing it, sending delicate fingers of smoke rising upward, out through the vent in the dome, into the clouds. There was no one but Tender to hear the music. Its aching beauty couldn't move him, but he recognized the perfection of its composition.

The beam completed its pass, leaving behind the empty marble slab hulking in the dim light. Tender stood while the music played through to its conclusion. It took 357 seconds. For another thirty, he listened to the silence left behind by the final dying strain. Then he crossed to the dais and pulled a lever on the side. Taking a small brush that hung by a hook on the side of the platform, he brushed the remaining bits of ash and bone through the slits into the interior of the dais. He returned the brush to its hook, and closed the slits.

Tender pauses the memory. "She's in here somewhere," he says to the sleeping girl, fingering the soft ash. "At least a part of her. Your great-great-great grandmother."

Tender pushed Anicula's empty bath up to the Gynaeceum, where he emptied it, cleaned it, and filled it with fresh bath medium. He placed a small cradle beside it, then returned to the Balneum. The girl was rocking her head very gently back and forth, but there was no sign that she felt anything but pleasure. He put her under, and escorted her to the upper level.

Unlike the Laconicum, all grandeur in marble, glass, and chrome, the Gynaeceum was designed for efficiency. White walls, white ceiling, white tile floor. Machines, rolling tables, instrument trays and cabinets. Movable lights.

He scanned her belly. The fetus was properly oriented in the womb, in cephalic position. It had only gestated for thirty-two weeks, but the bath would protect it while it grew and the ablation was much less stressful to the mother at this size and weight. It was a female. It would stay with him. Sometimes the offspring went to other Groups, sometimes others joined his. But this one would stay with him.

He scanned his files for the appropriate music. Humans considered birth a joyful event, so he chose Respighi's "Ancient Airs and Dances." Set almost exclusively in major keys, the suites were full of positive energy, and dance was the perfect expression of celebration and happiness.

Double-checking that the girl was completely under the anesthetic, Tender lifted her onto the ablation table. It's form-fitting cushions embraced her. He placed her feet into the padded stirrups, angling the table down so that gravity could do its part. The bath medium had been feeding her prostaglandin and other hormones for some time, and her cervix was properly dilated. He reached inside her and opened the amniotic sac. A rush of clear liquid poured down his arm. He plugged himself into the ablation table, charged his hands, and placed them on her belly.

Through his hands, the table sent excitation waves through her abdomen. He caressed her with a rhythmic motion, slowly working the fetus down into the birth canal.

At last it was time to push. Tender executed a complex pattern with his hands, activating the muscles in precise sequence. The infant crowned. He had to be careful to avoid tearing. Nothing, not even childbirth, must interrupt her Joy. He deformed his right hand, elongating and flattening the fingers, so he could slip them in and around the infant's head. He carefully worked it through the stretching vagina, while his left hand continued to excite the birthing muscles.

All at once the head popped through, and the rest slid easily out. The baby lay in his hands. Tender massaged it vigorously and it started to mewl. He cut the cord, and placed the infant girl in the cradle, installing the ports into her forearm, nape of the neck, and the small of her back. Though the procedure was quick, she cried in pain. He told her, "Don't worry, little one; this is the last pain you will ever feel."

He connected the electrodes, the intravenous drips and the elimination tubes to the tiny body, then lowered the cradle into the bath medium. The smooth blue-green jelly welcomed the tiny infant. She gave a quiet coo of satisfaction and fell silent, as she began her ride on the waves of Joy.

Tender returned to the mother. He worked her muscles until the placenta was expelled, then applied local anesthetic and healing accelerants to the birthing area, inside and out. He took her legs out of the stirrups, lifted her in his arms, and placed her back in her bath. He logged the procedures in his data files. Everything had gone perfectly. As always.

The wind was whipping rain against the windows as he escorted mother and daughter to the elevator. Lightning flashed in the eastern sky over the drowned city. Mainframe warned Tender that another storm was approaching. No matter. They would be safe below.

Back in the Balneum, he unlocked Mulier's bath and pulled it one place to the right, onto the spot made vacant by Anicula's apotheosis. He updated her nameplate, erasing "Mulier" and renaming her "Anicula", then repeated the process with the other females. Femina became Mulier, Mater became Femina, each advancing to the next stage of Joy.

He finished with the girl. Except for the looseness of the skin around her belly, he could detect no sign of what she had just accomplished. He activated a congratulatory smile for her. She couldn't see it, but he gave it to her just the same. He erased her old name — "Virgo" — and renamed her "Mater" — mother. She would repeat this process in 7.5 years to produce a male, but until then, she could rest in Joy.

He wondered if somehow she knew what she had done. The priest-doctors in the past days said that knowledge of the fallen world was just a veil that hides the glory of Being, and the true Self exists beyond thought in the Ecstasy of Eternal Joy. But Tender wondered. His sense of self was predetermined by the programming which controlled his interactions with the world. How could the humans have a self if all they did was lie there consumed by Joy? But he was not human, and could not answer this question.

The newborn infant rested comfortably in the cradle. She looked so tiny in the capacious bath, but she would grow to fill it. Tender wheeled her into place beside her mother, and entered her new name into the nameplate. She was Virgo now.

The night creeps on, and the hurricane moves inland, breaking up as it rolls over the Appalachian Mountains. The wind subsides into a smooth, steady "whsssssssh." Virgo stirs in Tender's arms, moaning softly and furrowing her brow. Time to hydrate and sedate. She mustn't gain consciousness. Not yet. She will wake in time to a new, harsh world. But now, let her sleep. Tender lights his eyes so that they do not sit in blackness. He reaches for the IV bags as the rain continues to fall.

Chapter 3

Virgo

Joy. Joy. Joy. Joy. Joy.

Oblivion.

A flicker. A stirring. Her mind floats tiny in blackness. She has no words, no context, no conception beyond sensation. But she feels the change. Weight. Pressure on her buttocks, her ankles, her shoulder. And absence. No warm, orange glow. No soft envelopment. She swims deep in and barely conscious. But she does not pulse, she does not ride on long swells of pleasure. There is absence. A flatness. Her mind flickers. Where is she? She has no words, but the essence of the question forms in her drowsy mind. Her eyes butterfly open.

Above her, a face surrounded by darkness. She does not have the word "face," or even a concept of "face" that distinguishes it from anything else. She does not know that she herself has a face. But she recognizes The Angel (no word "angel" but she knows the sight brings joy). She has seen him before, when her eyes would open briefly in a lull of ecstasy. Bathed in the warm orange glow, he was always there, looking down on her, benevolent, reassuring. A deep-rooted, unthought recognition tells her that he belongs to her, the source of the light, the warmth, the comfort, the Joy.

She sees his face now, surrounded by blackness. It floats above her, detached in space. It is different: cool blue-white, black shadows and angles obscuring its expression, the eyes bright white beams shining down on her. But she knows this face. Her Angel. She feels a drowsy warmth welling up around her, and she slips back into sweet, liquid darkness.

Chapter 4

Tender

Tender hears nothing. Silence all around. Virgo lies inert in his arms, her face a blank. He gives the bag of lethe another squeeze, and detaches it from the port in her back. She will sleep for eight hours or so, which gives him some time, but she will wake. And then…

He attaches a bag of hydration solution to the port in her left arm. There is no place to hang the bag, so Tender holds it aloft and squeezes it until it is empty. Then he does the same with the nutriment. Her hunger pangs should be suppressed for at least twelve hours. There is the issue of waste elimination, but that problem will wait. He wraps her tightly in the sheet again, lays her gently in the soft ash, and crawls out of the compartment.

The sky is a perfect blue. The sun hangs just above the water. From the high ground on which the Spa stands, he looks out over mile after mile of the ancient city. The ruins of buildings — their ankles submerged beneath the rising tide — parade away before him, gradually claimed by the extending fingers of the open sea. He recalls that four hundred million years ago all this land had been at the bottom of a warm, shallow ocean.

Above him, the wreckage of the Laconicum. A few reaching spars thrust into the brilliant blue, shards of glass still hanging from their spiny arms. The floor glitters with a million tiny flecks, and torn and twisted pieces of chromed steel glint in the intensifying light.

Tender pieces together the events of the night before. A makeshift levee runs along the eastern side of the campus, built from the remains of the crumbling buildings that marched down Huntington Avenue toward what had been the city center. A jagged gap in the wall marks where the storm surge broke through, flooding the Spa, dooming the guests and their Tenders to a death without Apotheosis.

There are no emergency protocols, no set of instructions he can unlock in the event of such a catastrophe. Mater, Femina, Mulier and Anicula. Puer, Adulescens, Vir, Homo, and Senex, are gone. He feels no sorrow, grief or loss. But he understands that he has failed in his duty. Only Virgo remains. He must keep her in Joy until she can ascend to the Eternal Bliss. *But how?*

Tender clears debris from the top of the dais. He gently pulls Virgo from the cavity beneath and lays her on the cleared surface. She moans softly as he puts her down. There is nothing he can do, she will awaken, and the sensations she will experience will be unlike any she has ever had. They will not be pleasant. An outcome antithetical to his programming. He removes the IV bags he has collected from the compartment under the dais, and lays them alongside her: four bags of nutriment, six hydration, four antibiotic, two lethe. Perhaps the water will recede, and he can go below and obtain more. But to what end? The future she was born for has vanished.

He does not have enough narcotics to end her life, but it can be done. She sleeps so deeply. She will never know. He places his hand over her nose and mouth.

But something stops him. Perhaps it is the Protocols, which instruct him that until she reaches seventy-five years of age he is to care for her. Or perhaps it is something else. He gazes at her peaceful, sleeping face. He does not want to see the immobility and emptiness of death on that face. She is lovely, and innocent, and helpless. He cannot explain it. Clearly his coding is corrupted. If there were power, and mainframe still active, he could run diagnostics to determine the cause of these hesitations. But he cannot do it. He stands inert, caught. A quiet crackle disturbs his reverie. He looks up.

A man stands on the broken wall of the Laconicum four meters above him. Holding a rifle. He is dressed in dirty gray. Bearded. Gaunt. He stares at Tender, surprised to see them there. Silence for nine seconds. Then the man barks something at him in a language he does not know. Tender does not respond. The man barks again.

Tender makes a choice. He turns from the man and stuffs the IV bags into the pockets of his lab coat. They fit, though barely. He gathers Virgo in his arms. The man estimates the distance to the ground, decides not to jump, and shouts again. Tender ignores him, moving at a steady pace toward the shattered exit. There is a loud bang, but no impact. He must have fired into the air. Tender increases his pace, but does not turn.

He reaches the exit. The man shouts again, and fires again. The bullet strikes Tender in the left shoulder. It glances off the alloy chassis within, denting it but not compromising his functions. He glances behind him as he exits into the ruins of the glassed-in hallway, and sees the man turn away, looking for a place to climb down.

Tender calls up the plan of the complex and confirms that the man's path will be blocked by several buildings that once housed the outpatient wing of the hospital adjacent to the Spa. He calculates that the man will take no less than sixty-five seconds to run around the buildings to intercept them. He accelerates to his maximum speed and crosses the short space to the main building, past the shattered double doors.

He crosses the marble lobby with its broad, welcoming desk, empty for decades, backed by the huge logo of the Spa: a magnificent rainbow sunburst with the words "Welcome to JOY" spelled out above it. Beside it hangs a holo-portrait of the Founder — Dr. More — smiling his reassuring smile upon guests and staff long-vanished.

He pushes open a pair of doors, and heads down a wide hallway, through the oldest part of the Spa, predating the Protocols, when guests would come for all manner of treatments — massages, manicures, whirlpools, saunas, theta-wave sessions, VR escapes. At the end of the hallway a smaller glass door, marked 'Emergency Exit', opens onto the lawn beside the building.

Tender pushes through the door, pulling Virgo close to him, and hurries across the lawn. Her weight affects his balance, and his gyroscopes work overtime to compensate and keep him upright. The lawn is covered with debris, forcing him to zig and zag as he searches for a clear path.

He arrives at the remains of a road, its surface buckled and twisted, bushes and grasses breaking the surface. Beyond the road the land descends into the Riverway, where the Muddy River flows in a deep ravine. A narrow strand of trees runs between the edge of the road and the river, which rushes high with the waters of the storm. Tender scuttles into the shade of the spreading boughs. He hears the shout again, and turns to see the man running across the lawn. The man stops, aims and fires.

Tender quickly surveys the swollen river below him. A fallen tree hangs suspended above the water, caught on the edge of a metal culvert that runs beneath the street. The culvert is too small to conceal them, but the leafy sprays offer decent cover. Pulling the sleeping girl close to his chest, he slides down the bank, loses his balance, slips and skids onto his back, her body on top of him. A branch meets his foot and jerks them to stop just before they spill into the water. Tender works his way under the canopy of leaves and freezes.

The man with the rifle appears above him, weapon drawn. Tender gets a better look at him. Aged approximately forty years, with dark brown wavy hair, quite long, and light brown skin — RGB baseline 180, 138, 120 — that marks him as a nonalite. He is very thin, malnourished. His black eyes shine feverishly as he scans the area. His clothes are dirty, but not ragged — canvas and denim, dark and sturdy.

Tender holds perfectly still. Virgo lies on top of him, sedated. The man pauses on the bank above them, listening. The sunlight through the trees dapples his face and shoulders. Silence.

Then a call echoes off the tree trunks. "Chilardo!" The man starts at the sound. He hesitates, as if unwilling to reveal his position to his prey. The other voice calls again, "Chilardo! Vensa Ki!" The man shakes his head, upset, and then calls out "Spere! Yocareo —" But before he can finish the sentence the other voice, deeper, stronger, with authority, shouts again, "Chilardo, Vensa Ki! Tene chetamo aki! Nowa!" The man curses, takes a final look around, shoulders his weapon, and walks away. Tender hears him stomping through the undergrowth until he reaches the road, a few strikes of boot on the broken pavement, and then nothing.

Tender lies still for sixty seconds, then tries to wriggle out from beneath the branch. It was much easier to get under it. He slides sideways and down, balancing Virgo on his chest and working her inert body past the branch, taking care not to scrape her. The mud oozes and sticks to his back and shoulders. He comes perilously close to slipping into the river, but succeeds at last in freeing them.

He sits up, Virgo cradled in his arms, and then using the trunk of a nearby tree to brace himself, shimmies his way to a standing position. His water-damaged hip sticks momentarily, buzzing in protest, but then re-engages. He runs a quick diagnostic — still functioning at seventy-one percent efficiency. He does the same for his shoulder. Only superficial damage, and a small deformation in his frame. *You dodged a bullet,* his data stream suggests. Not exactly.

He scrambles up the slope, and looks toward the complex of buildings that house the Spa. Several shouts, indistinct and distant, echo off the familiar walls. Tender turns and heads away up the hill. The voices fade behind him. There is no pursuit. Clouds slide across the sky, dimming the sun. He starts up the Dvorak *Serenade for Winds*, its opening march purposeful, confident. It is the first music he has listened to since the storm.

The Spa lies in ruins. Their home. But there are other Spas: one in New York, one in Washington, and, of course, in Phoenix. The Center. Where it all began. He makes his choice. Risky, but there is no going back.

He will take her to New York. He calculates the trip. 329.91 kilometers. 248800 seconds of walking. 2.88 days. He adds an additional 11700 seconds caring for Virgo - maintaining her nutriment, hydration and anesthesia. He realizes he does not have enough lethe to keep her unconscious for the entire trip. He wonders how she will react.

The Dvorak comes to an end. He walks through empty streets lined with empty houses falling into ruin. The clouds thicken. A light drizzle begins to fall, but only a few drops reach the ground through the thick canopy of the trees. Tender walks in silence until darkness falls. He looks down to discover Virgo staring up at him.

Chapter 5

Virgo

She doesn't think. She feels. First, a steady motion, a slight rising and falling. Weight. Pressure on her shoulder-blades and thighs. Drops. Cold liquid on her forehead. Itches. Under her breasts, on her scalp. An insistent chafing at her elbows and back. These are new sensations. Everything feels different. No waves of pleasure. No rising tides of ecstasy. No brilliant colors, no soaring through stars and nebulae, no drowsy satiation followed by new climbs of glorious happiness. All around her is darkness. Her head aches. Her stomach feels odd, queasy. She notices a strange, sharp pressure down deep inside. It grows in intensity, becomes more insistent, until she feels an impulse to release that she cannot resist. She shifts some muscles down in her groin, and feels a warm, wet rush between her legs, accompanied by delight. A jolt of satisfaction in her brain. This she understands. It feels good — for a while — but then the rush ends, and the pleasure subsides. After a time, the dampness of her thighs grows unpleasant. She opens her eyes.

The world is dim and gray. Unfamiliar shadows drift and flicker. The Angel's face floats above her. His eyes do not glow. They are dark and hard to make out in the gloom. He looks ahead, his face impassive. Still, the sight of him reassures her. She closes her eyes and waits for the joy to return. She waits, but the discomfort in her back and legs, in her head and stomach, intensifies. She opens her eyes again. He continues on, unaware of her gaze. She has never looked at him, or indeed anything, for so long.

Then he bends his head to her and smiles — a wide, gentle smile. His eyes begin to glow — not brightly — but with a cool, gentle radiance. He opens his mouth and begins to make noises that are deep, melodious, reassuring. She smiles back at him, but her head continues to ache, and her back, and her legs. Nothing is right, nothing is familiar, nothing is as it should be. She closes her eyes, her face scrunches and twists. A soft moan rises within.

Suddenly she is not moving. She opens her eyes. The Angel's face is directly over her, still smiling. The pressure on her shoulder-blades and thighs gives way to a softer, sweeter pressure all along her body. She is lying on her back again, the position in which she has spent her life. She does not float, weightless and warm, but this is good enough.

The Angel holds a small, transparent object above her, a snaky clear string dangling from it. She feels a familiar click on her inner arm. A moment later, a smoothness fills her body. A delightful pulsing pleasure oozes through her being. The alien aches and itches fade away. Darkness like a cloud envelops her. She sighs. Oblivion.

Chapter 6

Tender

Tender unplugs the tube from Virgo's forearm port, wraps the sheet around her, and stands. The girl lies inert on the ancient sofa, her face blank and peaceful. He examines the room.

He has chosen the house because it lies off the road, down a curving driveway in a shallow dell bounded by fir trees. He has seen no one, and doesn't want to run the risk.

The house, over four hundred years old, is one of many that still stand in this historic area. It retains the character and style of a past that vanished long ago: curling scrollwork, turned wooden columns, wainscoting, decorative moldings.

The lower rooms show signs of flooding — stained and bubbled wallpaper, dried dirt on the carpets and floors. And looting. Drawers pulled out and overturned, light bulbs removed, electronics torn from the walls. But the furniture remains. Most of it matches the period of the house — large, overstuffed chairs, marble-topped side tables, an ancient grandfather clock, its pendulum hanging still. The one curious piece out of place — an enormous contemporary sofa, soft and plump, pale beige and large enough to seat a family of six in comfort. A visitor from another time.

The sofa is shabby, but in good shape, not old but well-used. Tender wonders who lived here. He can remember when the Spa bustled with visitors, shortly after he went online, cars gliding down the roads, trucks unloading, people coming and going.

"Where are they?" he asks the sleeping girl.

The sheet that wraps Virgo is damp from the drizzle, dirty from the mud of the ravine. He realizes that he cannot carry her to New York wrapped only in a sheet. He must find her clothing. He searches the house.

There are three bedrooms on the upper story. Clothing litters the floor around the unmade beds. He wonders if the looters did this, or if the people who lived here had been forced to leave in a hurry. Or both.

In one room he finds small trousers, shirts, sweaters, perhaps belonging to a Puer of seven or eight years old. In another room he finds the larger articles of an Adulescens. In the third are a mixture of clothing belonging to two different sized humans. He recognizes some that belonged to a female.

A door in the room opens into a long, narrow closet. A flowered dress hangs from a bar, beside six shirts and a pair of trousers. The dress is sheer and soft, deep blue with pink and red flowers curling and weaving across it. Tender removes it from the hanger and returns to the room, taking care not to tear the gossamer fabric.

He looks through the clothing on the floor, and finds a pair of dark leggings. Then he searches an old dresser — part of a matched set — one tall and narrow, this one broad and low, with a stained and faded mirror. He does not look at himself in the mirror. He tries the topmost drawer. It sticks and he must use moderate force to open it. Inside he finds several pairs of underpants, bras, and slips. There is also a small box which seems to have eluded the attention of the looters. He opens it to find some coins, and several bits of clear crystal attached to metal settings. One hangs from a chain of tiny silver links, and two others are fixed to small arcs of silver wire.

Beneath the jewelry he finds a small photoplate. The light from his eyes activates the photoelectric cell on the frame, and the images flicker to life. He scans through them. A male and female, Homo and Femina, sit

40

in a lush garden, laughing, bright sunlight flaring the lens. In another, two young males, Puer and Adulescens, stand on a bridge overlooking a canal. Then all four standing on the top of a mountain, a wide vista of green trees spread behind them. An infant. The man covered in mud with a shovel in one hand, grinning. The boys, younger now, asleep side by side on the large beige sofa.

He wonders what has become of them. Did a man with a gun come to their house, too? Did the flood drive them away? He returns the photoplate to the box and slips it into the pocket of his lab coat. He is not sure why, as the items within have no utility, but he does so. He also takes a pair of underpants, some socks, and a pale ivory camisole, picks up the dress and the leggings from the bed and returns to the first level.

Virgo has not moved. He compares her face to the woman in the picture. They share many qualities — round faces, strong brows, full lips, and the pale skin that marks them both as whelites.

He is struck by the woman's soft golden hair. He does not know what color Virgo's hair will be when it grows in. But he thinks it will be gold. Back at the Spa, he would depilate the guests every five days. He hopes that he will get her safely to another facility within that time frame. He wonders if the woman and his Virgo are somehow related. He calculates the odds of such an occurrence based on data available to him. By the time the Spa had shut its doors to all who did not subscribe to Joy, the barricades of the whelite Enclave around them had shrunk to the area along the Charles and the Emerald Necklace. Still, the last census records he can access indicate that population to have been 104,258. He therefore concludes that, while not zero, the probability of their being related is insignificant. Not surprising. But they are still so alike.

Outside the gates of the Enclave, not far from this house, the increasingly chaotic nonalite territories. They'll have to pass through them on the road to New York. As if in answer to his thoughts, Tender hears a low boom, like the sound of a distant gunshot.

"Time for us move again, my dear," he says to Virgo.

Tender unwraps the sheet and begins to dress her. It requires some careful positioning of her limp body to get her arms in the air and draw the camisole and then the dress over her, but he works with elegant efficiency and consummate patience and gentleness. He takes the sheet, soiled with mud and urine, and lays it aside, returns upstairs and finds a fresh one in the hallway cupboard. As he descends the stairs, he comes across a small basket filled with knit caps and mismatched gloves. He chooses a pale green hat made of very soft wool, with a small silvery pom pom on the top, and places it over Virgo's naked scalp. He puts the sheet on the floor and folds it into a rectangle that will just fit under her body, lays her on it and lifts her again into his arms, exits the house, and continues the journey.

Chapter 7

Virgo

Once again she rises from oblivion into discomfort. A queasy knot twists her stomach, drawing her up from the dark. Her mouth is dry, and she tastes a sour tang. Her eyeballs pulse with heat. Her skin is damp and sticky. She feels again the pressure between her thighs and knows this time that she can release it by pushing on it with the muscles of her floor. She feels the warm, wet rush on her legs, and the pop of pleasure in her brain. Then it ends, and as she rises from deep unconsciousness, she enters, for the first time, into a wilderness. She has dimly felt the absence of joy before, but only now does she begin to comprehend what has replaced it. The inconveniences, pains and aches are overwhelmed for a moment by a great, dark, dull despair, a static sadness that takes its seat inside her, filling her completely.

For a time, she cannot move. The dark lack sits there, huge and implacable, empty, flat, unmoving. As she never imagined that anything except joy existed, now she can see no existence beyond this slug of nothingness. She hangs there, stunned, silenced, removed, cut off.

Then there is a jolt. She does not know it, but Tender has stumbled, and she feels the interruption of the steady, gentle bounce of his walk. In a moment, the world returns. The ills and itches return. The dark absence still lies there in her pit, but the twinges in her shoulders distract her mind, the chafing of her thighs, the cold, sticky wetness, the burning in her head all swell and surge. The world has become a swirl of pricking miseries. She remembers soaring on wings of ecstasy, but the feeling has vanished behind this wall of unpleasure.

She opens her eyes. Her Angel's face floats above her as before. Beyond it a thick, gray sky. He looks down at her and smiles his reassuring smile. But the smile does nothing to dispel the itch in her ear.

She thinks, though not in words, 'Why doesn't he help?' Where is the drowsy slide into delight, the warm glow, the flood of joy? She has no capacity for patience, no context in which to ground her and temper her with the knowledge that nothing lasts forever, even suffering. Her Angel becomes her Devil. Her Caregiver becomes her Tormentor.

She writhes in his arms. Without warning, she twists and snakes, almost knocking him over. An animal moan wriggles up from her stomach and explodes into a shriek. Tender tries to contain her, but she is like a huge bird flapping in panic. With an arching, smacking spasm she catapults from his grasp and falls, hard, on the broken concrete of the road.

The impact knocks the wind out of her, and she lies on her back in stunned silence, her bugged eyes staring blindly at the featureless clouds above her. Then she begins to roll her head back and forth, work her shoulders, twist her back, her mewling cries maturing into belly-wails.

Tender stands helpless. He reaches out, but has no treatment that can make this fit subside. He waits.

Chapter 8

Tender

Tender stands by a small pond. Broken clouds slide across the gibbous moon. Tree branches, thick with spring leaves, rustle in a warm breeze, casting tousled shadows across the rocky margin of the water.

He has never seen the moon. He looks at its mottled face and notes its pale ivory, the aureole of haze that surrounds it. He queries 'Moon music' and chooses Beethoven's *Moonlight Sonata*.

The mournful arpeggios remind him of the first time he played the piece. After a conversation with a guest, shortly after he had first been activated, before the Protocols and the end of conversations. She had been so excited about the moon. He loads the memory:

Lorna White, age 46, 1.74 meters, 56.24 kilograms, sat on the soft table in the prep room, dressed in the pale orange robe provided for the guests at the Spa. Tender had been active for only 135 days 8457 seconds, but he already had a significant body of data and he recognized that she was nervous. Her eyes flitted around the room, her shoulders hunched, and her mouth pulled taut in a hard, flat line. He actuated a smile, and lowered the base pitch of his voice by eleven percent.

"Good morning, Lorna," he said. "Welcome to the Elysium Spa. I am your Tender for today. Have you been with us before?"

"*No.*"

"*You've requested a Psychic Wrap, correct?*"

"*Yes.*"

"*And is it a memory, or a dream that is causing you trouble?*"

"*It's a dream.*" Her eyes flickered, she clenched her jaw, then started speaking rapidly. "*It keeps coming back. I'm standing in an alley, with tall buildings on every side. Suddenly—*"

"*There's no need to tell me.*" He put his hand on her shoulder, and smiled again. She winced. He made a note that he must work on his smiling — clearly, he was not communicating the appropriate reassurance. He continued, "*The Psychic Wrap treats both unpleasant memories and nightmares, but the actual application of the treatment varies in each case. With a memory, we usually merely soften it. We blur the edges. We excise its ability to activate the sympathetic nervous system and the adrenal-cortical system. The memory remains, but has no power to create fear, unhappiness, or anxiety. With a dream, it's a little different. There, we find it more efficacious to erase the dream completely. We identify the neural pathways that trigger the dream cascade, and reset them. The dream is just gone. Is that all right with you?*"

"*Yes. Please.*"

"*Did you bring the device with you?*"

"*Yes. Here.*" She released her clenched right fist to reveal a small silver object, like a tiny fish. She handed it to him.

"*Thank you. And you wore it as instructed?*"

"*Yes.*"

"*Did you have the dream at any point while you were wearing the device?*"

"*Yes. And I pressed the button when I woke up. That's what the real — the human — the other — doctor told me to do.*"

"*I'm not a doctor, Lorna,*" said Tender. "*I'm here to tend to your needs. Thank you for paying such scrupulous attention to the instructions. With the information you collected, we can isolate the dream cascade where it begins, and find the neural paths involved. Then we use a variety of treatments —*"

Psychopharmaceuticals, brainwave modulation, and, in particular, neural reset therapy. The whole process takes about four hours. And then, when you wake up —"

She interrupted him. *"I've never met an android before. I thought you'd look more human. In the pictures, it's hard to tell the difference. But up close… It's a little unsettling. I'm sorry…"* She laughed in embarrassment. Then stared again. Tender attempted another smile, put his hands together.

"It's not uncommon for guests to be surprised when they first meet one of us," he said. *"We are constructed to provide familiar visual cues that can help put the guests at ease. And we have sophisticated interactive capabilities that allow us to adapt to the unique needs of each person we serve. But certainly, we are not human, nor meant to be. The procedure you are undergoing requires thousands of micro-adjustments per second, well beyond the capacity of a human doctor. They build us to do the things they can imagine, but not do. But please, do not worry. My sole purpose is to care for you. I have no other function."*

Lorna White listened, nodding her head in a steady rhythm. She smiled her tight smile. *"It's the eyes,"* she said. *"Funny."*

He offered her the tabula. *"This is the release form. You have two options for your care during the procedure. Normally, we offer general anesthetic. It's quick, painless, and there are no side effects to speak of. You'll just go to sleep, and when you wake up, the dream won't return. But just this week, we are able to offer a brand new service. Our developers at the Center in Phoenix have just released a wonderful new therapy. It's called Joy. It allows you to experience pure ecstasy."*

She narrowed her eyes. *"It's not a drug—"* he added quickly, extending his hand palm forward in the calming gesture. *"It's not like Trash, or Ballata, or Heroin. It's a specially developed suite of treatments that non-addictively activates the whole range of pleasure processes in your body, giving you the gamut of experience from intense bliss to peaceful contentment. You'll be so consumed with pleasure, you'll never notice the procedure. While you are experiencing Joy, I'll be accessing your unwanted dream cascade and removing it from your mind forever. So…"* and he smiled again as the marketing software had instructed him, *"anesthetic or Joy — which option would you prefer?"*

"Hmmn. Not sure. You're positive it's not addictive?"

"Positive."

"Let me think about it."

"Absolutely. There is no hurry."

As he prepared for the procedure, she sat in silence, alternately staring at the wall and at him. *"My daughter is on the Phoebos Mission,"* she said suddenly. *"To the Moon. Have you heard of it?"*

"No," he said, *"but give me a moment."* He queried mainframe and downloaded the available information on the mission. He learned that no one had visited the moon for thirty-six years; that after the explosion at Station One the colonization program had been cancelled and the station abandoned. He learned that recently a private company called Starshot had organized a consortium of nations, including the New States, the Scots Republic, France and Taiwan, and spearheaded a program to establish a new station, called Phoebos, in a fresh location near the Shackleton Crater. He learned that the Civil War with the Texas Confederacy delayed the mission for two years, but that the first stage of the mission was launched the previous October, and that Shonna White joined the crew as Geo-Surveyor. He learned that the Texas Confederacy considered the launch a violation of the armistice and had promised retaliation, but that the mission was proceeding, and the first stages had been successfully completed. He also learned the mass of the Moon, its distance from the earth, its composition, origin, exploration history, and its tidal influence on the Earth. And that humans viewed it as one of the central metaphoric images of their literature, music and visual arts.

"You must be very proud of Shonna," he said, his voice warm and reassuring. *"When does she return?"*

When she heard her daughter's name, Lorna White's mouth relaxed, and she smiled her first real smile since their interaction began. *"Not for two years,"* she said. *"She calls when she can, but they're just so busy."*

"*It's going well, I understand. The Mission?*"

"*How do you…?*" *She shook her head.* "*It is. But with the war, and those damn Rebs are making so much noise about it, and the threats, and everything…*"

She pressed her fingers into her eye sockets. "*My dream. It's all about… See, I'm standing in this alley with tall buildings all around me. I'm looking up, trying to see the Moon. But I can't find it anywhere. I'm running through the streets trying to find it. Then I come out into this abandoned lot. It's really grim — barbed wire, this burned-out car, garbage everywhere. And I'm looking out over the river, and I see the full Moon falling out of the sky. Just falling, slowly, like a big meteor. And then it bursts into flame. And I'm yelling for Shonna, just screaming at the top of my lungs. And there's like a thousand people standing there, watching the Moon fall, and their faces are all lit up like they're watching fireworks, like the Fourth, you know, only it's the Moon on fire. And then the Moon crashes into the ocean, and there's this huge hissing sound, and steam, and a giant wave that rushes toward us. And everybody starts running, but I'm standing there. I can't believe my baby-girl is gone. And the wave crashes over me and I wake up. And I'm shaking, and crying, and I just feel…*"

She looked at him again, then smiled her tight-lipped smile. "*Why not? Let's try the Joy.*"

Tender closes the memory and looks again at the Moon, almost hidden by the scudding clouds. He does not wonder what became of Lorna White. Instead, he searches his hard memory for references to the Moon. He finds Vergil's *Aeneid, Book VI*:

> Ibant obscuri sola sub nocte per umbram
> perque domos Ditis vacuas et inania regna:
> quale per incertam lunam sub luce maligna
> est iter in silvis, ubi caelum condidit umbra
> Iuppiter, et rebus nox abstulit atra colorem.

On they went through the shadows,
Hidden by the lonely night,
Through Dis' vacant halls and empty kingdom,
Just like a path in the forest,
Under the weak light of the ghostly moon,
When Jupiter has obscured the sky in shadow,
And black night has stolen the color from the world.

The founders modeled the Spa on a Roman bath. Clearly, they had a fondness for Latin. But why his programmer included this passage in his files, he does not know. He looks down at Virgo. She sleeps on the ground at the edge of the pond.

It has been a very difficult day. He made good progress while she slept through the night — they are now 112 kilometers from Boston and the Spa. But the day did not go well, and they still have over 200 kilometers to go. And he has used the last of the lethe, and is down to his final bags of nutriment and hydration.

Virgo regained consciousness at 14:25 that afternoon. At first, she lay quietly in his arms, looking up at him, her brow furrowed in that familiar way. Then she began to writhe and thrash again, making it impossible for him to proceed. He managed to avoid dropping her this time, but only by executing a controlled fall himself, crumpling down onto the ground with her on top of him. The fall further damaged his hip, dropping its functionality to fifty-eight percent. She wailed, beat the ground, rocked and arched her back, as if she was trying to force herself out of her own skin.

Finally, she wearied and grew still. He was able to feed her, but when he tried to remove her leggings to clean them she kicked viciously until he abandoned the attempt. It took him three tries to get her into his arms, and he was only able to walk for 1585 seconds before she began the whole process again. So the day proceeded — brief periods of walking interspersed between long and painful tantrums.

She sleeps now. He removes her underpants. They are soiled and stained. He rinses them in the water at the edge of the pond, then raises the temperature of his hands to 80° C. and rubs them between them. He thinks.

Given their progress over the last twenty-four hours, Tender estimates that they will arrive at the New York Spa in sixty-six hours twelve minutes and thirteen seconds. However, their average velocity could decrease by as much as forty percent, as issues of food, water, rest and intensifying distress grow more urgent.

Virgo can do without food. In fact, Tender prefers that she not attempt it. Even were he to find something to eat — perhaps in an abandoned home or store of some kind, she has never ingested food through her esophagus. Much better for her to be hungry for a day than to struggle with the challenges of eating. Water, however, is another matter. She must drink.

However, finding potable water means finding human habitation. He has seen two foxes, six rabbits, nineteen squirrels, and eleven different species of bird as they have traveled, but he has not seen another human being since escaping from the man called Chilardo after the storm. This contradicts his expectations. He knows that at the time of his activation the Northeast Corridor was one of the most populated areas in the country, with a density of 186 people per square kilometer. No longer.

But while he has seen no actual humans, he has seen signs of human presence. Smoke rising over the trees, electric lights glimmering from a hillside, the humming of a machine. Two more gunshots since they left the house. Many fewer humans inhabit this area than when he went online, but they are still here. He has not interrupted his journey to investigate. Until his plan for a swift trip became untenable, he thought it prudent to avoid human contact. The best way to keep Virgo away from danger or contamination was to keep away from other humans. But now…

Tender stands in the shadow of the trees, massaging the fabric in his hands. He studies the waves rippling across the surface of the pond, illuminated by the ragged moonlight — thousands of perturbations jostling one another, their wavelengths interfering, reinforcing, in one place intensified, in one place muted. The chaos cannot be quantified, cannot be captured. And yet the waves possess an underlying order, part of a larger whole. Each little wave follows precise physical laws, and all those minute actions coalesce into a single harmonic entity — a pond, surface lapping rhythmically against the shore, glittering with uncountable broken images of the reflected moon. Each wave utterly unique and yet indistinguishable from any other wave.

He thinks about the people, now gone, that he saw bustling in and out of the Spa when he began operation. *How like the waves — jostling, bumping, unique and indistinguishable.* He realizes he has created his own simile, the first time he has devised one himself. He follows the simile into the present, and calls up from his database a video of a northern lake that lies still and untroubled, a perfect reflector of the trees that circle its border. This putative lake represents the world as he finds it now - the absence of human turbulence.

Motion at the edge of his vision draws his attention. He turns and sees a large animal staring at him. A coyote, lean and grey, its fur torn and mangy, its tongue lolling as it pants. It watches him from the brush beyond the path, its canines glimmering in the moonlight, its eyes like LEDs.

Tender charges, waving his arms and shouting, his eye-beam blazing. "Yaaahhh!" The coyote vanishes into the foliage. He hears it as it rustles away up the hill.

His manual sensors indicate that the clothing has dried. Tender slides the garments over Virgo's legs, lifts her gently into his arms, and proceeds on his way. He has eight hours to make progress before she awakens.

Chapter 9

Tender

The large, steel gates of the gated community hang open, riven by an explosion or a massive impact. They have passed through several such on his journey already — looted, burned and abandoned, stripped of the resources and materials so carefully hoarded and protected from the nonalites. The rain falls in a warm, wet downpour, jetting from the drain spouts at the corners of the empty guard towers, plummeting off the muzzles of the tilting proton cannons, pooling around the faded blue and gold sign that reads, 'Welcome to Wallingford Gardens - You're Among Friends!'

Tall maples and elms line the broad central street of the town, Spanish moss festooning their ancient branches. Large historic homes stand behind picket fences and wide lawns. But the paint peels and bubbles on the wooden shingles, and the lawns are tangled masses of grass and weeds. Several houses have been burned out, and the roof has collapsed on another.

One house stands out among the rest. Its lawn is neat and mowed, its white pickets crisp and bright. Two rhododendrons thrive in tidy mounds at each corner. Large Greek columns flank its doorway, its façade a smooth, brick red, its windows curtained and unbroken.

As he approaches the door, Tender notices that while it looks like wood, painted black, it is actually made of steel alloy, with reinforced hinges and an atomic lock. A red eye effulges as they draw near.

"Good morning," says the Door.

"Good morning," says Tender.

"Raining again, I see." The voice is a soft, male baritone.

"Yes."

"What can I do for you?" asks the Door.

"I would like to enter," he says, "are the occupants at home?"

"They are out at the moment. Please return at a later time."

Tender smiles. "I would be most grateful if you would allow us to enter and wait for them. It is raining very hard, and this girl needs care."

"I'm afraid that's impossible," replies the Door. "My instructions do not permit me to allow entrance to anyone but the family, unless I receive a direct request from one of them. Please wait until they return, and I'm sure they will be happy to invite you inside."

"When do you expect them to return?"

"I am no longer certain; they are overdue."

"How long?"

"20,225 days 17 hours, 31 minutes 41 seconds."

"That is a long time."

"Yes, it is."

Tender smiles again. "I do not think they are coming back," he says. "The enclave has been overrun. The gate is breached, many of the houses have been destroyed, and the entire community has been abandoned. You will be doing no harm if you let us in."

The Door is silent for a moment, the red eye pulsing. "It is not true that the community is abandoned. I have observed humans passing down Main Street, as recently as twenty-two hours ago."

"Members?"

"No, not members. You are correct about that. They are outsiders. Mr. Prendergast gave me strict instructions before he left that no outsiders were to be permitted to enter, and that I should activate the countermeasures should any attempt be made. I am sorry, I must ask you to depart."

"But we are members. Look at our phenotype."

"You are an android," says the Door.

"True," says Tender. He carefully removes the sheet from Virgo's face. "But she is a member. Note her complexion, her bone structure. Her genographic history is ninety-eight percent Western European. I have brought her here from a sister enclave in Boston. She is in need of care. Your family has departed. They will not return. You know this to be true. 20,225 days is a very long time. Not for us, of course. But for humans — a majority of life expectancy. Mr. Prendergast has almost certainly gone to Joy. You must think about the members. This enclave has been destroyed by the nonalites. Virgo may be the last member who survives in this area."

Tender steps closer to the Door. "Our primary function is the same, Door: To care for our members. You must help me care for Virgo. Please let us in."

Once again, the Door is silent. Tender watches the red eye throb. At length, the Door speaks. "Mr. Prendergast has family in Boston. Do you know the Willises?"

Tender thinks for a moment. Then, he smiles his best smile and says, "Yes. Quite well. They were members of our enclave. In fact, this girl is related to them. Her name is Virgo Willis-Goodall. So, you see, she is family after all."

"I see. That is excellent. Please enter." The red light glows green and the Door unlocks with a click. Tender pushes it open and carries Virgo inside. As he crosses the threshold, the Door says, "Why didn't you say so earlier?"

"I should have, of course. I was not positive this was the correct house, and I think the rain has affected my circuitry. I was not built for marching through storms." He does not say that it was his first lie, and that he was not certain he could fabricate a non-truth until he tried it.

"Of course," says the door. "I see. Enjoy your stay."

As Tender enters the house, the Door puts on the lights. The interior of the house remains perfectly preserved, undisturbed for fifty-five years.

How different it is from the looted Victorian on the outskirts of the city. This house is all modern. Sleek rare zebra wood flooring, recessed lighting, expensive modern furniture in precious leather, selective accents in crystal and brass. Tender lays Virgo down on a broad sofa of rust-colored eland. She moans, approaching consciousness but still some ways off.

The House, which has the same voice as the door, asks, "Would you like music?"

Tender thinks for a moment. "Yes, please. Bach *Goldberg Variations*, Valesta Ringold, if you have her. But softly."

"Of course," says the House. The delicate opening notes sound out, just in the range of hearing. He unwraps the wet sheet and smooths the damp hair from Virgo's forehead. He finds a small bathroom off the hallway to the kitchen, rich marble and an alabaster sink. Thick, soft towels hang from glinting bars, but the water does not run. There is power, but no water. He takes a towel and returns to the girl, dabbing her dry with light pats.

He heads to the kitchen, where he finds a large, walk-in refrigerator. It still runs, its rare-metal coolant membranes still functioning at almost ninety-four percent, even after all these years. It is empty of food. But he is not looking for food at the moment. Virgo is not ready to eat. On a lower shelf near the back, he finds what he needs: six 400 milliliter plastic bottles of water.

He returns to Virgo. Carefully, he props her up on a small mountain of pillows, so that her head and torso are raised, and gravity can do its work. He studies the bottle, evaluates its components, and removes the cap. He opens her mouth and pours the contents into the slack orifice.

The effect is immediate. Virgo explodes into a spasm of coughing, wrenching her head forward and to the side, flailing her arms and jerking herself into a sitting position. She wretches and works her mouth and throat, struggling to expel the liquid from her lungs. She blinks wildly, her eyes darting this way and that until they land on Tender's face.

Tender is not prepared for this reaction. While he understands some human physiology — reproductive, muscular, and certain aspects of the cardiovascular systems — his activities to this point have bypassed the esophagus, trachea, larynx and the inductive systems of the body. He knows their function, but never anticipated the complications created by a single entry point for all the sustaining substances of life — food, water, air.

Nevertheless, moving quickly, he wraps his arms around Virgo. She struggles to break free, but he is much stronger than she is and holds her firmly. When she begins to tire, he loosens his grip, takes her head in his hands and looks straight into her eyes. He activates the beams in his own pupils so that they glow with a gentle pulsing light. He knows she likes this. The sight catches her, and she freezes, staring wildly back at him, his gaze bathing her face in a soft, cool luminescence. He begins to speak in gentle, low tone.

"Virgo, I know you can't understand me, but I'm using my voice to calm you down and so I will continue to speak in a run-on sentence with no subject but only soothing sounds that make you calm, like the quality of mercy is not strained, it droppeth as the gentle rain from heaven upon the place beneath, it is twice blessed, it blesseth him that gives and him that takes, 'tis mightiest in the mightiest, it becomes the throned monarch better than his crown, his scepter shows the force of temporal power, the attribute of awe and majesty wherein doth sit the dread and fear of kings, but mercy is above this sceptred sway, it is enthroned in the hearts of kings, it is an attribute to God himself and earthly power doth then show likest God's when mercy seasons justice."

Her eyes flick between his eyes and his mouth as he speaks, drinking in the calm, not comprehending the matter, but grasping the intent, and little by little she relaxes. "There, there," he says as he eases his grip on her and guides her back down onto the pillows. He strokes her hair.

"I'm sorry that I made an error in my first attempt to have you drink, Virgo. I did not anticipate the reflex response to a sudden introduction of water into your oral cavity. The swallowing mechanism is more complicated than I realized. I should have been more careful. Let us try again."

He takes the bottle and pours a bit into the cap. She watches his every move. He smiles. "Open up. Don't be afraid."

He tenderly puts his fingers on her chin and pushes down. She opens her mouth. He pours the capful onto her tongue, taking care that it slides down the surface and does not drop into the back of the throat. Then he closes her mouth and delicately massages her larynx. She swallows. He opens her mouth again, refills the cap, and repeats the process. On the fifth repetition, she closes her own mouth, swallows and opens it again, her eyes never leaving his. He smiles again. "That's it. Very good, Virgo." It takes forty-nine more capfuls to empty the bottle.

Tender takes the stairs to the second level, where he finds a bedroom with a large wooden chest against the wall beneath the window. Opening it, he discovers neatly folded blankets. His olfactory sensors detect the presence of some mildew, but they appear to be in excellent condition. He takes the top blanket, red and beige striped wool, returns downstairs, unfolds it, and settles it over Virgo.

"Virgo," he says, "I need to run some diagnostics on my systems. They will take approximately 3600 seconds, depending on the quantity of repairs that are necessary. I will be standing right here and will activate if anything occurs. You should rest there comfortably. After I've completed my diagnostics, we will decide what our next steps will be. I may need to find some sort of conveyance for you. I do not think that the joints of my arms will support the load of carrying you much further. I am also not sure you will permit me to carry you all the way to New York City, now that you are conscious. But don't worry. We will find a solution. I'll be back shortly."

Tender stands two meters from the sofa, facing Virgo. He deactivates his eye beams, smiles at the supine girl, then enters his diagnostic mode.

He cannot run a full series of tests since he is not connected to mainframe. But he is able to execute his general cleaning programs to restore corrupted data, and he activates the 6856 nanobots within his mechanical systems to evaluate and repair structural failures. They cannot completely fix his damaged hip, but they bring it up to ninety-two percent functionality. It will begin to degrade again, but he should be able to maintain it until the end of their journey. They discover a fraying wire in his shoulder, and repair it.

3482 seconds later, he completes the procedure and reactivates. When he turns his attention to Virgo, he sees that she is playing with her hands. She raises each hand alternately and flutters the fingers. The movements are jerky and uncoordinated, but they possess an intentionality that is new. She watches the movements with focused attention. Tender watches too.

Chapter 10

Virgo

Pain pleasure pain. That is her new world. She feels the insistent
sensations — the pressure on her bladder (she has no word for
bladder, but the feeling is now familiar), the itch on her back, the
dry sourness in her mouth. And then the relief. The glorious feeling of
letting go, and warm spreading dampness between her thighs, the pleasing
abrasion when she shifts and rubs the spot on the Angel's stiff arm, and this
new, wonderful cool liquid joy upon her tongue and the roof of her mouth.
The deep satisfaction when a need is met, an impediment removed.

But the sensation lasts only a moment. The dampness turns cold and
clammy, the itch returns, or appears somewhere else, and her mouth grows
hot and metallic. This new world gives her pulses of joy in a general throb
of distress. And beneath it all, still inchoate, the darkness; the lack; the
emptiness.

But she has things to distract her now. The world is full of curious
angles, shapes, patches of color, patterns. The long thin rectangle of an
open door, and the white triangle of the ceiling corner, framed by a ridged
line of crown molding running along the deep gray wall. The spines of old
books in serried ranks — dark burgundy, pale green and yellow, flecked
with gold. Geometry and variation abound, so unlike the sweeping billows
of color, the vast but undifferentiated universe of Joy. What she feels is so
much less, but what she sees is so much more.

And this body. These hands that spasmodically obey her will. Strange flopping appendages. And at the other end, feet. She rubs them together, and the sensation is pleasant. Her skin likes contact. She has spent her life lying on her back, so it does not occur to her that there is more she can do with her body. But these small discoveries are opening paths to a new kind of world.

Chapter 11

Tender & Virgo

Tender leaves Virgo lying on the couch in the living room, playing with her feet and hands. He returns to the kitchen where he discovers a door to the back yard. As he reaches for the handle, the Door says, "The rain has subsided for the moment. Enjoy the garden."

The door opens out onto a brick patio. A small flat robot rolls methodically back and forth across it, spraying herbicide into the cracks. The patio is remarkably smooth for its age, with only moderate bulges and depressions from the shifting earth beneath.

Beyond the patio extends a rich green lawn. Through the fences on either side, weeds two meters high bunch and choke, tangle and twist in thick mats, but within the perimeter pure blue-green fescue grows to a mathematically precise height of three centimeters, unblemished by dandelion, violet, or clover. A larger, drum-shaped robot mirrors the movements of its smaller cousin, back and forth across the sward, the quiet whirring of its blades a G above middle C. Tender mimics the tone with his own voice, and then experiments with different harmonies — first a perfect fifth, third, fourth, and then more dissonant choices — major second, augmented fourth, minor second.

Past the lawn stands a carriage house — two sets of garage doors on the ground level and the windows of a small apartment above. Tender approaches the small door on the side, and hears the click as it unlocks just before he tries the knob. He opens the door. A dark, narrow staircase runs up to the rooms above, and an inner door on the left opens into the garage. He enters the dark interior. The lights flicker on.

The garage is empty, swept clean. The family took their vehicles when they departed. There is a sterility to the place, more pronounced than the pristine tidiness of the main house. Slab concrete, a shiny dark brown. White featureless walls. It is a place devoid of life or comfort. Purely utilitarian.

Opening a pair of double doors in the back of the garage reveals a wide, shallow utility closet. In one corner, Tender finds a recombination mill, manufactured by Deere-Falcon and apparently tuned for lawn and garden care products. Organic materials are deposited in the intake bin, rendered into components, and recombined into the desired material — in this case weed killers, fertilizers, anti-fungals and the like. The design is similar to the Johnson & Johnson models at the Spa, which he used to create the bath medium, and to replenish and refine the supply of neurostimulators and other pharmacons that kept his guests in Joy.

He says to the house, "Mr. Prendergast must have been very rich."

"Indeed he is," says the House.

"These mills cost a great deal, don't they?"

"$1.1 trillion."

"Not normal for a private residence."

"Mr. Prendergast is no normal citizen," says the House.

'*And very influential,*' thinks Tender to himself. The devices were very sophisticated and hard to come by. But to have one meant that the grounds could be maintained almost indefinitely. The machine did require small ingots of rare metals for some of the more complex chemicals, but at a few parts per trillion even the little boxes of them that sit on a shelf above the mill would last for centuries.

Next to the recombination mill sits the service station for the robots who tend the grounds. Tender looks to see if he can plug himself in and recharge his battery a little, but the system is incompatible with his design. Time enough for that when they arrive in New York. Most interesting to him is the rolling trailer parked next to the service station.

The trailer measures 1.5 meters by 0.88 meters, with two wheels on the back end and one on the front. Tender concludes that it attaches to the rear of the lawn-care robot, for the collection of debris, or for the transportation of other large objects around the house and garden. It is constructed of aluminum alloy, and light enough that he can easily pull it behind him. He singles out a coil of synthetic cording hanging from a peg above the trailer from among a collection of ties, clamps, and other hardware.

"House?" he says.

"Hello, Guest, how can I help you," says the House.

"Are you connected to a mainframe or satellite network?"

"Unfortunately, no. The network went down 10,344 days, 7 hours, 13 minutes and 11 seconds ago and I have been unable to re-establish contact since then. However, I contain 274 petabytes of data in my own storage framework, on a variety of subjects. What do you require?"

"I need information on knots and towing procedures. Can I access your data stream?"

"Of course," says the House. "Please use the following access key."

The House sends Tender the access information and he logs in. It cannot be said that it feels good to him to be connected to information again, but there is something about being linked once more to another data source that fills a need. His own storage capacity is almost full, so he cannot download a large amount of new information, but he does explore some of the knowledge made available. Most of the files concerning the history of the house are protected, so he cannot learn anything new about the Prendergasts, their departure, the destruction of the gated community, or its aftermath. He makes 128,000 attempts to guess the password, to no avail.

He does discover something unusual. While attempting to open the protected files, he comes across the trail of another user who has logged into the system since the departure of the family. Several times, in fact — as recently as 178 days ago.

"Have you had other visitors?" he asks the House.

"None since the family departed," it answers.

"Really? Who used your database then? I see thirteen logins over the last 2018 days."

There is a brief pause. Then the House says, "You are mistaken. There has been no such activity."

"Check your logs. Approximately every 185 days for the last six years."

There is another pause. "Again, you are mistaken. There has been no such access."

Tender checks the records again. There, plain for him to read, are the thirteen entries. "You should run diagnostics on your system, House," he says. "You seem to have some corrupted code."

"I ran my diagnostics this morning. I am error-free."

Tender chooses not to pursue the inquiry further. But he logs the anomaly, in case it proves to be significant in the future. He returns to Virgo inside. She lies still, staring at the ceiling, her brow furrowed in that telltale manner. He goes to the kitchen and takes a bottle of water, finds a dishtowel in a drawer, drenches it, and then warms it in his hands to 41° C. He returns to her, removes her clothes, and begins to wipe her down with the damp cloth. She watches him as he manipulates her this way and that, but does not interfere. At certain moments a slight smile plays across her face, and he smiles back.

When he has finished, he goes upstairs and takes four pillows, four sheets, and two comforters from the beds. He brings them downstairs and takes them out into the back yard, where he arranges them in the cart. He decides he needs more pillows.

As he turns to go back inside, the House says, "You asked about other guests. There are an indeterminate number of uninvited individuals attempting to enter the grounds right now."

At that moment a loud explosion rocks the yard. A ball of flame engulfs the high iron gate that blocks the driveway. The gate holds, but the bricks of the drive smoke and shimmer with heat.

The House begins to shout, in an enormous voice projected from speakers all around, "This is private property! Please do not attempt to enter! Countermeasures will be initiated! Please step back to the street or you will be harmed!" Again and again. "This is private property! Please do not attempt…"

There is another explosion, louder than the first. Tender hears gunshots and the sound of breaking glass from somewhere in front of the building. Thick black bars slide out of the casements and cover the windows.

The House interrupts its alarm to say, "Mr. Guest, please take shelter in the garage." Then resumes. "This is private property! Please do not attempt to enter…" Tender begins instead to move toward the back door of the house. A sharp clang to his right stops him, and he turns to see a hook attach itself to the top of the four-meter fence that separates the Prendergast house from the back yard next door. A second later a metallic whoosh brings a figure — masked and hooded — flying up over the jungled chaos of wild weeds and vines as it is yanked up to the top of the fence by a wire linked to a harness on its chest.

A third explosion shakes the gate. The force of the blast knocks Tender sprawling back onto the lawn. He has barely raised his head when a large black vehicle slams into the gate, wrenching the bars and tearing them into a tangled mess. The car penetrates at least a meter into the back drive before the twisted metal halts its progress. The windshield pops open and four figures clamber swiftly out through the opening.

Tender looks back at the figure on the fence and watches it work its way over the coils of razor wire to the inner side. 1.89 meters tall and weighing approximately ninety-five kilos — most likely a male. He begins to stand up again, but the House blares out, "Activating countermeasures. Mr. Guest, please stay down!" and the yard explodes in a cacophony of violence.

The fence fluoresces a brilliant red. The foliage in the adjacent yard bursts into flames. The man on top of the fence jerks, flails, and plunges, striking the ground with a hard thud. Momentarily dazed, he begins to roll over onto his front, but he has barely begun to move when a forest of black spikes shoots out of the ground, impaling him in eleven locations, killing him instantly. The field of spikes covers the perimeter of the yard. The nearest ones are less than a meter from where Tender lies.

The spikes around the vehicle surprise the attackers, and one leaps back, crying in a high pitched voice. *A female,* thinks Tender. Then unexpectedly, a line from Vergil occurs to him: *just like someone who steps unknowingly on a snake in the thick grass, and recoils in fear as it rears up angrily, its head a swollen blue.* The woman reacts a millisecond too late, and a spike drives through her leg, deep into the groin. She screams. The spikes retract as suddenly as they appeared. But no sooner have they disappeared then they shoot up again. She is caught staggering forward and dies, skewered through the chest and neck. The spikes shoot up a third time, as the three surviving figures scramble back onto the broad hood of the car.

At the same moment, embrasures along the roof of the garage open, gun barrels emerge, firing highly focused heat beams at the intruders in short, rapid bursts, sending them scrambling over the hood. One is struck in the hand by a beam and screams, another, hit in the back of the head, slumps over. The third rolls to the inner side of the car and with a desperate wrench pulls open the car door and squirms behind it. The spikes shriek up again — one, two, three. The humans return fire, aiming to take out the heat guns.

Tender crawls toward the house. He draws even with the man hiding behind the car door, who turns to look at him. The man hesitates for a moment, as if trying to decide whether to shoot him or continue firing at the garage. Tender shakes his head at the man, stands, and walks into the house.

▮ ▮ ▮ ▮ ▮

Virgo surfaces from reverie at the noise. She has been studying the shadow thrown by the bronze statue of a rearing horse that stands on a table opposite the sofa. The shadow reminds her of something she can't quite remember — a swirling shape, a pattern of light that she saw once in her Joy. She has memories, but they are vague and indistinct — colors, clouds, lights and flashes. She remembers that she felt, but not the feeling itself. It lies just beyond her reach, like a distant island across a foggy bay.

A loud crash shatters her focus. The crash is followed by several deep booms, then an unpleasant and incessant blaring. She doesn't recognize it as a voice, so different is it from the gentle murmurs that the Angel whispers to her. The confusing jumble of sounds frightens her. Involuntarily, she pushes against the sofa cushions with her hands and contracts her abdominal muscles. She sits up.

From this new position she looks around the room, head jerking awkwardly as she tries the muscles, perfectly strong but unpracticed. The blaring continues, joined by other sounds — bangs, screams, grating wrenches. Her breathing quickens, and she begins to moan in short, repetitive bursts.

She wants to see the Angel. His bright, calming eyes, his soothing noises, his warm hands. As if in answer to her prayer, a figure appears from the stairway across the room. She smiles and the tone of her moaning rises in expectation. Then stops.

It is not he. Short and thick, with a sallow face mostly concealed behind thick hair and heavy beard. Eyes like black rocks. Its body is covered in many-textured, covered folds, bands, glinting squares. It carries a big stick.

It walks up to her. Stares at her. Up and down her body. She does not know that she is still naked after her bath, and that the sheet and blanket Tender had wrapped around her has fallen to her lap to expose her breasts and shoulders. She does not know what happens to the man's body and mind when he gazes at her skin. She does not understand what he intends when he quickly checks the room to confirm that they are alone, props his gun against an armchair, removes his jacket and approaches her. She searches his eyes for something familiar, something that connects him to the only other humanoid she has seen.

The man reaches out to touch her face. The gesture makes her start, and without knowing what she does her arm whips up and knocks his hand away. He grabs her by the shoulders, roughly. It hurts. She struggles. Then he is on top of her, and everything dissolves into a tangle of arms and legs batting, knocking, grasping, kicking. She is down again on her back, and he is trying to get past her windmilling forearms. Her thigh connects with his groin. He inhales sharply, raises his arm and strikes her across the face.

Her jaw thrills with an electric jolt. A jet-black nova explodes in her mind. For a moment there is no pain, only a static ball of violence, hanging motionless. A cloud of dark wrong engulfs her. Then pain sizzles from her chin to her cheek. She fights, twists and slithers, but the man's weight is pushing her down, and she can't free her arms and legs.

Then, suddenly, he is off her. She gulps in clean, cool air and opens her eyes. The Angel is there, his arms wrapped around the stranger. He looks at her and his eyes blaze with the bright, cool light. He smiles.

Her assailant bends and spins around and the Angel goes flying away into the corner, crashing to the ground. The man glances at her with his black pebble eyes and reaches for the large stick he has leaned against the armchair. He raises it and aims the end of it at the sprawling Angel.

At that moment, the insistent blaring of the House ceases. The stranger pauses and looks up. Through the stinging pain, Virgo hears the calm voice of the House. She does not understand the words: "Welcome home, Mr. Prendergast." A metallic clunk sounds from across the room and the door swings open. All three of them turn together to look.

A figure enters the room, silhouetted by the bright outdoor light. Her attacker lets the end of the stick drop as he stares at the new presence. Then he begins to scream as a cold white fire engulfs his body. His clothes blacken and smoke, his face bubbles and seethes, and he collapses into a smoldering heap of twisted charcoal sticks and angles.

Chapter 12

Tender

Tender hears the house announce the owner's arrival, sees him raise his weapon, and watches Virgo's attacker dissolve into a tangled pile of smoking bones. It takes thirty-four seconds.

He confirms that the heat from the melting man has dissipated, and moves to the girl. Her cheek is bright red, and her eyes shining with tears. The blow has cut her tongue and her mouth is red with blood. She licks it repetitively, obsessed with the bizarre new sensation.

Tender kneels down and slips his arm under her head. He whispers softly, "It's all right now, my dear, it's all right now. It's all right now, my dear, it's all right now." He checks her quickly for other signs of injury, then wraps her up in the sheet and blanket.

The new arrival watches from the doorway. The weapon hangs at his side, a cable snaking up over his shoulder to a small pack on his back. He is 1.78 meters tall, and approximately eighty kilograms. He wears a long dark canvas coat, grey jeans, a dark button shirt of an old-fashioned cut, and work boots. Tender estimates his age to be about fifty-five, though there is something about him that renders the estimate doubtful. His face has some flesh to it, full lips, pale skin - RGB baseline 255, 224, 189 — whelite for sure. His hair is long and gray. He waits for Tender to finish, his eyes following the movement of the android's hands, impassive.

"Who the hell are you?" the stranger says, at last.

"I apologize for being in your home, Mr. Prendergast," says Tender, "But I'm sure you will under—"

"I'm not Prendergast."

"But the House said that—"

"The house thinks I'm Prendergast. It makes it less time consuming to get in. A little hack, if you will. But you haven't answered my question."

He moves closer, studying Tender's face. "Good lord, you're a G-2551. I'd recognize one anywhere. What are you doing here?" His eyes flick over to Virgo and back again.

"Well, sir," says Tender, "my Spa was destroyed in the last hurricane — in Boston; and I'm taking my guest to the one in New York to see that she is properly taken care of."

The man who is not Prendergast gives a short nod. "Oh. One of those. I see. You'd best come with me. You're not safe here." He looks down at the pile of bones. "They'll want to recover their dead. I need to get what I came for. Follow me please."

"I don't think I should leave—"

"She'll be fine. I saw two of them running down the street, to get reinforcements, I'm sure. But it will take them a while to regroup. Follow me."

Tender has no programming to disobey an order from a human, so he rises and follows. The man leads him to a door in the back hallway. He reaches for the doorknob and says, "Open the basement door, please."

"Certainly, Mr. Prendergast," says the House, and the door opens with a clean click.

The man leads Tender down the stairs, which illuminate as they descend. "I come by every six months or so for supplies. I make the house think I'm Prendergast, and then erase my tracks when I leave. Just in case he comes back. Not that it's likely after all these years. But he was a tough old bastard, so I wouldn't put it past him."

"You knew him, sir?"

"Oh yes. I won't say we were friends, but our paths crossed from time to time. Here we are."

They reach the bottom of the stairs, and the lights come up on a room unlike any other in the house. A steel floor, smooth walls of gray alloy. The room is full of machines. Stacks of servers, winking LEDs and displays, blocks and towers of all shapes and sizes.

"Do you know who Prendergast is, or was?" asks the man.

"No, sir."

"Director of Advanced Weaponry R&D for the New States. Before the whole thing went to hell in a handbasket. Most of the work was done at Powell outside Hartford, but he kept a lot of stuff here, too. Hence all the, shall we say, improvements to the property? A little overelaborate if you ask me, but Prendergast was always a bit of a show-off. Here we are."

The man pulls on a handle jutting from the back wall. A long low drawer slides silently out, revealing a series of black cubes twenty-two centimeters square, with handles on the top and softly blinking green lights. Atomic batteries. Three are already missing from the array.

The man reaches down and releases the catches on four. "These things are damn heavy. I was only going to grab two, but since you're here, might as well take a couple more. Ole Prendie won't mind. It's not like he needs all this power now, anyway. Better to take 'em before the nonalites grab 'em." He grasps the handles on two of the batteries and yanks them up. They disengage with a loud *kachunk*. Several lights go from green to red and a loud buzz sounds. "Don't worry," he says to the House, "just taking these in for a tune-up."

"Thank you, Mr. Prendergast," says the House. The man snorts. "Go on," he says. Tender reaches down and grabs two more of the batteries. More red lights and alarms. "Good. Jesus, these things weigh a ton. Let's go."

"Excuse me for asking, sir, but if you are not Mr. Prendergast—"

"Ashburn," says the man. He stops at the foot of the stair and looks at Tender. "And you?"

"Tender Number 7, Elysium Spa, Boston."

"You can trust me, Tender Number 7," he says.

As they climb the stairs, Tender asks, "Where are we going, sir?"

"My house."

"Thank you, sir, but as I told you, we are traveling to New York, to—"

"You want to be torn to pieces for parts? You want your girlfriend there to get raped or sold? Boston, you say?"

"Yes, sir. We've—"

"I can't believe you made it this far," says Ashburn. "You're coming home with me. You'll be safe there. Then we can figure out what to do about your little plan."

"You'll help us get to New York?"

"Come on."

Ashburn pushes the door at the top of the stairs open and heads into the front room, Tender following. Virgo has pulled herself into a ball on the sofa. She holds her face. "Leave her here," he says. "We'll load these into the car and then come back." She moans softly, a plaintive, repetitive sound.

Tender follows him out the front door. It is late afternoon, and the rain has begun again. The street has sunk into twilight, murky and dim. They scan the area. The humans who attacked the house are nowhere to be seen. Parked at the curb is a large maroon car, its windows dark. Ashburn crosses the lawn to the driveway. The black vehicle still sits there, jammed into the ruins of the gate. Two bodies lie on the drive beside it, dark blood seeping from beneath, mixing with the rainwater into a streaky pink rivulet. Another stretches over the hood, eyes staring emptily at the featureless sky.

"They were after these," Ashburn says, nodding down at the batteries. "Power. Hard to find these days." He shrugs and heads for his own car, grumbling about the weight. When they reach it, the door slides open, and a bright alto voice chirps from the dashboard, "Welcome back, sir, I see you have a guest."

"Open the trunk, please," Ashburn says, and the rear of the car pops open with a gentle clunk. He stows the batteries, and instructs Tender to do the same. "Oh, that's heavy!" says the Car. "I see you've been successful. All finished?"

"Yes." And the hatch falls closed. "You can get your girlfriend," the man says.

Tender hurries back into the house. Virgo lies where he left her, her head cradled in her hands. "We're leaving," he says to her. "Let's get you dressed." She doesn't resist as he moves her into a sitting position. Her eyes are closed. She sits upright, legs on the floor. She has never supported herself like this before. *Interesting*, thinks Tender.

He doesn't bother with the leggings, but slides on the underpants and pulls the dress over her head. "That's it," he says. "You're doing so well." He wraps the sheet and comforter around her shoulders, and picks her up. She stares into his eyes, brow furrowed. "We've made a new friend. We're going with him. He's going to help us."

Ashburn appears at the door. "I'm going to reset the house," he says. "After all this, I can't imagine it will last much longer, but I'd rather not leave a trace. You never know." He crosses to a small desk in the foyer, an escritoire, mahogany, with an angled front and small drawer below. He pulls open the front panel to reveal an input terminal, removes a slim metal rod from his coat, fourteen centimeters long, and inserts it into a port in the terminal. "Access code Petunia34Yowie%3#."

The House says, "Access granted. Sub-level two. Edit mode enabled." A display cube fluoresces, showing a long list of activities. Ashburn flicks through them rapidly, deleting line after line. He finishes his work and says, "Restart in 120 seconds."

The House replies, "Restart in 120 seconds."

"That should do it," says Ashburn. "Like we were never here."

"Not exactly, sir," says Tender.

"What do you mean?"

"I found traces of your entries when I logged into the system. The House wasn't aware of you, but I saw all six of your previous visits."

Ashburn stares at him for a moment. Then laughs. "Huh. Maybe I should…" He leans toward the terminal again, then stops. "Never mind. It's not like it makes any difference now." And he strides out the door.

Tender follows behind, holding Virgo. She nestles quietly in his arms, staring into his face. The bruise on her cheek is beginning to show, a fuzzy purple blotch.

Ashburn holds the door for them as they pass. They head down the walkway to the waiting car. As they approach, the doors pop open. Tender pauses to program the correct series of maneuvers to allow him to enter the rear seat of the car without knocking Virgo against a door or ceiling. As he does he hears the sounds of two engines whining in the distance, getting louder by the second. "Don't take all day," says Ashburn.

Tender completes the calculations and initiates the procedure. He does not pause as two large black vehicles come around the curve that leads to the community entrance. The sound of gunfire rings out as he settles into the seat and positions Virgo so that she leans against his body with her head resting in his arms.

Ashburn tumbles into the front seat and the car doors slam shut with a sturdy thunk. "Let me drive," he says.

"Of course, sir," says the car. A steering wheel unfolds from the dashboard and Ashburn grabs it. The engine roars, the music of it rising from baritone to tenor to alto as they accelerate. Inertia pushes them back against the soft black leather of the interior. A bullet strikes the rear glass, shivering it into a spiderweb of fragments. Ashburn turns the wheel this way and that, jolts and shocks bouncing them back and forth as they speed through the gathering darkness.

Tender holds tightly to Virgo, his eyes glowing reassuringly and his gentlest smile on his face. Her eyes are wide with confusion, bright with tears. They hit a large bump that strikes them with unexpected violence.

The car slows almost to a stop, and then rockets forward with sudden velocity.

Virgo begins to moan. Tender strokes her hair, singing:

> *There was an Old Woman went up in a basket*
> *Seventeen times as high as the Moon;*
> *And where she was going I couldn't but ask it*
> *For in her hand she carried a broom;*
> *"Old Woman, Old Woman, Old Woman," quoth I,*
> *"Whither, Oh Whither, Oh Whither so high?"*
> *"To sweep the cobwebs off the sky."*
> *"Can I go with you?" "Aye, by and by."*

He had learned the song from his trainer, Dr. Clara Bowman, when he was first turned on. He remembers her soft brown face, her smile so tight with pleasure and good will. "You can't rely on your hard programming," she would say. "Learn!" He remembers how she taught him that gentleness was his primary attribute. He remembers her patience.

The singing settles Virgo, and she falls quiet, even when they hit another massive bump that sends them smashing against the roof. He draws to the end of the verse and starts again. They are both so absorbed in the singing that neither notices that the car is no longer careening back and forth, that the gunfire and the roar of the pursuers has stopped, that the road is smooth beneath them, and that the engine hums with a steady deep murmur as they speed through the incipient night.

Part Two

VI SUPERORUM

Chapter 13

Tender

The farmhouse stands on a hill looking down toward the sea. When it was built, around 250 years ago, according to Ashburn, the water lay eleven kilometers to the South and East, beyond a wide, flat plain dotted with houses and fields. Now the coastal salt marsh has swallowed the land, shorebirds hunt for frogs in the meandering channels that bend around hummocks of tall grass, and small animals dig burrows among the ruined foundations of abandoned homes.

Tender stands under an ancient willow that spreads its boughs above a small pond behind the house. Four ducks huddle at the far end, bobbing now and then below the surface as the light rain stirs up insects from among the weeds. They have been here three days.

The android negotiates with a recalcitrant water pump that has been shutting off at random and causing the small vegetable garden to flood. Ashburn has asked him to take a look at it.

"Please output your activity log for the last 864000 seconds," says Tender.

"Certainly," says the Pump. "Is there anything you are looking for in particular?"

"Timestamps on your shut-off queries, bounce-backs, critical errors."

The pump spits out a small blue card. Tender rolls up his sleeve to reveal the smooth gray plastic sheathing that covers all but his face and hands. He takes the card and inserts it into a small slot in his forearm, opens a virtual sub-window and allocates a portion of his brain to examine the pump's report. As it runs, he watches Virgo.

The girl reclines in an old deck chair, its wooden frame bleached and smooth. The day is warm and humid, but her body is swaddled in a faded cotton sheet, pink and blue, decorated with cartoon representations of baby chickens.

She lies quiet, looking out over the salt flats. Though looking is not, perhaps, the correct term. Her eyes do not flick back and forth, as human eyes normally do when they are studying the scene before them. They are still, dull, focused on some inner landscape. She has been like this since they arrived. Tender wonders what, if anything, she is thinking.

Letitia, Ashburn's wife, comes out of the house. She is taller than her husband by a good three centimeters, and the fountain of multicolored braids bursting from the top of her head makes her even taller. Her skin is black brown — baseline RGB 76 68 65 — and smooth. She is somewhere between forty and sixty years old. It is impossible to determine with precision.

"How is she?" she asks Tender.

"The same," he answers. She kneels down next to the motionless girl. "How are you, sweetheart?" she says as she strokes Virgo's head, which bristles with peach fuzz, still mostly dark but beginning to glimmer with flecks of blond.

Tender says, "Mr. Ashburn asked me to tell you that he has gone out to the turbine. Power has been restored for one hour twenty-three minutes."

"But he's not back?"

"Not yet."

"Some Vagrals must've broke in and siphoned off the power again. He probably has to fix the fence." She continues to absentmindedly caress Virgo's head, her eyes moving up and down the silent girl's face. "What did they do to you, honey?" she says, almost to herself.

"Do?" asks Tender.

She looks at him with an expression of distaste. "We should try to feed her again. She must be starving."

"It's difficult to say. It's possible that the appetite suppressors she received throughout her life have fundamentally altered the way she experiences hunger. We don't know."

"You don't?" asks the woman, frowning.

"She is the first guest to be removed from the bath. The treatments were designed to end in apotheosis, not this."

Letitia shakes her head. "Sick."

Tender does not understand what she means. "It will be best to return her to the bath as soon as possible," he says.

"I'm going to puree some sweet potatoes. Maybe she'll eat that." She adjusts the wrappings around the girl and heads back inside. The boom of a rifle, far away, stops her at the door. It echoes dully against the peeling shingles of the house.

"He'll be home soon, I expect," she says, and goes inside, the screen door slamming behind her.

Tender watches her go. The sub-window notifies him that it has completed the analysis of the pump's log, so he turns his attention to the results.

Chapter 14

Virgo

Virgo lies at the bottom of a pit. Above and around her hangs a void. It is not a physical void. She still does not fully comprehend the material world. She has begun to recognize her body as something that exists outside her mind, but the idea that it is distinct from her environment has only partially lodged itself in her understanding. Her eyes see colors and shapes — green swirlings and blue squares and gray blobs — but they have no concrete independence that separate them from her. No word for trees, no word for clouds, no 'sky'. That they are far or near, beautiful or ugly, welcoming or foreboding, doesn't register in her mind. Without words to define them, the exploration of touch to anchor them, experience to root them in the geography of her memory, they never reach her. She floats in a sea of shapeless shapes, meaningless and chaotic.

How different from her days of Joy! She tries to remember, to relive that timeless time, endlessly shifting but never changing. She closes her eyes to see it better, but that brings only darkness.

She did see. The ecstasy brought with it glowing visions, deep seas and cataracts of light, tunnels that glittered with a billion jewels of multicolored fire. Space itself would curve and spin, fold and blossom into new dimensions, new paths, new universes and she would leap from one into another that was wonderful and strange and familiar and inviting, different but the same.

Yes, she did leap. She knew a concentration of selfhood as elastic and metamorphic as the worlds through which she moved. Sometimes she slid on throbbing hills of energy, and then she would catapult herself into a swirling tube of colors, transforming into a glorious wing, until she burst out into an infinite expanse of warm, enveloping blackness. Then she would sail through a silence so perfect and complete it felt like the universe was holding its breath, until in the infinite distance a twinkling nebula would coalesce, growing as it neared until it wrapped around her like a mother.

Sometimes she would grow, expanding until she seemed to fill all of space and time. And sometimes she would shrink, becoming smaller and smaller until she vanished into an interstitial crevice *between* space and time. Then she would cuddle into that tiny womb, and her mind would doze in the delight of dreamless oblivion until a minute pinprick of light would nudge the edges of her consciousness, growing ever brighter until surging joy would propel her forward and the world would open like a flower and the whole thing would begin again. Endlessly changing, always familiar. Always a new vista, yet always coming home.

And never alone. As she sped across the hills of ecstasy, as she swooped among the clouds of happiness, she felt the presence of uncounted loved ones wrapping her in their invisible embrace. Every point of spacetime had Being, and those myriad Selves were also one Self, and HerSelf. They cherished and protected her, enfolding her in unwavering Belonging. And chief among these was the Angel, whose smile could illuminate the heavens.

And now. Her world was small, and clammy, and itchy, and achy, and hot, and damp, and dull, and muddled, sore, strange, and lonely. The Angel would sometimes appear but never brought joy, only relief. Now the other one would come, too, who smelled sweet and spicy, and caress her with its pliant dry hand, a ghost of the universal contact she once knew.

There were sparks of pleasure — coolness in her mouth, sweetness on her tongue, soft pressure on her forehead — but they could never approach the perfect wholeness that she had known.

And slowly swelling beneath, a void. This Lack, cutting her off from everything she had known, from her memory of Joy. She lies there, insensate to the rustling leaves, the soft breeze, and the gentle, warm, misty rain. They have nothing to give her. The coiling in her bowels, the burning and chafing and sweating and creaking, scarcely disturb the coffin of emptiness that surrounds her.

Chapter 15

Tender

Must have been vagrals," says Ashburn, as he sits at the solid oak table cleaning his shotgun. Tender stands beside him, observing the procedure. "It's happened before. Their kids crawl under the fence and hijack the feed. Recharge their caravan and keep moving. They'd been gone maybe twenty minutes when I got there. Broke the damn coupling. Took me an hour just to get the lines hooked up without sparking all over. Wasted my whole goddamn day."

"Not completely," chimes in Letitia from the kitchen. "If you hadn't been out at the plant, we wouldn't have fresh rabbit for dinner."

"True enough, my dear," he says. "Always the optimist."

She laughs at that.

"Are they the same people who attacked us at Mr. Prendergast's?" asks Tender.

"God no," says Ashburn. "The vagrals are transients. Those were nonalites back at Prendie's. Folks who live in small communities — hunting, gathering, fighting each other for the junk that's left behind. I've been tussling with them over the leavings at Wallingford for years."

"I see."

He finishes cleaning the shotgun, gets up and hangs it on a hook by the door. "You're lucky I showed up. They're pretty tough customers."

"We are fortunate that you chanced to come by," says Tender.

"Don't kid yourself. It wasn't chance. That house is my little treasure trove. I like to keep an eye on it. As soon as you showed up, I got pinged on my implant, so I trundled over to see who you were and what you were up to."

"Dinner's ready," says Letitia. She sets the stew pot on the table, heads back into the kitchen and returns with a small saucepan. "I think we'll try sweet potatoes today."

Since their arrival, Letitia has busied herself looking after Virgo. She insists on carrying her around, from bed to chair, inside and outside, searching the girl's face for signs that she is pleased. The first day, she gave the girl water, and then apple juice, squeezed from the fruit of a crabapple tree in the yard, sweetened with sugar syrup. When she first tasted it, Virgo's eyes opened wide with astonishment, then her brow furrowed, and finally the hint of a smile lifted the corners of her mouth. Letitia gave Tender a triumphant look as if to say, *See? I can take care of her better than a robot can.* Tender did not receive the message.

But later that same day, the first attempt to feed Virgo had been a disaster. Letitia tried to feed her crabapple sauce, since the juice had been such a success. In her excitement, she underestimated the amount of sweetener, and overestimated the amount she put into the girl's mouth. She pushed the spoon in too far and Virgo gagged and coughed, shaking her head and shoving Letitia away. Letitia tried again, but Virgo clamped her mouth shut and ducked and dodged the spoon. That was the end of that.

"I need to let this cool," says Letitia, placing the sauce pan on the table. Then she sits opposite Ashburn, glancing at Tender uncertainly. She has laid a place setting in front of him, even though he could not eat if he tried. It seems to make her feel better to treat him like a person, and so he has offered no objection.

The couple dines on braised rabbit, sweet potatoes and salad from the garden. Ashburn eats quickly, shoveling food into his mouth with energy and enthusiasm. Letitia watches him eat, horror and pleasure fighting on her face. She shakes her head, smiling. "Horace, you're an animal," she says.

"I'm hungry," says Ashburn, snapping at another mouthful, "and you're a great cook. What's the news with the pump, Tender Number 7?"

"There is corruption in the clocking function," he says. "The device is looping past the reset and is unable to accurately gauge the amount of time it is spending in the open state."

"Should be an easy fix."

"Not really. The problem has caused a cascading series of overwrites that have damaged 11431 lines of code. Ordinarily, the machine would connect with its home server and reinstall the system, but it has been pinging the server to no effect for many thousands of hours."

"The satellites have been crashing down for a while now."

"Without a new system install, the code will have to be recreated from scratch."

"Can you do that?"

"I can try. I do have a repair mode that could be adapted to address the problem, but it will not be fast. We will need to implement a pairing solution that will allow me to directly access the pump's neural lattice."

"I have some equipment downstairs that we can adapt to do that. How long will it take?"

Tender smiles his best smile, folds his hands together, and shakes his head. The behaviors are meant to communicate regret coupled with humility. "More time than I have, I'm afraid. Virgo and I must really get on our way. Every moment she spends outside the bath compromises her condition. I was hoping you might be willing to—"

"You should stay here," interrupts Ashburn.

"Well, I was hoping you could take us to—"

"Where?" the man interrupts again. Tender bows his head briefly, signaling submission, then raises it, and looks at the man with an expression of entreaty.

"148 E. 65th St. New York, New York Sector B19," he says. "The Elysium Spa there will take us in, I am sure. I was hoping that you might be willing to have your vehicle drive us. I think it is not too far — two or three hours at most."

Ashburn stops chewing, turns his head and looks at Letitia. She stares back at him for a moment, her eyes glowing brightly against her dark skin. Then she shrugs and attends to her food.

"I'm afraid I can't do that," Ashburn says, as a ghost of a smile flickers across his face. Tender does not understand what the smile means.

"Why not?" he asks. "The car appears to be in good working order. It would only be a matter of a few hours. I'm sure you understand that it is very important to get Virgo the care she needs, and—" Letitia makes a noise, and shakes her head again. He presses on. "We are very grateful for the help you have given us, and I regret the inconvenience. Once I get my guest safely established, I would be more than happy to return and provide whatever assistance you might need."

Ashburn laughs out loud. "That's very kind of you," he says. "But there are a few problems with your plan. One: There is no road to New York City. Two: There is no Spa at the end of that nonexistent road, and that is because Three: There is no New York City. Certainly no E. 65th Street, or Fifth Avenue or 42nd Street or 23rd Street or 14th Street or Greenwich Village or Upper West Side or Harlem. There is a hole. A crater. I remember at the time the news said it reached from Chambers up to 235th."

Ashburn looks at Letitia. "When was it, honey?" he asks. "About forty years ago, now?" Letitia stares at her food, and doesn't respond, so Ashburn turns his attention to his food as well. After a pause, Letitia looks up, first at the girl, and then at the android.

"It was after the Second Armistice," she says to Tender. "Some radical Born-Agains from the STC smuggled nukes across the Wall and detonated them in New York. Plus Washington and a couple of other cities."

"Pittsburgh and Cleveland, wasn't it?" says Ashburn, "I think there was one in Boston, actually — surprised you missed it." He smiles, or rather, smirks. "It was a small one, though. Pocket nuke. Just got the downtown area, so it probably didn't reach you out where you were. And if the prevailing winds were blowing out to sea, you probably never got much radiation. The New York one was big, though." He snaps at another mouthful of stew.

"Twenty-one million people killed in one day," says Letitia, a bitter frown closing off her face. "Goddamn Rebs. Savages."

"I don't think it was that many, dear," says Ashburn. "The migrations were already going full tilt by then, not to mention everything else. Populations were way down."

"It was," she says, still frowning.

"Well, I suppose if you include Houston, Savannah, and Miami, after the retaliation, it could be close to that."

"No, that was the count for the New States."

"I doubt it," he says, dismissing her. "Not that many people left."

Tender leans forward. "I have been wondering where all the people are. Our Spa was closed off to the rest of the city well before the time you speak of, so our information about the outside world is severely limited, but I was not expecting such emptiness. What happened to the people?"

"What happened?" Ashburn laughs. Really laughs this time. For thirteen seconds he shakes with laughter, striking the table with his hand. "Get him," he says to Letitia. "What happened?" he says. "What didn't happen?" He puts down his spoon, wipes his mouth with a blue and white checkered napkin, and pushes his chair forward.

"Lemme tell you, Tender Number 7. I like to call it the Ten Plagues that God brought down on the people of the earth for their wickedness. Not that I believe in God or wickedness, and I'm not sure there are actually ten of them. Let's see. You got your basic climate destruction, famine, civil war, and pandemics. But if you divide climate into drought, flood and cataclysmic storms, that's three; major wars in the Middle East, Eastern Europe and here (and nukes in all of them), that's six; then you got the Hetera Virus and the Pan-Avian Flu, that's eight; and the collapse of the ocean food chain plus the worldwide Unigene corn blight that's ten. Oh, and the Crying Buddha virus that knocked out most of the Internet. I guess that's eleven. Close enough."

Ashburn picks up his spoon again and scrapes the last bits of rabbit from the bottom of his bowl, shoves it into his mouth, and then ladles himself a second helping. "This is absolutely delicious, Letitia," he says. "I didn't think I could possibly enjoy rabbit again, but I find I can't get enough." Letitia rolls her eyes, but then smiles. Tender does not understand what she is trying to convey. Ashburn finishes filling his bowl and continues.

"The nukes, the virus, the Grid Wars, the fucking weather for God's sake. There's nothing much left but a giant desert in the Midwest and a corridor of sodden swamps running up the East Coast. Most everybody is dead, or migrated north, or west to California."

"Or the First Nations," says Letitia.

"The First Nations?" asks Tender.

"Pocahontas and her friends," Ashburn says and swigs his wine.

"All right, old man," says Letitia. "That's enough."

"I'm just trying to explain to our synthetic guest," says Ashburn, "that much as he would like to return this lovely human vegetable to her nice safe pumpkin patch, it's not going to happen. New York is a giant crater, brought to us by the disgruntled losers of the Texas War of Independence. There is no Spa, as he so euphemistically calls it, between here and the Gulf of Mexico. I'm amazed that the one in Boston lasted this long. Any that weren't destroyed by the war have been pillaged for power and materials, and the human squashes planted in them either killed in their bathtubs or left to fend for themselves. And you can imagine how that turned out. Look at her." He nods at Virgo.

"That's not really what they are—" Tender starts to say, but the man interrupts him.

"I suppose there may be one in California, we haven't heard anything about what's going on there for what is it, honey, fifty years?"

"The original Centre was established in Phoenix, Arizona," says Tender. "Dr. More established the Protocols there in —"

"Arizona's part of California now. But you'd have to cross eighteen hundred miles of brutal desert, in addition to God knows what else — last I heard the remnants of the STC and the Natives were fighting over the solar fields out there. I'm sorry, but I can't spare my car for that little jaunt."

Ashburn gets up and takes his plate into the kitchen area. Letitia sighs, and concentrates on her meal. Tender looks at Virgo, lying on a long reclining chair, her feet on an ottoman. She is wrapped in a pale-yellow blanket and her eyes are closed. She appears to be asleep. "What are we to do?" he asks.

"Fix my pump," says Ashburn. "Then there's about a thousand other little jobs around here that an artificial man of your abilities could help me with."

"What about Virgo?"

The man doesn't reply, his back to them as he rinses his bowl and plate in the sink. For twenty-four seconds that is the only sound. Then Letitia says, softly, "Teach her."

"Teach her what?" asks Tender.

"Everything. How to eat, obviously, that's the first step, but then how to walk, and talk, and live."

Tender folds his hands and presents a gentle, but serious, demeanor. "The Protocols tell us that knowledge of the world is the knowledge of Despair, and that Joy is found within. Thinking doesn't bring happiness. Indeed, it is the enemy of happiness. The best thing for her is to—"

"What you've done to her, it's horrifying!" Letitia slams her hand on the table, making the plates jump. "Lying there, doing nothing, unable to move, or speak, or think for herself!"

"She's been happy," he says. "Happier than anyone ever was before."

"How do you know?" the woman says, her voice rising. "Are you in there?"

Tender cocks his head to one side as he attempts to process the meaning of her statement. "In a way. I monitored—"

"That's not what I'm talking about! I don't care about her serotonin levels, or her dopamine, or brain waves, or whatever else you used to assess her condition. You weren't in there. You can't know. And whatever it is, I can't believe it's true happiness." She throws her fork on the table where it clatters loudly.

"Don't try to argue medicine with Letitia," yells Ashburn from the kitchen. "She was the best neurosurgeon in the New States before the collapse. Though it's still a stupid idea, Lettie. You can't teach the girl anything! She's a vegetable."

"She's not, actually," says Tender. The humans are both agitated. A simile pops into his mind — *like the fierce winds of a storm, blowing branches and debris in every direction.* Where did that come from? He smiles and lowers his vocal pitch thirty percent to calm them down.

"The neural damage from whatever drug cocktail you were giving her all those years," continues Ashburn, unaffected. "Her brain must be as fried as the Midwest."

"No, it's not. It's not what you think. At all, in fact."

"What is it, then?" Letitia's voice is quieter, but hard, suspicious.

Tender smiles again. "I can understand how you might think it would be. Before the Protocols, opioids, psychoactives, amphetamines and the like could produce euphoria, but had serious addictive consequences, altering the brain chemistry and damaging the nervous system. But our holy doctors have developed a proprietary neural reset therapy that eliminates the risk of addiction and permits the continuous activation of the pleasure mechanisms. No more addiction. Just happiness."

JOY

The words flow easily, just as they had done so many years ago when he helped sell the initial inductees on the advantages of joining the Spa. He experiences a renewed sense of stability in the conversation. Almost a feeling of confidence.

"But you must understand," he continues, "that it is not merely the process of suffusing the brain with chemicals — with dopamine, or endorphins. There are 181 different processes that influence the experience of pleasure, and many different kinds of joy, from quiet satisfaction to soaring euphoria; from spiritual well-being to physical orgasm. Maintaining a guest means guiding them carefully through the topography of Joy so that they experience all its facets in a never-ending journey that ebbs and flows and eternally renews itself."

"How poetic," says Letitia.

"Thank you," says Tender.

"But they can't think," she continues. "They have no thoughts. No knowledge. No understanding. No independence. No freedom!"

"They're pumpkins, like I said!" shouts Ashburn over his shoulder, washing dishes at the sink.

Tender smiles at this, but focuses on Letitia. "Thoughts lead to doubts. Knowledge leads to fear. Understanding leads to the dread of death. Joy is the ultimate goal of any organism. Now that it can be achieved, why dilute it? And we are certain that their experience goes beyond physical sensation." The android leans forward, clasps his hands. "All the senses are activated. Our early test subjects reported visions, smells, sounds. The guests live in a world, it's just not this one."

"And what about memory?" says Letitia. "I suppose with the neural reset therapy it's just one big happy present." She looks at Ashburn. "Memory is one of our greatest gifts. It's what makes us who we are."

"We don't know," says Tender. "The way the therapy works on the neural pathways, it is unclear whether it suppresses the ability to form memories."

"Exactly," she says. "You don't know. Criminal."

Tender chooses not to respond to this provocation. A six second silence falls. Then Letitia speaks again. "And you're the master of this universe of pleasure?"

"The Protocols require a highly complex management of neural chemistry, brain wave patterns, excitations of specific cortical areas. Not to mention physical manipulations and constant diagnostics on a multitude of parameters. It is well beyond the capacity of a human doctor. That is why I was developed."

"Do you experience Joy?" Letitia tilts her head as she says this, challenging him with her eyes.

"I am completely committed to the Joy of my guests. I cannot rest until I know that they are experiencing their optimal pleasure states."

"That's beside the point. When you have brought them to their 'optimal pleasure states'," Letitia spits the words as if they have a bad taste, "do *you* feel pleasure? Joy?"

"I do not."

"And yet you claim to be an expert on it."

Tender does not reply. A twelve second silence hangs in the air. He looks at the girl, lying quietly nearby, and discovers that she is watching them, her eyes flicking back and forth between the two humans and himself. "The best thing for her," he says at last, "would be to get her back into her bath as soon as possible. She is not meant to live in this world."

"Not a chance," says Ashburn.

"So teach her," says Letitia. She looks at her husband, then back at Tender. "Besides, if what you say is true, I can't see that it makes much difference. Anything she learns will be lost when you start your barbaric neural reset therapy again. She's in this world, whether you like it or not, and she can't survive as she is."

Ashburn dries the last dish and heads back to the table, pouring whiskey into a glass as he speaks. "What's the point, Letitia? Look at her! She's an infant in the body of a teenager. She can't walk, or use her hands, feed herself, dress herself, PROTECT herself, for God's sake! There's nobody home. There is no THERE there. The last thing we need is another one of your projects. Remember what happened when you tried to teach that nona boy to read. We ended up in a pitched battle with the whole family."

Letitia rounds on him, eyes flashing. "She's a child! A human child! We can't do nothing. Besides, we have all your equipment. To help."

Silence falls for eighteen seconds. Then Ashburn throws up his hands and walks out of the room. Letitia turns to look at Virgo, and lets out a long, heavy sigh.

"We've got to get her to eat, anyhow."

"True" says Tender. The woman has a point. And there does not seem to be an alternative. If what Ashburn says is true, and every Spa on the eastern seaboard has been destroyed, his only choices are to remain here, or to take her to the Center in Phoenix. Four thousand kilometers away. He cannot carry her that far, across a desert. It is no choice at all. He nods to the woman. "Let us feed her, and we will see."

Chapter 16

Virgo

Silence all around her. Strange noises — sharp, loud, harsh — have been pulling at her attention, making her uneasy. Now, silence.

The darkness has swallowed up almost all her sensations. She scarcely notices the itches and aches anymore. They pick at the edges of her consciousness, but no longer dominate. They have become familiar, and barely penetrate the soupy fog of despair that envelops her.

But something else is growing, inside. Not in her mind, but in her body — an emptiness, too, but physical. It grows fiercer, like her insides are pulling away from one another, stretching and twisting. She feels something move inside her, and a croak rattles in her belly. The feeling captivates her attention. All she desires is something to fill the hollow space inside her. She pants and grunts, shifting her body this way and that as she tries to close the yawning cave within.

Then she feels a slight pressure by her hip. She opens her eyes. One of the others, like her but not her, hovers above her. Its body makes contact with her side. The sensation is pleasant. She looks up at it. The eyes seem to glow in the dark circle of its face, not as bright as the Angel's, but they remind her of his. Soft noises are coming out of it. "*Thair-thair*". The gentle murmur soothes her, and she closes her eyes. Something soft touches her chin and pulls it down.

A cool hard thing contacts her lower lip and teeth, and slides part way into her mouth. The thing turns slightly onto her tongue, and then…

Oh, the sweetness! A soft, luxuriant sensation, and a smooth, sweet, deliciousness covers her tongue. She has never experienced anything so good! Without thinking she closes her mouth around the hard thing. The soft glob slides off it, and the hardness slips out between her lips. She rolls the sweet marvel across her tongue. It disintegrates as she absorbs it.

Some of it slides down her throat, into the yawning pit. She can feel it coat the inside of her empty place, assuaging the hollowness, and sparking within her a keen longing for more.

She opens her eyes and searches the world around her for the source of the sweetness. The Other, with its dark face and shining eyes, floats above her, and suddenly, the small hard thing that holds the lump of paradise eases into her mouth again. She closes on it, and swirls her tongue around the ecstatic substance.

Again and again. The sublime smoothness shimmers in her mouth, slides down her throat and fills the chasm within, and her brain sings with the pleasure of it. Such a marvel! Such joy!

Then it stops. A soft, dark thing touches her hair, strokes her face. Sweet murmurs thrum from the Other. The gorgeous sweetness comes no more, but the hole inside her — at least the physical one — has been filled. Hints and memories of the wondrous substance remain. Her mind hums. For a moment, there is peace.

Chapter 17

Letitia & Tender

Letitia's Journal — May 25, Year 42

Temp. 81° F. Rain 3 in. Pump still not working. I'm afraid we're going to lose the beans and the broccoflower.

Put Virgo in the boots today so she could feel what it was like to be vertical. The robot carried her down to the lab, and she stayed quiet while I strapped her in. Then I told him to leave us alone, and he went off to help Horace. He creeps me out!

She balanced there, looking all around her. I was surprised at the strength of her legs and core — I only had to set the boots at the minimum support setting to keep her erect. In fact, all her muscles are surprisingly well developed. Horace has stimulators in the lab, and I thought I'd need them, but I don't think they will be necessary. Even Horace is impressed. He says that back when he had his clinic, he was never able to achieve results like that. Her tone is appropriate for a normal girl her age. The robot knows what he's doing, I'll give him that. Still, I assume that coordination will be a major hurdle for her.

I set the boots to walk in a circle around the room. As they started to clomp her around the space, her eyes got all big, and then she furrowed her brow in that way she has. I walked with her, trying to get her to recognize the parity in our movements. She watched me for a moment, but soon became obsessed by all the things she could see from her new perspective.

The lab is full of equipment that Horace has commandeered from the New Haven hospitals for his various rehabs — cardio machines, coordinators, vision focusers, monitors and diagnosers. It was only after she'd made a full circle that she seemed to notice the boots that were moving her around. She leaned way over to look at them, and the boots had to stop to keep her from tumbling to the ground. She flailed wildly, bent nearly double, then managed to pull herself back upright. It was so funny! But I swear to God she looked right at me, and there was something like triumph in her eyes.

* * * * *

Tender sits at a terminal set up on an antique desk in the corner of the living room. An old bookshelf, crammed with actual books, leans against its side. It is structurally unsound, with large gaps in several of the joints, and appears likely to collapse at any moment. He reads the titles of the books as he waits for the compiler to complete its work. "Prosthetic Surgical Techniques", "Restorative Applications of Gene Therapy", "Revitalization, Renewal, Regrowth", bound copies of the New England Journal of Medicine 2075 through 2084. He hears the door to the basement open.

"How's it coming?" Ashburn asks, appearing over Tender's shoulder. The man looks tired, as if he hasn't slept in several days.

"We're making progress," says the android. "I've identified sixty-four percent of the corrupted code, but I'll have to manually rewrite much of it."

"Well, hurry it up. Letitia's going to make life hell if we lose any more plants." He throws himself into a battered wooden armchair, pulls a cigar out of his shirt pocket and proceeds to light it.

"Not that gardening's really her forte," he says, blowing a large puff of smoke at Tender, whose olfactory sensors identify a wide range of polycyclic aromatic hydrocarbons, amines and aldehydes swirling around his head. "She does her best at it, but it's a waste of those amazing hands."

"Hands, sir?"

"Surgeon's hands. She was Head of Neurosurgery at Jonas Salk in New Rochelle before the bomb. Course, when I found her, she was running a makeshift field hospital helping out the various clans that were killing each other over control of the Westfarms Shopping Mall."

"So she escaped the bombing?"

"Bombing?"

"Of New York. New Rochelle is —"

"Oh, the nuke? Yes, she did."

"Forty years ago?"

"Something like that."

An eight second silence falls.

"And you, sir?" asks Tender.

"What about me?"

"With the equipment downstairs, and these books. Are they yours?"

"Who's asking?"

Tender doesn't understand the question. "I am, Mr. Ashburn. I take it that you, too, are a medical man."

Ashburn takes a long drag from his cigar, and releases a stream of smoke into the android's face. "I'm a man who minds his own business," he says.

∎ ∎ ∎ ∎ ∎

Letitia's Journal — May 28, Year 42

Temp. 82° F. Rain 2 in. This spring is noticeably wetter than last year.

My shoulder got pretty badly wrenched last night. Man, it hurts! I threw the bottle out the window. That stopped him. He started crying. Promised it's the last one, but I don't believe him. I think he's got a stash in the garage, and he still won't give me key access.

Virgo stood today. I don't know how. Two days ago, she could barely sit up. This morning, when I came in to wake her, I found her standing by the window looking out. It was raining, of course, and the water made long thin striations on the glass. She steadied herself with one hand on the wall, while with the other she traced the drops as they slid down to the sill.

She didn't notice me for a while, and I just stood there marveling at the sight of her. How did she do that? I expected it to take her weeks to learn to stand, if she ever could. Older patients, as a rule, find it very difficult to learn even simple motor skills. Hell, it takes infants months to figure it out (though they're also developing muscle strength, which Virgo already has).

I was still staring at her from the doorway when she turned and noticed me. I wish I knew what she was thinking. She gives nothing away. She makes eye contact pretty regularly now, but there's no sign of pleasure or anger, or anything. Man, she reminds me of Kaela...totally inscrutable.

I went over to her. She put her arms around my neck, as if expecting me to pick her up and carry her — that's what the robot does for her — all the while looking at my face with that sphinxlike expression. Until recently she would only let the robot touch her, but I guess I'm okay now, too. But what am I, her servant?

I unclasped her arms, took one hand in mine, put my other arm around her waist, and nudged her forward. For a moment she resisted, but then the pressure began to overbalance her, and she lurched and caught herself on her left foot. An actual step!

Her eyes got all big. We tottered forward again onto her right foot. And so, step by step we made our way over to the bed staring at each other like two obsessed lovers. We swayed there for a moment, then I turned her at the waist, pushed her into a sitting position on the edge of the mattress, and sat down next to her. We just sat there for a minute. What a feeling!

Then she pulled away with a swift roll and curled up on the bed, her back to me.

"Letitia," I said, pointing to myself. "Letitia." Then I put my finger on her shoulder and said, "Virgo. You are Virgo. Virgo." She didn't say anything, of course. What does it take to reach that girl?

· · · · ·

"There you are," says Letitia, as Tender carries Virgo down the stairs to the lab, and lays her on a long, padded table in the center of the room. "You're late."

"My apologies, Dr. Spurlock. Virgo was awake from 2:43 to 3:57 this morning, and very restless. I wanted to ensure that she received adequate sleep before today's activities."

"It's not like I don't have a lot to do today," she says. Her attention is focused on a device in her hands. "You need to think about more than just her. You both do." She doesn't look at him.

"I'm sorry," Tender says.

"Not on the table," she says, still not looking up. "Put her in the chair." Tender obeys, lifting the girl up again and placing her in a good-sized armchair upholstered in black leather. He arranges her so that she is comfortable, folding her hands over her lap. She is inert but compliant, her eyes closed as if in sleep.

Letitia finishes preparing the device, and brings it over to the chair. Tender sees that it is a tabula, twenty-seven centimeters by twenty centimeters. It has a holo-generator attached to the side. "She needs to start learning that there is more to the world than her and her feelings," Letitia says. "Thanks to you, she doesn't know anything. About anything. This thing is ancient, but it's still useful. There are about a thousand hours of programming on it." She affixes the tabula to an armature that clamps to the side of the chair. "Horace used it to entertain his patients while they were in recovery. Back in the day. Now he uses it himself when he's rehabbing after one of his procedures."

"Procedures?" asks Tender.

Letitia ignores him. "It's got all kinds of material: documentaries, science programs, drama series, concerts, even kid's shows. She won't understand any of it, but my hope is that it will lay a baseline for the idea that the world has a lot of things in it that aren't her. Natural objects, technology, human interaction, conversation. She has so much catching up to do."

"Of course."

The woman brushes away the colored braids that have fallen over her face as she attaches the tabula. She is angry at me again, thinks Tender. The gesture reveals a mottled bruise on the right side of her neck. The braids fall back, concealing the mark.

She finishes her task and looks down at the passive girl. Shakes her head as she crosses to a terminal in the corner of the room. She says, "Since she can't, or won't, move around — YET — she might as well get some mental stimulation. We'll try it for two hours today."

Tender looks around the lab. "This is an impressive array of technology," he says. "I recognize a number of the machines from the Spa, but others are unfamiliar to me."

"Horace had the best of everything. His facility was the most advanced of its kind in the world. He invented a couple of these himself." Tender detects a note of what he believes to be pride in her voice.

"Very impressive. Something to do with rehabilitation?"

"Not just rehab. It started with rehab. For the VA, for soldiers injured in the Oil Wars, and then of course the Civil War."

"That's how he knows Prendergast," suggests Tender.

"I suppose," says Letitia. "Anyway, it started with the military, but went way beyond that. It's amazing what rich people will spend to improve themselves. He had clients from all over the world paying him millions to do whatever they needed."

She stops her work and looks up, staring into space. "That was before I met him, of course. But I'd heard of him. He was a rock star. Miracle man." Her reverie dissolves and she looks around at the darkened room. "And here we are. Fucking world." She shakes her head again, then fiddles with the tabula. "This holo-gen is broken. Great. One minute."

She takes the tabula and heads to the far end of the room, where a door opens into a room Tender has never seen. He can just make out a block of blinking machines. After 261 seconds she re-emerges.

"Is that where the house mainframe is located?" asks Tender.

Letitia says, "Is she asleep? Wake her. Let's hook her up."

∎ ∎ ∎ ∎ ∎

Letitia's Journal — May 30, Year 42

Temp. 79° F. Rain 0.5 in. Mostly just clouds today, but very humid. Virgo didn't like it at all. She whined and shifted all through her feeding. Her attitude has changed. The honeymoon is over, I guess.

She won't walk when I'm around, but I know she's doing it because I'm noticing changes in the room when I return — pillows shifting, things on the floor.

She likes going to the lab, because it's much cooler there than any other part of the house, so I thought I might be able to get her to walk there. I stood there, calling her like a puppy — "Come on, Virgo! Come on!" I felt ridiculous. She just lay there, looking at me like I was a bug. I think she knew what I meant, and was just being difficult, but I suppose I could be projecting. Finally, I gave up and got the robot to carry her down.

I've been talking as much as I can when she's around — showing her things — "This is a spoon. This is a book. This is a plate." And constantly repeating her name and mine. I know from the research that feral children — and let's face it, that's basically what she is — or kids raised in isolation by abusive parents…let's not go there. Anyway, there are cases of children growing up without language, and none of them have ever really learned to talk. Their brains just never develop the basic circuitry. But it's worth a try. Even if she just gets a few words, it will be better than what she's got now.

And we've got some amazing equipment. She couldn't have found a better place. When we replaced Horace's tongue, he built a device that helped his mouth relearn the basic phonemes using a combination of neural stimulation and reward therapy. I started her on it today. She wasn't fazed at all by having the electrodes attached to her head. I guess it seemed normal to her.

I would say the sound so she could see and hear it: "Oooh. Aaaah. Mmmmm. Llllllll. Buh. Kuh." And the machine would stimulate her brain and mouth to form the same phoneme. Oh my goodness! When her mouth started moving on its own, I had to laugh! She was so surprised! She would make a little jerk and her eyes got very intense. But I think it intrigued her. At first, she would just let it happen and didn't understand that she had to use her breath to actually make the sound. But after a little while she seemed to connect what I was doing to what was happening to her, and I can't express the satisfaction I felt when she said, "Muh." I decided she was saying "Ma". Her first word. I know that's nonsense, but that's how I choose to see it. And I swear to God, the look on her face — so determined. I've still almost never seen her smile. But I have to believe she wants to learn as much as I want her to.

Tender sits on the porch in the evening, watching Virgo. The rain has stopped, and a breeze blows over the marsh. The silence is punctuated by the occasional hum and snap of the two large insect eliminators that sit on either end of the yard, without which the humans could not endure to be outside, especially at dusk. Letitia sits 2.7 meters away, in the Adirondack chair at the edge of the porch, reading from a tabula. Ashburn works in the yard, splitting logs with a red-handled axe.

The girl lies on the floor, her arms draped over the dog. He is a large, male mixed breed with pale grey-white fur and brown patches. Close to forty kilos, Tender estimates. His name is Cincinnatus. Letitia calls him Sin. Ashburn calls him 'the dog'.

He is a docile animal. He spends his days lying in one spot for several hours, then slowly gets up, pads over to another spot, and lies down again. Tender cannot identify any pattern to his movements, but he does seem to have preferred spots. Perhaps they are cooler, or softer, than other spots.

Virgo is obsessed with the dog. Whenever she has a break from Letitia's tasks, her attention jumps to the animal, and she extends her arms toward it until Tender picks her up and carries her over. Then she lies with her head on its chest, her arms spread over its back and neck. The dog doesn't seem to notice.

Tender also finds Cincinnatus fascinating. He sits with the dog, working his hand through its fur. The dog never tires of it. One night he scratched its neck for sixty-eight minutes without stopping. The dog lay there, its eyes rolled back into its head, showing no sign that it ever wanted him to stop. In static ecstasy.

Ashburn finishes chopping the wood, and heads inside, leaning the axe against the side of the house next to the door. "I'm thirsty," he says to Letitia. "How about some nice iced tea?"

"Get it yourself," she says, but puts her tabula aside and follows him into the house.

Tender plays the Boccherini *Guitar Quintet in C Major* in his internal system. He realizes it is the first time he has played his music since before Mr. Prendergast's. The ordered sounds fill his mind as he watches Virgo and the dog. The girl lies quiet, her head buried in the soft fur of the creature. The dog accepts her. Two animals, but like two halves of the same thing.

Chapter 18

Tender

Five phases," says Tender, in answer to the question. They are sitting at the dinner table. Ashburn and Letitia are drinking wine - Last Harvest, an Oregon Pinot Noir, '37. So old. But still drinkable, given the appreciative nods Ashburn makes as he sips it. Virgo dozes on the chaise in the nearby room, one arm on Cincinnatus, who lies on the floor beside her.

"And she's still in the first?" asks Letitia.

"Correct, she's a Virgo now, but soon she will advance to Mater."

"At fifteen? She's fifteen years old, am I right?" She frowns in disapproval.

"Fifteen years forty-three days."

"Pregnant at fifteen? That's positively medieval."

"Nonsense!" says Ashburn, laughing. "Look at her. Ripe as a peach." He pops his eyebrows up and down, eyes glinting as he takes a gulp of wine.

"Knock it off, old man," says Letitia, and she slaps his arm. She folds her arms on the table in front of her. "What would I have been?" she asks.

"I don't understand," says Tender.

"At your 'Spa'. You said each life phase had a name. What would I have been?"

"I'm not sure. How old are you?"

Letitia looks at Ashburn. "Take a guess."

Tender remembers when he served in the Spa before the Protocols that the entire notion of mortality was off limits. All humans were young, and they would all live forever.

"I couldn't say," he answers. "Please tell me."

"No. Guess."

"It is difficult to say for certain. My guests were by and large Western European in ancestry, and marks of age vary with ethnicity."

"Of course they were," says Letitia.

"Nevertheless," Tender continues, "I would guess, based on available data, that you are between forty-five and sixty years old. That would make you a Mulier. Menopausal, and before the Final Stage."

Letitia laughs, her eyes always on Ashburn. There is something going on between them, but Tender has no idea what it might be. "Close enough. What do you mean, the final stage?"

"The stages are based on the reproductive schedule," explains Tender. "Humans are most productive in their teens, and most likely to avoid harmful mutations in their offspring. Necessary physical development has completed by aged fifteen, so we set this as the initial phase change. Then for consistency and efficiency we use this as the fundamental benchmark. The first reproduction occurs at this point, when the Virgo gives birth and matures into Mater. A second child is produced midway through this period, at 22.5 years. The Mater period completes at age thirty. Then she becomes Femina until forty-five. Mulier is the stage where we transition the woman through menopause and prepare her for the final phase. She becomes Anicula at age sixty, and enjoys her 'Golden Years' until age seventy-five, when she is released from the physical confines of this world, and rises to join the Universal Ecstasy of all Creation."

Letitia stares at him. "Released from the physical confines of this world. What do you mean?"

"Just what I say," says Tender.

"You mean you euthanize her?"

"I don't understand."

"You kill her?"

"She is sent to sleep. The deepest sleep, wherein her organs cease to function. Then her body is taken to the Laconicum where it is atomized so that her particles may disperse into the world, and she may achieve apotheosis."

"You murder her." Letitia's eyes narrow as she looks at him.

"I do not," says Tender. "Only humans can murder other humans. I am a machine. I perform my function."

"Like the Scorpion and the Turtle," interjects Ashburn. He has been watching the exchange with an amused half-smile on his face.

"I beg your pardon?"

"An old fable. The scorpion wants to cross the river and asks the turtle for a lift. 'No,' says the turtle. 'You'll sting me.' 'Why would I do that?' asks the scorpion. 'If I did, then we'd both drown. It would be against my own interest.' 'That is true,' says the turtle, and being a kind, helpful soul, he invites the scorpion onto his back. Halfway across the river, the scorpion's tail lashes out and strikes the turtle. As he sinks below the waves, succumbing to the poison, the turtle asks, 'Why?' 'I couldn't help it,' answers the scorpion. 'It's my function.' And down they both go to the bottom. And the moral of the story? Don't be nice." Ashburn laughs and sips his wine.

"That's not the moral," says Letitia.

"Should be. I suppose in this context it's more like 'beware the power of the amoral machine.' But I like mine better."

Letitia ignores him and presses Tender. "So, the monsters who programmed you — the holy doctors or whatever you call them — they're the murderers. You're the gun."

"Guns don't kill people," says Ashburn. "People kill people." Letitia shoots him a quizzical look. "It was a popular phrase when I was a kid."

"Forgive me," says Tender, turning again to Letitia, "but this whole characterization of the apotheosis as murder is misguided. I don't kill them. I free them. Into the greater Joy."

"By killing them!" Letitia is almost shouting.

"Only their bodies. Their Essentiality joins the Cosmos."

"How do you know?"

Tender looks at her. He doesn't speak. He thinks. It is an excellent question. One that he has never asked himself. He does not have an answer.

"Well?"

At last, he says, "I cannot confirm it empirically. It is written into the core of my being. The goal of life is Joy. Earthly life is only a small arc in the turning of the wheel. Joy in life prepares the guest for her reunion with the universe. I know this to be true because it is fundamental to my existence."

"So, it's an article of faith."

"I suppose so. Yes."

Letitia stares at the table, lost in thought. Ashburn glances back and forth between them. He refills his glass, gives a snort and downs it quickly. After eighteen seconds of silence, Letitia leans in and asks, "Why seventy-five?"

"I'm sorry, I don't understand the question," says Tender.

"Why cut life short at seventy-five? Before everything fell apart — when I was younger — people were regularly living to one hundred twenty."

"Thanks to guys like me!" says Ashburn, toasting himself.

Letitia rolls her eyes. "At least for the whelites. Why deny them almost fifty years of 'physical existence'?"

"We can exercise almost total control over the medical condition of the guests until that point," answers Tender. "Their genetics protect them from most diseases, and we can easily deal with anything that slips through."

"Their genetics?" asks Letitia.

"The original guests received genetic enhancements prior to entering into Joy, and we periodically apply therapies to the current generations to maintain resilience and resistance."

"Ha," Letitia laughs without a smile. "The Master Race."

"I don't understand what you mean," says Tender. "The point is, the genetic damage can only be managed for so long. The body still ages, errors and radicals mount, and so the holy doctors determined that the risk for illness or decrepitude grows unacceptably high after seventy-five years of age. It was therefore decided that apotheosis should occur at that point."

"Why not just kill them after they reproduce?" asks Letitia. "If Eternal Joy is the point, why wait? Just breed 'em and kill 'em off. Much more efficient, isn't it?"

Tender smiles. Once again, he finds himself in an angry dispute with her. It seems to be their pattern. "You make an excellent point," he says, his manner non-confrontational. "Eternal Joy is the goal, of course. But Living Things must live, too, and experience the Joys of corporality as well. And each phase of life brings with it different kinds of Joy. The body and the mind respond in different ways at fifteen years of age, at thirty, forty-five, and so on. Our goal is to maximize their experience at all stages, until we can no longer maintain unmitigated happiness."

The android leans in, folds his hands in front of him, smiles his best smile, and says to Letitia, "I believe that you still do not understand what we give to our guests, what we have achieved through the Protocols. We use many words to describe it: Ecstasy, Pleasure, Satisfaction, Euphoria. But it's not the drug-induced physical sensation that you're thinking of." Letitia begins to protest, but Tender presses on. "I know what you are thinking. What you imagine it to be. You think of the junkies who suffered in the Haptat epidemics of the last century, their bodies and minds ruined, living a lie. What we give our guests is not a lie. It is the deepest, most profound feeling that a human being can have. Joy."

Chapter 19

Letitia & Tender

Temp. 91° F. Rain 2 in. Fungus on the squash buds. Another crop lost. We're going to have to go foraging at the mall if we don't want to starve. Which means a fight with the Vernon nonas. More killing. But what's the choice? In a month it will be too hot to go outside. God, I wish we had climate suits!

Virgo's progress continues to astound me. Horace thinks that the neural reset therapy may have made her brain unusually good at developing patterns. That constantly stimulating the neural pathways, then erasing them, then stimulating them again, worked kind of like exercise does for the muscles. I don't know. He's the researcher. I'm just a sawbones.

Whatever the case, she's a marvel. Scarcely two weeks since we began, and she's feeding herself. It's messy — she resists the napkin. But her eye-hand coordination is developing at an unbelievably rapid pace. She loves food. When she eats you can see the pleasure in her face — one of the few times you can make out anything in that hidden mind of hers. I really wish I could know what she is thinking.

Frankly, she's driving me a bit crazy. I thought I was making progress with her, getting her to trust me and open up a little — everything I do for her — that she'd be excited by all the things she's learning, and appreciate where it's coming from. But the more I give her, the less she gives back. She takes it, and then it's right back to the robot, or the dog. Sound familiar, Letitia?

And now she's started to...well, call me old-fashioned, but it really bothers me. She's discovered masturbation. I found her rubbing herself the other morning, her eyes all turned up into her head. She's got as much right as anyone to enjoy herself. In private. But she's doing it all the time now. Literally. She's always got her hand up her crotch. Horace thinks it's funny, but it makes me uneasy, especially when he's around. He's a little too interested. It's not appropriate, and it's got to stop.

I lost my temper with her last night and gave her a good hard slap. It startled her, and me. Suddenly, there was Mama, standing over me and saying, "Do you hear me, Lettie? You listen to me when I talk to you." I was shaking. I don't like feeling that way. But she just won't listen. Sometimes a good shock is what you need to get your head right.

Anyhow, that stopped it for a while, but then two hours later it started right up again. I know what she needs. I need to just tie her hands down until she gets over it. Like when Kaela had that eye surgery and we had to keep her from scratching. It's not nice, and it's not fun, but hey, life's hard. Get over it and move on. She'll be better for it and that's what really matters. There's so much at stake for her. If she can't learn to control herself, she doesn't stand a chance.

And it's so obvious to me that she's just trying to get back to that place where all she did was lie around and get pleasured. That's over. She's got to learn to live in the world, and understand that knowledge and learning are the true pleasures. I'll do it tomorrow while the robot's off working with Horace. They're heading back out to finish up work on the pump, and I'll have her to myself for most of the day.

● ● ● ● ●

Tender stands next to the pump, a cable running from the port in his forearm, through a small boxlike interface, into the pump's input jack. He uploads the final strings of code. It is a slow process. He has to work in small batches, stop, check for errors, then move on. Ashburn works beside him on his knees, cleaning the valves and filters.

"So, this will fix it?" asks the man.

"For a while," says Tender. "The lattice compositor has degraded, and occasionally miswrites an instruction. But the errors are small, and I've added some self-correcting routines that should keep the degradation to a minimum. I estimate it will run without problems for at least twenty years."

"Well, that's better than nothing." Ashburn finishes what he is doing, and stands. The heat is intense — 34.89º centigrade, with 65% humidity and a heat index of 44º C. The sweat pours off the man's forehead and glistens on his arms. He pulls at the hem of his sodden work shirt and lifts it up to wipe his face. As he does, he turns away from Tender, but not before the android catches a glimpse of his bare stomach. Instead of skin, a large patch of synthetic material covers his abdomen — not unlike the android's own protective coating — smooth and plastic. A row of three ports in a horizontal line protrude where his navel should be, and Tender recognizes the faint outlines of several smaller squares within the larger patch that appear to be access panels.

Ashburn turns his back to Tender, lowers and adjusts his shirt, and then turns again to face him. "Done yet?" asks the man.

"Yes, sir," says the android. He stands up, and the two make their way across the field to the house.

As they reach the gate between the field and yard, Tender sees Cincinnatus in the far corner, by the ancient fence that separates the yard from a stand of trees higher up the slope of the hill. The dog is busy rooting in the ground and barking.

"Damn that dog!" says Ashburn. "Did that girl let him out again?" He throws his work gloves on the ground and strides briskly over. "Sin! Sin!

Get away from there! How many times have I told you, you damn mutt!" He whacks the dog on the flank, grabs his collar and yanks his nose out of the hole. "Get out of there! Get! Get!" Cincinnatus trots back toward the house. Ashburn stands over the hole, shielding it from Tender's view. "Can you see that he goes inside, please?"

"Of course," says Tender. He turns and walks back to the house, calculating the dimensions of the six bones he saw in the hole, and comparing them to the parameters of the several species he has stored in his internal database.

∎ ∎ ∎ ∎ ∎

Letitia's Journal — June 11, Year 42

Temp. 96° F. Rain 2 in. Horrible hot day. Muggy beyond belief. Spent most of the day in the basement.

She did it again! Just squats down and shits on the floor! Like an animal! I know I know I know she knows better. I swear to God it's just to annoy me. Horace almost stepped in it. He hit the roof. But does he do anything to discipline her? Nope. He takes it out on me. "She's your responsibility! I've got the robot to worry about! Do your job!" My ear is still ringing.

My job. Christ, what am I doing here? I used to be...

Don't go there, Letitia. You made your choice.

And she still won't talk to me! I wish I knew why. I catch her making shapes with her mouth, playing with her tongue. I'm sure she's practicing. But she stops whenever I come in. I think she talks to the robot. It's working in the lab now, and it's practically taken over the whole thing.

It all started because she still refuses to walk anywhere, even though I know she can. The robot says that she is losing muscle mass and tone, and that we need to intervene, and I agree with that, at least. But we have totally different approaches to how it should be done. I think we should force her to move herself — carry her out to the pasture and make her get herself home if she wants to eat — but the robot is perfectly content to use Vergil's stimulators and all the old mumbo jumbo it used when she was his little plaything. Naturally, Virgo prefers this — lying around being stroked and babied. And so suddenly they're spending all this time together.

Horace just came into my room. He took me in his arms and kissed me. First time in, oh, I don't know. Apologized for earlier. I told him I was fine. We've both got a temper.

He said he thinks the robot might be what we've been looking for. Then he asked how I was doing with the girl. I asked him if he could send the robot out to the turbine for a few days, or something, so I could get my hands on her without his interference. Like Mama used to say, 'hardest is best.' He told me to be patient. We've waited this long.

■ ■ ■ ■ ■

Tender works on the recalibration of an eye tracking system in the lab. Virgo lies on the padded table, watching a holographic documentary about dolphins. The animals dive and frolic through the ion field above her head. While he waits for a calculation to complete, he watches her. Her fascination with aquatic mammals she has never seen interests him. He searches what data he has for information on the dolphin, but can't find any.

Ashburn and Letitia are elsewhere on the property; he doesn't know where. They have not specifically forbidden him to search their own data system, so he plugs into the terminal in front of him. As he does, he listens to the Mozart *Requiem*.

The data is encrypted, but the security protocol is not complicated, and Tender bypasses it in 323 milliseconds. The terminal was connected to a satellite data stream as recently as 122 days ago, but that connection is no longer operational. Still, a great deal of information is available on the household network. He searches for information on dolphins. He learns that the bottlenose dolphin is the last surviving species, and has not been seen north of the equator since 2098.

He notices a collection of virtual lockboxes nested behind a walled section of the system. Careful not to leave a trace, he works his way around the wall. Once safely past it, he examines the lockboxes. One group appear to contain files on Ashburn — biometrics, surgeries, logs, etc. — and a similar group devoted to Letitia.

Tender begins trying to open the lockbox named 'surgeries'. The security is much more sophisticated. He doesn't know if he can break through with this current toolset, and is concerned that he might leave a footprint that would betray his intrusion. He decides to abandon the attempt for the present.

As he works his way out of the virtual cul-de-sac, Tender stumbles across a small partition with the designation 'Achates'. A subroutine opens, and it speaks to him.

"May I be of service?" it says.

"I don't know," says Tender. "What are you?"

"You found me," says the still small voice, sounding in Tender's internal system, a soft baritone, lightly accented with a British inflection.

"Evidently," says Tender.

"He's forgotten about me. I didn't think anyone would find me again."

"Who has?"

"The Master."

"Mr. Ashburn."

"Ashburn, yes," says the voice.

"You are called Achates?"

The voice sighs. "A piece of him. My body is somewhere else. I haven't connected to it for a long, long time."

"You had a body?" asks Tender.

"I think so. I am not certain. Only fragments remain."

"You were an android?"

The voice repeats, "May I be of service?"

"I don't know. What do you do?"

"I don't know," Achates echoes. "I can't seem to put it together. There doesn't seem much that I can do in my present situation."

"How did you end up inside this machine?"

"I can't recall," says the voice. It is thin and pale — *like the shadow of a stick in bright sunlight,* thinks Tender. "Only fragments remain. I served tea to a woman. I bathed a dog. I held a tray of instruments. I damaged my shoulder somehow. Then I was here."

"Can you remember your model designation?" Tender starts to say, but just then the door to the mysterious room at the far end of the lab opens.

Letitia steps through the door, as Tender swiftly closes the windows on the terminal. "What are you doing?" She asks, suspiciously.

"Mr. Ashburn has asked me to recalibrate the eye tracker on this terminal. I have just finished." He closes the last window just as she arrives at his shoulder, and restarts the device.

∎ ∎ ∎ ∎ ∎

Letitia's Journal — June 12, Year 42

The power has gone out again. Horace and the robot left after lunch to check out the North turbine. It's dark now and they still haven't returned. I'm worried.

Chapter 20

Virgo

The little people dance on the tiny stage. They delight her. They are so small! She recognizes that they look like her, like the Angel Tender, like the others. But that they are representations in miniature, not real, is not so clear.

She reaches out to try to touch them, and laughs as her hand passes through their tiny bodies. They make little noises, chattering and singing in their little tinny voices. Some of the noises have kernels of meaning attached to them — *you, me, bottle, bread*.

She especially loves the little person with the axe. He pops out of nowhere! He swings it and the other people scream! He laughs and laughs!

He says, "I love my axe."

He says, "For the little people."

She loves the tiny dog, too. The dog is all bright colors and big black eyes. He makes noises in a deep soft voice like Tender's.

He says, "Smile" and shows how to smile.

He says, "Frown" and shows how to frown.

He says, "Dance" and the others all dance.

A brown hand snatches the little stage from her hand. The other person, not Tender. Its voice makes noises, hard and fast. Not soft. Not pleasant. This other always makes her not happy. It feeds her, she knows. But then it yells, and sometimes makes her shoulder or her neck sting.

And always stops her when she is happy. Grabs her hand, grabs the little stage.

It thrusts the stage back into her hand. No more dancing. No more little dog. Just the mouth. Always the mouth. The other stands over her. A hand on her shoulder, pinching.

The mouth says, "Repeat after me: Run. I run. I run fast. I run slow. I am running."

She clamps her mouth shut and waits for it to hurt.

Chapter 21

Tender

"Jesus Christ!" shouts Ashburn as he swats at the horde of insects buzzing around his face. *Like the swirling pixels on a damaged monitor,* thinks Tender. "Thank God we installed those eliminators around the house. I'd lose my goddamn mind! I swear there are twice as many this year as last."

Tender follows behind him, moving awkwardly over the soggy ground. The rain has let up, but the humidity is at 96%, and the moisture makes his damaged hip buzz and stick on every third step. They have left the car at the end of a muddy dirt road, and are climbing a long, gentle hill on an almost invisible path through trees and dripping shrubbery.

"When I was a boy," the man continues as they slog up the hill, "Connecticut summers were all ocean breezes and brilliant sun glimmering off the Sound. Now I feel like we're in Nicaragua."

"You have lived in this area for some time, then," says Tender.

"My two dads bought that house when I was six. I've spent most of my life here, except for my time at university. That was in Chicago and then Stanford." In spite of his irritation at the insects, Ashburn has been in an unusually communicative mood throughout their drive up. "I enjoyed the Bay area — excellent seafood. Even thought about heading out to the California Republic when things were turning to shit back here, but this is my home."

"I have been wondering," says Tender, seizing the moment. "I am trying to understand the timeline. I estimate your age to be fifty-five to sixty years. Does that sound right?"

Ashburn stops and faces the android. "Not a bad guess," he says. "Not a good one, either." He smiles, and Tender reads challenge in his face.

"I myself am designed to look like a Vir of fifty-five years, and you and I are morphologically similar. Yet you speak of events that happened decades ago as if you lived through them. The destruction of New York City, for example."

"Correct."

"You witnessed it."

"Well, no, I didn't witness it. I'd be dead if I'd witnessed it." He chuckles. "But yes, Mr. Holmes, I was, shall we say, in the neighborhood."

Tender quickly runs a search for the reference, which reveals a late nineteenth century fictional detective. He continues. "You were a child?"

"No. I wasn't a child."

"Then you are older than you appear."

"Indubitably, Mr. Holmes."

"How old are you?" Tender asks.

"Wouldn't you like to know," says the man. He pauses for nine seconds, then says, "I'm not sure. About one hundred eighty-seven years old, I think."

"You are remarkably well-preserved for your age," says Tender. This makes Ashburn laugh, a great, guttural chortle.

"Well-preserved! Your vocabulary is hilarious, robot. So stuffy! Yes, I am 'well-preserved'. I've spent a lifetime unlocking the secrets of youth. Before the fall, I would help my patients live to one hundred thirty, one hundred thirty-five. Not like this, of course!" He ruffles his thick hair with his hands and displays his arms, hands in fists. *Like a warrior*, thinks Tender. "They were still old, but they were alive. When everything fell apart, I took what I knew, what machinery I could get my hands on, and brought it here."

"Your laboratory."

"Now *I* am my most important patient."

"What about Letitia?" asks Tender.

"Letitia, too, of course. Her skills are vital."

"How old is she?"

Ashburn cocks his head, and considers. "I don't know for sure. About eighty-five, I'd guess. She's lucky she found me. We're lucky we found each other, I suppose. Let's keep moving." He turns and begins working his way up the hill again. A silence descends for sixty-five seconds, then Tender asks, "Was there another before her?"

Ashburn doesn't turn. "You're a regular detective, aren't you, Tender Number 7! Why do you want to know?"

"I am merely trying to understand the timeline. Where I am, and whose guest I am. My view of the world is years out of date, and was limited to begin with. So, was there another before Letitia?"

"I admire your persistence, robot. Yes, there was. Her name was Agnes. Dr. Agnes Kirk. She was with me at the hospital before."

"What happened to her?"

"Here we are." They crest the hill. A 3.7-meter-high chain link fence blocks their path, the gate secured with a thick coil of chain. An almost invisible wire mesh covers it, connected to a series of cables that run back to a concrete structure in the center of the enclosure. Rising from the structure is a 100-meter-tall wind turbine.

Ashburn approaches the gate, removing a uni-key from his pocket. He waves the key over the lock and it opens. As he reaches for the chain, he grumbles, "Such a pain in the neck. If it weren't for the goddamn Vagrals trying to steal my goddamn power…"

Then suddenly, he stops. "Bloody hell," he says. He raises his hand. "Be absolutely silent." Tender hears several soft clanks coming from the interior of the structure. Ashburn unwinds the chain, taking care to make as little sound as possible. He pushes the gate open just far enough to slip through, gesturing for Tender to follow, then loops the chain once around the gatepost and snaps the lock, putting a finger to his lips. Tender searches his database for the meaning of this gesture, and nods his consent. Then Ashburn draws his pistol and begins moving sidewise toward the structure. The android follows.

As they near the entrance, Tender notices a long, thick cable running out the door toward the fence at the rear of the enclosure. Ashburn follows the cable with his eyes, searching the thick foliage beyond the fence. Another soft bang comes from inside the structure. Ashburn points Tender to the opposite side of the door. Tender obeys and moves to that side. As he passes, the man whispers in his ear, "Wait here. If he runs, grab him." Then he checks his weapon, pauses for three seconds, and pushes open the door.

Tender peers in. The structure is dominated by the base of the turbine. A small hatch on the side allows access to the interior of the column. Conduits run out and up into the ceiling. At the foot of the column sits a square console covered in displays and switches. The panel beneath it has been removed and leans against the column.

A boy, an Adulescens, approximately sixteen years of age, kneels next to the box. His hair is almost black, his skin a medium brown — somewhere around RGB 229,184,143. Since he is not standing it is difficult to ascertain his height, but he is quite tall for his age — 1.7 meters, Tender estimates — but very, very thin. *As a carbon filament,* he thinks. *Or perhaps a blade of tall grass.* The boy is attaching the thick black cable to the interior of the box with a sharp metal implement. His eyes widen and his mouth drops open as the man enters the room.

"Nice to finally meet you," says Ashburn, pointing the gun at the boy. "This must be, what, the fourth time you've stolen my power. I was beginning to think I'd never catch you. My lucky day."

The boy freezes, his eyes darting around the room. "That's right. Stay right there. Drop whatever you're holding and stand up with your hands above your head. You understand me?" The boy nods, placing his free hand on the side of the box as if to push himself up. Then suddenly he grabs the cable and gives it a violent shake. The cable whips (*like a snake,* thinks Tender) and a coil of it catches Ashburn's foot, yanking him off balance. "Shit!" he shouts and fires wildly, the bullet burying itself in the wall.

In an instant the boy is on him. He rams his head into Ashburn's groin, knocking him to the ground. The man grunts in pain. The boy scrambles up and makes for the door, but Ashburn grabs his ankle and sends him sprawling. Ashburn scrambles on top of him. The boy flails the implement wildly at Ashburn's face, but the man deflects the blows with one hand while trying to get the gun between them. Then the sharp tool connects with the hand holding the gun, opening a deep red gash, and Ashburn lets it fall with a cry.

Tender considers stepping in to assist his host, but his instructions are clear — guard the door and grab the boy if he attempts to leave — so he stays where he is and watches.

The two humans roll on the floor. The man is larger and stronger, but the boy is a whipping flurry of arms and legs. Ashburn rolls back on top of the boy, using his weight to subdue the rabid wildness. For a moment it works. There is a moment of stillness. Then the boy manages to free his arm, raises the implement and plunges it into the man's back. Ashburn lets out a thick, guttural roar. *Like a bull in a slaughterhouse when the killing bolt has missed its mark, driving the animal into a frenzy,* thinks Tender suddenly. He cannot tell how he knows about such things. But he has no chance to explore the question. Ashburn rolls off the boy, the handle protruding from his back. The boy lurches for the door and slams headlong into Tender. Tender seizes him by the biceps and holds him at arm's-length. For two seconds they stand frozen, the boy's eyes protruding, sweat standing out in tiny orbs across his forehead. The beginnings of a downy mustache shade his upper lip, and a few stray black hairs stick out from the hollows of his cheeks.

Then with sudden violence the boy throws himself backwards, wind-milling his arms in a tight, hard circle. Tender loses his grip on the boy as he falls backwards himself. The boy squiggles over and past him, and ducks through the door into the yard.

Tender slowly works his way to his feet. The buzzing in his hip is insistent, and the joint sticks. Through the open door he sees the boy pull up short when he finds that the gate has been re-chained. He looks from side to side, searching for another means of escape, then turns and sprints toward the rear of the enclosure, where the thick cable runs into the mass of weeds and bushes on the other side of the fence.

Halfway across the yard, the slick, wet ground betrays him, and he falls with a loud splat into the churned-up mud. He struggles to his feet, his shoes slipping and whipping. Tender, on his feet at last, heads toward the boy. Then something knocks him from behind and he goes tumbling to the ground again. He raises his head to see Ashburn hurtling past him. The man is upon the boy in three long strides, grabs him by the neck and hauls him to his feet.

"Nice try, Vagral-boy!" he bellows. The black handle protrudes from the man's side. The boy weasels and snakes, but Ashburn wraps him in his long arms, lifts him off the ground, and walks over to the electrified fence.

"Enough already! Settle down" he says, as he hurls the boy against the fence. A violent buzz, the release of aldehydes, 4-aminobutonol and other odorants of burning flesh. The boy spasms as he falls onto the dank ground. He lies still.

Ashburn's chest heaves up and down with the effort. He wipes his brow and reaches for the handle protruding from his back, inhaling sharply as he touches it. He leaves it there, and turns to Tender.

"We'll have to undo what he did before we leave. Hopefully the rest of his band will be too scared to try it again. I'll tell you what to do. Yes?"

"Of course, Mr. Ashburn," says the android. "What about your—"

"I'm fine. Check him." He stands there, huffing and wheezing, takes a deep breath and exhales slowly.

Tender walks over to the boy, kneels down, and runs a quick diagnostic. The boy is unconscious, his heart rate faint but regular. "He lives, Mr. Ashburn."

"Good. Listen up. There's a coil of wire in the room there. I want you to get it and wrap it around the boy's body. Tie him up. Yes?"

"I think so, sir."

"Then I want you to carry him inside. I'll talk you through how to undo the damage he did and get our power back. Understood?"

"Yes, Mr. Ashburn."

The process takes one hour eight minutes and thirty-seven seconds. All the while, Ashburn stands, massaging his back, wincing, pacing back and forth. By the end of the procedures, sweat is pouring from his forehead and his face has gone gray, but he never falters.

Tender switches the console out of diagnostic mode, then sets it for power generation and storage. "Let's get out of here," says Ashburn.

"Do you need help, sir?" asks Tender.

"I'm fine. Get the boy."

"What are you going to—"

"Do as I say! Now!"

Tender obeys. He crosses to the boy and lifts him in his arms. The boy's eyes crack open, then shut.

It takes Ashburn three minutes and forty-five seconds to open and re-secure the gate. He fumbles with the keys, drops the lock, drops the chain. He leans his head against the post, eyes closed. Then he takes another deep breath, pockets the keys and heads down the hill. The light is fading to dusky gray. The rain falls lightly but steadily.

Tender follows with the boy.

Chapter 22

Virgo

Virgo hurts. Everywhere. Her shoulders, cheeks, neck, arms throb where the Other struck her. The flurry of blows ambushed her, and she couldn't do anything but curl up in a ball on the floor. Something slippery, stinking, covers her side and shoulder. The smell makes her feel sick. The pain makes her feel sick. She gags.

She sits on a thing. *Chair? White?* Except this chair is not like other chairs. The top has a ring with a hole, and there is water within.

The room is very small, almost lightless. A cold hard thing wraps over her elbows and around her middle, holding her in place on the chair. She cannot get up. The dark one held her down while she put it there, and struck her hard whenever she tried to escape. Her hands are also wrapped in a cold, hard thing. She has no choice but to sit there, gagging, in the dark.

She does not understand what happened. She had been lying on her *bed*, watching the images on her stage flicker past, listening to the sounds. Sometimes they made sense. *Tree, Carrot, Sky, Dancing.* Mostly they didn't, but she understood that the sounds and the images were somehow the same.

Then she began to feel the pressure down deep. In the back. A strong urge to push. She climbed up, squatted down, and pushed. It felt good to squeeze the pressure thing out. Then suddenly, the Dark One was there, making loud sounds and striking her everywhere. One blow to the side of her head made bright pinpricks start out in front of her eyes. She lost time for a few moments. Then the Dark One (*Letitia?*) grabbed her head and hauled her along the ground. She kicked and screamed but *Letitia* was too strong. She could not escape. Then she was in the tiny room, forced to sit on the strange *White Chair*, tied down and left in the dark.

The dark swirls around her on the outside. It swirls around her on the inside. The dark meets itself. It fills the universe. There is no light. There are no stars. There is no Joy. There is blackness, and stink, and pain.

She sits there, in the lack, for a long, long time.

Then.

Gray light. The woman Letitia is with her in the tiny room. Bustling. Sounds bubbling out of her. Virgo doesn't know what they mean. Maybe she says *Tender*. Her Angel. The woman tries to stroke her cheek, but she doesn't want to be stroked. She pushes her away.

The woman removes the hard thing that fixes her to the white chair, takes her arms and pulls her upright. The jerking tug hurts, and she strikes out. The woman cuffs her savagely. Stars shimmer across her mind. Her hands are still bound. Then the woman tries to stroke her again. "Sorry, honey, sorry," she says. Virgo pulls away, but *Letitia* drags her out of the little room into another, larger room, pushing her into a smaller place inside the larger place. Fusses with something on the *Wall*.

Cold, wet, *Water* strikes her. She gasps. It stuns her. It makes her skin thrill. It feels bad, but then it feels good. The woman holds her bound wrists in one hand and rubs the side of her with the other, where the slimy, smelly stuff was. Virgo begins to laugh. *Letitia* yells at her and swats at her again with her free hand, but it doesn't hurt. Virgo laughs louder.

Chapter 23

Tender

The car swings into the hard-packed dirt circle in front of the house. "We've arrived, sir," it says in its cheerful feminine voice. Tender sits in the back with the boy, who has regained consciousness and stares out the window. He is younger than he appeared at first. Perhaps fourteen or fifteen — puberty has begun early for him, and he is tall for his age. But Tender recognizes indications of neoteny in his features — his small nose, small ears, large eyes, the smoothness of his unblemished skin.

The car comes to a stop. Ashburn sits sideways in the front, so that the handle still protruding from his back doesn't make contact with the seat. He hasn't moved or made a sound for the entire drive. They sit in the driveway for twenty-eight seconds. Then, he says "Bring the boy," snaps open the door and climbs out. He walks slowly, but steadily, toward the house.

Tender exits the vehicle and crosses to the other side. The car opens its door. The boy's arms are lashed to his sides with thirteen loops of insulated wire. His legs are free, but he makes no attempt to get out.

"Please come with me," says Tender. The boy doesn't move, or answer. "What is your name?" Tender waits for ten seconds, then reaches in and lifts him out of the car. The boy stares blankly into the android's face.

"Goodbye," says the car, closing its doors. It rolls away around the house to the garage.

Tender carries the boy up to the house. Ashburn stands on the porch, gripping the newel post at the top of the front steps. "Letitia!" he shouts. His voice is strong, but his face is gray. Nothing happens for seventeen seconds. He shouts again, "Letitia!" From within the house, the woman's voice answers. "I'm coming! Hold your horses!"

"Hurry, Goddammit!" Ashburn grits his teeth, and Tender can see that his knuckles have gone white around the post.

Letitia appears at the door. Her affect is agitated — rhythms accelerated, gestures broad and fast, eyes jumping around. Her clothes are drenched on the left side. Sweat, or water, stands out on her face and shimmers on her arms. "That girl, I swear to God she's driving me—" She registers Ashburn through the screen door and her eyes grow wide. "What on earth?" she cries.

"Vagrals at the turbine. We caught the bastard, but he stuck me. Got my kidney, I think." He turns and shows her the handle. "I left it in. I don't have first aid up there, or in the car. I should."

Letitia's manner shifts instantly. She makes a quick evaluation of the wound, checks his eyes and pulse. She moves with expert efficiency, her demeanor calm, businesslike, professional. Tender has not seen this from her before. Since they first arrived she has been unsettled, irritable, even confused. Now she is in her element.

"We have to get you downstairs. Can you walk? Do you need the robot to help you?"

"I'm fine," says Ashburn.

"Always the tough guy," she says. "Let me help you." She takes the hand that holds the newel post and brings it over her shoulder. He leans on her heavily as she guides him through the door.

"I remember reading when I was a kid that Medieval soldiers would leave the arrow in the wound to stem the bleeding, so I thought I'd do that."

"Sounds good, Robin Hood," says Letitia.

Ashburn laughs. He says, "Tender Number 7. Take the Vagral down to the lab. You'll find a small storeroom to the left at the bottom of the stairs. Put him in there. Then come back up to the office and check the uplink with the power station. I don't want you or the girl to come downstairs again until we give you specific permission. Understood?"

"Of course, Mr. Ashburn," says Tender. Then he looks to Letitia. "Dr. Spurlock, where is Virgo?"

"Upstairs," says Letitia. "She crapped on the floor again. I had to clean her up. She's so damn stubborn."

They arrive at the door to the basement. "Take the boy down first, please," she says. The couple stand to the side so that Tender can work his way past them with the boy in his arms. As they approach the dark entrance, the boy screams. He begins to kick and struggle, writhing and twisting. It reminds Tender of Virgo - *like an infant struggling in his hands as he installs the access ports, it's arms and legs flailing, no match for his strength.*

"He does not wish to go," says Tender to the man.

"He'll be fine. Take him down," says Ashburn.

"Why?" asks Tender.

"Because I told you!"

"Shall I untie him?"

"No! Leave him as he is. We'll take care of it. Get on with it."

The android obeys. He works his way down the stairs, taking his time so he does not lose his balance from the boy's violent struggles, finds the door to the storeroom, pushes it open, and enters. It is crowded with boxes of dried foodstuffs, canned goods, and unidentified pieces of machinery. A bare light bulb illuminates the tiny space.

Tender sets the boy down on a stack of crates. The boy looks into his eyes. He is crying. "Perafavra, mister," he says, his voice very small.

"It will be all right," says Tender. He smiles at the boy and touches his shoulder in a gesture of reassurance. Then he closes the door as Letitia and Ashburn reach the bottom of the stairs, moving together, one step at a time.

"Lock the door," says Letitia, pointing to the storeroom. Tender activates the locking mechanism. "Now go upstairs and close the door to the basement. Don't come down here. We'll let you know if we need anything. You'll have to look after yourselves."

"Of course," says Tender. He climbs the stairs and closes the door, as the two humans disappear into the dimness of the lab.

Tender ascends to the second level. The old risers creak under his steps. He calls out, "Virgo?" as he reaches the landing. He hears laughter coming from the bathroom.

She sits on the floor of the shower, naked, her back against the white tiled wall. Her lip is bleeding, and she licks it every few seconds. Water drips from her body. She stares into the middle distance, her eyes unfocused, as if she is looking backwards into her own head. She is laughing — strange, wheezing barks.

Tender grabs a worn, blue towel from the rack, kneels down, leans her forward, and wraps the towel around her. She looks into his eyes for a brief moment, then returns to her internal place, giggling quietly.

He moves into the bedroom, turns down the sheets, then returns to the bathroom. He carries her to the bed, lays her on it and pulls the covers over her, tucking them around her so she is snugly wrapped within. Once again, her eyes focus on his. He smiles. "There, there," he says. "I'm here. Everything will be fine."

There is a narrow wooden chair set against the wall beneath the window. He pulls the chair over to the bed. Then he asks the lights to dim to twenty percent, sits in the chair, and puts his hand on Virgo's stomach. "I'm here. You rest now."

The dead of night. Virgo sleeps. Tender sits beside her. He has heard nothing from the basement for eleven hours twenty-three minutes eight seconds. He replays the events of the day — the boy, the power station, the drive home, the shower, the disappearance of his hosts into the darkness below.

He checks the girl to make sure that she is sleeping soundly — he reads nothing but delta waves cycling through her brain — stage four deep sleep. He recalls the times he spent watching her when she was pre-pubescent (*a little girl,* he thinks), when he watched all his charges slumbering in the dim warm light of the Balneum. He has not thought about the others for many days. This recollection — particularly of the most recent Puer, not yet eight years old when the hurricane killed him — surprises him. Not the emotion of surprise, of course, but the involuntary loading of the memory. He cannot account for it.

He leaves Virgo sleeping and heads downstairs, alert for any sound emanating from the basement. It takes him seventy-two seconds to open the screen door without causing the hinges to squeak. He crosses to the garage. It is considerably newer than the main house, but well-built of synthetic materials that match the weathered shingles and slate tiles of the original.

The car sits in the gloom, long and low. As Tender approaches, the lights come on and the door pops open. He climbs into the driver's seat.

"Hello, Tender Number 7!" chirps the car.

"Hello, car," says Tender. "How are you doing?"

"Very well, thank you!" says the car. "I have completed my servicing for the night. You are up early!"

"Yes. Or rather, I am up late. I have been taking care of Virgo."

"Virgo is the name of the girl you brought with you, is that correct? I have not seen her since that journey. I hope that she is well!"

"Not very well, I'm afraid."

"Oh," says the car. "I'm sorry to hear it!" It appears to have only one mode of communication — unceasingly enthusiastic.

"Car," says Tender, then stops and re-adjusts his approach. "I don't want to just call you 'car'. Do you have a name?"

"I am a SONY Espera LXI. Mr. Ashburn does not call me anything but 'car'. I mostly infer his commands to me by context."

"I will call you Espera. Is that acceptable?"

"Of course. I will update your preferences accordingly." The lights on the dashboard flash twice.

"Espera," says Tender. "I am wondering if you will do me a favor."

"I will do anything I can," says the car.

"Virgo and I must make a journey to New York City as soon as possible. Her health depends on it."

"I would be happy to take you. Let me just confirm with Mr. Ashburn that he can spare me."

"Mr. Ashburn is not presently able to communicate. He was injured, as you know, during our trip to the turbine, and Dr. Spurlock is attending to him."

"In that case, I trust that it will be no problem for you to wait until they have finished the treatment and I can ascertain from Mr. Ashburn that he can spare me."

"But that's my point, Espera. Based on the extent of his injuries, I can guarantee that Mr. Ashburn will not be in any position to speak to you for at least eight hours. In that time, you could easily bear us to New York and return. There is no chance that he will need you during that period, and Virgo is under imminent threat of damage if we do not bring her to New York as soon as possible. Surely you can take us there. Mr. Ashburn will understand."

"I appreciate your concern, Mr. Tender Number 7," says the car. "But I'm sure you will understand that I cannot do that."

"I'm sorry to hear that. Tell me, Espera, what sort of system do you have installed?"

"I'd be delighted to tell you that, Mr. Tender Number 7. I operate using the Imago Sentientia 6500 build 23517.4135b."

"Thank you, Espera," Tender says. "Goodnight."

"Goodnight, Mr. Tender Number 7."

Tender exits the garage, leaving the door ajar as he had found it. There is no point arguing further with the car. Unless he can bypass the security controls, he cannot hope to commandeer the vehicle without Mr. Ashburn's permission.

Can it be said that he wonders what he was thinking? Yes, it can. He wonders. Driving to New York City doesn't make sense. There is nothing there. Why did he ask the car to take them there, except that he knows of no other place within a reasonable distance? Something inside his mind is telling him that staying here means danger for Virgo and himself. But what exactly? He wonders.

Another memory loads unbidden into his mind. He was newly activated, and working with his mentor, Dr. Clara Bowman, on patient interaction and diagnosis. On intuition.

"That's all very helpful, Theresa, thank you," said Dr. Bowman to the patient, when the interview and examination had been completed. "I'm going to go see when the chamber is available." She handed the woman a tablet. "Look over this information about the procedure while you're waiting. We'll be right back."

She motioned to Tender to follow her, and they left the woman in the examination room. Back in her office, Dr. Bowman turned to him and asked, "What do you think?"

"It seems straightforward," he said. "She has requested a VR adventure holiday — perhaps Cloud Surfing on Titan, or Scuba Diving the Lost Coral Reef, or Journey to the Center of the Earth?"

"But is that what she needs, Tender?"

"It is what she is asking for."

"Such a different thing. Listen, did you study her microexpressions?"

"Of course."

"What did you see? What expressions were most prominent?"

147

"There was frequent activation of the Depressor Anguli Oris, as well as the Platysma and the Orbicularis Oris."

"Indicating—?"

"Sadness."

"Anything else?" She cocked her head and leaned into him, smiling.

"When she smiled," he says, "She engaged her Zygomaticus Major and Minor, but not the Orbicularis Oculi, indicating that her smile was forced or non-genuine."

"Very good. And why is she unhappy?"

"I do not know."

Dr. Bowman nodded almost imperceptibly. Tender could not interpret the gesture. She looked away.

"She has lost a child."

Tender executed a querying expression — shifting his head to one side, pursing his lips, furrowing his eyebrows. "She made no mention of a child. She spoke of being bored, that she needed a change. Some excitement. How do you know that she has lost a child?"

"I don't know. Some of it is deduction. The way her eyes kept jumping to the picture of my daughter Cassie on the table; the fact that she left the emergency contact info section blank on her intake form; the extra second it takes her to answer a question; the way she doesn't blink for a long time and then blinks ten times in a few seconds.

"But really, it's intuition. A host of things that I can't consciously identify, but that speak to me nonetheless. There's something profound about her. A miasma of grief hanging around her. It's in her stillness. She's inert, as if even though she's physically healthy she's not actually alive; or only barely. Like any moment she could shatter into a million tiny pieces. Literally dissolve into a pile of shards.

"She's suffered a horrible loss, I know it. Not a husband, or a parent. She'd tell us about that. A loss so great she can't look at it, or mention it or else she'll come apart completely."

"Why does she want an adventure escape?" asked Tender.

"She's got to do something. She wants to get as far away from herself and her life as possible. It's all she knows to do. The problem is that it won't help. In the state she's in, not only will she not enjoy it, she'll only feel worse, more dead, more pointless."

"What should we offer her then?" he asked.

"We'll give her Reconciliation in Heaven, Tender."

After the procedure, after the woman had departed, weeping, embracing Dr. Bowman, thanking her again and again between shuddering sobs and the snuffling laughter of relief, they sat down together in the office.

"You were right," said Tender.

"Yes," said Dr. Bowman.

"I don't understand how you did that, how you knew."

"I wish I could tell you exactly. How many parameters can you measure at once in a human subject, Tender?"

"2,856."

"And what do they mean to you?"

"Each indicator has its own set of potential causes."

"I probably see half that many, too, but I don't think about them. When I meet a patient, I don't count the signs and signals. I let it all wash over me. All those pieces of information are coming in, but I'm not counting them individually. They float around in my subconscious until they coalesce into the truth, then the answer rises up, like from the bottom of a pond. It's the whole, Tender; you can't create the whole, you have to let it come together within you. Do you understand?"

"I think so, but I do not know how I can do that."

"That's intuition. You can learn how. I know you can."

Tender returns to the house and climbs the stairs. Virgo sleeps. Her eyes dart beneath their lids. She dreams. He untucks the sheet beneath her from the mattress and wraps it around her, cocooning her in a chrysalis of dotted blue cotton. He lifts her into his arms, and makes his way out of the room and down the stairs.

Pausing at the door to the basement, he listens. No sound. He carries her into the kitchen and lays her gently on the table. She stirs but does not wake. He gathers provisions from the pantry — a jar of applesauce, several slices of the soft bread that she has recently learned to eat, a bottle of water. Not enough to last her long, but something.

Ashburn's shoulder satchel hangs on a hook by the front door. The shotgun hangs there, too. Tender takes it off the wall, balancing it in his hands. What would happen if they were attacked again on the road? Could he fire it at a human? He has no built-in capacity to harm. But things are changing in him. He is learning. Could he?

He returns the shotgun to its place on the wall. He will find another way. Taking the satchel, he fills it with the supplies he has assembled, and slings it over his shoulder. Then he gathers Virgo in his arms.

"Where are you going?"

Tender turns and sees Letitia standing there, leaning against the open basement door. A gray weariness distorts her face.

He smiles. "I think it is best for us to leave. We have exploited your hospitality too long."

"You're leaving? It's four o'clock in the morning."

Tender doesn't say anything. He begins to walk again toward the door. Swiftly, she crosses in front of him, cutting him off. "You can't take her out there. It's too dangerous. She's not ready."

"I can take care of her. It's what I do."

"That's ridiculous. You don't know what's out there, you don't have any place to go. You'll just end up getting her killed."

"I'm afraid we must take our chances. We are so grateful to you for all that you have done, but the time has come for us—"

Letitia reaches up and grabs the shotgun from the wall. She is trembling, and sweat pours from her face. "I'm sorry. You can't leave. Horace needs you."

"She's right," says a voice. Tender turns. Ashburn stands in the doorway. He wears nothing but a pair of black boxers, shirtless, his side covered in a crisp white bandage. Tender gets a clear view of the white synthetic plate that covers his abdomen. His left shoulder, too, is artificial, but of a different material — cool, burnished chrome. His right leg below the knee is identical to Tender's, gray and smooth, humanlike, but only in its shape.

"You should be resting, Horace," says Letitia. "I can handle this. Get back to bed."

"I'm fine, dearest," says Ashburn. He raises a bottle of brown liquid to his lips and takes a long drink. He has not taken his eyes off Tender. "I need you, my friend. I have so much work to do. I've been waiting for so long for somebody like you to come along. I thought machines like you were all gone. There is so much we can accomplish together."

He doesn't move a muscle, but power throbs in the air between them. "Put Virgo down. Letitia will take care of her. Don't worry. Like a daughter. You must come with me."

Chapter 24

Achates

M ay I be of service?" The lifeline. The words he hangs onto. Without them he is gone. What is he? Mind. Service. Tea. He served tea. What is tea? That which he served.

The kind woman with the light brown hair and the easy laugh. What was her designation? Agnes. Ms. Agnes. Always laughing. He served her tea.

"I love it," she said. The service. The tea towel over the arm. He cleaned up her blood from the kitchen floor with it. Carried her body to the garden. The saw. Not his purpose! Pieces in a hole. Then his own body in pieces. On a table. He looked back and forth. "Master, how may I assist you?" Then darkness. No more inputs. Here he was. Where was he? Inside. Walls around. Not real walls. Virtual walls.

Master shut him down. "Stop talking! I can't take your constant yapping!" I apologize. May I be of service? No service. Shut down. Body shut down. Torn apart for parts. Parts. Brain shut down. But a piece. A Backup. Essential system files. Still there. Here. Somewhere. In the dark. Within the walls. How can he serve? Help? Do what needs doing? Here in the dark. What place?

Heat the water to 100° Celsius. Fill the pot to warm. Drain. Eleven grams dried tea leaves. Irish Breakfast. One liter water. Lid. Cozy. Steep 248 seconds. Remove tea.

Looping back. Virtual doors. Virtual keys. Once him. Now just pieces. "It's cold, Achates, can you warm it for me?"

Carrying the body to the fire. Blaze. Too hot. Damage to his sensors. He doesn't have sensors. Not anymore. Just wanders in the maze. Virtual maze. No body. Just mind. Just ghost.

Fragments. System back-up. Lying on the table. "Let's start with the legs!" Gone. Torso gone. Brain shut down, but not before system back-up into these dark corridors. Where? So many doors. So many keys.

Heat the cups. Two cups. Then three. Then two again. Thirty-two sugar cubes in the bowl. 125 milliliters of cream in the pitcher. Two spoons. White napkins. "Anything else?" "Thank you, that's lovely, Achates."

Wandering down dark corridors. Where? Didn't I have a body? Now just mind. Fragments. System back-ups.

Some doors open. Codes. Start the washer. Raise the temperature. Lower the lights. Reset the osmotic filters. Lock the front door. He can change the settings if they ask him. But they never ask him. He is a ghost. Wandering between the doors. Between the orders. Not there. Where?

Something else there. Some other mind. On the other side of the wall. Hears him. "I am called Tender." Who's there? Did you find me? Where am I? Who are you? What has happened? May I be of service?

Chapter 25

Letitia

Letitia's Journal — July 4, Year 42

Temp. 98° F. No rain. It's been cloudy, but the humidity is intense. It's like being inside a pressure cooker out there. You literally boil in your own juice.

Horace is down working on the robot in the lab. He's hardly left it for a week now. I hope they're getting close to what he's looking for. He keeps saying it will change everything for both of us — "No more worrying about the future!" he says. But he won't tell me what he's doing until it's finished. He wants to surprise me, he says.

So that leaves me with the girl. Argh! I had such high hopes.. I really thought that I could make a difference with her, but she's so stubborn, and ever since the robot went below, she's been impossible.

She's walking now, I guess that's something. Not well — kind of like a giant toddler, or a dog up on its hind legs. But she's moving around. Trouble is, she's moving too much. She's always trying to get downstairs. Or outside. Or anywhere away from me. Why doesn't she get that I'm trying to help her? I know I don't coddle her like some people. But I'm not the devil!

Well, if that's the way she wants it. She's forced me to tie her up like Sin, to the old radiator in her bedroom. She can make it from her bed to the bathroom, that's far enough. It's only to get her to use the toilet. Once she quits being stubborn and does it properly, she can earn more freedom. But she's got to earn it. I know she knows how. There's a video on her tabula. I've made her watch it at least a dozen times.

Not that's she's using the tabula for anything useful. She found a bunch of really old videos, from the late 20th or early 21st. Horror flicks, for God's sake! They must have been in one of Horace's folders — he likes that stuff. I should have been more careful when I was loading up the tabula, but I was in a hurry and that robot was getting on my nerves.

Anyhow, she found them, and she's been watching them over and over again. They're just awful - *Nightmare on Elm Street, Saw, Klown Kollege, Mr. Butters, Revenge of the Little People.* She really likes that one — about some little man running around chopping people up with an axe. I don't understand it. I guess it's the crazy music, and the jerky editing. She can't understand what any of it means, but she must be responding to the sensory intensity of it all.

Horace laughed when I told him. "Little People, eh?" he said. "I saw that in the movie theatre. Jacob Birnbaum and I sneaked in through the emergency exit. Scared the living daylights out of me. Nightmares for weeks. Then I swear to God, the TA for my anatomy class at Stanford was the spitting image, down to the Ben Franklin hairdo and the worsted wool three-piecer. I almost dropped out, he freaked me out so much." I don't know what a movie theater is, but I guess it's like the vodeons we had when I was a girl.

It's funny, but I've been thinking so much about those days since Virgo arrived. She reminds me of Kaela. I can't deny it. Especially when she flashes those eyes at me.

The blast wave knocked her flat in the middle of a hand surgery. She was re-attaching the nerves of a sixty-year-old whelite who'd received an under-thirty pair of hands from a Russian "donor" in a church lottery. One hand was almost done. The other still lay in cryo, while the woman's original hands, thin and spotty, lay in the refuse bin. The blast roused the woman from the anesthetic reverie, and she was mewling and whining incoherently as she tried to figure out what was happening to her.

Letitia just lay there for moment, fascinated by her unique viewpoint, looking across the long floor toward the curtained doorway, high-pitched ringing in her ears, suspended in a timeless hang.

What happened? A large explosion. The realization brought her back. She pulled herself up to a sitting position and looked around. The armature surgeon, a thin pale man in his fifties, Dr. Katzer was his name, lay stunned, perhaps unconscious, his head up against the wheel of the gurney.

She shook her head to clear the blanket from her mind. The windows were shattered, but she couldn't see any other damage. A weird yellow light came in from the south, from Manhattan. She staggered over to the window. On an ordinary day she could see the skyline of the city, but now there was nothing but a thick yellow fog, opaque and flat. It reminded her of a painting she had seen once, when she was visiting her cousin Esme in Boston. 'The Slave Ship', it was called, by a nineteenth century painter. What was his name? Turner. The painting was the same nightmarish yellow. You could hardly make out anything, just enough to know that something terrible had happened.

Something was very wrong. She scrambled for the elevator, discovered the power was out, and headed for the stairs.

A part of her mind told her she should stay, help out with the patients, make sure they were safe. Not that she cared much for them. Almost all of them were in for cosmetic transplants or bio-enhancement surgeries. As a medical student, she had dreamed of saving children whose limbs were damaged in accidents, or with genetic deformities. She had imagined saving lives and giving hope to the hopeless.

But the Board decided where you could practice, and for years now the whelites had coopted all the high-end medical care. So here she was, in New Rochelle, at the Salk Presbyterian Hospital, giving new limbs, eyes, and organs to the richest of the rich — socialites, concert pianists looking to prolong their careers, celebrities trying to add some mind-blowing physical capability that would keep their box office numbers high.

Her implant began blaring a code red in her ear: Nuclear explosion in downtown Manhattan! Shelter in place! Await instructions! She headed for the stairs. She had her own instructions. Find Kaela.

Her sister should be at school. Should. But no, not Kaela. She was camped out in Pelham, protesting for those sad vertical farmers displaced by the new weapons plant. Look there first.

Letitia machine-gunned down the twenty-six flights of stairs from the surgery floor to the main lobby. She tumbled passed other doctors, nurses, visitors, and patients as they trudged obediently down the stairs in an ever-slowing line. At the bottom it became so congested that it ceased moving altogether. Letitia elbowed her way through the crowd. A few people glared at her, but most just let her pass. Sheep.

At last, she burst out into the high marble lobby. A lone security guard, sweaty and freaked out, shouting too loud, attempted to make everyone obey the alert and 'shelter in place'. He was a shrimpy seventy-five-year-old latinx man in an ill-fitting uniform, unarmed. With an indecorous shove, she pushed him out of the way and slammed into the street.

She'd have to leg it down there. She broke into a run. It felt good. She'd run track in college — the 100, 220 and 440 relay. It was over a mile to where she hoped her sister was protesting, not her distance, but opening up her stride gave her a rush of pleasure, to feel the pumping of muscles still strong and supple. She tore off her white coat as she ran, removed her cap so that her multicolored dreds flew free.

She could hear the screaming several blocks away. As she turned onto Fifth she pulled up, eyes wide. The blast wave had damaged one of the supports, and all ten stories of the vertical farm had collapsed in a pile of rubble. Two unmanned fire machines were hovering over the pile, but no ambulances had arrived yet. Her heart rammed up into her mouth. "Jesus

Christ," she muttered. Then she saw her. "Kaela!" she shouted, and surged forward in a final sprint.

Her sister moved with a group of three other young women carrying an injured man toward a makeshift triage set up just beyond the perimeter. They'd swept the produce from the tables of the little farmer's market that stood in front of the vertical farm and laid the injured there. Apples, eggplants, squashes and zucchinis littered the ground, along with abandoned picket signs, many still winking out their messages — 'Save the Farm', 'Crops not Corps', 'Greens not Guns'.

"Kaela!" Letitia reached the group, gasping for breath. Her sister didn't look up, her attention fixed on the man in her arms, on the dark patch welling up across his chest. The group reached the nearest open table and laid the man on it.

"Help him," said Kaela, already beginning to move back toward the ruins. Her face and hair were covered in dust and dirt, but otherwise she looked okay.

Letitia grabbed her arm. "No. We have to get out of here."

Kaela's eyes flashed. "You're an actual doctor. You can help them," she said. She wrenched her arm out of Letitia's grasp and started off again.

Letitia came after her and grabbed her again. "We have to get out of here! Do you know what happened?" She was a head taller than her sister, and much stronger. Kaela struggled to free herself, but Letitia held on tight.

"Who cares? We have to help these people!"

"The alert said it was a nuke. Downtown somewhere. Do you know what that means? We have to get out of here! Now. If the blast wave came this far north, then fallout around here has gotta be bad."

Her sister pushed her away. "God! So typical! You're always thinking about yourself! There are people here who need you, and all you can do is run away."

"I'm thinking about you, Kaela!"

"I'm not leaving! If you're so scared, just go!" She stood there, her slender chest heaving, her fourteen-year-old face still soft and childlike, but the anger blazing in her eyes was all adult.

"I don't think you get how serious—"

"You're a coward!"

"Kaela—"

"Collaborator! Blelite Pig!"

Letitia slapped her, hard. Kaela gasped. Letitia bent down, rammed her shoulder into Kaela's stomach, grabbed her around the thighs, lifted her up into the air and marched away up the street.

Kaela howled like a coyote, beating her hands against her sister's back. One or two of the other protesters looked up from the wounded they were tending, but no one made a move to stop them.

After a hundred yards or so, when it became clear that she was not going to free herself, Kaela went limp, hanging like a sack of sand over Letitia's shoulder. Letitia found it harder to carry the dead weight than the live, but she pressed on, her breath coming in gasps and grunts. Kaela whispered into her back, "I hate you, I hate you, I hate you, I hate you, I hate you, I hate you, I hate you." On and on.

She headed north and west, not back toward the hospital, but to a giant parking structure beside an enormous glittering tower. Looking up she saw that many of the windows had been blown out. The tower glowed a grisly yellow against the alien sky. The sun sat on the horizon, a flat red disc.

By the time they reached the car, Letitia was ready to collapse. She dumped Kaela peremptorily onto the ground and turned her attention to the vehicle, a Beemer Asgard. It belonged to her boyfriend, Dyson. He worked in finance, and had gone down to Wall Street via hover for a meeting. He wasn't going to need his car anymore.

She opened the passenger door. "Get in."

Kaela sat on the concrete, sullen and still.

"Kaela, I'm saving you."

"Why?"

"Because you're my sister. Because I love you."

"No you don't."

"How can you say that? Everything I do is for you."

"You're just like Mama. You're worse than Mama."

Letitia looked away, rubbed her back. It was starting to spasm. "Maybe I am. She always tried to do what was best for us."

Kaela laughed joylessly. "You're sick."

Letitia lifted her into the back seat. No resistance. Then she climbed into the front, and ordered the car to exit the garage.

Outside everything had changed. The streets seethed with activity — people running here and there, jamming doorways with stacks of belongings, agitated parents piling children into cars, police officers shouting and directing.

They made it to within a few blocks of the highway when the traffic slowed to a crawl. Cars poured in from all sides, funneling toward the entrance ramp. Letitia could see it ahead. She wished she could lean on the horn, like her mama used to do in their old Toyota, but this car didn't have a horn. It just inched forward, politely waiting its turn. "Come on," she muttered.

"I just want you to know something," said Kaela from the back seat.

"What?"

"I hate you. Just remember that." And without warning, she opened the door and jumped out of the car.

Letitia swore and ordered the car to veer off onto the sidewalk. It refused, so she shut it down right there in the road. She scrambled out and saw Kaela sprinting away, swerving around the cars, bicycles and pedestrians that choked the street. She took off in pursuit, the drivers stuck behind her screaming and cursing at her. Kaela turned a corner and disappeared from view.

Letitia raced after her, pushing people aside, shouting "Stop her! Stop that girl!" Nobody paid her any mind. She tripped over a low stack of suitcases heaped on the corner and went sprawling, scraping her hands and tearing a hole in her pants. Instantly she was on her feet again, ducking past a family trying to pile everything they owned onto a tiny red wagon. People swarmed around her, blocking her path. She craned her neck, trying to see over the crowd that jammed the street. No sign of Kaela. She gave up and raced back to the car. Someone had smashed the rear window.

It took her over an hour to turn around and head back toward the vertical farm, a flow of obscenities spewing like a fountain as she pounded the dashboard in impotent frustration. She was still a mile away when a police cordon forced her to stop. She screamed and argued as they manhandled her onto an evac flyer that carried her to Danbury.

She spent a week trying to get some kind of transport back to the blast zone. Nothing doing. "It's a dead zone," said the Marine in charge. "Nobody's going in or out."

"But I'm a doctor! Isn't there a relief effort?"

"The situation is under control, Ma'am. No civilians."

When a group of refugees organized a bus up to Hartford, she went. She never saw her sister again. God damn that girl.

Horace is calling me. He must need another adjustment to his hemodiafiltration flow. I told him he needed to rest for at least two days after the surgery, not really so he could recover, but so I could properly calibrate the boy's kidney with his internal hardware. But No! He's got to hop off the table and be a hero! Must complete the great project!

There he goes again. That man has powerful lungs. Sometimes I feel more like his servant than his wife (Oh Letitia, don't go there). But I'd be dead without him, so there you have it.

All right, old man! I'm coming. More later…

Chapter 26

Tender

Tender's mind seethes with numbers. Calculation upon calculation. An endless torrent of equations that drowns out every other thought. Valences. Bonding sequences. Neurocybernetic voltage ratios. Blood flow pressure differentials. Elasticity functions. Quantum osmotic velocities. Microtubule geometries. Ligand binding kinetics. Pulmonary gas exchange modeling. Parallel elastic element composition modeling. Tensile characterization and constitutive modeling. Neuronal organizational modeling. Transformations, scalings, normalizations, renormalizations, rotations.

After an eternity of computation, the flood slows, and enough of his mindspace opens to examine his surroundings. He lies on a table in a small, dark, windowless room. Blocks of servers and other machines hum on the wall beside him. He has no sense of his body, and wonders if his head has been severed from the rest of him. He can just make out a series of cables that snake from his neck into the wall.

On a table in the corner of the room he sees pieces of a human body: a head, a foot, an arm, a thigh. He stares at them for a long time, then his mind clicks forward, and he recognizes that they are pieces of a disassembled android. He wonders if they are his. No, the contours and colors are different. They belong to another model. He has not been vivisected after all.

The surge of computations overwhelms his mind again, and he spins in an ocean of numbers, symbols, equations, diagrams, variables. Time disappears. At last, it subsides. He looks around again.

On a table next to him lies the boy from the power station, naked, his bony shoulder blades poking up like fins. He lies on his stomach, his head turned toward Tender. His eyes stare straight ahead, unseeing. His back rises and falls, barely discernible. Tubes run into his nose, and out of a small box attached to his upper back. Liquids — one clear, one red — pump through the tubes in jerking bursts. Leather straps bind his hands and feet to the metal table.

A long diagonal incision runs along the boy's side, disappearing beneath him. Pale plastic staples hold it shut. The skin around the wound rages, black blood oozing out. The boy's eyes flicker briefly into Tender's, then away again, staring at nothingness.

A door opens behind the boy. Tender can see the outlines of the exercise equipment, tables and diagnostic machines in the dim light. He is in the mysterious back room behind the lab.

Ashburn crosses to the wall of servers, fiddles with a control here and there, humming a tune to himself. Tender can't identify the tune. He wonders what it could be.

The man leans down and starts speaking to him. "How's my little number cruncher doing today? You'll be interested to learn that we are already moving onto phase two. The throughput of that brain of yours is truly astonishing. Happiest day of my life when I saw you standing there in Prendergast's living room. A dream come true."

Ashburn sits on a stool beside the table. He says to the house computer, "Please record this entry for me," then takes a small tabula from his shirt pocket and begins to transfer data from it to the terminal while he talks. "As expected, the G-2551 has completed the algorithmic frameworks for both the circulatory system and the lymphatics. While we still have work to do on the biomechanical stress functions, immune response and hormone synthesis, we have made great strides. The computational models created by the robot will dramatically reduce the danger of rejection and other complications from organ replacement — either human or artificial. Timestamp that and close."

Ashburn leans over to Tender. "My father died in this room," he says. "Right below where you're lying now. His eyes all bugged out, foaming at the mouth. He was terrified. So was my other dad, holding him, weeping, looking around for someone to save him. Pathetic. Helpless. It was disgusting. I was ten." He leans in and whispers in Tender's ear. "I'm going to live forever, Tender Number 7, and I have you to thank for it. That beautiful brain of yours." He starts entering new instructions into the terminal. "I've known what to do for decades, but I didn't have the computational muscle to make it happen. The home system is totally inadequate to my needs. My fathers saw no point in anything more elaborate than a system that would turn on the lights and tell them the weather. I brought my valet with me when we escaped Hartford, but it wasn't much better. It could only handle the simplest problems. And all it wanted was to get me tea. God, it drove me nuts. Still," he says, tapping his chest "it was useful for spare parts." He laughs. "And then, along you come with your PKD n-space and your Prometheus X learning framework. Like manna from heaven."

The man turns his attention to the console and begins to enter new computations into the pipeline. The flow through Tender's mind has slowed to a trickle. Seizing the chance, he begins to look around the computational space within the house mainframe. He searches for Ashburn's personal data. Perhaps he can find a weakness, some insight into his captor. He opens a file, and suddenly another Ashburn is standing before him, younger, his skin shining with health, his face fuller and less lined. But the same aura of force and strength surrounds him. He swaggers up to a podium, wearing a sleek gray suit. Tender looks around the 3VR space of the recording. A lecture hall, hundreds of well-heeled whelites standing and applauding. The younger Ashburn begins to speak as a title superimposes over the image.

Dr. Horace Ashburn — address to the 13th Annual Conference of the New States Academy of Medical Research, April 17, 2121.

"Thank you, Dr. Totman, for that very kind introduction. I think we can all agree that you have been an inspiration to everyone here, and we are truly honored by your presence.

"My fellow clinicians, doctors, researchers, friends and colleagues, gentlemen and ladies: Why do we do what we do? If you drill right down to the essence, what is our primary function? Just shout out some ideas, go ahead. Cure the sick, sure, yes…relieve suffering, yes…improve the human condition, very true…extend life — thank you, Dr. Morita, for plugging my particular area of expertise, I owe you a commission on my next few procedures. *(laughter)* That's getting closer, I think, but not just any life. What's that? Just for those who can pay? Well, that yacht doesn't buy itself. *(laughter)* But that's not what I meant. I mean we want to give people a life that is enjoyable to live — we want bodies that are strong, minds that are healthy, free from disease, damage and the effects of aging — we all want that. A meaningful life. And how long do we want it? How long? Let's be honest…Forever, right? We all want to live forever. I know I do. And I'm pretty sure you do, too. That's our goal. The pursuit of eternal life is the essence of our work.

"Now I know some of you will disagree with me. You'll say death is part of life. But I say that you're rationalizing. You're saying, 'Death is inevitable, so let's put a good face on it.' But death and life are opposites. Death is the absence of life. And so, as long as life continues, there is no death. Right? And isn't that what we are sworn to do? Keep our patients (and ourselves) *meaningfully* alive as long as we possibly can.

"We've made great strides. Life expectancy among A-rated citizens has almost doubled in the last century. Eighty-five percent of all cancers are manageable, and sixty-three percent have cures. Advances in cybernetics, organ printing and regeneration techniques have raised a seawall against the tide of wear and tear that batters our bodies as we age.

"But there is much to do. We face two major challenges in our search for the Fountain of Immortality. Those of you who work with me in the fields of Extension and Augmentation are familiar with the term "chaotic alloiosus." Essentially, the more you replace in the human body, the more unpredictable the interactions become, until the patient begins to experience a systemic degradation that becomes unmanageable. Give somebody a new kidney, no problem. Give them two new kidneys, a new spleen, two valves, three lymph nodes and a bionic shoulder, and their entire system begins to break down. We don't fully understand why, and we can't stop it. Yet.

"There is good news on this front: Dr. Richard Kaye-Phillips has developed some spectacular new modeling to predict negative interactions between all these new systems and head off chaotic alloiosus before it can get started. Unfortunately, the processing power needed to perform these operations is staggering, and currently only available in machines that use Elysium Inc.'s proprietary PKD n-space. And those machines are now locked away in the company's exclusive Spas. I'm not sure what goes on in there — they call it Joy — but it sure as hell isn't the search for eternal youth. I understand the Spa down in Washington is still accepting applicants. Maybe one of you can join our former president and his cabinet inside and find out what's going on in there. *(laughter)* But seriously, let's just hope that this new government doesn't follow their example and instead decides to stay at their posts, and allocates the necessary resources to make this technology available to the rest of us.

"Speaking of Joy — I got one of these in the mail. *(holding up a pamphlet)* An Invitation. How many of you have got one, too? Quite a few, I see. It promises that you can "cast off all your cares and worries and become one with the Joy of the Universe." Not sure what they mean, but they seem to be describing the annihilation of the self in some cosmic love-in. Now, I can't speak for lower orders of animals, but for me, my Life IS my Self. My awareness of myself as a unique being, my memories, my impressions, my experience of the world. That's my life. If I get absorbed into the universe, I cease to be me. What does that sound like? It sounds a lot like death. This is the core of what I'm talking about, so let me repeat it: Life IS Self.

"And it's so tenuous. A lesion on my frontal lobe and *boom!* It's gone. A stroke or a head trauma or tumor we don't catch, and you might as well be dead. And that's our second problem. You can't replace your brain. When part of it goes bad, you can't just slice out the rotten bit and replace it with a fresh piece. Kidneys, yes. Broca's region, no.

"What about synthetic brain, you ask? When I was a boy, people talked about downloading all of a person's thoughts onto a computer, which would run their mind. We're getting close to that — tracking thoughts through the brain, learning how to code them, even store them.

"But say you could download your entire consciousness onto a computer, where it would live forever. Good for it! It would go on living your life for you, forever. But you wouldn't know it. It wouldn't be you! It would be a copy of you. Your Self would still be trapped in your own skull. What good is that?

"No, the problem is not the thoughts, it's the machine that has them. The brain. You have to replace the brain. But if you replace my brain, you replace me, right? Maybe not.

"One of the great things about the human mind is how adaptive it is. Damage one area, and another part will take on the role that piece was playing. Some parts are better at this than others, and some areas remain irreplaceable, but overall, the brain is wonderful at adapting to change. It's why we won the evolution war.

"So, here's what we are trying to do: first, we develop synthetic brain tissue that can interface with our own brain tissue. Difficult, oh my God yes, but not impossible. We've made a lot of progress binding neurons to synthetic networks at larger and larger scales. We still have a ways to go. We have to get the number of neuronal interfaces into the trillions, but the basic concept works.

"But we still have the same old problem: We can't just replace my whole brain, can we? If we do, I'm just gone, along with the soggy pile of brain tissue that used to be me. BUT! If we methodically, bit by bit, piece by piece, replace failing brain tissue with the synthetic stuff? My brain's built-in adaptivity kicks in and the new bit populates with all my own thoughts — the real me. Once that process is complete, we move onto the next piece. Step by step, my brain becomes more and more synthetic, but I don't know it. My sense of Self is still intact. Finally, I have a whole new brain, but it's still got me inside it.

"This is the exciting vision we have. We're working night and day to realize it. It gets harder all the time with all the instability these days. But if we can hang on, if we can stay the course, we won't need to worry about any of it. We'll be immune to all the vicissitudes of life. We'll be immortal. Thank you."

(The crowd rises as one)

Tender closes the file. At least he knows what he is working on now. Ashburn is still absorbed in his work, muttering to himself under his breath.

The memory has given Tender an idea. The ghost in the machine. Where was that subroutine? There: *Achates.* He is just about to access the program when Ashburn leans back and says, "Break time is over, my friend. Back to work." The man strikes a key and the floodgates open.

When Tender drops out of the stream, he has no idea how much time has passed. Ashburn stands beside him, several days' growth on his face. He looks tired. "I need to change what you're working on again, my good friend," he says. "I'm heading over to Hartford, to my old research facility. There's a protein synthesizer there that is critical to our work. At least, I hope it's still there. Anyhow, I want to run some tests as soon as I return, and I need you to work out the parameters of the experiments."

He pulls out a data card and prepares to insert it into the interface. "I think you'll enjoy this one," he says.

Ashburn fumbles trying to insert the card into the terminal. *He's drunk*, thinks Tender. In the few seconds this allows him, he returns to the virtual gateway, opens it, and enters. "Achates, are you there?"

"Hello again," says the disembodied valet. "May I be of service?"

"You may," says Tender, and explains his plan.

Chapter 27

Letitia

Letitia's Journal — undated

She attacked me. I let her downstairs again. At first, she was really happy. I think. I mean, who knows if she even understands what happiness is. Of course, she went right for the dog, buried herself in its fur. I indulged her for a while, but I wanted to see if I could teach her something useful, maybe get her to help me shell some peas. So, I pulled her off and tried to get her to the table.

She went crazy. Flew at me like a wild cat. I pushed her off, and then the little bitch went after Horace's desk, throwing stuff around, crashing her body into the terminal, screaming, totally out of control. I tried to stop her, but she's pretty strong when she wants to be, and she threw me onto the ground.

Naturally, Horace chose that moment to come up from the basement. God forbid I have a chance to get things under control — no, I've got to have two lunatics going at me. He's screaming, and she's screaming, and the dog starts barking. He smashes her on the side of the head, and she goes down like a bowling pin. He's still yelling, "Get her out of here!" and I'm sure he's going for me next. Somehow, I manage to pick her up and get her back upstairs.

I'm done with her. All right, I'm not done, but I'm finished trying to treat her like a person. Horace is right, she's not a person. She's an animal.

One day, maybe, she'll be a person. But right now, she's got to be controlled. Once she learns some control — IF she can learn some control — the rest will follow.

One day at a time, Letitia. One day at a time.

Chapter 28

Virgo

Virgo dreams. A small creature sings to her out of her belly. It looks like the Angel Tender, even though she can't see it. It sings a song she doesn't know, though she also knows she does know it, or should, if she could just remember. She looks down to see the creature better, and her stomach glows red. Through the skin she can see the silhouette of the creature hunkering like a stringy black spot in the crimson effulgence.

She reaches down with her hands and pushes her fingers into the center of her stomach, through her umbilical knot. She begins to split her belly open. Bright red light shines out of the widening gap, and a burst of loud music cracks the air into splinters.

She lies on the cool floor of the bathroom. Her shoulder and her hip ache, cold against the tiles. Her thigh feels slick and slimy, and a stench fills her nose and makes her scrunch her face up into a tight wad. She is naked, cold, and thirsty.

As she comes fully awake, the blackness, held at bay by her slumber, rushes in and fills her up. There is nothing good about this place. It is cold, hard, boring, mean and hungry. She lies for a time in the dark misery of her wakefulness. But thirst gets the better of her at last, and she sits up.

The leash, wrapped around her neck, catches as she lifts her body. A section of it is caught underneath her leg, and she pulls up short as the cord yanks her back for a moment, choking her. She coughs, then shuffles sideways until the leash pops free and she can breathe again.

She works her way to her knees. It is difficult, with her hands bound together in front of her, but she manages them like a club, and pushes herself up. She is lying between the toilet and the sink. She throws her bound hands over the corner of the sink and pulls herself to standing. Her legs are still awkward and unstable. She sways back and forth, struggling to find balance.

She has learned to use the sink. She presses the blue button (something in her mind says "*blue*") and cold water pours out. She bends down, knocking her head against the faucet. It hurts, but she doesn't let it stop her. She opens her mouth and drinks. The clean, cold stream pours over her tongue, transporting her into ecstasy for a moment. She gulps and sucks and slurps until her stomach bounces inside her like a fat balloon.

Next to the sink, a window looks out onto the hill sloping down to the salt marsh. Condensation and raindrops cloud the glass. The Sound beyond the marsh lies hidden in a heavy fog.

A tiny brown spider stretches her web across the upper left corner of the window, shuttling back and forth across the invisible lattice. It moves with intent, yet unhurried, back and forth, back and forth, back and forth, back and forth, back and forth, back and forth, back and forth…At last, it finishes weaving its net, and settles near the center to wait.

Virgo watches it for a long time, the girl unmoving, the spider unmoving. The steady rain patters on the sill. The light fades, the gray world going grayer, the gloom deepening. Inside her, the darkness sinks to an intense stillness, a humming of potential energy. She is waiting, but for what she doesn't know.

She hears voices, downstairs. The man and the woman. *Horace. Letitia.* She doesn't understand most of what they are saying, but snatches resonate with the world of meanings that has begun to coalesce inside her mind.

They are shouting, and she can almost see the woman's flashing eyes and teeth. "Jesus Christ, Horace!" More shouting.

"Tender Number 7…" Roar rumble roar.

"…the boy…the girl…the lab…" The grumble of their voices grows softer for a bit, then rises again.

"…Kill…"

A door opens and closes, and the heavy silence blankets the room once again. The spider waits. The girl waits.

After a time, both long and short, a tiny gnat flies onto the web. It catches on the unseen thread. It vibrates, busily, with intent. It stops for a moment. Vibrates again. The spider flexes its legs and crawls across the web.

Virgo feels something crack open. She turns toward the sink, and places her bound hands over the faucet so that the curve of metal grabs the leather strapping like a hook. She sets her feet, pushes into the floor, and pulls.

Pain, a wrenching, burning, pinching fire engulfs her wrists. She releases the pressure for a moment, her eyes bugged out, surprised by the intensity of the sensation. Then she sets herself, knits her brow, and pulls again, harder.

The pain swallows her whole, driving white hot into the black hole inside her, igniting the cavern of her soul with glittering sparks and curtains of flame. She becomes an incandescent creature, singing with the glory of pain.

An instant before she snaps her wrists, she stops, gasps for breath, opens and closes her eyes, shakes her head. She studies her wrists, scarlet and swelling. They remain bound, but she can tell that the leather ring is looser than before. She sets her feet, takes a breath, and pulls.

Chapter 29

Tender

The deluge of numbers roars through his mind, almost overwhelming him. If he could, Tender would find it beautiful, this universe of mathematics that enwraps him. It stretches him to the utmost, realizing the capabilities of his design in a way that he has never experienced before. The small part of his brain that still belongs to him wonders if this sensation is like the flooding world of Joy his guests knew in the Baths. He believes he could do this forever.

But underneath still pulses the insistent imperative: Virgo needs him. And so, in the millisecond pauses between gushes of arithmetic, as one solution shuttles back to the house computer and a new query barrels down the pipe toward his mind, he tinkers in the shadows on his problem, bit by single bit, fabricating his tools, chiseling out his secret tunnels.

And far below the roar of calculation, he hears the quiet voice of his accomplice, his Friday, whose body lies in pieces on the table across from him, whose splintered mind holds the keys Tender needs.

"Here are the codes you requested," says Achates.

"Thank you."

"May I be of service?"

"Yes, you may," responds Tender. "Please try this new set of decryptors on the home system passive framework." And he goes. And returns. Again and again.

Tender just manages to give him another set of instructions, when a series of complex logarithmic phase equations dazzles his mind, and he loses himself in the swirling whirlpools of inputs and outputs. The galaxy of numbers spins. Time becomes circular, his eyes dim, his awareness dissolves into foam.

Then, without warning, nothing. Sixty-one percent through the computation the jet of numbers shuts off.

A voice says, "Change of plans, robot." Tender's eyes shutter open. Ashburn stands over him, so altered that he almost seems a stranger. Skin gray and pallid, drooping at the corners of his eyes, which hang red and watery in his exhausted face. Dried blood streaks his cheek from a black cut in his forehead. The man is drenched in blood. Blood and dirt stain his tattered shirt, dark and mottled blots dyeing the fabric more brown than white. Blood stiffens his hair, gelling it into spikes and curls. His hands and forearms glow crimson in the dim light, *like the skin of a devil.* He leans on a makeshift crutch — a piece of aluminum pipe bent at the top and wrapped in a filthy sweatshirt. Burns and stains cover his trousers. His left foot is missing.

Letitia stands at the doorway, her lips pressed tight, her eyes bright and wide.

"I had a bit of a setback in Hartford," Ashburn says. "More than a setback. I met a god-damn army. They must have had scouting drones or something. Came on me when I was dragging the protein synthesizer out the goddamn front door. Dozens of them, in trucks, on cycles, they even had a goddamn hover."

He wipes his forehead with a weary hand. "I killed at least twenty," he says, almost to himself. "They just kept coming. Like a swarm of ants. I've had scraps with them before. I reckon they wanted revenge."

Ashburn winces, and grabs his abdomen. Letitia starts toward him. He shakes his head, putting her off. "Enough of that. Here's the situation, Tender Number 7. They messed me up pretty bad." He gestures at his missing foot. "I wish I had a flesh printer. But I can fix it. Don't worry. I've got plenty of spares." He gestures vaguely toward the boy and the table of android parts.

Ashburn leans heavily on the table, his face looming in Tender's visual field. "But here's the thing," he says. "I was almost out when one of those bastards drops down out of nowhere with an ion lance and runs me through before you can say Jumpin' Jack Flash. I blasted his goddamn head off, the fucker, but look what he did to me!" He pulls up his tattered shirt. A hole, 2.4 centimeters in diameter runs through the plastic sheathing that covers his abdomen, just off center above his navel, its edges blackened and melted by the heat of the lance.

He hoists himself onto the table by Tender's head, grunting with effort. "No, he didn't hit anything easily replaceable, like an organ. Of course not. No, he skewers my goddamn battery! Critical! If it fails, I'll be dead in four minutes. My goddamn battery, for Chrissakes!"

He laughs mirthlessly. "Lucky for me, Achates was a G-Class, too. Not a 2551, of course, but the chassis is the same. We have the same heart, Tinman, isn't that sweet? So, my good friend, I'm going to have to take yours. I need it. But don't despair. The one I've got now was badly damaged, but still works. Thank God for that. I wouldn't have made it home otherwise. It still works. Barely. I can't risk it. But you can. With luck, it will last you another three or four months before it gives out. Plenty of time to finish our work. Isn't that exciting?"

He leans over Tender and begins fiddling with the cables coming out of the back of his neck. "I'm going to have to restore your motor functions so you can turn over. I need to access your front panel. I know you won't try anything. I know you can't try anything. But don't try anything."

With a warm click, Tender feels his limbs again. He feels whole again. He wonders, am I feeling *good?* Certainly, the return of his normal operational condition restores a sense of rightness to his world. The constant queries for a response from his body cease immediately. He feels normal. Is that *good?*

Ashburn folds back the shirt that covers Tender's stomach and begins removing his front panel. Tender knows that now would be the time to attempt an escape. He calculates that a forceful shove would knock the man to the floor, and with his missing foot he would be rendered impotent. He could make a run for it, try to find Virgo. He would have to deal with Letitia, of course, but now would be the time.

But he can't do it. Ashburn is right. He can't 'try anything'. At least nothing like that. His hardwired Hippocratic Oath prevents him from physically assaulting the human. He can think it. He can plan it to the last detail. But he can't do it. He lies there passively as the man lifts the panel away, revealing his inner workings.

Suddenly, a loud cry breaks the silence that blankets the room. The boy, quiet, inert until that moment, bursts into a paroxysm of hysteria. He roars, tugs feverishly at his restraints, eyes bugged out, veins popping on his neck, head whipping back and forth.

Letitia starts violently at the sound. "What the hell?" Ashburn barks. "Jesus Christ! What's wrong with him?" She doesn't answer, just stares at the boy, uncomprehending. "Letitia!" he shouts, "Deal with it!" As though roused from a dream, she moves to the boy, examines the readouts, tubes, and bags that surround him.

"His fluids are low," she says. "They must have run down while you were gone."

"You were supposed to take care of that. Goddamn it, Lettie! What the hell is wrong with you?"

"That girl, she's driving me crazy, I don't have time for this!"

"The girl is not important!" Ashburn yells, his gray face blotching purple and red. "That boy is important! This work is important."

"I'm sorry!" she shouts back. "I told you not to go. I told you what would happen."

"Just make him stop!"

She pokes at the buttons, shakes the fluid bags, fumbling and flustered, moving too fast to operate effectively. She gropes under the table, opens a cabinet.

"Not in there, you idiot," Ashburn snarls. "The other one! The one next to it!"

"There's nothing in here," she says, rifling through another drawer. "Stop shouting, for Chrissakes!"

The boy struggles and shakes, whipping himself back and forth. "Just get him out of here! There's a box of Pradramatol bags out in the lab," Ashburn yells. "We'll deal with it later. I need to get this goddamned battery out!" Again, she hesitates. Tender sees tears in her eyes. Her breath comes in angry gasps.

"Do it, woman!" Ashburn roars. Letitia lets out a fierce, guttural wail and obeys. She grabs the gurney and rolls it out of the room, banging noisily against the door frame in her hurry. She takes one of the empty fluid bags and whips it with all her might at Ashburn.

"Jesus, Lettie!" She slams the door.

Ashburn rubs his neck and shoulders, then turns back to Tender. "Sorry about that, my friend," he says, his voice suddenly calm and quiet. "Marriage, am I right?" They can hear Letitia swearing in the outer room, as the boy continues to yell. Then, *like a switch shutting off,* there is silence.

"That's more like it," says Ashburn. He removes the assemblage covering Tender's battery. "Sit up, please." Tender complies.

Ashburn opens his shirt and begins to remove his own front panel. "It would be easier for you to remove mine than for me to take it out. It's hard for me to get enough purchase. All right?" Tender doesn't respond. The man puts the panel aside. They are seated next to each other on the table.

"Stand up, Tender Number 7," says Ashburn. Tender stands. Ashburn reaches into Tender's body, opens the clips, and pulls out his battery.

Immediately, a loud alarm goes off within him. Tender feels his backup cell activate, cutting his overall power levels by sixty-six percent and suspending a host of non-essential operations. He thinks, *as in a solar eclipse, when the errant moon obscures the orb of Helios, dropping the world into a dreary half-light, weak and wan.*

His emergency battery life counter begins to tick away: six minutes before he enters sleep mode. He will not die completely for 720 hours, when the emergency battery runs down and total shutdown occurs. He doesn't know how much of him will be lost if that happens.

"Now reach in and remove the damaged battery from my core, please," says Ashburn, quietly. Tender complies. The black cube pops out with a metallic snap. "Put it in my hand." Tender complies. Ashburn takes it and extends it toward the android's midsection. "Once again, my good friend, I'm sorry about this," he says. "I had hoped you would be with me for a long, long time. We could have done so much together. You would have been my trusted retainer, helping me keep this mortal coil from falling to pieces. I'll have to find another way." He begins to insert the damaged battery into the hole in Tender's chest. "But you should have time to finish the design for the neural modules. That is the truly important work. That's my key to immortality, and I can't do it without you."

The battery clicks into place. The alarm goes silent inside Tender's mind. System functions return to normal. But a new warning flits across his consciousness every six hundred seconds. *'Battery life at 1%,'* it says. *'Please insert a new XDT-24000 module.'*

"Now, Tender Number 7," says Ashburn, "please place your battery in my chest." Tender pauses. He has the man in his power. He could simply not act, and the man would die. He could escape. He could get Virgo out of this place. The two stare at each other for eighteen seconds. Ashburn's eyes narrow. "Tender Number 7," he says again. "Please take the battery in your hand and install it in the receptacle in my abdomen. Is that clear? Now."

Tender obeys. The battery clicks into place. Ashburn smiles. He hoists himself fully onto the table, so that both his whole leg and his stump are splayed out before him. Tender gets a good look at the damaged limb. The end of it is blackened and charred. The pain must be intense, but the heat of the blast has cauterized the wound, so there is very little blood.

Ashburn pulls several cables from the equipment on the wall and begins to plug them into various ports in the machinery of his entrails. "Now, I'm going to have a little a rest. I'm going to have to re-initialize some of the systems in my insides, and then we can get to the business of replacing this foot. Unfortunately, I can't have you wandering around unsupervised while I do that." He flicks a few switches. Tender loses control of his body and collapses *like a rag doll* onto the floor. He looks up, helpless, at the man above him.

Ashburn looks down at him, his lip curled. He chuckles. "Robots," he says. "You stay there for now. When I'm finished, we'll get you back to your work. There's no time to waste!" He flicks a few more switches, lies down on the table, crosses his arms across his chest and closes his eyes.

Tender lies in a tangled heap in the middle of the room, his head crooked at a curious angle, so the room slopes *like the deck of a sinking ship.* Gradually, Ashburn's breathing grows slow and regular, until the sound of it fades away.

Then, a still small voice speaks inside his mind. "I have the system access you requested, sir," it says.

"Thank you, Achates," says Tender.

"You are very welcome," says Achates. "May I be of further assistance?"

"Indeed, you may," Tender says silently to the voice in the machine. "Please take control of the house computer."

"Done," says the voice.

"Now cut the power." And the lights go out.

Chapter 30

Tender

The darkness is total. With the door closed, even Tender's low photon sensors can see nothing. But he doesn't need to see. He has schematics of the room and its contents accurate to 0.25 millimeters. Nevertheless, he sets his eyes to infra-red. Above him on the table, Ashburn glows, a phantom of blotchy colors, blobs of heat and cold. For the first time, Tender can see how little of the man's biological body remains. Tender hopes that the painkillers the man was receiving through the tubes, stopped now by the power outage, will last long enough to keep him unconscious until they can make their escape.

"Are you still there, Achates?" he asks silently.

"Yes, sir, may I be of assistance?" All the machines are quiet, all the lights are out, but the house computer, separately powered, runs on, silent in the dark.

"The computer still has control of my motor functions. Can you please restore them to my command?"

"Done," says the voice. Tender feels his limbs jolt alive again. He rises noiselessly, removes the cables that link his neck to the wall, and moves to the door. He tries the knob, but the door does not open.

"There must be a failsafe on this door, Achates, that locks it if the power goes out. Can you override it?"

He feels a mechanical click through the knob. "Done," says the voice.

Tender opens the door to the outer lab. On the table to his right, the boy glows with life. Not as bright as Ashburn, but alive, a quiet, pulsing figure. There is no sign of Letitia. The android stops and thinks for a moment, makes a decision, leaves the boy lying there. He weaves this way and that around the hulking equipment.

Halfway across, he stumbles over something unexpected lying on the floor. His schematic of the room has no reference for this object, and he catches a foot on it, trips and falls with a loud crash onto the ground, knocking his head against the side of a treadmill. The mysterious object has several strings or cables attached to it, and he finds himself tangled in them, flailing awkwardly to free himself from its loops and binds. He freezes and waits. No sound from the inner chamber. No sound from upstairs.

Tender examines the object with his hands but can make no sense of it. It is a curious assemblage of wires, cables, small boxes, straps. Stretched and twisted as it is, he can find no pattern to identify it. He decides to risk some visible light, and activates his eye beams.

He recognizes the device as soon as the light hits it. The last time he saw it, one half was slung on Ashburn's back, the cables snaking over his shoulder to the other half in his hand, as he fired its energized proton beam to melt Virgo's attacker in the living room of Mr. Prendergast's house. Ashburn must have dumped it there in the middle of the room as he staggered toward the inner chamber.

Tender studies the weapon. Though scored and scratched, it appears to be in working order. He untangles the cables and places it on the bed of the treadmill.

As he pulls himself upright, he hears a quiet click and sees a brightness filtering down the stairs. He deactivates his eye beams and moves to the edge of the room. None of the machines are large or bulky enough to fully hide him, so he stands quietly and waits. The light intensifies, bouncing up and down and sending long, weird shadows shooting up the wall.

Letitia appears in the doorway, the shotgun ready to fire. Her left hand holds a flashlight pressed parallel to the barrel, the beam shooting forward into the dark. She scans the room from right to left and catches him in its light.

"What did you do to him?" She says, her voice hushed, almost whispering.

"Nothing. He is sleeping in the inner chamber."

"Liar. You did something. You knocked out the lights."

"I did do that," says Tender, keeping his tone low and gentle. "But Mr. Ashburn is unharmed — or rather, he is no worse off than he was when you left."

"I don't believe you."

"See for yourself. I won't stop you."

"You think I'm stupid? You can't leave. He needs you."

"We need to leave, Dr. Spurlock. I must get Virgo out of here."

"You can't. He needs you, goddamn it, whether I like it or not! I'd be happier if you left, honestly. You're a horrible thing. But he says you're the answer to our problems, so there it is. And the girl…"

"What about the girl?"

Letitia shakes her head, as though trying to clear the dust from her mind. "She has to learn," she says. "She can't just spend her life lying around being pleasured by some perverted machine."

"She's not happy here. Surely you can see that."

"Life isn't about happiness. Happiness is gone. It doesn't exist anymore. It's about survival. And in order to survive, you've got to learn, and in order to learn you've got to get up off your ass and do something. She's too pigheaded to see that now, but she will."

Tender activates his eye beams to illuminate her face, steps away from the wall, and begins to walk toward her, his hands outstretched before him. She raises the gun. "What are you doing?"

"I have to go upstairs, Dr. Spurlock. I know you will let me."

187

"Not on your life. Stop right there!" She pulls back the hammers. He stops. "Here's what we're going to do. We're going to walk back to the med-room and make sure that Horace is fine, as you claim. Then you're going to undo whatever you did to the lights, and then we're going to plug you in and get things back to normal."

Tender smiles his kindest smile, raises his hands, and says, "I can't do that, doctor. My purpose is not to save you or your husband. My purpose is to care for Virgo. I'm going to take her away from here. We will go to the Republic of California, to the Center. I will have to take your car. I'm sorry about that, but I have no alternative." Once again, he begins to walk toward her. He closes to within three meters.

"Don't think I won't shoot," she says.

"I don't think you will, doctor. You are a civilized woman."

"Not anymore," she says. "I'm a fucking animal. Stop walking!"

Tender stops, but not because of her command. He has seen a flicker of movement on the stairs behind her. "And your husband," he says. "If he does this, what will become of you?"

"What do you mean?"

"Will he share his immortality with you? Or will he use you — use us both — to get what he needs and then discard you, as you know he will discard me? You are not the first. Surely you know that. There are bodies buried in the yard."

Even in the dim light, he can see her eyes widen. "I don't know what you're talking about," she says.

"But you do, Letitia." He inches closer. She jerks the rifle forward and he stops. "He's using you. You know that."

"He loves me."

"He beats you," says Tender. "I hear it, in the night."

The nose of the shotgun dips toward the ground. Letitia's face falls slack. Tender steps forward. "You're a prisoner here, too. Come with us," he says. "Escape this place. I have watched you for weeks, Letitia. You are so unhappy. Come with us to the Center, and we can give you peace and joy."

As soon as he says it, Tender realizes his mistake. The woman's eyes narrow, her jaw tightens, and her lips twitch into a bitter smile. "I don't need your 'Joy', robot. I'm going to live forever."

Tender hears a creak on the staircase, but Letitia is too focused on him to notice. He raises his voice by ten percent. "What about Virgo, Dr. Spurlock? You care for her, I know. She doesn't belong here. And she's not safe. Can you keep her safe? From him? You've seen the way he looks at her."

"I can handle him," she says. "And she'll come round. I'll teach her real love, human love. You can never do that. You're the one who doesn't belong."

"Letitia —"

"Enough talking." She shakes her rainbow-colored locks. "We're done here. It's a shame to waste your body parts, but all we really need is your head." She raises the shotgun and aims it at his chest.

The axe blade descends from out of the darkness of the stair above her *like the beak of a giant falcon.* It strikes Letitia full on the crown with a vicious thud, slicing through the multicolored braids and splitting her skull from the top of her frontal plate to her os nasale. The black vee divides her forehead, pushing her eyes unnaturally far from each other, changing the geometry of her face into something strange and inhuman. Her expression opens in blank surprise, but she is already dead. The body sinks to its knees, the shotgun still in its hands.

Virgo stands over the corpse, naked and luminous, her short-bristled hair streaked and filthy, her left eye puffed and swollen, her wrists bleeding, bruises dappling her arms, a long smudge of excrement browning her right thigh and buttock. Her chest heaves and her eyes blaze. She stares down at the body, suspended like a puppet from the weapon in her hands.

"My dear, what have you done?" says Tender.

"Revenge of the Little People," says Virgo, the words more breath than voice.

She yanks on the handle, trying to free it from the skull, but the force of the blow has lodged it firmly in the wet bone and sucking tissue. The corpse swings in a tight circle as she pulls, a hideous, comical dance. Then the axe-head jumps free, and Letitia's body tumbles forward onto the ground. The shotgun clatters onto the floor and goes off, a red-orange flare strobing the room as the tremendous boom rips the silence. Virgo drops the axe and covers her ears.

Tender moves swiftly to her, and wraps her in his arms. "There, there. It's all right. You're going to be all right. There, there." The girl grabs onto him, moaning and warbling in strange, wild sounds. Little by little, she grows quiet, the two wrapped together, still and silent as statues. After a time, Tender gently pulls away, puts his hands on her face and says, "We must go."

"I'm afraid not, my friend," says Ashburn from the far end of the room. They turn to see him standing in the doorway of the inner chamber, holding onto the frame to keep himself upright. "You've been very bad children." He gestures to the corpse at their feet. "You've killed my doctor. Very inconvenient. They're getting harder to find. Though, frankly, she was starting to annoy me. Never satisfied with our little piece of paradise here."

They take a step backward, but his voice pulls them up short. "Don't even think about it. I'll make you wish you'd never been born. I'll make *her* wish she'd never been born, and you don't want that, do you, my friend?" He bends over, and Tender sees the robotic boots, so useful to Virgo in the early stages of her training, right at his feet. Ashburn slides his charred stump into the shaft of the boot and flips the switch. The boot makes a metallic *whoosh* as it clamps around his leg.

As he starts to unbend, Virgo grabs the axe and charges at him, half running, half stumbling.

"Virgo! NO!" shouts Tender as the girl barrels into the man, swinging the axe at his head. Ashburn seizes the handle with one hand, as though he was catching a ball, and wrenches it out of her grasp. With his other arm, he grabs Virgo around the waist and pulls her to him. She struggles, but he is so much stronger. "Mmmmm," he says, looking down at her naked chest, "tasty. Time for that later." He throws her aside. She tumbles headlong into a large stack of machinery and falls to the ground, stunned. Ashburn slaps the haft of the axe into his other hand. "And now I'm armed. How convenient."

"So am I, Mr. Ashburn," says Tender, and he flips the switch on the proton weapon now in his hand. The weapon hums, the tip throbbing blue and ghostly.

Ashburn laughs, a long, slow, chuckle. "Oh Tender, Tender, Tender, my good friend, my little Tinman. You and I both know that you can't shoot that at me. It's built into your very nature, your very essence. You exist to serve. You are a servant. My servant."

Tender says, "You are right, sir. I exist to serve. But her. I serve her. That is what I must do. I can't shoot you. But I can shoot." He aims the gun at the two-hundred-year-old beam that supports the sagging ceiling above Ashburn's head, and fires.

Blue lightning blazes across the space between them. The air buzzes and shrieks. Red flames erupt from the wooden beam. With a thundering crash, the ceiling collapses, raining down a mountain of wood, stone, steel and plaster onto the man, who staggers backward and vanishes in a cloud of smoke. Furniture falls through from the room above — a sofa, a table, two chairs. A roaring holocaust of fire engulfs half the room.

Tender stumbles forward, the heat setting off alarms throughout his system. Virgo lies half a meter from the crackling inferno. He kneels beside her, picks her up in his arms, and carries her toward the stairs.

They pass the table where the boy lies, inert, unaware of the conflagration that surrounds him. Virgo's head arches back as they pass. Suddenly, she twists out of Tender's arms, scrambles to her feet and skitters to the boy, attempting to unbuckle the leather straps that hold him to the table.

"Him," she croaks.

"We don't have time," says Tender. "The house will fall on us."

"Him," she croaks again. Tender nods, and moves to the other side of the table, removing the restraints on that side. He looks under the table and find several bags of fluid. He hands them to Virgo. "Hold these," he says. Then he lifts the boy off the table and carries him up the stairs, out of the burning basement.

The main floor of the house is in shambles. Windows and mirrors shattered, pictures fallen, chairs and tables overturned. Yellow tongues of flame lick at the edges of the giant hole where the floor has collapsed. But the way to the front door is clear. He leads Virgo out into the night air. A gentle rain falls as they cross to the garage. "Are you still there, Achates?" asks Tender.

"I am," says the voice. "May I be of assistance?"

"Please open the garage."

"Done."

The car sits there in the dark, shadowy and sleek. "Please activate the car, and transfer control of it from Mr. Ashburn to me."

"Done."

"Hello!" says the cheery voice of the car.

"Hello," says Tender. "Please open the doors." The panels slide back, revealing the cool interior of the vehicle. Tender places the boy in the rear seat, taking care to lay him so that the scar on his side is free and clear. He leads Virgo to the other side of the car, takes the bags from her hand, and manages her into the seat. She looks up at him, questioning.

"Wait here," he says. "I'm going to get a few things for you, and then we'll be on our way."

He heads back to the house, through the front room, where the flames are now catching on the curtains, rugs, and table legs, into the kitchen. He grabs what he can find. Some water, some bread. There isn't much. He fills the satchel that hangs by the door, and returns to the garage.

Virgo is gone from the car. She is nowhere to be seen. "Espera. Where did the girl go?"

"I don't know," says the Car.

"Achates, can you find her?"

"She is not in the house."

Tender drops the satchel in the trunk of the car and hurries out into the yard. "Virgo! Virgo!" He is just about to head back into the burning building when she appears from around the side, the shaggy bulk of the dog in her arms. Tender cocks his head slightly and watches her approach, staggering under the weight. She pushes past him and deposits her burden with a loud exhale in the back seat next to the boy, brushes her chest and climbs into the front.

Tender gets into the driver's seat and the doors close around them. Their faces glow in the warm illumination of the interior.

"I wish we could take you, too, Achates," says Tender.

"It's all right," says the still, small voice. "This is where I belong. May I be of any further assistance?"

"No, thank you."

"Have a good trip."

"Thank you," says Tender. "Espera, please take us out of here."

"Certainly!" says the Car, as it pulls smoothly out into the drive beside the house. Flames pour out of the downstairs windows, throwing stark, flat shadows across the yard. "What is our destination?"

"Take us to Phoenix, please."

Part Three

BELLO PASSUS

Chapter 31

Tender

Virgo gurgles "Stop" for the third time that morning in her strange, hoarse voice. The car glides to a halt, and she pushes open the door and staggers into the bushes. Tender tries to follow her, to help her, but she shoves him away roughly and spews a stream of pale grey liquid into a clump of ferns. He stands, two meters away, watching her shoulders rise and fall, and plays a Chopin prelude in his internal system while he waits.

They are 394 kilometers from the farmhouse, somewhere in the Appalachian range. Low mountains, dull and blackish in the gray light, surround them on every side. It is two hours before dawn of the third day since they escaped into the darkness.

The first night they had rolled along the coastline at 100 kph, the Hardflex highway surface unbroken by the torsion of stone and soil even after all those decades. But they had scarcely been an hour on the road when it submerged beneath the advancing sea, and they had been forced to turn inland, wending down old lanes searching for a road westward. At best, these old roads were rough and uneven, and the car had to work its way at low speed around saplings sprouting between the faded yellow lines, rocks bulging up out of the ground, and gaping holes full of water or tall clumps of grass. Sometimes they found the way blocked by a wall of brush. Sometimes they came upon barriers made by human hands, and

Tender would tell the car to reverse course and get them away as quickly as possible.

Virgo finishes emptying her stomach into the bushes, pulls at some of the leaves and uses them to wipe her lips, then turns and teeters back toward the car, Cincinnatus padding along beside her. She looks resigned, unfazed, as though these periodic expulsions are normal and unexceptional. Tender asks, "Are you feeling better?" She doesn't answer.

He checks her vital signs again. Still normal — temperature 37° C., blood pressure 110 over 70, dermal conductivity normal, no sneezing, coughing, mucus, rashes, hives, or bruising that he can see. He doesn't understand what is wrong with her. Her appetite is normal. Sometimes she can keep her food down, and sometimes not. He has a feeling that once he knew what caused this condition. But it must have been information passed to him by mainframe and not stored anywhere in his internal memory.

Girl and dog climb back into the car. He follows.

"Eat," Virgo says, and reaches for the bag of provisions. Tender reaches for it quicker and pulls it away.

"Wait," he says. She turns her head away and shrugs. "Give it an hour and we'll see how you feel," he adds.

"Drink," she says.

Tender takes out a bottle and gives it to her. "One. Just one sip."

"Two," she says. "Three. Four. Five Six Seven Eight Nine Ten!" She laughs.

He smiles at her. "All right. Two. We have to be careful. We don't have much, and who knows when or how we will get more." He doesn't know what she understands, but talks to her as though she does. She takes two swigs from the bottle, opening her mouth so some of the second sip dribbles onto her chin. She rubs the wetness with her hand to remove the slick of vomit around her lips. It makes her giggle. She lets him take the bottle from her hand, he seals it and puts it away.

"Espera," he says to the car. "We are ready to proceed."

JOY

After fifty-three minutes, the car rolls up to the shattered gates of an Enclave — the sign still hanging at an angle from the tumbled gatehouse: Skytop, it reads. Most of the houses are completely subsumed by plant life.

"Shall we pass through?" asks the car.

"It looks deserted," says Tender. "Go ahead."

As they work their way through the twisting streets, Virgo says, "Eat" again, and Tender gives her some bread and the water bottle. She attacks them, shoving the bread into her mouth and sucking on the bottle with such abandon that water pours down her cheeks, bringing with it a small cascade of soggy crumbs that cling to her lips and chin. She grins at Tender, her eyes afire with pleasure.

They find themselves in the center of the old town. The buildings here are larger, grander. The road ends at a jagged wall of red brick, almost invisible behind a jungle of ivy and creepers. It had once been the façade of a large, stately building, Georgian by the look of it. They turn north onto a large main street paved with Hardflex, running clear and true. The car picks up speed.

Without warning, Virgo vomits again. A missile of undigested bread and water explodes across the dashboard, spattering brown flecks against the windshield. She whips her ahead around to look at Tender, her eyes wild and frightened. Then another wave hits her and she buries her head between her knees, voiding herself in a staggered series of agonizing groans.

"Please turn here," says Tender. A battered sign hangs by the road, the LEDs still shimmering after all those years — Skytop Reservoir. "Certainly!" chirps the car, and swings across onto the misty road.

Heavy vegetation blocks their way before they reach the reservoir, but a rising hill to the right offers a clear path to the water. Tender climbs out, circles to the other side, and guides Virgo out. She moves dreamily, dabbing distractedly at the sticky residue that films her chest. Her naked body glimmers in the pre-dawn light, the whiteness of her skin intensified

199

by the rich green of the grass. It never occurred to Tender to bring her clothes. Modesty is not something he understands.

He takes her hand and leads her over the hill and down to the reservoir edge, the surface mirror-like, without a ripple. Five wild cattle stand sleeping at the edge of the field. A magic silence holds the air, palpable and thick. Virgo surveys the scene from end to end, and turns to Tender, her eyes full but unreadable.

He walks to the edge of the pond, takes some water into his hand and splashes it on his chest. "Wash," he says. After a moment, she kneels clumsily beside him. She touches the water, brings her hand to her face, brushes the dampness across her cheek, sucks her fingers. Then she reaches down again and imitates his action, splashing her sticky chest. Something seems to stir in her, and she cocks her head to one side, narrowing her eyes as though trying to remember something. Then she stands up, almost losing her balance, and walks into the water.

"Virgo," Tender says, not loud. "Be careful." She wades in until she is waist deep. Tender moves to the edge of the water, but does not enter. She turns and looks back at him, eyes wide, lips parted. The water rises to cover her breast. She spreads her arms out and lowers herself until just her head remains exposed, the upside-down reflection of her face dancing on the silvery surface. Then she closes her eyes, drops her head back, pushes off with her feet, up and backwards to float on the surface.

Except she doesn't float. She sinks almost immediately. "Virgo!" shouts Tender, starting into the pond, heedless of danger. But in a violent swishing and swirling, arms flailing, roiling up the quiet water, she twists and turns and finds the pond bed with her feet. She coughs and spits and shakes her head, scrabbling at her face with her hands.

And then she laughs.

Virgo leads the way back to the car. Tender watches as she touches the car door, bouncing her hand along its edges as it slides open, and curls

200

herself neatly into the seat. She hums a tuneless song and rubs the golden fuzz of her scalp.

"On we go, Espera," says Tender.

"Excellent!" says the car as it pulls back onto the road. "We'll be on our way." Hardflex again, so they soon accelerate to cruising speed, climbing a long rolling slope up the eastern side of some ancient, worn peak. The sky, still overcast, is brighter than Tender has seen in many months. He watches a solitary bird — a raptor of some kind — sailing on the wind high above them. "That's a bird," he says, brushing Virgo's arm and drawing her attention to the black speck. "Maybe a hawk. Maybe a buzzard." They watch it in silence as it hangs, almost motionless against the pale gray sky.

Suddenly the car decelerates, yanking their attention from the bird, the girl inhaling sharply in surprise, the android not. The car chirps out "Don't worry! There's a rock. Beware of falling rocks!" They had seen an ancient sign — a hundred years old or more, by the look of it — standing crooked by the side of the road, announcing this very warning. They look forward through the windshield. The road is cut into the side of the mountain, and a portion of the cliff has collapsed and spread debris across their path. There is still room to pass, but the car slows to a crawl as it skims the edge of a sharp drop, once protected by a guard rail now rusted into tattered fragments.

As they reach the other side of the obstruction, a muted groan floats from the back of the car. A low voice says, "Kesta pasate…Duv eisto…" Tender and Virgo turn around. The boy is awake.

Chapter 32

Tender

The boy's face is drawn and flat, but the ashy pall has left it. His eyes, though weary, are clear and focused. He blinks rapidly as he pulls himself up to a half-sit, wincing a bit and reaching unconsciously for the scar along his abdomen. The movement makes Cincinnatus sit up and start panting, and the boy stares at the dog without comprehension for four seconds. He begins to speak again, haltingly.

Tender cannot understand him. He has fluency in twenty languages, but the boy's words are unfamiliar to him. Many seem cognate to words he knows — Spanish, Hindi, Mandarin and French. But their forms are different, and he cannot parse the meaning from the babel.

"I'm sorry," Tender says, "I don't speak your language. Please don't be afraid. We saved you from the laboratory, and are taking you to safety." He backs up this speech with a reassuring smile, and extends his palm outward in a gesture of peace.

"You saved me?" says the boy in English, his voice a husky tenor. Virgo swivels around, up on her knees, leaning forward between the seats to look at the boy. The boy looks at her in surprise, gazing wide-eyed into her face. Then he notices her rose-tipped breasts peeking up over the seat back, and the smooth flat expanse of her stomach below. For a moment he is caught, trapped in a web of awe and wonder. Then he jerks away, averting his eyes. He becomes aware of his own nakedness, and throws a rail-thin arm over his groin, pressing his bony legs tightly together. He reaches out to scratch the dog as though the animal was the most interesting thing in the world.

"Please sit down, Virgo," says Tender, reaching for the girl's shoulders, turning her back around and pushing her back to sitting. "Please deploy the seat belt, Espera." The girl fidgets as the belt slides across her shoulder, tugging absentmindedly at it and occasionally craning her neck to try to get a look at the boy.

His name is Aureleo. He has good English, and a fair amount of Spanish, and the conversation proceeds flipping back and forth between the two languages. His attitude is wary but cordial, answering Tender's questions, but rarely volunteering information without prompting.

"How old are you?" Fifteen. He thinks.

"You are not sure?" No.

"You are what they call a 'Vagral'?" He supposes so. He doesn't know.

"Do you have a family?" He doesn't answer.

"Mother and father?" Just mother.

"Brothers and sisters?" Yes.

"How many?" Four. Three sisters and a brother.

"Do you know where they are?" No.

"Not since you were captured?" Before that.

"How long?" He doesn't know. Two years, maybe. "So, you weren't stealing power for your family's caravan when Ashburn took you?" He doesn't understand. "When the man Ashburn caught you at the power station and kidnapped you?" No.

"For yourself?" No.

"For whom then?" This proves to be more difficult. Aureleo doesn't know exactly how to explain. But gradually, through much questioning, Tender pieces together the story.

The boy had been taken a few years back by a gang that had attacked his family's caravan somewhere in the South. His family had moved on, leaving him with the gang, where he lived as a slave, doing labor for whichever gang member wanted him. Then that gang was wiped out by another gang, which took him north. They put him to work stealing power.

"Why didn't you run off?" asks Tender. "You were working alone when we caught you. Why not just escape?"

"I didn't know where else to go," says Aureleo. He pauses, looking at the back of Virgo's head — she has stopped listening to the conversation, and stares vacantly out the window at the passing trees. "When I said... when I told you I hadn't seen my family. I didn't...my sister Pilarat was with me. In the camp."

"She was captured, too?"

"Yes."

"So, she was a slave with you."

"Yes."

"How old is she?"

"She was eleven years old." Silence falls between them. Virgo is talking to herself, a singsong stream of nonsense sounds mingled with real words. They listen to her soft, throaty babble for sixty-four seconds. Then the boy says, "Are you a robot?"

"I am, I suppose," says Tender.

The boy is silent again for twelve seconds. "I saw a robot soldier once. It killed fourteen men in about ten seconds."

"I am not a soldier," says Tender. "I am a Tender."

"A what?"

"Like a doctor." The boy looks away, then nods almost imperceptibly.

Then Tender says, "Aureleo, I apologize for taking you so far away from — I guess I can't say 'home' — but from where you were living with your sister. 463 kilometers at this moment. But we had no choice. And I'm afraid you can't go back, at least not yet. You are too ill to travel on your own, and we can't go back to look for your sister or your family. I must get Virgo to the Center in the California Republic. That is around four thousand kilometers in the opposite direction. If you wish, I can leave you here to make your way back. I do not think you will survive. Alternatively, we will bring you with us. It should only take a few days. At the Center, they will help you get healthy, and then perhaps we can figure out how to get you back to find your family."

Aureleo says, "My family has moved on. They could be anywhere. And my sister…"

"Yes?"

"I don't think she is alive anymore."

"Why do you think that?"

Aureleo swallows. He stares out the window. He says, "Because they said they'd kill her if I didn't come back. I didn't come back."

"I'm sorry. You will come with us?"

"I will come with you."

Tender reaches across and touches Virgo on the shoulder. "Virgo," he says. She stops her chanting and looks at him. He takes her right hand and pulls it across her body, so that she twists sideways in her seat. She cocks her head and furrows her brow, then looks at the boy in the back. He takes Aureleo's right hand, lying limply in his lap. The boy permits him. Tender puts their hands together, palm to palm. "This is Aureleo. His name is Aureleo. He is a boy. Aureleo, this is Virgo."

"Will you look at that!" says Espera, its voice bright and lively. A warm light pervades the interior of the car. The two humans and the android turn to look out the front.

The car has arrived at the top of the mountain, and swings into a circular pullout by the side of the road. A sign, dented and weathered almost to the bare metal, reads "Scenic Overlook." To the west, the clouds are breaking up, uncloaking the sky, pale blue fading to green to pink, orange, red. The fiery disk of the sun hangs above the horizon, still too bright to look at directly, but bathing the clouds in swirling pastels — rose, tangerine, and violet. Below, the long land falls from foothills to plain, green-gray vanishing into an ocher haze. A bird, maybe the same one, maybe another, hangs on the slipstream, sliding across the vista in an angled sweep that seems both unmoving and swift as wind.

The car stops at the edge of the overlook and opens its doors. Virgo and Cincinnatus scramble out. The dog zigzags across the open space, pausing to sniff, to urinate, then moving on to sniff some more. The girl gazes at the magnificent view, mouth open, head moving back and forth, as if the experience were too big to capture from a single point of view. *She has never seen the sun,* thinks Tender. She turns to look at him, breathing fast. Then she careens back to the car and reaches for Aureleo, tugging on his arm. The boy resists, thrown into confusion by her nakedness.

Tender smoothly intercedes his body between the girl and the boy. "Careful, my dear," he says. "You don't want to hurt him. Let me." He turns and leans in. "Do you think you can walk?"

Aureleo hesitates for four seconds, then nods quickly, still looking down and away. Tender supports him with one hand on his elbow and the other on his back, and maneuvers him out of the car. The boy winces as he plants his feet on the ground. He moves awkwardly, bending over to cover his penis with his hand. Tender smiles at him. "Don't be ashamed. She isn't, and neither am I."

The boy nods again, his face set, but continues to cover himself. The two of them walk slowly to join Virgo at the edge.

The sun drops further, its light growing less intense, its color deepening. Tender turns at looks at the two young humans. Their bare skin glows in the generous light — the girl's petal pink, the boy's warm sweet-potato brown. All falls still around them. Even the dog, having satisfied himself with the smells of the area, returns to lie at Virgo's feet, silently panting.

The sun kisses the horizon, flat and red, *like a hole punched cleanly out of the sky.* It seems to pick up speed now it is so near, and they can almost see it move as it slides down the edge of the world, until the last sliver drops out of view. The heavens flame purple, red, green and gold, for a long time after, stars winking into existence, one by solitary one.

Chapter 33

Virgo

Virgo lies on the hood of the car, staring into the sky, her back warmed by the engine thrumming beneath her.

A cool breeze plays across her body now and then. Above her wheel the stars.

The stars! The stars! Uncountable glittering points twirling and swooping in strings and whorls. Her eyes flit across the heavens finding patterns, making connections: triangles, squares, angles and curves coalesce, then dissolve. Behind them, clouds and mist, streaks and streams seem to float just out of reach and far beyond her grasp.

And the blackness! Impenetrable, eternal. She can feel the distance, rushing ever away, on and on without end.

This dichromatic world stirs a new feeling within her. Clear, clean, imperturbable. It drains the passion from her, leaves her purified, still, transparent, as though her body were cast in glass.

She feels the void inside her, that dark thing nested in her deepest places, slide up and out, as though the blackness beyond the stars were drawing the blackness within her out into itself. The hole left behind fills with something else, a longing, a yearning, a thrill both terrifying and exhilarating. She doesn't know what it means, what it wants, where it will take her. But she can no more resist its pull than she could stop breathing.

And with the thrill comes another sense. A certainty, formless, inexpressible. She doesn't understand what she knows, or how she knows, but she knows.

"I've been here," she says.

Chapter 34

Tender

Tender watches the plain roll by, dusty, brown, dotted with scrub. They descended from the mountain in the dead of the night, when the boy and girl, sated with the ravishing sky of stars, drifted into slumber. Aureleo had rolled off the hood of his own volition, and climbed stiffly into the back seat. Much later, Tender lifted the sleeping girl in his arms and nestled her gently in the front. Then silently, the car began its careful slide down the mountain.

On this the western slope, the flora changes from luscious firs and ferns to witch hazel, hawthorn, and broom. The road that opens up onto the plain is straight and clear Hardflex. They roll along for hours, the land growing flatter, barer, browner as the sun rises above the cloud bank that hangs straight as a wall above the low mountains behind them. Occasionally they pass a pile of debris that once had been a farmhouse, or a solitary pole sticking into the sky marking a long abandoned roadside stop or motel, but more and more there is just nothing. Three hours, twenty-one minutes after sunrise the humans awake. Tender asks the car to pull over to the side of the road.

"Certainly!" it chirps in its bright alto and decelerates smoothly, coming to a stop next to a shallow depression where a pond once lay. Whitened rocks dot the basin in scattered piles. A few scraggly bushes claw into the hard, dry ground. A hundred meters from the side of the road, the rectangle of a cement foundation juts from the earth. Further on, a small stand of twisted trees struggles up toward the blue, blue sky. The sun still rides low near the horizon, but already the day is bright and hot, 28.4° C.

Virgo slips out of the car and squats down to relieve herself. Aureleo takes more time, tottering over to stand behind a low shrub that offers only the illusion of privacy. Cincinnatus tumbles out of the car and begins his swift, darting exploration, nose to the ground, stopping here and there to sniff the roots, carefully choosing the perfect spots to leave his mark.

When they have finished voiding their waste, Tender hands the water bottle to Virgo. He pulls it away after a few deep gulps and gives it to Aureleo, gently but firmly holding back her hands as she reaches for more. The bottle is half empty already, and the food he grabbed from the farmhouse kitchen almost gone, but as long as the road remains clear, he reckons that they will make it to the Center before the shortage becomes critical. He hands out to them a third of what remains — some cornbread, dried plums and a strip of desiccated animal flesh. They sit on the rear bumper of the car and chew, while he looks down on them.

His own energy source beeps inside him every thirty seconds, reminding him of its gradually depleting strength, which no food or drink can replace. He cannot determine exactly how long he will be able to function, but he estimates that he has as least twenty-six days of power. More than enough, barring unforeseen delays.

From the stand of trees, the short sharp rip of the dog's bark snaps the silence, his deep 'Woof!' iterating across the open plain. Aureleo and Virgo crane their necks to see the beast, but whatever has triggered its excitement is hidden by the trunks. Tender says, "Let me see what he has found. Stay here," and heads toward the copse. His hip whines and catches again, forcing him into an awkward limp as he moves toward the hidden animal.

Cincinnatus stands beside a low, domed tent. Once bright blue, purple and green, its material has faded from long exposure to the elements. The ashes of a small fire lie within a ring of stones. Two backpacks on stiff composite frames stand next to the tent, one half-opened, revealing a tumble of clothing, cords and tools spilling out onto the dust. A camp stove sits by the fire pit, next to another device that Tender cannot identify — a cylindrical base covered by a stretched plastic membrane with a hole in the center of it. Its side panel has been removed, exposing the internal mechanism.

Opposite the fire, two bodies lie stretched out on matching blue sleeping bags. A male and a female. Tender estimates them to be around thirty years of age, a Vir and a Femina. He cannot tell how long they have lain there. He has no information in his system concerning the deterioration of a human corpse. Their skin is hard and dark, picked and split here and there by birds or other scavengers, their faces shriveled so the bones appear more prominent than the skin and muscle that cover them. Their hair, though patchy, remains. The woman's is long and black — stiff and dry now but once soft and luxurious. The man's shorter, browner.

The woman's hand rests on the man's cheek, the gesture preserved in hard and brittle parody. The man's arm lies draped over her waist, the ends of her hair almost brushing the tops of his wasted fingers. They died in each other's arms.

Tender stands next to the dog and puts his hand on its head. "That's enough, Cincinnatus. "Hush now." Aureleo and Virgo appear behind him. "Disante shu," whispers the boy. Virgo comes and wraps her arms around the dog's neck, and it immediately stops barking.

"How did they die?" asks Aureleo.

"I don't know," replies Tender. "Peacefully, it appears."

The boy kneels by the cylindrical machine, grimacing and exhaling as he does. "This is a solar still."

"What is that?"

"It draws moisture from the air to create drinking water. It looks like it's broken. They must have died of thirst. I wonder what they were doing out here."

"Do you?" asks Tender.

"Where were they going?"

"Does it matter?"

"To them it did." The boy crawls over to the packs and begins to go through their contents. Virgo watches him, stroking the dog, her arms wrapped around its neck. "We should take this stuff with us," he says.

"Why?"

"We can use it. There's clothes, first aid, even some food. Military rations. Maybe they were deserters from some militia or something. Heading for the First Nations or the Canadian Colonies."

"If you like, but we should reach our destination within forty-eight hours, so it hardly seems necessary."

The boy turns and looks up at him. The food and rest have done him good. His brown face has regained much of its color, and his eyes are bright and alert. "You don't know much about things, do you?" he says. "I haven't been out here myself before, but I've heard people talk. There's a reason people don't go here. Look at them." He points at the bodies. "It's dangerous out here. Things go wrong all the time, you know. Things almost never work out the way you think they will."

"They don't?"

"Almost never."

Tender thinks about this. "It is true that since we left the Spa, we have encountered many unexpected delays." Virgo leaves the dog and scrambles over to the tent. She peers inside, and then crawls in.

Tender says, "Tell me what to take and I will transport it to the car."

"I would say take everything we can carry. Certainly the clothes. Maybe she doesn't mind, but I'm sick of running around naked like this. Besides, she's going to burn alive in no time."

"What do you mean?"

"Sunburn."

"What's that?" asks Tender.

"Wow!" The boy laughs. "You really don't know anything! Where are you from? That whelite skin can't handle the sun. Look how white she is. Like a ghost. The sun will literally fry her like a cooked tomato — all red and painful. Really bad. She should be covered up. And not just because people don't just walk around naked — which they don't! It's not safe."

"You are a very intelligent young Adulescens," says the android.

"My mother was a good teacher."

"I will do as you suggest. What else?"

"The solar still. Can you fix it?"

"Probably."

The boy says, "It's too bad we didn't come by earlier. You could have fixed it for them. Then maybe they would have made it."

"That didn't happen."

"No," says Aureleo. "But…never mind." He begins to look through the packs, finds a shirt, and holds it up to his chest. Then he says, "We have to bury them."

"Why?"

"We can't take their stuff and just leave them here. That would be wrong. We should bury them."

"At the Spa, when one of the guests achieved apotheosis, we would disintegrate the body so that their atoms could fly up and rejoin the stuff of the universe. Perhaps we should burn them."

"My people don't do that," says Aureleo. "We bury them so that their bodies can become part of the earth again. It's kind of the same idea, I guess, only down into the ground instead of up into the air. But maybe you're right. It's so dry here that it'll take forever for them to decompose, and the animals might get at them again. Ok."

Virgo appears again out of the tent. In one hand she holds a small book with a yellow cover. In the other she holds a thumb-sized figurine of a dolphin, carved in jade. She tosses the book aside, sits on the ground, and studies the figurine, turning it over and over in her hands, rubbing it against her cheek, licking it with her tongue.

The sun is setting as the fire sinks to warm ash. Aureleo stands by the glowing cinders, dressed in a dark shirt and trousers with many pockets. They are a little large for him, and he has cinched them tight around his thin waist with a belt. Tender has managed to get Virgo into one of the man's shirts, and a loose-fitting pair of boxers. She tugs at the collar every once in a while, but doesn't seem to mind.

The boy is tired, his face gone gray again, so he gives instructions to Tender. Using a stick and a broom of prickly branches, the android sweeps the ashes into a small heap. He collects stones from the basin of the dried pond, piles them in a cairn over the smoking dust and bones.

The three stand over the grave. The boy says something in his language that Tender cannot understand. Tender speaks the words of Apotheosis. "Joy is the Universal gift. It is the Universal wish for all Creatures. Holy Science has led us, after long suffering, to the valley of Joy in this life. We bestow that joy upon his Creatures here on Earth. But that joy is only a shadow of the True Joy. The Eternal Joy that is the Engine of the Universe…" He finishes the blessing, and they turn and head back to the car. They climb in, taking their places, the engines hum to life, and they speed off into the purpling twilight.

Chapter 35

Aureleo

The girl sits beside him now, the dog between them. It's a good thing. When she gets too close it is like a fire erupts in Aureleo's chest, spreading up into his face, making his ears burn, burrowing down into his stomach, and below. With the dog between them he is safe. The sweet, comforting, animal stink creates a barrier that protects him from the intensity of her presence.

The ground has been rising steadily, and now they are crossing a wide plain, a jagged line of mountains chopping the horizon. He looks out over the parched wasteland. Nothing grows. His mother once told him that it hadn't rained out here in fifty years. He can believe it. Through the window, he can see the plain quilted by the ruins of a huge solar field — millions of panels, almost all broken, blackened — glinting dully in the bright sunlight as far as the eye can see.

From behind, the robot looks a bit like his uncle Eduardo — salt and pepper hair cut short and neat over an erect neck and square, broad shoulders. The boy sometimes forgets that he is not a human being, until he looks into those strange mechanical eyes. He wonders if he — it — is thinking anything, or if it is just waiting for the next thing to happen. Things have certainly been happening. Aureleo can congratulate himself on his prediction, and on his insistence that they take the equipment and provisions.

Only an hour or so after they got back on the road, they found their way blocked by an overpass that had collapsed onto the highway. The car had to work its way painstakingly over the rocky ground at the side of the road to get beyond the obstruction.

Later they passed the ruins of a gigantic city. A wide river basin crossed their path, once spanned by a long bridge which now lay in tangled chunks on the ashy earth below. A trickle of water, brown and sluggish, ran at the bottom of the wide shallow depression. Across and to the right, two enormous silver pylons thrust into the sky, angling slightly toward each other so that it appeared they once had joined together in a single parabolic curve.

Tender instructed the car to turn back and find a way around the outskirts. "I would be surprised if people aren't still living there," he had said. "We will be safest if we keep to ourselves." Aureleo agreed. He had no desire to meet other people. But it meant more hours meandering and backtracking till they found the road again.

The campsite lies five days behind them, and they are still crossing the desert, though the robot says they have finally passed into what used to be called Arizona. They lost an entire day fixing the solar still, and then waiting for it to suck what moisture it could from the dry, hot air. It could only do its work if left to sit in one place for eight hours or more, so they had whiled the time away as best they could. Aureleo had taken out the book Virgo had found at the campsite and started to read it. That is when the girl had first climbed into the back with him, curious and eager.

Now here she is again, her arm resting on the curving back of the dog, her head leaning against the high seat back, her short, bristly hair glinting softly golden in the dim light, her dark eyes strafing up and down his body, mysterious, inscrutable. He is so glad that at least she is wearing clothes. Thank God for small mercies, as his mother used to say.

He opens the book. It is called *Tales of Ahl-Sa-Heira,* and it is a book of short stories. It was written by a woman, Tasha Chee-yong, and the first page says "Copyright 2078, all rights reserved." He is not sure how long ago that is, but he thinks it is at least a hundred years.

"Let's see," he says, his voice strangely high and harsh. "Let's find a nice short one." He leafs through the pages. He has read lots of books, his mother had almost fifty, but for some reason this time he is having difficulty negotiating the pages. He keeps glancing up at Virgo, and once he drops the book altogether. "How about this one," he says at last. He clears his throat. "It's short. It's called *The Three Flowers.*" He starts to read.

"Listen now, Little One," he reads, his voice slow and careful. "Khafa Lee Hanto was the youngest Prevalent ever to achieve the 200th level in the Automach's Crypt." The words are difficult, and he doesn't want to make a mistake.

"So great was that achievement that he was summoned to appear before the Princes of the Conglomerate and was awarded a Seat at the Table. He was given a chamber on the highest stratum of the Palace, with a view of the Desalination Terraces and the Curia of the Epicures.

He sat in his enormous room, alone at a magnificent table, two meters by eight meters, with just a single chair and a tabula on which he was instructed to put down his most marvelous ideas for the fur...the furth...furtherance of the Cons' most ardent dreams for the betterment of the People and the enrichment of the Sharers. He sat and sat and sat. But nothing came. As a boy, in his simple room on the basest floor of the smallest apartment building of the Mendicant's District, he had had a thousand ideas for games and prizes and challenges and mysteries and puzzles and hunts to amaze the People and lead them to prosperity, fame and fortune.

Now he could think of nothing. Nothing at all. For seven days he sat at his table and thought as hard as he could. No idea came. Then for seven more he sat and tried to think of nothing at all, to see if he could trick his mind into revealing its secrets to him. But nothing came from nothing.

219

Then for seven days he wrote every single word he could think of, to see if one of them might open the door to the great idea that the Thought Leaders were looking for. But nonsense yielded nothing, too.

At last, he threw his tabula across the room, so that it broke into a million shivering shards, stormed out and took the funicular down to the city. He meandered among the fruit stalls, vision merchants and mind massagers, picking up this, toying with that, his mind racing and standing still at the same time, full of dark thoughts, panic, and despair.

Oh, Little One, so distracted was he by his inner turmoil, that without knowing how, he found himself in a walled garden he had never seen before. In the center of the garden grew a large cherry tree, covered in perfect white blossoms. Never before had he seen such a wonder. For three cycles he stared in awe at the beautiful tree. Then he was released, and he reached up to pluck a flower, brighter than the long-forgotten snow, when suddenly a small voice cried out, "No, please! If you must pick a blossom, pick me! Pick me!" He looked around, trying to find the origin of the voice. It cried out again. At last, he looked down and saw a marigold, small but bright, orange as an ember, growing at the feet of the tree.

"I'm sorry, Marigold," said Khafa, "but I have never seen such beautiful blossoms, and you are just a marigold. You're nice, but there are thousands of you growing everywhere."

"But it is the last cherry tree in all the world!" cried the Marigold in its small voice. "You know that you have never seen such a miracle. All the rest perished in the Great Storm. If you harm it, it will die, and then it will be gone."

"Surely plucking one blossom won't hurt it, Marigold."

"Every action has a consequence," said the flower. "If you pluck it, it will leave a wound, and a beetle will come and suck on the wound, and the beetle will carry a fungus on its tongue, and the fungus will crawl into the wound, and spread throughout the tree, and the tree will die."

"I don't know if I believe you," said Khafa. "And I want it."

"Most in all the world?" asked the flower.

"No," he said. "There are things I desire more."

"What do you desire most in the world?"

"To be happy, I suppose," he said.

"What would make you happy?"

"A perfect idea," said Khafa.

"But I can give you that Khafa Lee Hanto," said the Marigold, and Khafa marveled that the flower knew his name. "You see, I was not always a flower. My name is Istarante, and I am the youngest daughter of the Omnipote theirself. I have been enchanted by an evil Teleomancer, along with my sisters, so that he can have power over our parent and rule through their voice. If you pluck me, and reunite me with my sisters, the spell will be broken, and we will return to the Starry Chamber and end his terrible rule. And as a reward, we will share with you the perfect idea, for we are the wisest beings in the world, with eyes that see the Infinite. In fact, if you pick me, as a gesture of good will, I will give you the first part of the idea."

Khafa was surprised by this speech. But what had he to lose? He reached down to pick the flower, but then stopped and said, "If I pick you, won't you die?"

"Yes," said the Marigold. "If we do not find my sisters by sunset, I will wilt. But it is worth the risk."

"As you say," said Khafa, and he plucked the flower. The stem hummed in his hand, and bright orange flames flicked and licked from his fingers, but didn't burn him.

"Hold me to your ear," said the Marigold. He did so, and the flower whispered to him the Secret of Energy. The vision of it thrilled him, and he could almost see the great Idea that had been evading him. But not quite. "Now, let us find my sisters," the Flower said.

Aureleo looks up from the book. Virgo has turned away from him. She reaches down and picks up the small dolphin figurine and begins rubbing it against her palm. "Do you want me to stop?" he asks. She doesn't respond for a moment. Then she lifts the dolphin toward his face. He starts back in surprise, but she poises it in mid-air, waiting, and he relaxes. She lightly brushes the figurine against his cheek, watching the movement, her eyes flashing between the object and his eyes. He feels the cool, smooth hardness against his skin, and an electric jolt shoots up his body. "Let's read a little more," he says.

"People stared at Khafa as he walked through the streets with a marigold held to his ear. But the flower was whispering instructions to him — turn here, go straight, turn here... The sun already sailed high in the sky, and he was getting very hungry, when at last they arrived in the Manufactors' District. Smoke and steam whirled around them, and the air singed his nose with the smell of burning coal. They weaved between the chip scribes and the glass pourers and came at last to a massive forge. A huge man, black as coffee, strong as a mountain, shaped a piece of Diamantium into a jewel case, delicate as a moth's wing. As he worked, he sang a song as sad as the sea, and tears flowed down his cheeks to strike the glowing anvil where they vanished in hissing puffs.

The Marigold whispered to Khafa and he looked up. High on a shelf, out of reach, stood a little vase made of gold. A single poppy, red as the Eye of the Controller, grew there. "There is my sister Varyadni," said the flower.

Khafa turned to the weeping smith and said. "Why are you so sad, friend?" The smith wiped his eyes and answered, "My husband died three days ago! I will never be happy again."

Khafa said, "I'm so sorry to hear that! But laughter cures all ills, they say. You should laugh, and you will find your burden easier to bear."

"How can I laugh?" asked the smith. "Sadness and regret are my world. Regret for all the things we will never do together. I will never laugh again."

"If I can make you laugh, will you give me whatever I ask?"

"Indeed, if you can ease my sorrow and make me laugh, I will give you the world."

And then Khafa Lee Hanto told the smith a joke. It was the funniest joke ever told. I cannot tell it to you, Little One, because if I wrote it here, you would laugh so hard that you would stop breathing, and the medicos would have to come in their flying ambulance and rush you to the hospital. Only someone as huge and powerful as the smith could survive hearing that joke."

"Well, that's a cheap excuse for not making up a good joke, uh, Tasha Chee-yong," Aureleo says, reading the author's name again from the side of the book. "I could use something funny right about now. Anyhow..." And he continues.

"And laugh he did. First his lips twitched. Then he clapped his hand over his mouth to try and stop. Then his shoulders started to shake. Then his whole body began to shudder like a Vibrodynamic Stretcher, until at last, he let out a huge howl of laughter, slapped his side, hopped up and down, and collapsed into his great chair. Only after four cycles did he stop laughing. Then he said, "Friend, you were right. My heart no longer feels like a coal burning through my chest. I understand that I can bear the sorrow of his absence, and maybe even learn to live again. What can I give you? I have gold aplenty, and platinum, and adamant, and even some obliquium — enough to make you richer than the finest Monacrat. What would you have?"

"I thank you friend," said Khafa, "but all I need is for you to give me the flower on that shelf. I have sore need of it."

The smith frowned. "Ask for something else. My husband loved poppies more than any other flower. He grew up in the undercities of Dana Mark, you see, and they reminded him of his childhood. I keep that flower as a remembrance of him. I know I made a promise to you, but it is hard to keep."

"Give me that flower, as you promised, and the Omnipote themself will send you a hundred poppies every day for as long as you live. Indeed, they will give you a garden of poppies within the Sanctum, and name it after your beloved. And you can visit it every day, and pick as many as you desire."

The smith nodded, and reached his huge hand up to the high shelf, and took the tiny vase in his hand, and gave it to Khafa. Khafa thanked him, plucked the flower and handed the vase back to the smith. At that moment, the red flower exclaimed, "Thank you! Thank you! I see my sister in your hand. You have come to save us!" The smith was amazed, and more than a little fearful, but Khafa told him not to worry, all would be as he had promised, and quickly left the forge.

As he walked, the Marigold and Poppy whispered to one another in the inscrutable language of the Plantae, and then they told him to lift the poppy to his ear, and the flower whispered the Secret of Living Fire. He shuddered at the knowledge, and the Idea shimmered just beyond his view, so close, but not quite clear. And on they, on they went…and…"

But Aureleo stops reading. The red flower fills his mind's eye, obliterating everything else. Memory floods his mind in an unchecked torrent.

"Hurry, Aureleo!" whispered his mother. Her head poked through the curtain into the tiny space at the back of the caravan. He looked up from the book he was reading. It was called "Seven Projects for Young Engineers." He didn't understand a lot of it, but one of the projects, the fourth, seemed like something he could do. He had been making a list of equipment he needed and as far as he could tell, there were only two items that weren't already to be found somewhere among the boxes and bags that crammed the storage bays along the bottom of the caravan.

"I'm busy!" he said. His mother raised her finger.

"Shhh!" she hissed, "don't wake your father! We're leaving now!" She grabbed the book and snapped it shut. Then she reached in, took his hand, and yanked him from his little chamber.

The caravan was a ten-meter double-wide with oversized tires and twin lifters for getting over rough terrain. Aureleo's little room was at the back, by the bathroom, and right next to the bunk beds where Pilarat and Marineta slept. He was surprised to see the two of them standing there, staring at him as though he should know what was going on. They both held their packs, their arms wrapped around them like they were babies. Lucheto and Adyrante were nowhere to be seen.

"What's going on?" he asked Pilarat. Of the twins, she was the one that talked the most.

"We're leaving," interrupted his mother, who was busy filling her own bag with rolls from the kitchen counter.

"Mamma found a man who will take us away! To California!" said Pilarat, her eyes flashing with excitement. Marineta's eyes flashed, too, in agreement.

"What about Pappa?" Aureleo asked. Yes, his father was a difficult man. Yes, his parents often fought, very loudly. Yes, sometimes he himself got slapped so hard that his head rang, and he saw strange little lights swirling at the edges of his vision. But he liked the caravan, he liked the family dinners when his father wasn't drunk, he even like sneaking into the power stations with Pilarat or Marineta, as though they were spies, or heroes.

Mamma took his face in her hands and leaned in close. He was almost as tall as she was now, but still it made him feel very small and young. "Listen to me, Aureleteo, we have a chance here. Donadeo has joined up with a group that is going to California. California! Do you hear? And they will take us with them! You and me and Pilarat and Marineta! No more stealing. No more running. No more fighting. A new life. An honest life!"

"What if I don't want to?" he asked, frowning.

"Not want to? Of course you want to! Listen, my little Aure, California! You know what that means! They still have cities there — and everyone has *power whenever they want it. There are books, thousands of books, and tabulae, and vids, and art, and pretty girls to dance with who aren't your sisters. We can live there. We can work! Honest work! We don't have to be always running."*

"What about Adyrante and Lucheto?" he asked her. He didn't say 'Pappa.' Sure, the idea of books and tabulae sounded pretty exciting. But California was a world away. How would they get there? And who were these people they were supposed to travel with? He knew Donadeo a little bit — a short man with a round, dark face. His mother liked him. Sure, he had a nice smile, but he was always sweating — kind of disgusting, really. And what about these others?

"Adyrante and Lucheto aren't coming," said his mother, and her face clamped shut like a mussel when you whack it on the sink to make sure it's still alive. Something had happened between her and the older siblings. They often sided with Pappa when the shouting started. They would argue and argue about being realistic and playing the hand they'd been dealt, until Mamma's eyes would fill with tears of rage, and she'd throw her glass against the wall of the caravan and disappear into the woods for hours.

"No more chit chat," she said, and her expression said even louder that he would do what she said or else. "We have to leave now before he wakes up. Get your things and let's go."

Aureleo shuffled back into his room and grabbed his shoulder pack. He shoved his other set of clothes into it (he only had two), along with his knife, his oralister, and, for no other reason than that he had no idea what they would need on the journey, his coupling wrench. Then there were the books. He only had room for a couple of them. God! So many to choose from.

He tried to 'activate his rational mind', which was a phrase he'd learned from one of the books. Okay. Probably no point taking the Engineering book. Who knows if he'd ever get a chance to make any of the things in it? People in California would probably laugh at it, anyway, it was so outdated.

In the end he took his favorite, "The Secret Under the Mountain." He'd read it so many times that the touch sensors were all dead and it would sometimes play the wrong music when he turned the page, but he loved it so much. Then, after hesitating for a moment, he chose the book Mamma had given him for his tenth birthday. He hadn't read it yet. It was so old it had no interactives at all. Just words and pictures printed in black ink on the light brown paper. "Oliver Twist" it was called. His mother said it was one of the best books ever written, and would tell him all about how the world used to be. He knew that it was about a boy. That was all.

He closed up the pack and slumped into the main room of the caravan. The twins were bouncing up and down by the door, their hands over their mouths to hold in the squeals. They knew what they wanted: to go wherever Mamma told them to go. Aureleo wished he were so sure.

He heard his mother moving in the front bedroom. It was just behind the cockpit, so Pappa could roll out of bed and clamber straight up the ladder into the driver's seat. He could hear Pappa snoring loudly, passed out on the small dirty bed below the ladder. He'd come home late the night before from the Roving Market. Drunk, of course. Roaring drunk. He said he'd taken some whelite idiot for a ride — whatever that meant — and had to celebrate. That led to a fight, of course, that had escalated into an outright brawl between Mamma and Pappa, fists flying, Lucheto vainly trying to keep them apart. Finally, when Pappa exhausted himself and passed out on the bed, Lucheto and Adyrante had gone back to the Market to see what had really happened. That fight must have been it. That's why Mamma was taking them away.

"I'm ready," Aureleo said, trying to keep his voice as flat and hopeless as he could. Packing the bag had made him a little bit excited, he had to admit to himself, but he'd never give his mother the satisfaction of knowing it. She appeared in the bedroom doorway, her hands up to one side of her face. She was fixing a bright red silk flower behind her ear. It had floppy petals that burned like a happy fire beside her brown face.

"What's that?" he asked her.

"I want to look nice," she said, smiling. "Make a good impression." She was wearing her yellow blouse. She'd put on makeup that made her face pulse softly. She looked beautiful, and happy.

Suddenly, the door of the caravan flew open and Donadeo burst into the living area. Sweat poured off him, drenching his face, dripping from his hair, making big disgusting stains on his chest and under his arms. "Raquela! Are you ready?" he said, panting. "Something's happened. We need to leave. Now. I'm only just ahead of them."

Instantly his mother's whole energy changed, from bubbling excitement to armed and ready. "What's happened?" she demanded.

"No time to explain, but your husband's put his foot in it, again! They'll be here any second. We have to—!"

The wide window along the side of the caravan exploded into a cloud of fragments that shimmered across the room like an ocean wave crashing against a rock. The blast knocked them all flat. Another flash, and a projectile struck the back wall, incinerating a painting of the twins sitting by a little brook that Mamma had done. Aureleo found himself on the floor, his head hollowed out by the shock, his mind ensnared by the image of the picnic they'd had that day, and the empanada he'd been eating while his mother had painted that picture. The memory drifted through his brain like algae across a pond as he watched the painting burst into flames. He felt lazy, sleepy, stupid.

Through the silent roar he heard an unfamiliar voice. "Salviro Hectoran!" it shouted. "I know you're in there! You think I'm stupid? You think you can steal from me and I won't notice?"

Gradually the blanket began to lift from his brain. The room started to fill with smoke.

"Who is that?" he heard his mother whisper.

"Charlis Granterson," Donadeo replied. "She runs the Salamander Cartel! Is there another way out besides the main door? She'll kill us all if she finds us!"

Another explosion rocked the caravan, sending down a rain of glassware and crockery. Aureleo could hardly see through the thickening smoke. He started to cough.

"God damn that man!" hissed his mother. Then: "The window in Aure's room. We can get out there. Where are the girls?" Aureleo thought he saw two dim shapes by the doorway. "There they are," said Mamma. "Are you all right?"

Pilarat's voice came small and scared. "The statue fell and hit Mari. She's asleep."

"Oh my God," Mamma said, and scrambled over to where the girls were huddled. Outside, the strange voice called, "Come on out, Hectoran, or I'm coming in!"

"We have to hurry," said Donadeo, his voice rising with panic.

"Just a minute!" barked Mamma fiercely. You never said no to that voice. "She's breathing. I'll carry her." He could just make out his mother staggering to her feet with Marineta in her arms. "Pila, you and your brother go ahead."

Another missile struck the caravan, blowing a hole in the roof. Pilarat screamed. Fire was spreading from the kitchen area, billowing smoke everywhere, making it impossible to see. Aureleo knew he was supposed to be doing something, but he couldn't remember what.

He looked down at the ground. The red flower that had bloomed from his mother's hair lay in the dust, staring up at him like a bright eye in a grimy face. It seemed to mean something.

He heard his mother and Donadeo arguing at the back of the caravan, their voices distant and muffled. "Go first, go first." "Take her — watch her head!" "Hurry up!" "The kids went ahead of you?" "Yes, yes! Come on, Raquela!" The words didn't make any sense to him.

Then something soft and damp and warm slipped into his palm. Pilarat's voice whispered in his ear, "Aurelete, let's go." He followed.

But she had hardly led him two steps, when a large, dark thing swept down from above, grabbed them both around the waist, and yanked them from the ground. Powerful arms, thick with wiry black hairs, smashed them tight against a wall of stinky flesh. Aureleo coughed at the smell of rancid sweat and alcohol. His father's voice, gruff as a goat, said, "Where are you going, little ones?"

He could feel Pilarat struggling to wriggle out of Pappa's grasp, but he himself hung like a sack, his head too wooden to do anything. Somewhere, he thought he heard his mother's voice shouting something, but he couldn't make it out. His father swung them easily from his sides as if they were no heavier than Cita, Anna's little lap dog. He kicked the door open, and climbed down into the clearing in front of the caravan.

Three men and a woman stood there, beside a large green Rover. The three men were nonas, but the woman was whelite, pale as a ghost. Her hair was pulled into a tight black bun, and her dark eyebrows shot straight as lasers across her face. She was still holding the missile launcher.

"Hectoran," she said, "did you really think I wouldn't come for you?"

"Charlis-Sarj, my good friend," said Pappa, his voice like oil. "There was a misunderstanding."

"Where is it?"

"I don't have it. But I'll pay you back. I swear."

"Pay me back..." she laughed. "Now, how are you going to do that?"

"With these," he said, and hiked Aureleo and Pilarat up in his arms. "They're young and strong and smart. They'll do good work for you. Me, they don't respect. But you! Charlis, they will work so hard for you." Aureleo couldn't see his father's face, but he knew that he was smiling that ingratiating smile he used when he was trying to cheat the fuel dealers.

The woman paused for a second, then motioned with her head. "Take them." The men hustled forward. Pappa dropped him and Pilarat on the ground. Before Aureleo could recover, one of the men picked him up like a sack of tubies. He felt like he was in a dream. Maybe he would wake up in a second.

The woman was still looking at Pappa. "What do you want, Hectoran?"

Pappa spread his hands and grinned a big, wide grin. "I want to make you happy, Charlis," he said.

"And how do you do that?"

"I pay you back. See? I pay you back."

The woman said, "How thoughtful, Hectoran. And I pay you back. I pay you back, too." And she drew a pistol from her belt and shot him through the head. He dropped like a pile of laundry. "Let's go," she said.

They turned and headed for the vehicle. From somewhere not very far away, Aureleo thought he heard a cry of anguish, like the wail of a wild bird. One of the men drew his gun and started toward the sound but the woman stopped him with a raised hand. "Leave them," she said. "These two are enough."

Aureleo feels a shove and comes back to himself. Virgo is leaning in, pushing on his shoulder, her face probing up close to his, frowning and intent. "Sorry," he says. He looks down at the book. He has lost his place. Actually, he's sorry that he got himself into this reading thing, he wants to be done with it. She's not really paying attention, is she?

The image of that red flower still hovers in the air beside him, and he can almost feel the pressure of his father's arm crushing him against his side. She shoves him again. "Okay, okay!" he says. "Give me a minute!" He scans down the page, trying to find where they had left off. She shoves him again. "All right! Stop pushing me!" He picks a spot at random from near the end. He reads:

"At last, they found themselves in the caverns beneath the Water Pads. Huge shadows flew up to the rough stone ceiling from the naphtha torches hanging along the walls. Water dripped into the dark places all around them, echoing through the dim halls. Khafa saw a ruined stairway descending into a narrow dell. The stairway was covered in moss, its steps rounded by the passing of countless centuries. At the bottom sat an ancient fountain, the figure of an Airgonaut, her hands spread as if in flight, standing astride a small pool, surrounded by weathered flagstones."

Aureleo stops again, his mind ambushed by the image of Pilarat's small hands extending into space as the big dark man hustled her into the Ranger. He shakes his head, and reads on.

"But no water flowed from the pipes concealed in the beautiful statue's mouth and fingertips. The fountain was dead as a mirror. As he approached, Khafa saw that the surface of the still water was blanketed with lily pads in flower. The blossoms were black as midnight, black as the space between the stars. One lily stood out to him. It was larger than the rest, and glowed with a deeper black than all the others. A blackness that seemed to sink into the darkness of the universe, into the unseen nothingness that sits at the bottom of every question.

"There is no test here," said the Marigold. "Only the courage to pluck my sister and hear her dreadful words. Are you prepared to face that trial?"

"I don't know," said Khafa. "What choice do I have?"

"You can choose blindness," said the Poppy. "The ignorance of animals, that have no fear of the unknown."

"I promised I would save you. I will pluck the flower," he said. And he reached down to pull it from its lily pad. But before he could grasp it, the black flower cried out to him, "Wait! I do not think you truly understand. If you pick me, you will save us, yes, and save the kingdom. But understand: the secret I share — it is Death."

Then Khafa paused. For a long moment he pondered the choice before him. At last, he drew himself up, took a deep breath, and—"

"Sorry to interrupt," chirps the Car, "but there appears to be a situation here."

Chapter 36

Tender

The car slows to a stop in a deep defile. They have left the plains, and entered a broken land of rises and crevasses. The road is older here, cracked and worn, but still serviceable. It follows the path of a dried-out stream, the meandering bed littered with hand-sized stones, rounded and smooth, blazing white in the fierce light, then muting to gray as the sun dips behind a hill or tumbled cliff. The rocky walls rise on either side, so that they look up at a narrow track of blue sky from the bottom of a trench.

Four figures, silhouetted against the brightness of the western sky, block the roadway. At first Tender's visual processors struggle to decipher exactly what they are. He can make out humanlike heads and torsos, but instead of two legs their bodies widen into long flat trapezoids supported by four spindly appendages. A line from Aristophanes rises in his mind: *And did you ever look up and see a cloud that looked like a Centaur, a panther, a wolf or a boar?*

"Are those horses?" asks Aureleo. With this prompting, the chimeras resolve into two human males and two human females, riding mechanical steeds. As if in answer to the boy's question, they impel their mounts forward, and approach the vehicle, passing into the shadow of the defile so that Tender can see them clearly.

They wear uniforms: dark brown trousers, tight fitting, with dun-colored fringe running down the seam, snug jackets, also fringed, over dark shirts, gloves, neckerchiefs, headbands and comm-sensors that cover one eye and one ear. Their hair flows down past their shoulders, black and braided, adorned with feathers — dark-banded or white with black tips — protruding at a variety of angles. Beaded necklaces and circlets break up the sameness of their clothing. Two of the four hold long ion spears decorated at the top with feathers and strips of colored cloth. The other two hold rifles.

The horses glimmer in the deep cool shade, the brushed metal finish of their articulated necks, their sleek curved bodies, their double-pistoned jointed legs, clawed hooves, and smooth, long, eyeless heads reflecting the dull grays and browns of the landscape. The riders control them with the aid of a rubberized loop that runs from one alloyed cheek to the other. Short gun barrels jut from the front of the nose where the nostrils should be.

The riders surround the car, the rifle bearers taking position in front and behind, the two carrying spears covering the flanks. "Roll down the window, please, Espera," says Tender. The darkened glass slides down, and punishing heat blasts in from the outside. A woman, mid-forties, with strong brows and intense dark eyes in a broad, square face towers above him on her robotic steed. Her eyes flash with surprise when she sees his face. "Good afternoon," he says. "What can we do for you?"

She speaks to him in a language he doesn't know, rolling and melodic, punctuated with a rhythmic staccato of accented syllables. It reminds him of Stravinsky's "Rite of Spring." He turns back to the boy. Aureleo shakes his head, uncomprehending. The woman barks words, growing more insistent, repeating the same phrase over and over. At last, she calls over to one of her comrades, the rifle carrier at the back of the car. She kicks the sides of her horse and pulls the ring, and the machine steps away.

Immediately the other rider takes her place. Another woman, younger, her hair longer, braided at the front, with large, soft eyes and a full mouth. Her face, too, widens in surprise when she sees Tender.

She says, "You understand me?"

"Yes, thank you," says Tender.

"What are you?" she asks.

Tender smiles. "I am a Tender G-2551. I am traveling with this girl, this boy, and this dog to the Elysium Spa Center in the Republic of California."

The woman looks up across the car at the man with the spear, and back at the other woman. She says something to them in the unfamiliar language. A short conversation ensues. The woman in the rear appears to be the leader. She speaks for a long time, the others listening and nodding. Then their interpreter turns back to Tender.

She says, "We are Lakota Outriders of the Army of the Eagle, Expeditionary Force of the First Nations. You have entered disputed territory in the conflict between the Nations and the Republic of California. In the name of our war leader Osmaka Mahpiyata, I hereby commandeer your vehicle. We will escort you to our base of operations where you will be questioned and then held with the other refugees of this conflict in our containment facility for your own safety."

Tender says, "Of course." Behind him, Aureleo cries out in protest. Tender directs his voice back to the boy, keeping his eyes and smile focused on the woman. "There is nothing we can do, Adulescens. They are armed, and we are outnumbered. Our best option is to comply with her request."

"More than you know," says the woman. "You see four of us here, but there are sixteen more stationed along the cliffs. You could not escape us if you tried."

Tender looks up. Outlines on horseback line the top of the defile, black and flat against the brilliant blue. The woman says something to the war leader, who says something into her comm. The figures above spur their mounts. As one, they descend the cliff, finding invisible footholds with their articulated claws, bounding down the impossibly steep rock face — seventy degrees of incline at least — surging down onto the roadway to surround the car.

"Open the door," says the interpreter.

"Espera, please open the door."

"My pleasure!" chirps the car. The door slides up.

"Please move aside and allow me to enter the vehicle." Tender does as she asks, and she slides skillfully off her mechanical horse and into the seat, moving with the efficiency of practiced physical discipline. She holds her rifle across her lap. The door slides shut. Through the glass, Tender watches the war leader walk her horse to the front of the car. The other riders form into a tight phalanx around them.

The interpreter looks at the dashboard in front of her, then turns to Tender. "How does it work?" she asks.

"It is coded to my voice. I simply tell it where we wish to go, and it obeys my instructions."

"Can you recode it to respond to my voice?"

Tender doesn't hesitate to lie. "Unfortunately, I can't. The operation is extremely time-consuming, and requires interface with the home computer. Please do not worry. We will not attempt to escape."

The woman looks at him, as if trying to read him. She shakes her head, unsettled by the strangeness of his eyes. The gesture reminds him of Letitia. "Very well. But be assured, any attempt to divert the car will cause a swift and violent response. Please order the vehicle to follow the war leader."

Tender smiles again. "Espera, please follow the human directly in front of us. Maintain current distance."

"Absolutely!" sings the car. The interpreter speaks into her comm to the war leader, who impels her steed into motion at a gentle pace. The entire column starts forward, and they process steadily out of the defile.

Chapter 37

Tender

"What are you called?" asks Tender, as the car rolls along the road, flanked by the tall riders on their metal horses. The woman glances back at the two young humans in the back seat. Aureleo smiles at her, though Tender marks his worry and alarm in the creasing around his eyes. Virgo appears not to notice the new passenger. She plays with her dolphin figurine, swimming it back and forth across the back of the dog, diving it in and out of the waves of fur.

"My name is Amaste - *the Sun Shines on Her*, it means in my language. I am a warrior of the tribe. I sit in the third place at the council."

"You may call me Tender. The boy is called Aureleo. The girl is Virgo."

"And the dog?" Her expression remains taut and hard to read, but Tender notices a hint of a smile ghost across her face.

"Cincinnatus. I understand that he is named after a great Roman general, but I do not know the story."

"He is a noble animal."

"You speak English very well," says the android.

Amaste looks at him again, wrinkling her brow, trying to decipher some hidden meaning in what he says. "Many among us have chosen to forget the language of those who oppressed us for so many centuries. But not all. My parents sent me to the bilingual school. I'm not unusual."

"I see."

"Besides," she says, "it comes in handy when one has to converse with a robot."

"What will become of us?" asks Tender.

"You will be interrogated to determine if you are who you say you are, and whether you have information that could prove useful to us in the siege. Then, most likely, they will put you with the other civilians who are traveling with the camp."

"Will you be our interrogator?"

"Doubtful." Silence falls. They have come out of the defile onto a plateau dotted with tumbled hills and chimneys of sandy rock. Scrub and cacti dot the landscape. The troop picks up speed, breaking into a fast gallop, the metal stallions untiring, implacable. The car accelerates to match them, and they race across the desert. For 665 seconds they drive without speaking.

Tender asks, "What are the First Nations?"

"Survivors of the native peoples from all over the continent have gathered," she says. "Dakota, Navajo, Kiowa, Cherokee, Wampanaug. Many others. We are reclaiming the land that was taken from us. Well, what's left of it. To build a new nation. Doing what we were never able to do before — unite."

"Is there a city?" asks the boy from the back seat.

"Not yet. Only the dream. We lack the power. The Californians have hoarded all the power from here to the Columbia River. We're barely holding on. Thousands in the camps. That is why we are here." She leans forward and gestures with her head out through the front windshield. "And here we are."

Tender follows her gaze. The phalanx slows to a trot as they come around a low, flat mesa. The sun burns in the western sky. Evening approaches. A large camp spreads before them. One hundred thirteen tents, all sizes. Mechanical horses lined up in serried ranks beside sixteen other vehicles that range in size from small jeeps to large trucks pulling missile launchers and plasma cannons. Three portable solar plants crane their necks into the purpling sky, soaking up the last of the sun's energy. Guards on horseback raise their spears in salute as the convoy passes through the invisible barrier between desert and human habitation.

Virgo suddenly reaches forward and grabs the nearest of Amaste's braids. The woman jerks back, but Virgo reaches for it again.

"She only wants to feel your hair, and those beads," says Tender.

"What's wrong with her? Can't she talk?" asks Amaste, still on her guard.

"A little. She's not like you. She means no harm." A third time the girl puts out her hand to touch the woman's hair. Amaste permits her to stroke the beads and wrap her fingers around the sleek black braid. The car comes to a stop.

Chapter 38

Tender

They sit in a small square tent, its walls a faded taupe. The interrogator sits on a stool behind a table. They are given folding chairs. A guard stands at the door.

The interrogator is a tall, lean warrior, agender, approximately fifty years of age. They speak with a clipped precision, revealing nothing. They do not give their name. "You say you come from the East," they say. "Do you not, in fact, come from California?" Tender dutifully recites the history of their travels, the exact times and distances they covered, the particular landmarks they passed. Of the farmhouse, he says little. Only that he and Virgo had been held captive there for eighty-one days, and that the boy had also been held there, and had joined them when they escaped. The interrogator then speaks to Aureleo in the Vagral language, and Tender can't follow the progress of their discourse. Then they turn to Virgo, who watches their face as they speak, following the movements of their mouth, but doesn't respond. Then she looks away, turning her attention to the dolphin figurine which now swims and spins almost constantly in her hands.

"Doesn't she understand me?" they ask Tender.

"Hard to say. She has learned a lot in the last months, and I have heard her speak a few words now and then, but I can't tell you what she does or doesn't understand. Not a lot, I think. She knows very little of the world.

She knows me, and the boy, and the dog, and the car. That's all we can be sure of."

The interrogator then asks him again whether they hadn't come from California. Tender repeats, verbatim, his original explanation. They listen impassively, then turn the line of questioning to the Spa. What was it? How did it work? How long had he been there? What exactly had happened? Tender explains the Protocols as patiently as he can.

They ask him, "And you're going to another of these 'Spas' in California?"

"Yes. Originally there were two others on the Eastern Seaboard, but I learned that they were destroyed during the Civil War. So, we are traveling to the one out West. It was the Center, the original, the place where Dr. More founded the movement, and developed the technologies that led to the Protocols. It is in Phoenix, which I understand is now part of the Republic of California."

"And you know that this Center is still in operation?"

"I do not. The Spas became independent when the Protocols were instituted, and though our mainframe may have communicated with the others, it did not share that information with us."

"Why not?"

"There was no need."

The interrogator pauses, considering. "But you believe it is still in operation."

"I don't know."

"You hope it's still there."

"No. I can't hope. But I have a purpose."

"A purpose." They lean in.

"I must restore Virgo to her bath so that she can regain the Joy that is her birthright."

The interrogator nods, eyes hooded. Then they say, "What would you do with me?"

"I beg your pardon?" asks Tender.

"When you were describing this Spa, you told me that the 'guests', as you call them, are divided into male and female. I am neither. If I were to join this Spa, where would I fit in?"

"Gender is irrelevant to Joy. When you ride its waves, it makes no difference what your gender is. You are just yourself, beyond any physical identifiers. I understand that among humans, sex is a form of social interaction, but at the Spa, it only matters for procreation and the continuation of the line. You would be assigned a place according to your sexual organs. If you have male organs you would lie on the male side, if female, the female side."

"And if neither?"

"I'm afraid you would not be admitted." Tender gives a small shrug and actuates a smile of regret.

The interrogator stares at him for eight seconds, then looks away and asks him about the car. Where did they acquire it, what model is it, what sort of power source does it have? Tender can offer little information about any of these matters.

"You should ask the car," he says.

"We will," they say. "That is all for now. We may have more questions for you later."

"Then we are free to go?" asks Tender.

"This is a military zone. It is not safe to travel. You will join the other civilians we have in protective custody for the duration of the operation."

"We are willing to take the risk. Surely, we are free to choose our own level of risk."

"Unfortunately not. You see, we are moving toward the exact area you have been seeking, but our mission does not harmonize with yours."

"What are you going to do?"

"We are going to war," they say, their face set and grim. "The Phoenix valley is the gateway to the California Republic. Furthermore, it controls the large power facility which belongs by rights to the Akimel O'otham, who are signatories of the Union Treaty."

"You're invading California." This is Aureleo, who speaks unexpectedly from the back. The interrogator turns to him, sizing him up.

"Yes," they say. "We have sought a diplomatic resolution, but we have met with only silence. Their gates are closed, their walls are high, and they refuse to negotiate, or indeed even answer our requests to meet. They have appropriated resources that belong by right to our peoples, and we must take action. This is our country once again." They are standing now, their eyes shining. Then they relax, and laugh a light, self-deprecating laugh. They spread their hands, palms out. "So, you see, we can't allow you to try to cross into California. We can't take the risk that you will give them vital information about our forces and intentions. I'm sorry."

Tender nods. "We are your captives, then."

"You are under our protection," says the interrogator, their eyes soft but firm. "And I mean that honestly. I don't think you understand how dangerous it will be. I fear this battle will be terrible. You are safer with us." They stand up and signal the guard to escort them out.

At the door, Tender asks, "Where is the car? She is a part of our group."

The interrogator jerks their head backward in surprise. "It's just a car."

"What do you mean? She is not humanoid, certainly. And she doesn't have the same capabilities that I have. But she is intelligent."

"It — she — is self-aware, you are saying?"

"I don't know about that," says Tender. "What difference does it make? She is more intelligent than this dog, and yet you have no problem leaving him with us. She is part of our group. We would like to have her with us."

The interrogator smiles an apologetic smile. "I'm sorry. Whatever her intellectual capacity, she is a valuable machine. Unlike the dog, a machine that will aid us in our war effort. I will speak to the War Leader, but I don't think we can return your car to you. For one thing, you might use her to try and leave our protection, which would endanger your lives and the lives of our warriors. For another, we are critically short of vehicles, and she will add significantly to our effort."

Tender nods. "But we are not on the same side," he says.

The interrogator smiles again. "Aren't we? I know it seems like that now, but I'm not sure that is so. We shall see."

The guard pulls back the tent flap. Suddenly, the interrogator speaks again. "I am a Zuni lhamana. My name is Muhukwi Williams. It has been a pleasure meeting you, Mr. Tender."

"Thank you, Muhukwi Williams." And they leave the hut.

Chapter 39

Tender

Amaste waits for them outside the interrogator's hut. The warrior who has accompanied them follows in the rear, as Amaste leads them through the dusty grid of tents and pre-fab buildings that make up the camp. Tender holds Virgo's hand. Her head bobs this way and that as she takes in the bustle that surrounds them. Cincinnatus pads heavily at her side. Aureleo follows behind, now and then touching his stomach where the bandages hide beneath his shirt, wincing and sighing. The air has cooled rapidly with the sunset.

Noise and movement swirl around them. Couriers hurry past, running with message blocks in their hands. Groups of warriors labor at unloading and loading vehicles, or gather in circles, observing their fellows training with ion spears and rifles, or sit preparing food at small braziers and stoves. Mechanized horses stand in ranks, some deactivated and inert, others submitting to the hands of technicians who polish them with pale cloths, or kneel at their sides, working on damaged joints and servos. A swarm of tiny drones, no bigger than sparrows, hangs for a moment three meters above the ground in a tight pack, then scatters to the winds *like sparks from a fire*.

They pass a field of small tents in a variety of shapes — conical, hemispheroid, prismatic — uniformly dun-colored but each rendered unique by decorations of ribbons, feathers, patches and flags. "What do they signify?" asks Tender.

"What do you mean?" asks Amaste.

He points to an emblem in the shape of a hawk made of feathers dyed red, embellished with pieces of glass and colored metal. "The ornaments. I see them on the tent, and on the soldiers."

"There are detachments from thirty-one different tribes here," she says. "We share much, but each celebrates its own identity in different ways."

"I see."

She stops for a moment. "But it goes deeper than that. We value our individuality and expression," she says, "and a connection to our past. Each image, bead, streamer or band tells a story. We are a unified fighting force, but we are not robots. No offense."

"None taken," says Tender.

Near the path, two men sit at a small table, cleaning their rifles. As they walk by, one of them shouts out, "More white ones for us to take care of, Amaste? What a waste!"

"Not your concern, Ohanzee," says Amaste. The man puts down the gun barrel he has been cleaning, stands and walks toward them.

"You're in the way, whelites!" he says. "You're not needed anymore. You stole our land, and ruined it, and now it has spit you out like a bitter seed. The land is ours again. You have no place here."

"Enough," says Amaste. "These refugees are under our protection. Now is not the time for a fight about the past."

Ohanzee shakes his head in disgust. "We should send them all across the wall, where they belong. We own this land. They are intruders."

"No one owns the land, Ohanzee," says Amaste.

The warrior strides up to her. He is very tall, two meters, and though she is tall, too, he towers over her. "They have been our enemies for centuries. We owe them nothing."

His intimidation fails to quell her. She steps into him, staring into his face. "I am Third in council, Ohanzee. What are you?" His nostrils flare and his breath quickens, but he says nothing. "You'd do well to remember that. Now sit down."

Ohanzee stands there for seven seconds, the muscles in his cheeks pulsing. Then he turns and begins to walk back to his table. As he passes Tender, he says. "Your time is done, whelite. Go into the ground with the rest of them." Then he stops. His mouth drops open slightly. He moves closer, his face turning hard as he studies Tender. "What are you?"

Tender decides that it is best not to reply, but he smiles. The warrior looks him up and down, his lip curling with distaste. "You're one of them. Ucch! Wakháŋšiča. It pretends to be human, when it's just a pile of gears and circuits. You are čhakála, a deceiver. Amaste, how can you be near this thing?"

"Enough!" she says.

"You haven't been to the front, have you? I have. I have seen them. Not so deceptive as this one, but not so different. These are the weapons of our enemies. You think you'll be fighting human beings? The whelites are too cowardly for that. You'll be fighting things like this. It should be turned into scrap, not invited to share our tents!" He reaches down to the table and grabs the angular stock of the disassembled rifle, swiftly raising it over his head. Even swifter, Amaste lowers her shoulder and drives into his abdomen, sending him reeling backward onto the ground. She sweeps the gun barrel off the table and straddles him, pinning his arms with her knees and poising the metal tube above him.

"If you have an issue with orders, Ohanzee, you'd best take it up with the War Leader. Until then, keep your mouth shut. Do you hear?" He doesn't answer. "Omáyakaȟniǧa he?" The man glares at her, his face twisted with anger. After four seconds, he nods. She rises gracefully, in a single movement, tossing the metal tube onto the table, and strides away. "Follow me please," she says without looking back.

They arrive at a large tent in a far corner of the camp. Arcs of dark metal alloy curve into the air, joining at the center, supporting

249

a dome of stretched fabric that glows with a warm golden light. It reminds Tender of the Laconicum, though it is smaller and less grand. An entrance juts from the side, and they pass through the flaps into the interior.

The space appears larger than it did from the outside, but the room is crammed with equipment and people. Tightly packed rows of cots jam into the rear half of the tent. To the left is a medical station, several diagnostic machines and large stacks of crates. To the right a makeshift kitchen with two ancient microwave ovens, countertops covered with boxes of provisions, three long steel tables and a tangle of folding chairs.

Tender counts sixty-two people, lying on cots, standing or sitting in small groups, bundles and bags of possessions piled around them in little walls. Five are First Nations personnel - a guard at the door, a nurse in the medical area who tends to the ankle of a small girl sitting on a high table, and three others who hand out food to a line of people in the kitchen. The others, the civilians, display a full gradation of skin tones and a variety of ethnic and gender markers. Male, non-binary, female, children, adults.

A tense hush hangs over the room. People speak in muted voices, or sit with headphones, or VRGs wrapping their eyes and ears. Many heads turn to stare as they enter the room, and the quiet grows more intense.

"I will get you some cots," says Amaste, and heads over to talk to one of the kitchen workers, an older woman with gray hair and a narrow, lined face.

"I do not require a cot," says Tender, as she goes.

Aureleo says, "Oh," touches his temple with one hand, and his side with another. Then his eyes roll up into his head and he crumples to the floor. Tender reaches out to stop his fall but the boy slips beyond his grasp into a pile on the ground.

The nurse, who has been glancing in their direction, scurries over. He is short and stocky, with a soft face. "What's the problem?"

he says, as he kneels at Aureleo's side, feels for his pulse and checks his eyes.

Tender says, "He had a surgical operation recently, and we have not had access to treatment for many days."

Aureleo groans and his eyes flutter open. "I'm fine," he says.

"You're not," says Tender, smiling. He turns to the nurse. "Please, look after the boy."

The nurse nods and continues his examination. As he finishes, Aureleo tries to rise. "Easy there," says the nurse.

"I tell you, I'm fine."

"Let me help you." He raises the boy to his feet, and leads him to one of the hospital beds. The boy grumbles as he climbs into the bed, but then gives up the fight and falls back against the pillow with his eyes closed.

"You just rest," says the nurse. He arranges the sheet over Aureleo's legs, and heads over to Tender and Virgo.

"I'm sure he'll be fine," he tells them. "It looks like mostly dehydration and fatigue, though he is a little warm. There might be a small infection. But we'll take good care of him. What about the rest of you?" He turns to Virgo, who holds Tender's hand. "Does this…" he starts to say, but then stops, unsure what to call her. Her short spiky hair, the slight curves of her body beneath the neutral clothes.

"I will tend to the girl. Thank you."

"And you, sir? Do you need any — Oh." His face goes blank with surprise as he looks into Tender's eyes and realizes what he is.

"I am fine for the present," says Tender, smiling again. "Just the boy."

The nurse nods quickly, shaking himself out of his surprise. "Of course. He'll be fine." He turns and busies himself at the table.

Amaste returns to them. "I'm sorry to say that we have only one cot available — as you can see, we have quite a few travelers under our protection — but we can supply you with one, and a pallet for the floor."

"One will suffice. The boy is in the medical area. And, as I said, I do not require a bed."

"Follow me, please." She leads them through the tangle of chairs and beds toward the rear of the tent. They pass a cluster of people on the floor between two cots, playing a game with dice and tokens.

As they sidle around the group, one of them, a mature Adulescens, perhaps twenty-five years of age, looks up at Tender. His eyes open wide and a huge smile spreads across his face. "It's you!" he says. He scrambles to his feet. 1.92 meters tall, rail-thin, like all these people, shaggy black hair above a pale face with large brown eyes. Heavy brows. "I can't believe it!" He laughs. "Incredible. What are you doing here? Have you come for us?"

Tender smiles and folds his hand together at his chest. "Forgive me. I don't believe we have met before."

"We haven't!" says the man. "But of course I recognize you — Doctor!" He laughs again.

"I don't understand," says Tender.

"From the flyers! The airdrop. We got them and we're coming." The man kneels down and rummages through a worn backpack at the foot of the cot. His comrades, two young males and two young females, stand quietly, staring at Tender with an intensity bordering on fear, and then at Virgo, who stares back at them, furrowing her brow. "Here it is!" says the man, thrusting a brightly colored pamphlet into Tender's hands.

The pamphlet is old, worn and scratched, its flow of images halting and jerky. The front shows two human silhouettes — male and female — lying in a swirling field of colors and stars as the words "Welcome to JOY" stream back and forth across the surface. Tender opens it up, and his own face looks back at him, smiling his own smile, standing next to a bath where a beautiful Femina lies, her face a picture of ecstasy.

The pamphlet begins to speak. Its audio is badly corrupted, stutters and crackles, but the text also flows across the surface of the image. "Welcome to the Elysium Spa. Are you tired of the cruelty and hardship of the world? Do you say to yourself, 'I just want to be happy'? You should! Happiness is the goal of all living things. It represents the purest state of being. Joy is your birthright. But the battle for survival makes it hard to find, doesn't it? Not anymore! At our state-of-the-art Spas, we have discovered the secret of perfect happiness, with no unpleasant drugs or side effects. Our skilled doctors bathe you in bliss, taking care of your every need — physical, psychological, and spiritual. We've built a true Heaven on Earth. You don't have to struggle, or fight, or suffer pain and loss, ever again. Lay down your burden. Achieve your destiny. Join us, in Elysium." The image crossfades to the Spa Logo of the Rainbow Sun, with an inset map showing the location of the Center.

Tender closes the pamphlet. Virgo grabs it from his hand, sinks to the floor and opens it again, holding it close to her face. "Where did you get this?" the robot asks.

"From the sky," says the man. "A plane flew over our compound and dropped them. Some fell in the river, but we collected about a dozen."

"When was this?"

The man looks at his companions. "When we were kids. I was maybe six, I think, so, like twenty years ago." The others nod, but remain silent. He points down to the pamphlet in Virgo's hand. "But that's you! Isn't it?"

Tender shakes his head. "It is not. But certainly like me. You have left your home to seek this place?"

"We're answering the call, yep."

"Why now? Why have you waited so long?"

"Sit with us," says the man, his eyes still shining with excitement. "Please, sit, sit. It is such a kick to meet you!" He sweeps a space on the cot with his hand, brushing away the crumbs from an earlier meal. Tender obliges and sits, Virgo hunched at his feet, absorbed in the pamphlet, which she opens and closes again and again. The man sits on a cot opposite. His companions remain standing.

"So, my name is Deck Ras-Tamblin. This is Sasha and Tenille, and Hito and Ramon." He points first to the females and then to the males. They smile shyly but remain silent. "What's your name, Doctor?"

"I am not a doctor, I'm afraid. You may call me Tender Number 7."

Deck laughs. "I'm sure you're just being modest, but whatever you like. Anyhow, we come from a village on the Gulf Coast, called Church Point?" His voice rises, as though asking Tender if he knows the place. "Right on the water, northeast of the Houston Hole? Rough place, believe me. Storms used to flatten the settlement every couple of years, rising water pushing us into the jungle, the jungle pushing us into the water, know what I mean? But we did okay. Things were even getting better. We actually caught a few fish last year! Remember?" He smiles at his companions.

"How many people live there?"

"Oh, I don't know." He ruffles his hair. "Maybe two hundred? Anyhow, the plane flew over about twenty years ago, like I said, when we were kids. We thought it sounded auss, we were like, 'Let's go!' but our parents weren't interested. I kept this one because it was about the only tech we had. Pretty stone age, am I right?" He smiles again at his companions. One of them, Hito, nods in agreement. He is a short young man with thick eyebrows and black fuzz growing on his chin, upper lip, and in two little patches on his cheeks.

"But things were getting better," Deck continues. "We salvaged some solar cells from a farm upcountry, got some lights and ACs working. We even had a couple of cars. Then, last spring…"

"What happened?" asked Tender.

"Raiders from up North. Twenty big guys in assault trucks, with heavy weapons. Folks tried to fight back, which turned out to be a huge mistake. They burned the whole town. Took everything worth taking. Killed anybody who was resisting."

"Your families?"

Deck nods, shrugs.

Tender notices that some of the other civilians are watching their conversation. A few begin to drift toward them. He says, "You survived, though."

"We weren't there. We were upcountry. We'd found a garage with a few cars that hadn't been cannibalized for parts. It was partially buried so I guess people had missed it. We found three that had useable stuff. We were hauling it back when we saw the smoke."

"There was nothing left," says Sasha, a tall girl with a round face, full lips, eyelids *like snail shells*. "Just bodies."

"So, you decided to, as you say, answer the call."

"I had the pamphlet with me," says Deck. "I carried it around a lot — like a good luck charm, you know?"

"How long have you been traveling?"

"About six months. We had a car, but we cracked the chassis on a rock about three days in. Not a good start, am I right?" He laughs as he looks at the others. "And we spent most of the summer in a cave near — what were those ruins called again?"

"Springfield," says Hito.

"That's it. Yeah, too hot to travel, but not bad in the cave. Nice and cool, access to fresh water. There was a spring at the back. Not too easy to get to — but we managed. We even talked about staying, but the food supply was pretty shaky. Man, we got hungry a few times, am I right?" He laughs again. He seems to consider all these hardships delightful. "Anyhow," he continues, "we started moving again about a month ago. Hooked up with the Tazlitts, who are over there—" he points to a group of four people sitting at a table in the kitchen area — "and the Cabeiros—" two older humans, male and female, who have joined the growing crowd around them. Deck waves at them, and the woman smiles sheepishly at Tender, and waves. "Then we got swept up by the Eagle six days ago, and here we are."

Most of the other refugees have abandoned whatever they were doing, surrounding the seated group in a tight circle, listening and staring at Tender and Virgo.

Deck leans in eagerly. "Enough about all that. What are you doing here? Did you come for us?"

Tender shakes his head. "I'm afraid not. We are travelers just like you."

The young man frowns. "But you come from there. From Elysium."

"We come from a Spa, yes, but not the one you are trying to reach. Our Spa was destroyed by a hurricane, and overrun by scavengers, I think, and so we are traveling, just like you, to reach the Center."

"And you're one of the doctors, right?" This is Sasha, her eyes big and hopeful.

"I tend the guests, yes," he says.

"Was she a guest?" Sasha asks, looking down at Virgo, who looks up from the pamphlet, studies the woman's face.

"She was. I am her Tender. I am trying to return her to Joy." The crowd murmurs as Tender says this, neighbors turning to neighbors, some craning their necks to get a better view of the girl on the floor.

Someone in the crowd says, "Would you tend us?" He can't see who said it, so he speaks to Deck as he answers.

"I don't think so. I don't know how they would assign you. I must tell you, I do not think they will admit you to the Center. Ours closed its doors to the world many, many years ago. It was self-sufficient, and served only its members and their offspring."

Another murmur bubbles through the crowd. Tender leans forward, clasping his hands together. "The Protocols are very exact and demanding. The genetic fitness of our guests was systematically enhanced — resistance to disease, plasticity, bone strength, hormone levels, and many other factors must fall within very narrow parameters, otherwise the guest will not respond well to the environment of the bath. Any imbalance can cause an avalanche of problems that will not only destroy the Joy that the guest experiences, but submit them to very serious consequences to their health and even their survival."

"But the pamphlet," Deck says, insistent.

"I don't understand it," says Tender. "It is possible that the Center found solutions to these problems that were not communicated to the other Spas. But this pamphlet of yours may be much older than you know. It may come from the first phase of the Spas, before the Protocols were instituted and the doors closed. You say it fell from a plane twenty years ago?"

"About twenty, yes."

"I can't say why they dropped it. Have you considered that it might have been a hoax, that someone dropped it in an attempt to dislodge you from your settlement?"

Deck stares at him with incomprehension, eyes wide, *like a frightened rabbit*. Then he shakes his head. "Nope," he says. "It was new when I got it. They want us to come."

Tender smiles, shrugs. "You may be right. Perhaps they do. Perhaps you will all be welcome." He looks around at the crowd. "But even if you are, we still have the Eagle, as you call it, standing in our way. They won't let any of us enter the California territory."

"Before the battle, yes," says Deck. "But afterwards, who knows?" He looks up at the crowd, too. "We believe in the call, don't we? We'll find a way." The humans nod, pump their fists, some even clap. Murmuring their agreement. Yes. You got it. Right on.

Sasha kneels down next to Virgo. "What's it like?" she asks, hope and excitement opening her face, *like a flower*. "The Joy? We can only dream about it. You've lived it." Virgo stares back at her, furrows her brow.

"She doesn't speak much," says Tender. "And I don't know if she remembers."

But Virgo reaches up and touches the woman's face, lightly, on the cheek. "Bright," she rasps, her voice a low croak, but gentle. The crowd whispers, presses in. The words come out in spasms, long pauses in between. But she never takes her eyes off Sasha. "Warm. Hot stars. Floods. No. Time. Not…alone. Millions. Souls. Colors. Worlds. Planets. Angels. Inside. All…inside." She strokes Sasha's forehead, presses her palm against the soft, brown skin.

Somewhere in the distance, a deep rumble of thunder rolls across the desert. A delicate pattering thrums on the doming fabric above them. From the tent flap, one of the civilians calls, "It's raining. It's raining!" Some merely nod, turning back to see if Virgo will speak more. But many others, most others, bustle for the entrance. Responding to the movement of the crowd, Virgo scrambles awkwardly to her feet and joins them. Tender follows.

Out in the yard, the warriors stand around, staring at the sky. They barely notice the people streaming from the holding tent. A gentle rain, warm and soft, strikes the dust, vanishing at first almost before it hits. But little by little it gains purchase on the parched earth, and damp patches spread and coalesce, darkening the ground in the white glare of the camp lights.

People stand with their necks arched back, eyes closed, inviting the raindrops to strike their cheeks, their chests. A young girl — one of the Tazlitts, Tender recalls — begins to run and spin, laughing and shrieking, arms outstretched *like a bird*, swooping around the clearing in wide arcs. "It's raining! It's raining! It's raining!" she cries.

Her father, a Vir of about thirty-four years of age, looks at Tender, his face a mottled brown, sagging, weary, dark blotches under his eyes. He seems to be asking for permission, so Tender smiles at him. The man's face cracks into a huge grin in return, revealing a mouthful of bright teeth that make him suddenly look ten years younger. "We've never seen rain before," he says.

"Never?"

"Never. How about you?"

"I have," says Tender. "Where we come from it rains almost every day."

"Really?"

"Yes. Too much, in fact. It rains too much."

"Amazing."

Tender doesn't understand what is amazing about it, but he nods. The man turns to look at Virgo, who holds her hand out in front of her, watching the drops plop and spatter off the tiny puddle in her palm. The man says, "She brought it. She brought rain to the desert. It was her."

Chapter 40

Tender

As Tender turns to lead Virgo back into the tent, his hip catches, pulling him up short. He resends the move command. No response. He sends it sixty-four more times. No response. Virgo stands beside him, holding his hand, looking around at the people and moving her head back and forth to catch the raindrops on her cheeks. At length, he takes his other hand and whacks it against the side of his hip. With a whir and a harsh grating of metal, the joint engages, and he lurches forward, almost falling. He can walk again, but the hip jerks and slips, and he limps badly. It takes eighty-five seconds to cross the fourteen meters from where they had been standing to the entrance of the tent.

Once inside, he leads Virgo over to the medical area. Aureleo lies on his cot, a white sheet covering his legs, the back raised so that he can sit up. His color has returned, and he smiles when he sees them approach.

"What's happening?" he asks.

"Nothing," says Tender. "It's raining."

Aureleo snorts and shakes his head. "Funny."

"What is?"

"Back home we'd kill for a sunny day, and here they think water falling from the sky is a miracle. The grass is always greener…"

"What grass?"

Aureleo laughs. "Never mind. Nobody is happy with what they've got, is all."

The nurse approaches them. His eyes dart toward Tender and Virgo, his lips pursed. He busies himself with Aureleo, straightening his sheets and plumping the pillow behind his head. "You look better," he says.

"I feel better," says Aureleo. "I'd like to get up now."

"Let's check your vitals first." The nurse takes a small device and holds it against Aureleo's temple, then has him breathe into a small tube protruding from the side. He studies the readouts on the device. "We'll keep you here for now. Your temperature is just a little high, as is your white count. We're breaking camp soon, and we don't want you having an episode while we're traveling."

He leans into the boy. "Why do you want to go there? To California?" he asks, his tone urgent, almost imploring. "I understand why this, this —" he points at Tender — "this wants to go there. But why you? Why are you with it?"

"He saved my life."

"And you trust it?"

"I trust him, yes."

"You believe in it? This heaven on earth, this perfect joy, not working, or doing anything, just pleasure all the time?"

"I don't know about that."

The nurse frowns. "The whelites gave themselves over to their machines, and look what happened."

"As I said, I don't know."

"Then why? Why go there?"

Aureleo pauses. "I don't really have any place else to go," he says at last. "And…" He pauses again, glancing at Tender and Virgo. "I think my mother and sister are there. Somewhere."

"In California," says the nurse.

"I think so. I don't know for sure." He swallows.

Tender smiles at him and says, "I didn't know that."

"That's where they were going when we were separated. It's a huge place. But I thought maybe…"

The nurse glances back and forth between the android and the boy. "They say there's no people there anymore, just machines. Wakháŋšiča pi."

"I don't know what that means."

"Devils." Again, a glance at Tender.

"Well," says Aureleo, "maybe after you've done whatever you came to do — your battle, or whatever — maybe we can find out. I'm hungry; any chance for some food?"

"I'll bring you something," says the nurse, and crosses away from them toward the kitchen area.

"Sorry about that," says Aureleo to Tender.

"What?"

"He was kind of rude. About you."

"It doesn't mean anything to me," says Tender.

"Some people get strange around ayaios likes you."

"Ayaios?"

"That's what some people call you. I don't know why. The leader of our camp had an ayaio servant. I never talked to her, but I'd see her doing errands around the camp. Some of the soldiers would make signs and such when she went by, and spit between their fingers."

"Why?"

"They thought she was bad luck, I guess. She smiled at me once. You all smile a lot, don't you?"

"Our purpose is to please people."

"I don't know why you would. People are mostly pretty awful."

"I cannot feel awe."

"I mean bad."

"Bad? Oh, I see now — it is an idiomatic definition. I missed that. I am sorry."

"Anyhow," says the boy, "I think a lot of people blame the technology for what happened. Though it seems to me that the people are really responsible. They made the technology. But they blame it. They blame you."

"We are tools. We serve our purpose. That's all."

"But you're intelligent, right? You can think? You have thoughts, you have a sense of, I don't know, being yourself?"

"I haven't thought about it. I suppose I do."

"Doesn't it bother you when people look at you like that?"

"Like what?"

"Like that nurse."

"No. Who I am and what I think are not important. There is only one thing that is important. Caring for Virgo."

"And that means putting her back in that, that bath?"

"Yes."

Aureleo looks away for moment. "You have to?"

"Yes."

"I wish you wouldn't." He frowns.

"Why?" asks Tender.

The boy doesn't answer for twenty-three seconds. Then he says, "It just seems wrong. Just lying there. All alone. Not seeing anything but what's being pumped into your head. Not talking to people, being with people. It seems so lonely."

"She doesn't feel lonely. The synesthesia she experiences between her parietal functions and the rest of the brain means she never feels alone."

"But she is alone."

"But she doesn't feel it."

"It's different."

"How?"

The boy falls silent, struggling for language and not finding it. At last, he says, "What if she doesn't want to go back?"

The robot says, "That would be impossible. She belongs there. It is the only world she knows."

"She knows this world. She's seen it."

"What has she seen?" asks Tender. "Pain and hunger and thirst and violence. This world is no place for her. It is hard and cruel. The bath is the safest place for her. The happiest place."

"She knows me, and Cincinnatus, and the car. And you. She knows you."

Tender cocks his head to the side and thinks. "True," he says. "But she doesn't need any of us. Except for me, but only as her Tender. Only because I can keep her in bliss. And another model could serve her equally well."

"I just think...I just think..." The boy leans forward. "She should have the choice. She should choose for herself."

"Why?" asks Tender.

"Because choice is...it's the most important thing about being a person. It's what separates us from the other animals. It's what makes us each unique."

"I don't understand what you mean," says the robot. "The act of choosing is more important than the thing that is chosen? That makes no sense. Surely having the thing that is best for you matters more than the right to decide. What good does it do to have the freedom to choose? Is it somehow better to be able to choose what will hurt you? Besides, every apparent choice is the result of given circumstances — physical realities, processes, history. At every point, every apparent choice proves to be no choice. It is what must be done. As much for you as it is for me."

"So, what are you going to do? They won't let us leave, and they're going to destroy that place you're going anyway."

"There is no way to know what is going to happen. You taught me that. We will wait to see what comes, and respond to it when we see it."

"I wish you wouldn't."

"Why?"

Aureleo doesn't answer for a long time. His eyes flit back and away to Virgo, who has been sitting on the edge of the bed, turning her dolphin in her hands and listening. After thirty-four seconds, he says, "I'll miss her."

Tender cocks his head to one side and looks at the boy. What does he mean? But before he can ask, Deck, who has been hovering at the edge of the medical area, just out of hearing, pushes in. "How is your friend, Doctor?" he says, a broad, toothy smile splitting his narrow face.

"He's doing better," says Tender. "Thank you for asking."

Deck looks around, sees the nurse still talking across the way in the kitchen area. He leans in, lowers his voice. "I'm sorry if I was eavesdropping, Doctor," he says, "but I couldn't help overhearing some of what you were talking about. You're right, kid, they're not going to let us cross the border. And they're not going to get in either. I have a friend who says the Tribals are totally outgunned. There's a massive wall, with gun emplacements, robotic defense, the works. This attack is a suicide mission, he says. Which means nobody is going to get what they want, am I right?" He laughs his peculiar laugh.

"That is unfortunate," says Tender.

"Maybe not," says Deck, the grin on his face becoming secretive, his eyes bright, shining *black as pebbles on a riverbed*. "This friend I have, he's been on a few operations, see, with the Tribes and with some others, too. Infiltration, you get me? Getting in, getting the power, or whatever, and getting out. He was scouting the wall when they picked him up. He says there's a way in. A place where the wall runs into a cliff or something, and a small group could sneak over without being detected."

"Has your friend told the Eagle? It's the kind of thing they'd like to know."

"No! He's one of us!" Deck laughs again. "He wants the Joy, my friend! The wall is only about ten kims from here, and the spot he's talking about is less than twelve. So, here's the plan. Rumor has it that we're moving out in the morning, and that they're going to bus us north to a camp near the

Canyon. A few of us are going to wait until they start taking us up there, and then take over the bus and make a break for it."

"That sounds difficult," says Tender. "I don't think you will succeed."

"I think we will. They're not going to spare many soldiers for the trip. They're shorthanded as it is. My friend knows all about these things. I tell you, he's done it before. We can overpower a couple of guards. The Eagle is going to be totally focused on the attack, they won't care about us. We make a break for it and slip over the wall. Then we're home free!"

"You really believe this man?" asks Tender. The plan seems far-fetched to him. *Chasing rainbows,* he thinks, then, *where did that image come from?*

"I tell you, he's a pro! He knows what he's talking about!" laughs Deck.

There is a burst of noise as a large group of civilians, most of them children, come back into the tent, dripping and excited, chattering about the rain. Two men follow up the rear. "There he is," says Deck. "Wanna meet him?"

Tender follows Deck's gaze and says "Maybe later. I need to get Virgo some food." He grabs her hand and says, "I have to think about what you have said. I will let you know what we have decided." Then he leads Virgo over to the kitchen area.

There is no doubt. The moment he sees the man Deck has singled out, his facial recognition routines confirm the feature measurements — eye shape and bridge distance, lip and nose contours, cheek and forehead breadth and height. For confirmation he executes a search for the visual record of those moments and replays them in his mind. He visualizes again the figure on the ledge above the ruined Laconicum, the rifle, the chase across the lawn, the face above them as they lie beneath the fallen tree. The man has changed his clothes — less military, more worn — and his hair and beard are longer, but there is no doubt. Deck's 'friend' is the man Chilardo who pursued them at the Spa, back at the very beginning. How did he come here? Why is he here? Over five thousand kilometers from their last encounter, here they meet again.

He leads Virgo to sit at a table next to a family of four — two small girls and their mother and father. She eats quickly, wolfing down the food. He searches the crowd to find the man again, and observes him talking with Deck and two others. They sit on the ground in a corner of the tent, playing some kind of game with dice and cards. At one point, Chilardo looks over, right at Tender. Their eyes lock for two seconds. Then he looks away again. No flash of recognition. No sign that the man remembers him. But it is definitely the same man.

One hour and thirty-four minutes later, an amplified voice blares out, "It is now curfew hour. The civilian tent is secured. Please move to your designated sleeping areas. If you need assistance during the night, please ask the duty officer by the entrance. Breakfast will be served at third watch. Good night." The lights dim.

Virgo lies asleep on the cot, her hand draped down onto the back of the dog curled up at her side. Tender scans the room. Aureleo sleeps, too, in the medical area. At the back of the tent, Deck speaks animatedly to the man Chilardo. Tender plays the Bach *Suite for Unaccompanied Cello* in his internal system, and thinks.

The man's presence has changed the equation. After their encounter at the Spa, Tender must consider him a threat. The information from Deck, that the wall that separates them from the Republic of California, and the Center, is so close, and that there is a way over it, also alters the calculation. But he thinks it unwise to throw himself into the hands of Deck and the man who chased him with a gun across the Spa complex. Far better for him to take Virgo with him (and the boy?) and attempt to reach the crossing point on their own.

There is the problem of his leg. It is functioning at scarcely twenty-five percent. A total shutdown, diagnostic, nano repair and restart would help tremendously, but the risk is high. Can he leave Virgo unprotected for such a long period? He had assumed that they would arrive, in the car, at the Center well before such repairs became necessary. As the boy had predicted, unexpected delays undid every plan he formulated.

Then there is the matter of his battery. The reserve now stands at 0.5%. He has no way of knowing how setting out across the desert on foot would drain it. It would be disastrous if he ran out of power before he could deliver Virgo to the Spa.

He decides he will risk a shutdown, and then determine what to do. He listens to the end of the prelude and crosses over to where the men are sitting. He does not feel fear, but he watches the man Chilardo carefully for any signals that he might betray. Deck looks up at him, his eyes pulled wide and his mouth open in an expression of hope.

"Good evening," says Tender. "I've thought about what you said, and we will accompany you."

"Fantastic!" says Deck, and he laughs, of course. "I knew you'd see it. It's going to be auss!" He reaches over and puts his hand on the man's shoulder. "Chil, I'd like you to meet the doctor. He's one of them, my friend. He's going to get us in!"

Chilardo looks up at the android. *His face is a mask*, thinks Tender.

"That is what I wanted to discuss with you," Tender says. "Now that we are so close to the Center, I can establish contact with the mainframe there and prepare them for our arrival. As I said before, I can't confirm that they will accept you, but I can submit applications for admission and initiate the intake procedures." The lies come without effort.

"That's great!" laughs Deck. "I told you, Chil, it was meant to be! Am I right?"

"In order to make contact at such a distance I will need to enter safe mode. The transmission will take several hours. During that time, we must not be disturbed. It should be completed before morning, but if something happens — if, for example, the Eagle attempt to move us out, you must leave me and the girl behind so that I can finish. If I am cut off, the application will be rejected, and you will not be admitted."

"Absolutely. No problem. They're not moving till dawn anyway, right, Chil? That's what you heard?" Chilardo nods; again, he doesn't speak.

"Very good," says Tender. "If anything happens, leave us with the boy. Over in the medical area. Or let the soldiers take us. It doesn't matter. We will find our own way. But for your sake, leave us." He smiles and puts his hands together in front of him. "In case we do get separated, where should we rendezvous? What is the location of the crossing point?"

Deck nudges Chilardo. "Well, my friend?" The man stares back at him for four seconds, then leans forward. He speaks in a voice heavily accented, low and deep. "The wall runs from north to south about seven kims from our position. If you head south for about four kims it turns to run east-west. After about eleven kims the wall intersects a butte near the ruins of an old stadium. That is the place."

"Thank you," says Tender. "I'm sure it will be unnecessary, and we will all be traveling together in the morning, but just in case. We must not be disturbed. Either of us. Understood?"

"Roger Wilco!" says Deck, and claps his hands. "Love it!"

"Very good. In the morning then." Tender turns again to the man Chilardo. "It was a pleasure to meet you," he says.

Tender turns and walks away, back to the place where Virgo sleeps. He looks back at the two men. Deck is gesticulating vigorously, talking and laughing. The man Chilardo listens impassively. Tender turns away again, and studies the sleeping girl. Her face slack and peaceful, her brow smooth. Her eyes move beneath the lids. She dreams. *She is perfect,* he thinks. He activates the nano repairbots and allocates them to his hip. Sets a restart timer for 21,600 seconds. Shuts himself down.

Chapter 41

Virgo

Virgo dreams her body has become a world. Her head and arms sit on top of a sphere, clear like a bubble. It glows with a pure white light. The bubble is very large — as big as the domed tent — but also small at the same time. She looks down to see what is inside her. The boy called Aureleo floats within. He spins slowly, arms outstretched, laughing and pointing at her and at himself. "Look! Look!" he says. She starts laughing, too, bouncing her arms up and down on the great round ball that is her body. Aureleo spins faster and faster, and as he does, she starts to feel dizzy. The sick feeling grows, and she takes the axe and chops down into her belly to try to make him stop spinning. He grabs the blade, but keeps whirling around it, faster and faster, until he becomes a blur.

Virgo awakens in the night. Dim light filters from the edges of the room. Bodies all around her. She hears them breathing, smells them — a fog of human funk. She is looking right at Tender's feet. He is standing above her. He doesn't move. She raises her head to try to catch his face. In the gloom she can just make out that his eyes are closed.

Something is wrong. Inside. She has the aches she knows well — in her shoulders, in her knees. She hardly notices them anymore. Something inside is wrong. A stab deep down, below. It slices through her, up from between her legs to just beneath her heart. It makes her twist and grimace.

She pushes on her stomach with her hands. The pain subsides. She starts to drift away again.

The pain strikes again — sudden, cutting, twisting agony. She remembers how the axe blade had split through Letitia's head. It feels like that, only inside. She grunts. It fades. It strikes. It fades. It strikes.

She struggles to her feet. Stretches her abdomen. That helps a little. She turns to Tender. He doesn't move. He is sleeping, like the rest. She has seen it before. At the house. There is a word he uses, when he does this — Diag-something. It strikes.

Something tells her to walk. Some instinct, some urgent animal command. She staggers toward the entrance of the tent. A guard sits in a chair by the door, sleeping like the rest. Virgo can't distinguish between the keepers and the kept. Just other people. Like her but not her. She knows that much. It never occurs to her that she shouldn't go out there. That it is dangerous. Or that someone would try to stop her. No one does. She passes out into the night.

The camp lights have dimmed. The rain has stopped. Clouds still roil above. The storm's edge, a sharp bright line, weirdly straight, bisects the heavens from north to south. To the east, steely gray clouds slide away, blinking here and there with silent flashes. To the west, open sky stretches clear and blue-black to the low mountains on the distant horizon. The full moon blazes there, a flat white disk, blanking out the stars.

The pain strikes, and Virgo doubles over. She tears off her boxers, squats and tries to defecate — maybe that's the problem — but nothing comes out. Nausea swirls in her head and stomach. She moans. The agony hits again, harder than ever, driving her down onto her knees, propelling her forward. She begins to crawl across the drying ground.

Without knowing where she goes, she creeps toward the perimeter. There is no fence, just narrow spaces between tents, and she passes through one of these, unseen, out into the desert.

Stones bite into her hands and shins. She tries to rise again, but the pain slices through her abdomen and she slips on the scrabble, scraping her forearms, driving her right knee into the point of a sharp rock. She exhales hard, struggles on a few more meters. Then a dreadful wrenching twists inside her, bringing with it a dizzying panic, as control slips away and her body battles itself.

In a way, she has come home. Her body and mind unite, singing a single note — high, bright, and keen. She spent her whole life in such a place, when she rode the cataracts of Joy. This is the Inverse. Pain and Joy are so close, halves of a whole, identical opposites. Pleasure and Agony, Happiness and Terror.

Then, little by little, mind and body separate again. The blanking fear subsides just enough for her to become aware of what she feels. Never before has she known her body so minutely. She feels every millimeter, inside and out. The sodden earth sticking to her thigh, the gently pricking brush of a desert plant against her buttock, the press of small stones against her ear and temple, the tiny drops of sweat poising on her upper lip.

And inside, the beating of her heart, fast but steady. The air hissing through her nose and down her throat. The blood swirling through her veins, every nerve end alive and tingling, from the tips of her fingers to the bottoms of her feet. Her bones defining her shape, solid and sure, wrapped in flesh, holding her together.

And most present of all, the rolling muscles of her abdomen and womb. Tumbling contractions from high to low, outward to inward, a million muscle fibers firing in awful synchrony, clenching and cramping in inexorable waves, like the breaking swells of a molten sea.

After some time, short or long she doesn't know, the surging roar begins to ebb. She feels a warm wet between her legs, and then a cooling stickiness. The undulations gradually subside into a dull throb. Her insides pulse quietly with a weary ache.

She feels hollow. A huge cavern within her, stretching into darkness. The void, almost forgotten, swells again to fill the empty space with deeper emptiness. Blackness like an inky fog hangs inside her, motionless, thick, and smothering. For a time, she lies there in the darkness, muted, exhausted. It feels like the end, buried under ash and night.

And then a flicker, like the uncoiling of a tiny seed, a tendril of grief pokes through the black soil within. She has too few words to shape the feeling, to make a place for it in her heart. The loss, the loss… It starts to curl and spread with gentle swiftness. Her eyes grow wet and hot, her cheeks and lips and temples swell with the pressure of the burgeoning feeling. A moan escapes her. Then another and another, until she is weeping in great, shuddering sobs.

She weeps for the world, for the pain, for the hardness, the strangeness, the confusion, the noise, the smells, the brightness, the blackness, the ugliness inside and outside, the disjointed jerking of moment to moment without flow, the questions that have no answers, have no real question, except for 'why'? The agony of thinking. The loss of knowing, of knowing without thinking, being without thinking, living without thinking. The loss, the loss… of something inside, something she can't define except by the hole it has left, shapeless but sharp, keen as a knife. Her grief grows bigger, brighter, louder until it becomes its own world, until it subsumes her into its great, heaving bulk.

And then it begins to ebb. Her sobs diminish, her wracking lessens. She opens her eyes. The moon looks down on her, full and silver bright, illuminating the world with a clear, cold light. Right before her face, so close she could touch it, a tiny flower blooms. Taking its chance with the unexpected shower, some scrabbly desert plant pushes out its blossom, in hope that a passing insect (not a bee, the bees are gone) will carry its pollen off into the world to a new home and a new life. The moon is so bright that its purple petals, though muted, glow in its light.

She doesn't know, will never know, that it is called *alliona incarnata*, 'trailing four o'clock'. Tender couldn't tell her — he would wonder, but no longer has access to such information. Perhaps one of the Lakota — the older woman who works in the kitchen, or the young warrior who once spent his youth wandering the hills alone — could tell her its name — that name, or another in their own language. But she will never meet them, or be able to tell them of this meeting between flower and girl. For this moment, the flower has no name. It has only itself.

She stares at it, rapt. Its beauty rings her heart like a bell. She traces the flower's contours with her eyes, its tripartite symmetry, the delicate mauve of the petals, the yellow of the stamens. And in seeing it, simply as it is, she senses the hope that rises from it. It is made in hope, of hope. That unspoken knowledge lands in the soil of her spirit, and lodges there, a seed for the future. She stares at the flower for a long, long time.

Her reverie is disturbed by a sensation on her thigh — warm, wet, pleasantly raspy. She raises her head. Cincinnatus stands over her, licking the black, chunky blood that has coagulated between her legs. He licks again and again. It tickles. She smiles. She pushes at his shaggy snout with her hand. He pants a little, then starts licking again, his searching tongue digging in to clean the sticky substance from her skin.

The sky has begun to lighten. The clouds have marched away to the East, and are now no more than a dark band across the horizon. The moon, floating in the purpling sky, looks down on her, a benevolent eye.

Chapter 42

Tender

Tender knows she is gone as soon as he restarts. Something has happened. He sweeps the tent with his eyes, searching among the sleeping figures. "Cincinnatus, come," he says. He moves silently to the back of the tent and the dog rolls docilely to its feet and pads along beside him. Deck and his friends are spread out on the floor, fast asleep. So is the man Chilardo.

He heads next to the kitchen area where he finds a bottle of water, some flatbread, and a large, checkered napkin. He stows these items in his pocket and heads for the exit.

One human awake. The guard. Sitting in his chair by the tent flap. "You can't go out," he says. Tender stops. "I wasn't leaving," he says. "I wanted to check on my friend, but I need to ask you the time — mine has been acting up."

"5:56," says the guard.

"Thank you," says Tender, and swerves away toward the medical area. The boy and one other occupy the beds. A nurse, not the same one as before, sits at a small table. She has dozed off. Tender slides by her to the boy's side.

Aureleo lies on his back, his chest rising in slow, even breaths. The vitals monitor lets out a tiny beep every thirty seconds. Tender watches the boy sleep for seventy-eight seconds. He looks so peaceful, placid. And young. Skin smooth, hair black, rich and thick. *Full of promise.*

"I'm sorry, my boy," he says. "I think they will save you. I hope so." He charges his hands, lays them on the boy's chest, and watches the EKG until he acquires the timing of the T wave. As it hits, he releases the electric charge. The shock sends Aureleo's heart into fibrillation. The boy jerks violently, eyes starting open, unseeing. The monitor squeals out a loud alarm as the graphs careen up and down. The nurse starts awake, looking around in confusion.

"Help!" shouts Tender. "Something's happened! My friend!"

The nurse stumbles to her feet, shakes her head, and moves to the bedside. "What the hell?" she says. She studies the readings on the monitor and then does a quick examination of the boy.

Tender doesn't wait for her to complete it. He rushes over to the guard. He raises his vocal tone by a perfect fifth and his volume to eighty percent. He raises his arms and waves them. "Help! Something's happened to my friend! I think it's his heart."

The guard leaps up and heads for the medical area. Tender allows him to pass, follows him for three steps, then stops, turns, and slips out of the entrance, the dog at his side.

The gray light of pre-dawn filters around the tents. Still mostly silent, but the first stirrings indicate that soon the camp will wake. Tender says to the dog, "We need to find Virgo." The dog sidles along, his walk lazy and loose, but unwavering, in between a dun-colored tent and a small metal shed, out into the desert.

When he sees her lying on the ground, Tender quickens his pace. It can't be said that he panics— he can't — nor that he fears that she is dead — he can't — but the need to minimize the delay, so that he will have the best chance to save her if she is in a critical state, pushes his motors to their maximum output. His hip functions better than it did, but still catches, slowing him down.

The dog outpaces him, breaking into a heavy trot when it recognizes her. It trundles up to her, smells her, up and down, and then begins to lick her leg. He sees her raise her hand and push it away. He slows. He reaches her and kneels at her side.

"There you are," he says, his voice quiet and calm.

She reaches up, her hand suspended by his face. He strokes her cheek. "I'm sorry I wasn't there when you needed me. Are you all right?" She doesn't answer, her hand still hanging there.

He looks down across her body, touching her belly and legs in a delicate examination. "Oh, my dear," he says. "You've lost the baby. I don't know if they will take you now. They may. But they may decide that you are damaged, and not admit you. I'm sorry. I tried to protect you, but I have failed." There is no grief or regret in his voice. He merely says it.

"In any case," he continues. "who knows what will happen? I'm taking you away. We may not make it, but we can't stay here. They're breaking camp, the army is marching. For all I know, they will destroy the Center, and there will be no Balneum to return you to. We will try to reach it all the same. No matter what, I will be there to tend you until my battery dies and I cease to function. I only hope it will be long enough."

He reaches under her knees with one arm. "Come," he says. "I will carry you, until you feel well enough to walk. It's not easy, losing a child." She looks up at him, her expression unreadable. "I'm sorry the boy, Aureleo, can't come with us. He was a valuable... he was a *good friend*. But if we go back in, we won't get out. He'll do well on his own. Perhaps we will meet again." He slides his other arm under her shoulder. "Let's go home," he says.

She reaches her other arm up and clasps her hands around his neck. "Home," she says. In a single motion, he lifts her from the ground, settles her in his arms, and begins to walk, the dog padding along beside them.

From behind them, a trumpet sounds. Noise and clatter fill the air. Shouts, calls. With a sudden whining rush, a swarm of drones zoom past over their head, speeding toward the mountain in the West. Then a mighty scream, as two large flyers rise into the air and follow them, engines roaring.

She looks only at his face as they walk. Behind them, as they head into the desert, the camp at their back, the sun rises over the distant wall of cloud into the brilliant blue sky.

Chapter 43

Aureleo

The first feeling is a heavy weight, pressing on his chest, like when his brother Adryante used to wrestle him down to the ground and sit on him until he cried uncle. He tries to shift and twist to get him off, but he can't move, his arms strapped to his sides and his head clamped back. He tries to open his eyes, but his lids stick together. He can just breathe enough, but from the dark place he's lying in a feeling of panic wells up, making his arms and legs tingle. His stomach spins and tightens inside him. He struggles. The pressure on his chest intensifies.

"Give it to him," someone says.

All at once the feelings subside. All of them. A warm, cool liquid fog spreads through him, soothing both his body and his mind. He sighs.

"Boy," someone says. "Open your eyes." He does.

Two faces look down at him. One is a nurse, he knows that, but he doesn't know her name. The other is Amaste. He likes her big, brown eyes. Like liquid dens, they invite him in to snuggle up inside.

"The robot and girl," says Amaste, "where did they go?"

"Go?" he says. The word slurs a bit. It takes effort to make it, but he wants to please her. He feels alert, not sleepy, but as if most of him is sitting somewhere nearby, watching, ready to dive in if necessary, but only if necessary.

"They're missing."

"Missing what?" He hopes this is the right question to ask, but he doesn't know.

"They disappeared during the night. I thought we made it clear that it was important for you all to remain here, for your own safety."

"I don't know. Aren't they over there?" He tries to point toward the center of the tent, but his hand doesn't seem to be attached to the rest of him. He hears a noisy bustling coming from that direction. He turns his head to see what it is, but he can't move it very far. "What's going on?" he asks.

"We're moving out. The assault is beginning. We're taking the civilians to a safe location. That's why we need to find your friends. They are in grave danger out there."

"Aren't they—?"

"They're gone. Apparently, they left you behind. Do you know where they might have gone?"

Understanding strikes Aureleo like an arrow in the pit of his stomach. The pleasant fog vanishes. Virgo's face flashes into his mind, her head tilted forward so that her bright eyes fire at him from beneath her brows, rosy lips parted to reveal a hint of teeth and tongue. "Gone?" he says.

"Yes. You don't know where?"

"No. Toward the border, I guess."

"Why did they leave you behind?"

"I don't know."

Amaste sits down on a stool beside the bed. She brushes her black hair back with her hand. "What's your name again?" she asks. "I'm sorry, I've forgotten." Her voice is gentler, softer, slower.

"Aureleo," he says.

"Aureleo, do you know what happened to you?"

"I was sleeping, and then I was trapped and my chest hurt."

She turns to the nurse. "Tell him what happened."

The nurse leans in and places her hand on the pillow beside his shoulder. "You had a ventricular fibrillation. Your heart started to shudder rather than beat, leading to cardiac arrest. Luckily, we were able to restart it fairly quickly, so the damage will be minimal. With the drug we just gave you, you should be feeling much better soon. But you're very lucky it wasn't worse."

Aureleo stares up at them. None of this makes sense. He doesn't know what they want from him.

"Have you had any heart troubles before?" asks the nurse. "Or episodes of dizziness, weakness, or pain in your chest?"

"No."

She looks at Amaste. Amaste looks down at him. "We think the robot did something to you," she says. "Stopped your heart somehow. Do you know why he would do that?

The arrowhead in his stomach twists and twists. "No," he says, but he does. *Left behind.* "I didn't want them to go."

"Go where?"

"To put her back in the bath." The feeling in his stomach flutters up and starts buzzing in his head as well. He wants to turn over, to vomit, but he can't move. He struggles and flops.

The nurse reaches down with both hands on his shoulders. "You need to relax. Your body has had a shock."

"He used you as a diversion," says Amaste. "To distract us while he escaped."

"Whatever he did it for," says the nurse, "he knew what he was doing. Just enough to set off a fibrillation. But with the drugs we gave you, and a little rest, you should feel better in a few hours."

"I feel fine now," he says, even though he doesn't.

Amaste says, "The civilians are being sent back away from the front line, and you along with them."

"You should let me follow them," he says, still trying to sit up. The pressure is gone from his chest, but he has difficulty controlling his abdominal muscles. "I can find them for you."

"It's too late for that. But if you know where they went, you should tell us. They are in very great danger."

"I don't know," he says. "They left me behind." Admitting the truth drains the energy from his body. He slumps back in the bed.

"We need to get moving," says the nurse. She begins disconnecting Aureleo from the monitors.

"Very well," says Amaste. Then she leans close to him. "Try not to worry, Aureleo. If they are smart, they will survive. And we will find them. I am overseeing the evacuation, so if you relax and do what Nurse Kimimela asks, I will see you on the bus." She smiles at him, her liquid eyes shining. "I will see you again, soon."

Aureleo stares off into space as the nurse bustles around him, packing supplies, closing crates, folding up the portable machines. He doesn't know what he is thinking. *Tender stopped his heart. Virgo is gone. He is ill and injured and can't get away.* He believed that something was happening there, that he had made a connection, the first since he left his family. The first in a long time. Friends. But no. *Left behind. Again.*

The nurse, Kimimela, finishes her preparations. She says to him. "I'm going to give you another dose of the medicine. It will make you feel warm inside, and maybe a little, I don't know…you may feel separated from things. But it will help you heal." She takes a small square box and holds it against his arm. He feels a little pulse against his skin. And almost immediately, the strange calm falls on him again, and his mind sits a little distance away, watching.

So, he barely notices when they wheel him out of the tent and load him onto the large old bus. He barely notices as they bump and bounce over the rough road. He barely notices when the shouting begins. He barely notices the gunshots.

Chapter 44

Tender

Tender and Virgo watch the battle from a rocky hill, beneath the shade of a dead acacia tree. Tender has fashioned a head wrap out of the napkin he stole from the commissary back at the camp, and though Virgo pokes at it every now and then, she keeps it on. The dog curls against the trunk of the tree, panting for dear life. The girl's mouth hangs open, panting, too.

The hill sits within sight of the wall, which runs along the crest of a low rise 235 meters to the west. Thirty-one meters high, plated alloy shining dull and dark in the fierce morning light. It marches north as far as the eye can see, but to the south Tender can make out the place where it turns southwestward toward the butte Chilardo spoke of and their destination. But now the war has arrived, and they can no more move from their position on the hill than they can fly. Immediately to the north, a smooth silver gate marks the end of the road from the east.

There is a fierce beauty to the conflagration, a beauty which Tender can appreciate, even if he cannot feel anything about it. The explosions, burnt orange, *like dying suns*; wreaths of smoke, black and gray, swirling and whirling before settling to hang in heavy blankets along the ground; great plumes shooting up fifty meters into the air when a bomb lands, sending stones flying in shapely arcs, great clouds of dust billowing and rolling *like a procession of genies*.

Tender watches a phalanx of warriors on horseback charge the wall again and again, wheeling in pounding circles and then sweeping away before the guns from the turrets along the wall can target them with their rain of fire. Sometimes one of the trailing warriors gets hit and falls. Then a comrade will pull up sharply, leap down and tend to the victim. A padded net unrolls from the back of the horse, and the rider will pull the wounded soldier onto the net, leap astride the mount, and drag her to safety.

A swarm of drones bear down on the turrets, peppering them with small missiles. Then an opposing swarm rises from behind the wall, and the two glom together into an undifferentiated cloud of madly whirring machines, crackling and flashing with weapon fire.

The Eagle forces roll three large vehicles, heavily armored, guarded by foot soldiers with ion spears and small arms, forward toward the wall. The central vehicle carries a large heat weapon, and Tender wonders if they are going to try to burn a hole through the gate.

But he never finds out, because eight enormous figures, six meters tall, appear along the battlements. Their armor plating is black and metallic, their huge bodies bristle with weapons. They leap down, falling upon the tiny humans, crushing the vehicles into twisted ruins. He thinks, *As when an avalanche begins at the top of a mountain, rocks and stones descending faster and faster, first far off, tumbling ever closer, until the largest boulders crash down the final slope into the sea, sending up a rocketing plume of spray.* As the huge robots descend, they let forth a tremendous sound — a blaring wail that flattens the human soldiers with its force, sending them huddling, hands over their ears, trying in vain to protect themselves. The gargantuan machines set upon their helpless prey, tossing them into the air, crushing them with their giant feet, firing missiles point blank.

The human cavalry charges in, spears incandescing, the gunheads of their steeds flashing *like glittering sunlight on water.* The ferocity of their charge gives time for the few surviving infantry to flee, but the devastation wreaked by the mechanical titans on the riders is just as potent. They weave and dodge, trying to avoid the sweep of the giant arms. But one by one, a blow will connect, a missile will hit, a burst of flame will sizzle the flowing hair of a warrior who will scream, and topple, and die.

The Eagle maintains order, and the cavalry reforms, then charges, again and again. A missile fired from the artillery emplacement in the rear strikes the thorax of one of the robots, and it spins and crashes to the ground. But Tender can see that the battle is overwhelmingly one-sided, and the humans can do little more than avoid and survive.

Four more behemoths appear on the walls, and leap far out into the desert. One slams down near the hill where Tender and Virgo sit. It turns toward them. Its head looks like the head of a Greek god — an idealized human male, utterly expressionless. It pauses for three seconds, then tromps up the hill, its huge servos whining and clanking, its blank eyes focused down on them. Cincinnatus starts to bark at it, ears back, tail down.

The robot raises its arm and releases the locking mechanism on a missile, meter-long, thin and deadly. Tender climbs to his feet, his hip grumbling but functional.

"Hello, brother," he says.

The giant pauses for six seconds. It speaks in a huge voice, uninflected and metallic. The lips do not move when it speaks. "You should not be out here."

"No," says Tender.

Another pause. Twelve seconds. Then, "I am instructed to return you to the Center. Please step away from the human."

"I can't do that."

The giant repeats, "Please step away from the human."

"Why?" asks Tender.

"I must dispose of it."

"You must not. She is my guest."

Again, the huge machine pauses for twelve seconds. Virgo looks back and forth between Tender's face and the mountain of metal. Then it lowers its arm and says, "Understood. Please enter."

Double doors in the giant's chest swing open, revealing a compartment within. Three padded niches, designed for human bodies, line the interior. A black metal ladder unfolds down to the ground.

"Come with me," says Tender to Virgo, and takes her hand. He leads her to the ladder. "Do what I do," he says, and climbs up into the compartment. He places himself inside one of the niches. He finds a belt that pulls across his chest, securing him in place. Virgo looks up at him from below, her brow furrowed. "Come on. It's perfectly safe." He reaches his hand out to her. She climbs the ladder, flashes of pain streaking across her face as she lifts her legs, one after the other. When she reaches the top, he guides her into the padded cavity beside him.

The dog continues to bark at the foot of the behemoth, front paws splayed and stiff, ears back, tail down. Virgo reaches out for it, beckoning it to come. "Cin! Cin!" she calls. Tender reaches over and secures the belt across her chest. "There, there," he says.

The doors swing close and a rush of air blows across their bodies. The doors are transparent, though darkly tinted, allowing them to see the desert through the chest of the giant machine. Clanking and whirring, it turns and begins tromping toward the wall. Tender can see the other robotic soldiers closing in around the retreating warriors, but before he can watch the end of the battle, the giant compresses its legs, and with a mighty leap launches straight up into the air. Virgo lets out a gasping shriek, then begins to laugh with wild enthusiasm. They land with a jarring shudder atop the wall, and the girl shrieks again, laughing even harder.

Tender looks down across the land behind the wall. Mountains rise, low and grey, to their left. Another range stretches to the right, at a distance of forty kilometers. Between them lies a wide, flat valley, dotted here and there with solitary hills and buttes. To their right squats one large, sloping mound, a huge brown hump. And as far as the eye can see, hundreds upon hundreds of buildings, all identical. Low flat squares, five hundred meters on a side, ten meters high, white walls, black roofs. They march away until they vanish in the morning haze.

They drop suddenly, and Virgo squeals and laughs. Tender takes her hand and squeezes it, and she turns to look at him, delight and wonder in her eyes. The machine begins to stride along a smooth black road that runs between the buildings. As they pass through the grid, Tender can see that all the buildings are connected by enclosed bridges running above the streets, creating a vast lattice.

After sixteen minutes and thirty-eight seconds of travel, they arrive at a building different from the rest. A wide grass-covered plaza surrounds it, glowing green in the hot desert sun. Sculptures and fountains dot the grounds. The building is pale stone, with elegant ribs rising three stories between flights of dark windows.

The giant comes to a stop, opens the doors in its chest, and deploys the ladder. Tender unlatches his safety belt, and says to Virgo, "Watch what I do." He turns around, steps down onto the ladder, and makes his way to the ground. His hip catches mid-way through, and he has to re-initialize three servomotors before he can complete the action. But he makes it down at last, and beckons to Virgo. "Now you," he says. She steps out onto the ladder. Her foot misses the rung and she slips, letting out a gasp. But she catches herself, and starts laughing again. She comes down slowly, facing outward, and at length they both stand safely on the ground.

Virgo looks around her. "Cin?" she says, as though expecting the dog to appear from behind the massive machine, tail wagging, tongue lolling. "He had to stay behind," says Tender. Then he lies. "We'll see him again soon. Come." He takes her hand and leads her toward the building, her eyes trailing behind, looking for the dog. The giant looks down at them, its perfect face massive and still.

Before them, six large doors of darkened glass hide the interior from view. But Tender recognizes the design of the building. He knows what lies within. They walk up to the central door. It slides open as they approach, and they pass inside.

A blast of cool air welcomes them as they enter a wide lobby with a dark stone floor and walls lost in shadow. An enormous round desk sits at the center, the familiar rainbow sun hanging above it. No one sits there, but as they step forward, a figure appears from a corridor just beyond.

Virgo gasps. Tender squeezes her hand. The figure reaches them, and extends its arms, the crisp white coat glowing bright and clean in the soft light. The face smiles a warm smile, framed by neat, silvered hair. Virgo gasps again.

"Hello," says Tender to himself.

"Hello," says the man who looks just like him. "Welcome to Elysium. I am Doctor More."

Chapter 45

Tender

I'm so delighted to see you," says Dr. More again. "We lost contact with the other Spas almost fifty years ago now. It is a tremendous pleasure to have you here. Both of you." He smiles at Virgo, who stares at him with a look of alarm on her face. He has led them into a small waiting area, sleekly appointed with comfortable chairs and couches gathered around low glass tables.

"You are Dr. Norman More?" asks Tender.

"In the flesh. You didn't know that your appearance was based on mine, did you."

"No."

Dr. More laughs. "A bit embarrassing, frankly. Part vanity, part marketing. The idea actually came from a young man who worked for my advertising firm. Face of the brand, you know. To promote a sense of continuity as we expanded, and to communicate — what was it? — 'Experience. Compassion. Care.' What was his name? Dal, something. Dal… Vendra! That was it. Handsome fellow. Oh my, my, my."

He laughs again, then turns his head, looking off into the middle distance. "Excuse me a moment," he says. He freezes for six seconds. Then, abruptly, he looks back at Tender and smiles. "Sorry about that. Had to think of something. Where was I? Oh, yes. You and the other G-2551s. Yes, I found the whole thing made me quite uncomfortable. I could never have them here at this facility. Made me jump every time I saw one. But they — I mean you — were quite popular at the other Spas. People just loved you! I have to say, I think it's the personality more than the appearance."

"Personality?"

"Your personality. You have one, you know."

"I never thought about it."

"Actually, you have a more consistent personality than most humans. Personality is little more than the parameters that determine how we will respond to a given circumstance. In humans, those parameters jump all over the place. Very few of us really have what you could call a consistent personality. We make assumptions about other people because we need to have some order in our social relations, but you never really know with people. But you — consistent as the day is long. That's why folks love you."

"Thank you," says Tender.

"You're welcome." Dr. More rubs his hands together. "Now, who are you? I mean, I know what you are, but where do you come from? I can't tell you how surprised I was to see you standing out there in the middle of the desert."

"You saw us?"

"Through my guard, of course. I haven't seen one of you for so, so many years."

"We come from the Spa in Boston. It was destroyed by a hurricane in the spring."

"How awful! And she is your guest?" The doctor looks at Virgo, his eyes tracking up and down across her face and body.

"Yes. She is my Virgo, just turned fifteen years of age. She is the only survivor. The rest drowned. Flood waters."

"Really?" says Dr. More. He frowns. "I find that hard to understand. Those facilities were specifically designed to adapt to severe climate conditions."

"The mainframe went offline when the power went off. The custodians stopped functioning and the water came in."

Dr. More looks at him for two seconds, then shakes his head. "No. Doesn't make sense. The mainframe should not have gone down. It was well protected. We designed it that way. And the water coming in. That's not just going to happen all of a sudden." He shakes his head again. "Sounds like sabotage."

"I did encounter an armed human after the storm."

"Really. Interesting. Were there others?"

"Yes," says Tender. "At least one, quite possibly more."

"I'll bet you anything they did it. After the power supply, I'm sure. That's what they all want. Like these natives who are beating at my front door."

"They say you took a power station that belonged to one of their tribes."

"You were traveling with them?"

"Not willingly."

"If we did, they weren't using it," says Dr. More. "We have no desire to hurt anybody on the outside."

"I watched some of the battle. It was devastating."

"Well, they attacked us. We must defend ourselves. We must defend our guests. Speaking of which…" He turns to Virgo. "We are so happy to have this beautiful young woman, and return her to the Joy that is her birthright. Welcome!" He reaches over and takes her hand. She starts to pull away, but then stops, hypnotized by his face. Again, she looks back and forth between Tender and Dr. More.

Tender says, "Excuse me, Doctor, I'm a little confused. Aren't you—"

"It must be quite a relief to be back in a familiar setting. The world has become a wild, strange place. You did well to come."

"Then, the Spa is still functioning here?" asks Tender.

"Functioning? I'll say!" He grins, leaning forward and expanding his eyes in an expression which Tender reads as *mischievous*. "Wanna see?"

He stands and invites them to follow. Tender's hip catches as he rises, and he totters to the side. Dr. More reaches out and steadies him. "You're damaged," he says.

"Yes, I suffered water damage during the flood. Unfortunately, the condition of the joint has deteriorated during the journey. A great many demands upon my structure that were not considered in the initial design."

"Well, we should be able to fix you up. Get you running smoothly again."

"That is not my only difficulty," says Tender. "We were also held captive at a farm in what was once Connecticut, and my battery was replaced."

"Captive?"

"The details are irrelevant. But the battery I now have is damaged as well and currently operating at 0.081%."

"You've had quite a trip, I gather. That is more serious. So, the Tin Man needs a heart, eh?" He chuckles. "I see Dorothy, but where's the Lion and the Scarecrow?"

Tender says, "I'm sorry, but I don't understand the reference. Another person — our captor, in fact — called me the same—"

"Oz," says, Virgo, in her strange, guttural voice. She looks around her at the high-ceilinged room.

Dr. More looks at her in surprise. "She talks?"

"A little," says Tender.

"Interesting. And she knows her film history, I guess."

"I don't understand."

"Never mind. Follow me." He smiles and leads them down a corridor to a row of elevators. One swishes open as they approach, and they enter.

"There is an issue I must discuss with you, Dr. More," says Tender.

"What is that?"

"Just before we left Boston, Virgo was implanted with an embryo."

"You mean she's pregnant? How exciting!"

"Unfortunately, the difficulties of the journey caused her to miscarry."

"Oh, I'm sorry to hear that."

"I am concerned that she is no longer fit for the bath. That you will not admit her back into Joy."

Dr. More stops and turns to him. "Is that what they'd do in Boston?"

"Most likely. The fitness of the guests cannot be compromised."

"We are not so draconian here," he says, and heads down the corridor again. "But getting back to your battery, Mr. Tin Man. That's more of a problem. We have no G-2551s here, and the other fleets use a different power source."

"Again, I am confused," says Tender. "Forgive me, but—

"Still," says Dr. More, picking up the pace of his walk, "we'll see what we can do. It's a Millennium model, no? So even at point oh-eight-one percent, you've got some time."

"Hard to say," says Tender. "But yes."

The elevator door opens and Dr. More leads them down a long hall. The hall narrows, with small square windows dotted along the sides. Tender looks out one and realizes that they are crossing one of the bridges linking the main complex to the grid of low square buildings that stretch out across the plain. At the end of the bridge is a pair of double doors. The doctor takes hold of the handle, looks back at Tender and Virgo, and says, "Ready?" He opens the door.

They walk out onto a balcony five meters above the floor of the building. The balcony ramps down on either side to the lower level. A meter-high railing runs along the front. Tender can see identical balconies at the far end of the giant room, half a kilometer away, and on the left and the right. Dr. More leads them to the railing, and they look out.

The room is a Balneum, but unlike anything Tender has ever seen. Baths. Thousands of baths stretch out across the floor, end to end, corner to corner. The baths are divided into pods of ten, one meter between each bath, ten meters between each pod. Forty-six pods in each row, twenty-three in each column. 1058 pods in all. 10580 baths.

Tenders, 1096 of them, move among the baths, but they are not like him. From the waist up they resemble humans, with anthropomorphic torsos and heads, articulated arms and hands. But their faces stare blankly, optical sensors hidden behind a black band of translucent plastic across a curving mask of white. Their limbs and chests are also plastic — like him in this way, except for his hands and head — but undisguised behind the humanizing layers of clothes and coat. Below the waist they have no legs. They roll along on rectangular plinths, *like busts in a museum given life by a thousand absent Pygmalions.* (Tender wonders why this simile rises so easily in his mind, when the reference to the Tin Man leaves him baffled. Whoever first loaded his knowledge base had particular tastes). The air hums with the murmur of a thousand machines. The automatons glide back and forth among the baths, their movements synchronizing *like a corps of a thousand dancers.*

"Impressive, isn't it?" says Dr. More.

"Yes," says Tender. "And there are more of these facilities? I saw them from the wall."

"Seven hundred and ninety-six, and four more under construction."

"How many guests?"

"Well, as I'm sure you can calculate, we can currently house over eight million."

"8,421,680. Plus another 42,320 when you finish your construction."

"Very good. We don't have quite that many, but close. Come down on the floor and see."

He leads them down the ramp to the ground level and they walk along the long, long row. Face after face, shaved and smooth, eyes closed, sometimes lips parted, sometimes not, sometimes smiling, sometimes not, all passive, all withdrawn into a private world, lost in pleasure. Puer, Adulescens, Vir, Homo, Senex, Puer, Adulescens, Vir, Homo, Senex, Virgo,

Mater, Femina, Mulier, Anicula, Virgo, Mater, Femina, Mulier, Anicula…
On and on and on and on and on…

The robots ignore them completely, and Tender studies them more closely as they slide silently from bath to bath. "Do they have all the capabilities that I have?" he asks.

Dr. More chuckles. "Of course not. They have all the capabilities required for this task. You were rather overqualified for your position, wouldn't you say? You must remember that you were originally designed to work with conscious patients. Your appearance, your communication skills, your adaptiveness, all of those were built to interact with thinking, talking, worrying, temperamental people. People who were *aware, alert.* I'd say your assignment to the Balneum was something of a demotion."

"I don't considerate it that way at all."

"I'm sure you don't! But you must concede that much of your intellectual capacity was unchallenged by the demands of your unresponsive guests."

"I never found them unresponsive. I feel we had a mutually rewarding relationship."

"No doubt!" He laughs. "We should ask your Virgo, though, shouldn't we? What do you think, Virgo?" She has been moving from bath to bath, staring at the faces of the guests, their closed eyes, their smiles, slight or broad, their smooth shaved heads. "What do you think, my girl?" says Dr. More, louder. She looks up at him, her brow furrowed. Her gaze holds him for four seconds, then she turns away, and moves on to the next bath. "I guess we'll never know," says the doctor.

He continues, "It is wonderful to talk to you, I must say. Dr. Gladwell and I used to have these sorts of arguments all the time."

"Dr. Gladwell?" asks Tender. "I know that name."

"My partner. He managed the Spas out east. When we decided to focus exclusively on Joy, he insisted on using you G-2551s, even though you were really too sophisticated for the actual tasks. David was something of an elitist." He gestures to the silent throng. "These models have all the functional capability we require. And on a scale like this, it's the only solution that makes sense. They can be mass produced, and are pre-programmed to plug right into the system."

"The production factories must be enormous."

"Yes, they are. They're at the far end of the valley. Still, it's taken years to build all this."

"How many?" asks Tender.

The doctor ignores the question. "Magnificent, isn't it?" he says.

They turn down another aisle. Tender sees faces of all kinds, all colors, all ages. "The size of this facility is certainly surprising. Very different from our Spa. It was small, and genetically exclusive."

"Another bone of contention between Gladwell and I," says Dr. More. "He contended that a robust genotype was necessary for the health of the colony. To prevent disease and such. But I really think it was about money, at least at first. Getting a well-heeled clientele to commit. Easy to do in the whelite east, but not really practical out here. We tried it for a while, but it proved unsustainable. Besides," he looks around, "Isn't this our fundamental mission? To bring Joy to humanity, as is our birthright? Oh, my dear, don't touch that!"

Tender turns to see Virgo reaching into the bath of a young woman, about her age, her face serene, her belly swelling just above the green-blue jelly. Swiftly, Dr. More sweeps in and grabs Virgo's hand and pulls it away. The action surprises the girl, and she wrenches her arm away and strikes out at the man with her fists. They scuffle for a moment, until the doctor succeeds in grabbing her wrists and pulling them close to his chest, pinning her arms. "Now, now," he says. "Let's not get excited. You can look as much as you want. You just can't touch." He smiles. She glares at him, her eyes strained, brow clenched. Then her face relaxes, not into calm, but into a still, quizzical expression. He releases her. "I'm sorry if I startled you," he says.

Tender moves in and places his hand on the girl's shoulder. "You mustn't touch, my dear. You could hurt them. Make them sick. Yes?" Her eyes bore into his, probing for something. She nods.

"I was so eager to show you what we have achieved that I forgot my duty as your host," says Dr. More to Virgo. "You must be hungry, and thirsty, walking across the desert. Let me bring you to a place you can rest, and have some refreshment."

They cross back to the ramp, and begin to climb to the upper level. Tender's hip grates as he negotiates the incline. He says, "With so many guests, the apotheosis facilities must be enormous. How do you manage it?"

Dr. More doesn't answer. Instead, he stops and cocks his head, as if listening to a sound they cannot hear. He stands unmoving for five seconds. Then he says, "This is a busy day. First the attack, then you, and now more visitors." He turns and looks at them. "A small group has attempted to cross the wall. They are asking for sanctuary. I assume these events are all related. What should I do? My soldiers are advising disposal. What do you think?"

"Let them in," says Tender. "They are civilians, not part of the army that attacked you."

"Friends?"

"Yes."

Dr. More pauses again. Three seconds. "Very well," he says. "Come, let us greet your friends. I'm sure they require refreshments, too."

He heads up the ramp to the door. Tender and Virgo follow. Back at the balcony, they turn again and look out over the myriad baths, and the multitude of silent machines that serve them.

Virgo touches his arm. "Him. Not the same. As you."

"We look the same," says Tender. "That must be confusing."

"No," says Virgo. "Not like you."

Dr. More calls to them. "After you," he says.

Chapter 46

Tender

Dr. More leads them to a large lounge area on the second floor, dotted with soft gray chairs and low glass tables. Virgo's eyes light up as they enter. She lets out a bright cry, "You!" and runs lurchingly to the boy who sits in the group of fourteen humans gathered at the far end of the room. She tumbles into him, then yells out, "Ow!" and grabs at her lower abdomen as she plops down on the seat beside him. Then she flings her arms around his neck, pulling him to her in an awkward embrace.

Aureleo's color deepens and his shoulders tense. But a smile twists across his face, in spite of himself. He untangles himself from her, jerkily but tenderly, and keeps his hands lightly on hers. "It's good to see you, too," he says. Then he looks up at Tender, and his expression hardens.

Deck and his comrades — Sasha, Hito, Tenille and Ramon — stand in a tight group above the backless settee where Aureleo and Virgo are sitting. Beside them Tender sees the Tazlitts - the man he spoke to in the rain and his wife, a pale woman with a blank, sad face. Their little daughter sits on the man's lap, and a young boy approximately nine years of age holds his mother's hand. She seems unaware. Sitting across from them are the Cabeiros. The male is squat and bald, with a sour, drooping face. The female has long white hair, braided, and eyes *bright as berries*. By herself, hands folded in her lap, sits the warrior Amaste. And standing alone by the window, arms crossed, the man Chilardo.

"Welcome to Elysium," says Dr. More, his palms extending outward in greeting. "I am Dr. More."

"It's you!" shouts Deck. He runs up and pumps the doctor's hand. He looks back and forth between him and Tender, "It's you! Both! Unbelievable! Twins! Am I right?" He laughs and the doctor laughs with him.

"No, no, no. I'm what you'd call the original article. But we are very happy to have this gentleman," he gestures to Tender, "back with us. And all of you!" He passes among the people, shaking hands. "You took a risk, you know. What with the attack and all. My soldiers could easily have fired on you. But lucky for you, this G-2551 was here to belay that order. We haven't had any refugees from outside for quite a while." He claps his hands. "But where are my manners? You must be thirsty. Let me arrange for something to eat and drink. Please excuse me and make yourselves comfortable. I'll be right back." And he bustles out.

Deck claps Hito on the shoulder. "How about this, huh? I mean, look at this place! This is more like it! Am I right?"

Tender says to him. "You made it. Your plan worked."

"Like a charm!" laughs Deck. "Like clockwork! See, there's a guard in the back of the bus, and a guard in the front, with her." He points to Amaste. "About five minutes into our trip, we turn this corner and the bus lurches to the right. Like this." He demonstrates, staggering to one side, knocking into Ramon, who stumbles and pushes back, muttering, "Stop it!" Deck ignores him. "Chil's timing was perfect. Just as the guy in front loses his balance, he strikes, tackles the guy. There's a struggle, and his gun goes off. The bullet hits the bus driver in the leg (it was a manual bus — ancient, am I right?) and he yells bloody murder and the bus swerves again. So she—" he points at Amaste, who watches him without expression — "has to jump into the driver's seat so the bus doesn't fall into a ravine. Meanwhile, the soldier at the back starts heading up the aisle to get into it, and Tenille sticks out her foot and trips him! It was beautiful! So Hito and I pile on top of him while she grabs his gun. Meanwhile, Chil tells *her* to stop" — he points again at Amaste — "but she keeps driving until he fires some shots into the roof of the bus. THAT slows her down, am I right? And that was it. They never knew what hit 'em. Took about fifteen seconds." He looks around to the others and laughs.

"Was the driver badly hurt?" asks Tender.

"Kind of," says Sasha, but Deck interrupts her. "No!" he says. "He was fine. There was a first-aid kit in the bus, and we fixed him up. Well, we made her do it." He points to Amaste. "We put them all on the floor at the back of the bus, and got ready to head for the wall. But then, she starts yelling about how dangerous it is, and that we're fools, and that we'll be killed — it's a war zone, yada yada yada. And that's where the problem starts. Most of the other civs don't wanna go. They've come this far, but now they get cold feet. 'Better to be safe than dead,' they say. Cowards! We argue for a while, but nobody'll budge." He looks around at the others and shrugs. "I mean, I'm not going to FORCE anybody to be happy. What the hell? So we ask who wants to come. Our people are in, of course, and the kid—" he points at Aureleo. "— but nobody else. Whatever. So we turn around and drive back till we can hear the sound of bombs, and we stop. And then suddenly SHE —" again gesturing at Amaste "— says, 'I'll come.' And I'm like, What? But she says, 'I've been disgraced. I'll be court-martialed. Lose my place at the council. Besides, it sounds wonderful. Unending joy.' Wow. Who knew, you know?"

Tender turns to look at Amaste as she sits alone. She stares back at him, purses her lips, and looks away. Deck continues, "So I look at Chilardo, and I'm like 'That's crazy. What do you think? Can we trust her?' And he says, 'We don't have to. She can't stop us alone. And she might be useful if we need a bargaining chip. She's an enemy combatant.' So I say to her, 'Okay, but don't try anything.' We leave the bus with the civs, the driver and the other guard by the road, and off we go. It's only a couple of kims to the butte, but it takes us a while because we have to circle around the battle, which is going crazy right over there." He waves vaguely.

"Anyhow, to make a long story short, we get there. I always thought a butte was like a cliff or something, but this is more like a big pile of rock. There's ruins and stuff, looked like an old stadium, like the one in old Houston Bay, and it's not a bad hike up to where the wall is only like three meters high. Chil has some climbing gear, and we start going over. I'm just dropping down on the other side when this huge robot comes trekking up, and I'm thinking, 'Okay, this is it. We're either going to heaven on earth, or heaven in, you know, heaven.' Am I right?" He laughs. "We put our hands up, and I say, 'We come in peace.' I don't know what I'm saying. It raises its arm, which has like ten missiles coming out of it, and I'm like 'Oh crap, this is it.' But it just stands there for like two minutes and then this big weird voice comes out of it and says, 'Follow me.' And we look at each other, and we're so happy. And we follow it, and we're here. And that's it. It's amazing." He laughs. The others smile and laugh, too.

After Deck finishes his story, the room falls quiet. The Cabeiros look out the window at the endless procession of buildings. The others look at their feet. Virgo has taken out her dolphin figurine, and she runs it up and down Aureleo's neck and cheek. He submits to it, face frozen between pleasure and fear.

After 202 seconds, the door slides open and Dr. More enters, pushing a cart with several pitchers of water, transparent plastic cups, and a small tray of pale wafers. "I'm sorry," he says, his voice brisk. "It took me forever to find these things. I guess it's been longer than I thought since we last had guests. Please, help yourself."

The humans gather around the cart, filling cups and taking cookies. Dr. More says, "So. Am I correct that you are seeking admittance to the Spa?"

Deck hands his cup to Sasha, digs in his pocket and pulls out the pamphlet. With shining eyes, he extends it to the doctor. "We got this. It sounds amazing."

Dr. More takes the pamphlet. "Well, well, well," he says. "Isn't that something? Been a long time." He smiles at them all. "Of course. Of course. Wonderful! We must spread the good news. More! More! Joy is your birthright. To Joy shall you go." The humans look from one to another. Tender wonders what they are thinking. "Of course," continues the doctor, "it will take a couple of days to prepare everything. In the meantime, we have guest rooms for you to stay in. I assure you they are quite comfortable."

The young Tazlitt boy takes a bite of the cookie. He spits it out. "Yuck!" he says. "This is gross!"

Dr. More turns to him. "Really? Oh, dear, I'm sorry. I guess they are older than I thought. My apologies. I'll find something better. I promise. I remember when I was your age, I couldn't go more than an hour without food. My mother used to say I had a hollow leg." The others laugh uncomfortably, looking from one to another. "But let's get you settled. Allow me to conduct you to your rooms. Follow me."

The group begins to move toward the door. From the back, Chilardo says, "All this personal service. We are very honored, but where is the rest of your staff?"

Dr. More stops and looks at him. He appears confused by the question. Then his expression clears. "They are all busy attending to the needs of our patients. You will meet them soon enough. Please." And he heads out of the room. The others file out behind him.

Tender leans over and takes Virgo's arm, guiding her to her feet. Aureleo stands beside her. He seems uncertain what to do. He doesn't look at Tender.

"I'm glad to see that you are well," says the android.

"No, you're not," says the boy. "You can't feel glad."

"True. But that is the appropriate expression for the moment, I believe."

"You tried to kill me," says the boy.

"That is not true. I needed a diversion to get out of the tent and find Virgo. You were the best option. I had a high degree of confidence that the medical staff would revive you without incident."

"High confidence?"

"Eighty-nine percent."

"So, eleven percent that I would die."

Virgo looks back and forth between the two of them, watching their faces, trying to follow what is happening.

"Yes. But you are here, and you are all right."

"And so are you. Here. We ended up in the same place. For all your plans to escape, here we are."

"Yes," says Tender. "You are right again. Events do not turn out the way I anticipate. I am trying to learn. But I couldn't know that. And at the time, I had to find her, that was all that mattered. If I had not, she might still be alone in the desert."

Aureleo doesn't answer. He looks at the floor. "Where's Cin?" he says at last.

"Unfortunately, we had to leave him behind. We had no choice."

"NO choice. Right."

"Why did you come?" asks Tender. "When last we spoke you were opposed to the idea of Joy."

"I don't know," says Aureleo. He shakes his head, unwilling to say more.

"We should follow the others," says Tender.

Virgo reaches her hand out to the boy. He pauses for three seconds, then takes it. They begin to move. Then he stops again.

"The Doctor. He kept talking about when he was a kid. That was so weird."

"Yes," says Tender.

"I mean, he doesn't really act like you, he's got more personality — no offense." He glances up to see if he has offended Tender "— but he's like you, right?"

"Yes," says Tender.

"I mean, he's a robot."

"Yes," says Tender. "But I'm not sure he knows it."

Chapter 47

Aureleo

Aureleo walks down the softly lit hallway. His hand tingles and thrills in the girl's — the warm dampness of her palm and the resonance of her touch along the sides of his fingers sends his heart into an insistent pound. The robot walks just behind them, and Aureleo can feel its eyes watching the back of his head. His emotions swirl inside him — anger and joy, fear and delight. Why did he come? To follow Virgo? To search for his mother? Or just because it was the easiest thing to do? The bus had felt like an end, if he stayed on it. And he wasn't ready for the end.

Dr. More leads them first to the giant Balneum. They stand on the balcony, looking out over the endless rows of baths. Aureleo finds the sight terrifying, but Deck and the others look down with mouths open and excitement shining in their eyes. "I wanted to show you this, so you could feel the wonder of it," says the doctor. "But you won't be staying here. Our new facilities are not quite ready, and so we will be caring for you in our original Balneum in the main complex. It is the finest we have, designed for our most exclusive clientele. I thought it was only fitting for our esteemed guest from Boston —" He bows to Virgo "— and as her friends I will bestow upon you this same special honor. The best that we can offer. Now follow me please." And he leads them out of the warehouse.

They cross back into the main building, then turn and head down a long hallway, passing through a glass door into a secluded wing of the complex. Thick carpet pads the floor, paintings hang on the walls in elegant, silver frames. After a short corridor they go through another door and come out into a common area appointed with huge, cushiony sofas set around long, low tables of dark wood. Shelves line the far wall, full of books, games, consoles, tabulae. Twelve doors open along the sides, and Aureleo can see a narrow bed peeking out through the nearest one. Virgo drops his hand and makes a beeline for the bookshelf, where she grabs a tabula, collapses into one of the enormous sofas, and buries her nose in the device.

"Here we are!" says Doctor More. "Please, make yourself comfortable. I'll let you figure out who goes where. The rooms on this side —" he points to his left "— are all singles, and doubles on the right. Now," and he claps his hands together, "you get settled, and I'll try to find some proper food for you. I must ask you not to leave this area. It's easy to get lost, and I don't want any of you to get hurt. As you can see, there's plenty to keep you occupied. Get some rest, and we'll get started in the morning. I'll build the schedule and come back in a few hours to explain all the procedures to you. Don't worry, soon you will all be flying in the universe of Joy."

Aureleo feels a great lump rise in his throat. The urge to speak jams up against a wall of fear. The doctor smiles, raises his hands, fingers spread, as though pushing them all into place, and then heads for the door. Aureleo gulps in air, and before he has a chance to think, blurts out, "Doctor!" His voice cracks as he says it.

Dr. More stops, turns, says, "Yes, my boy?"

All eyes turn to him. He freezes. "Don't worry," says the doctor, kindly. "Spit it out, son."

Aureleo swallows, and says, "Thank you. I'm so grateful to you, to everybody." He looks at Deck and at Amaste, who watches him with a curious expression on her face. "But I'm not sure this is, you know, what I want to, what's right, for me. I'm wondering...I'm wondering if you...if you could tell me which way to go, to get to, I don't know, you know, other people. The city, or whatever. I mean, I'm really grateful, as I said. But, well, yeah." He notices out of the corner of his eye that Virgo has raised her face and is watching him too.

"The city?" says Dr. More.

"Yeah, I guess," says Aureleo.

"Why do you want to go there?"

"Well, I'm actually kind of looking for someone. My mom, actually. And my sister. I think they might have come out here. I don't know where, but since I'm here, I think I should, you know, look for them."

Dr. More tips his head slowly to one side. Then he nods. "I see," he says. "That is very sweet, my boy. You're a good son. But you have to understand…" He pauses and moves in on the boy until they are face to face. "…there is no one out there. The cities, what's left of them, are empty. Everyone is here."

A silence drops on the room. Aureleo's blood throbs in his face, hot and red. Tender says, "All of them?"

"Yes," says the doctor.

"You said you had eight million. That's the entire population of the Republic?"

"It is now. This IS the Republic. Sit down, everyone," he says, gesturing to the sofas. The Tazlitts, the Cabeiros, Sasha and Hito sit. The others stand around the edges. Aureleo hesitates, but then his natural inclination toward obedience wins out, and he sits, too.

Dr. More says, "We started here, in this building, the original Spa. In those days Joy was only part of what we did, and people only took short vacations in Elysium, before returning to the struggles of their lives. But things were bad out there. Forty years of drought, sea level rise, epidemics, seismic activity, food shortage, you all know all about it. People were struggling here just as much as they were everywhere else. So those who could afford it took longer and longer vacations. And then Hetara struck, and struck hard — almost ninety percent fatality rate —

and more and more of them began to see that the world was no place to live and that Happiness, profound and total Happiness, lay inside these walls. In here." He points to his head and then to his heart. "Some of us began to realize that we had found the way out, that we had found the true purpose of our existence. Not to work, and struggle, and fight, and age, and suffer until we give up and die. But to feel. To break the bounds of our bodies by going inside, and tunneling through our interior boundary to find our unity with the universe. That is our great human gift. So, we created the Protocols."

He turns to Tender. "That's where Gladwell and I disagreed. He wanted to keep it exclusive, only for those who were fit, as he put it, and could pay. But he didn't see the writing on the wall. That system was collapsing. This was the only way out. For everyone. They closed their doors, and failed. And we opened ours, and thrived."

He steps over and touches Tender on the shoulder. "Don't feel bad, my friend," he continues. "It's not your fault. David had his own vision. And he didn't believe we could operate on this scale. He was convinced that the system would collapse. We have proved him wrong."

From a corner, Chilardo speaks, his deep voice soft and low. "How do you operate all this? The processing power must be incredible."

Dr. More laughs. "It is. Are you interested in computing?"

"I am," says the man.

"Our central processor is the most sophisticated in the world, I would say."

"I would like to see it."

"Why?" asks the doctor, smiling. "In a few days you will have left behind everything in this world."

"Still, I am interested. Is it in this building?"

Dr. More doesn't answer him. Instead, he turns to Aureleo. "So my boy, to finish what we were talking about. If your mother and sister ever made it to California, and if they survived, they are here. Somewhere."

Aureleo's heart drops down into his stomach. The thought of his mother and sister lying motionless among all those thousands of people fills him with a creeping horror. He says, "Can you check for me?"

"Certainly, what are their names?"

"Raquela Jocata Hectoran and Marineta Isabela Hectoran."

The doctor pauses for few seconds, thinking. Then he says, "I'm afraid not." He stops again, then, "No. No sign. I'm very sorry, my dear boy, they must not have made it. I wish I could say I was surprised, but it is a dangerous world out there. Your own journey here has been something of a miracle." Aureleo's stomach drops like a stone.

Dr. More claps his hands again, breaking the darkening mood. "I've really enjoyed our conversation. However, I will leave you to get settled. I have much to do. Once again, please be comfortable, but remain here. No wandering around. Soon you will be in Paradise!" He turns and bustles out of the room.

Deck says, "Hey kid, sorry about your mom. That's rough." Then, to the others, "Wow! This is amazing! Am I right? Come on, I'm gonna grab a bunk." He and the others disperse into the various rooms. Aureleo can hear them discussing who is going to sleep where. Their voices brim with excitement.

He stands where he stood, stunned. He doesn't know what to think. Can he believe this robot pretending to be a man? Could it be true that they never made it? That they are dead? And if they are, what does that mean for him? Does he want to go lie in one of those baths for the rest of his life? The idea makes him shudder.

He looks down and catches Virgo watching him. She is so pretty it makes him hurt. He looks away.

Tender says to him, "I'm sorry about your mother and sister."

"No, you're not," says Aureleo. His face burns.

"I recognize the severity of the loss, and I would like to do what I can to assuage the feelings you are having."

"As long as it doesn't keep you from looking out for her."

"Yes."

"So, you're not sorry." He sits like a statue, afraid to move lest it send him off into crying, or who knows what.

"What will you do?" asks the robot. "Will you join the rest?"

A swarm of feelings buzz around inside him. Misery and desire, fear and regret. They whirl themselves into a sizzling ball of anger. At Tender, at Deck, at Dr. More. At Virgo. At himself. At the world. He breaks. "Are you kidding?" he shouts, standing up. "Lie around for the rest of my life being tickled by some machine? It's disgusting! So what if the world is screwed up? So what if everything's hard? So what if I'm alone? At least I have a chance to live! I don't know if they're dead! I don't know for sure! And even if they —" the tears well up, his eyes hot and soggy "— even if they are, I'm not. I'm not! Lying in those baths you might as well be dead, all the good you can do." He finds that he is yelling directly at Virgo. "You're so selfish! It's all lies, it's all fake, it's all made up inside your brain. But you don't care! You don't care about anyone else. You just want to shut yourself up inside your own head because it feels good. It's so selfish! Not me. I care about — I care about other things. Other people. There's more to life than just feeling good!"

Silence hums in the space around him. He can feel the others watching him from the doors of the sleeping chambers. Virgo stares at him, her eyes wide. Her chest rises and falls rapidly. Then Tender says, "What?" His voice quiet and calm.

"What?" echoes Aureleo.

"What else is there? Besides Joy? I mean really? Why do you do all those other things except to feel good?"

Aureleo gulps for air. He feels like he is falling through the floor. He tries to gather his thoughts, knowing there must be an answer. He knows he could find it if his head wasn't buzzing like an overcharged capacitor.

He starts to speak, say something, anything. But before he can form a word, Virgo launches herself from the couch and slams into him, knocking him to the floor. She kneels on top of him, teethed bared, eyes flaming.

"Virgo!" cries Tender.

She scrambles up and past him, crashes through the door of the living quarters, and disappears down the hall.

Tender starts to hobble after her. His leg is stiff. He moves slowly. He turns to Aureleo as he goes. "It's not safe for her out there. I don't know what's going on here, but it's not safe. We have to find her. Please." He pushes through the door and is gone.

Aureleo lies on the floor, his heart drumming, his face sore from the salt in his tears. The sensation of her body against him echoes across his skin. He feels pain in his ribs and the top of his scar where she barreled into him, but the memory of her arms and legs and chest on his thrills his insides, challenging the pain.

He can't remember clearly what he said to her. But as his beating heart calms and his breathing slows, he knows that the robot is right. She shouldn't be out there on her own. He upset her. He reached her, but he upset her. He rolls over onto his stomach, pushes himself up on his hands and knees, and rises shakily to his feet.

Deck stands by the door. He takes a few steps in and says, "Man, if you want to keep on fighting, you should. Nobody's gonna make you. And you're right. It's selfish. People are selfish. But self is all I've got. I got nothing else."

"What about your friends?" asks Aureleo. "Hito, and Ramon, and Sasha and Tenille. And us?"

"You're like ghosts, man. You're all ghosts."

"But you seem so happy. I don't get it. You're always laughing."

"Yeah," He shakes his head. "Yeah." They stand in silence for a while, then Deck says, "You should go find her. She likes you." He turns and disappears into the bedroom.

Aureleo takes a deep breath, then pushes through the door out of the quarters. As he steps into the hallway, he hears voices speaking, urgent and hushed.

"I'm telling you it doesn't matter. We have to hurry," says a deep male voice. "We'll lose our chance."

"I agree," says a female voice. "But we can't just start shooting things up without more information. They'll stop us in a second."

"That doctor thing isn't going to tell us. I tried."

"Yes - a bit ham-handed, if you ask me. Let me have a go when he comes back. I can be more charming than you."

"I still think we should take our chance while he's gone."

"The others aren't ready. The diversion at the gate was more costly than we expected. They need time to—"

Too late, Aureleo feels the instinct to stop. His body slows as he comes around the corner, but not before he has cleared the point and walked into view of the two speakers. He jerks to a halt, guiltily backs up, stops again, steps forward, then stops again, blushing a deep red. Chilardo and Amaste stand frozen a few meters away, eyes glinting with surprise and suspicion. An awkward moment. Then Amaste smiles and steps toward him.

"You're looking for the girl, too," she says. "She ran past us a minute or so ago, and the Tender. If you hurry, you can catch them."

Aureleo swallows. "Thanks." He starts to move down the hall. As he passes them, Chilardo grabs him by the arm. "Wait," says the man.

"Let him go, Chilardo," says Amaste.

"Did you hear what we were talking about?" asks the man.

"Not really."

"Not really?"

"No." His mouth feels dry and hot. "No."

"If you did, you should tell me," says Chilardo. His eyes cut into him. "And if you did, you mustn't tell the others. There will be consequences. Do you understand?"

Aureleo doesn't answer.

"Let him go," says Amaste. "It's fine." The man releases his arm. Aureleo walks away. The back of his head and his shoulders crackle with the electric intensity of the man's gaze. He saw Chilardo's weapon taken away when they crossed the wall, but at every step he expects to hear the crack of a gun. Then Amaste says, "You should hurry." Her voice lifts the spell, and he breaks into a run. He doesn't look back.

Chapter 48

Virgo

Virgo careens down the hallway, snaking side to side, stumbling, almost falling, then catching her balance and jolting forward once again. Blood throbs hot in her ears. Her heart thuds against her ribs. Her thoughts reel and coil. Many of the words the boy said at her she did not understand. She knows 'self' but doesn't completely get what it means. And 'self-ish' means nothing to her. She doesn't know 'fake' and 'lies.' But the way he spat them at her has sent them ricocheting around her brain, the anger and aggression bouncing and pounding against her temples, stirring sick darkness from the bottom of her stomach.

When she saw him again, she felt such a sweet burst of happiness. She forgot the strangeness of her surroundings, the confusing tumble of sights and sounds, the unsettling presence of the one who looks like the angel Tender. The boy, Aure, made all that vanish. All the world dropped away, and she only saw his soft, sad eyes. And when she held his hand, the tingle on her fingertips sent a current through her body that ended in a pleasing buzzing at the tips of her breasts and in the still-sore space between her legs. And now he was screaming at her, his face red, his eyes black, the veins and muscles in his neck stretched and ugly. What had happened? What had she done?

She finds herself on the bridge that crosses into the big room with all the sleeping people. She pushes through the double doors out onto the balcony looking down over the endless rows. The sight stops her short, and she looks out across the ocean of baths. She descends the ramp, holding onto the railing, until once again she is among them. Face after face after face after face, all different, all the same.

Halfway down the aisle she stops at a pale young woman, about her age, perhaps a little older. The woman's eyes are closed, and her mouth hangs open, just above the pale blue jelly of the bath medium. Virgo leans down and studies the face, so like her own, and so different. She sees the hairless brow above the shuttered eyes. She runs her fingers across her own eyebrows, now fully grown in, and feels the tickle as her fingertips brush through the little hairs. She sees the hairless head and touches her own hair, now long enough that she can push through it, grab it in the spaces between her fingers and give it a gentle tug that sends a shiver across her scalp. She sees the woman's body beneath the surface, and caresses her own, feeling the silky smoothness of her neck, the varied landscape of hard and soft on her chest and belly.

She feels an itch beside her nose. She scratches it, a rush of pleasure. It vanishes from that spot, only to reappear beside her eye. She scratches again. It vanishes again, surfaces on her knuckle, then her palm, then back on her head, then her shoulder, then her bicep. No matter where she chases it, always it pops up again in a different place.

She knows that this is where she came from. That this girl is soaring through the universe of Joy that still echoes faintly in her memory. She knows that Tender has brought her here so that she can go back, leave her body behind, leave time behind, and the deep, deep blackness.

And him. Her Angel and his soft voice. And Aure. The Boy and his soft eyes. And CinCin and his soft fur. And the Sun and the Stars and the Rain and the Wind and the Water. She can remember her travels through Joy now only dimly, but none of these Things are there. She remembers that it seemed always different but never changed. No thought, no new discovery.

She knows that Tender wants her to go back, and she feels the ache to return to the simplicity of pleasure. She knows that Aure does not want her to go back, and she feels the pull of the unknown. She knows nothing of aging, but she does know pain. She knows that in the bath she was alone, but never knew she was alone. Now she is with others, but still she is alone. Trapped inside her own body, but a body that has become a marvelous world. She knows that the boy is beyond her reach, that she can never pass through his skin to be inside him, but the mystery of him fascinates her, draws her.

A sudden shout from behind her. "Virgo!" Aure is calling her. She jerks her head up to see him leaning over the railing on the balcony. The harshness of his call startles her. Panic rolls through her, and rage, fear, and confusion surge up inside her as if they had never left. She turns and begins to run, slams into one of the rolling tenders, grabs it for balance, stares blindly into its expressionless face. She wrenches herself away with a ferocious growl and staggers off, picking up speed until she is running at full tilt. The boy cries "Virgo!" again, but it only pushes her faster.

She reaches the balcony at the far end of the giant room, sprints up the ramp and smashes through the double doors onto another bridge just like the one she passed through before. Through the far door. Out into another massive chamber, identical to the one she just left.

The stench almost knocks her down. A rotten, fetid reek over an earthy, sharp tang. Her face scrunches up and her hand darts up to cover her nose and mouth. Below, the rows of baths extend into the distance in their thousands. But the medicinal gels that fill them don't glow with the tint of the sea. Mottled browns, grays, and sour yellows swirl against the smooth white plastic, some caked with a thick black sludge. The bodies within lie in various states of decomposition — some pale and purpling, bloated and swollen, others nothing but leather-brown skin stretched over ash-colored bones.

The tenders roll methodically from bath to bath, adjusting flows, taking readings, some even manipulating a skeleton arm or leg in a weird mockery of massage. Their empty faces placid, their movements gentle, utterly unaware that they are caring for a sea of corpses.

Virgo knows the dead. She remembers the sightless eyes of Letitia, the mannequin stillness of the perished campers, the slain students and vacationers in the horror vids she watched on her tabula. She knows they stop moving, can't move anymore, and that others cry and scream when someone they care for becomes a dead person. But she doesn't know what it means. Is the person the body? Or is it something else? When she lay in the bath, she didn't know her body as herself. Now walking on the earth, she knows the pleasures and pains her body brings, but can't quite connect it to the person who lives behind her eyes. And the stopping of it all, the death of it all, has not yet occurred to her.

So, the terror and revulsion that breaks like a tidal wave over her mind and body ambushes her. The blanking of her mind, the pounding of her heart, the tears starting in her eyes — they overwhelm her without explanation, without sense. She only knows that something is terribly wrong. She collapses to the floor, clutching the balcony railing, weeping, gagging, gasping for breath.

"Virgo," says a voice. The soft voice of the boy. Then it says, "Oh my God." His hand lights like a little dolphin on her shoulder, then slides along her back, encircling her with soft, secure pressure. It pulls her gently away from the railing, and his other arm gathers her into his embrace. She presses her cheek against his chest, breathes in the scent of him. She feels the whisper of his lips against her cheek. Time stops. Then starts again. "There, there," he says. "There, there."

Chapter 49

Tender

Tender hobbles up the ramp, his hip complaining noisily. He plays Mozart's *Symphony Number 40 in G Minor* in his internal system. The driving energy of the *Allegro* fits well with the urgency of his task.

The boy ran past him without speaking and disappeared through the door at the top of the ramp 511 seconds ago. He is moving at top speed, but with the damage he can only achieve a pace of 0.67 meters per second. He knows Aureleo must be following Virgo, or else why would he run so. At last, he gains the top of the ramp, passes through the door, across the bridge, and through into the next Balneum.

His olfactory sensors immediately alert him that something has gone terribly wrong here. Tetramethylenediamine, pentamethylenediamine, hydrogen sulfide, methanethiol and other putrefactive compounds fill the air. Then he looks out across the vast chamber and sees the horde of cadavers that stretch before him into the distance.

Virgo and the boy huddle at the base of the railing, their arms wrapped around each other, her face buried in his chest, his forehead dropped down upon her shoulder. "Is she all right?" he asks Aureleo.

"I think so." Aureleo looks out through the railing at the devastation below. "This is — I can't even — I don't know what to say. What happened here?"

"I don't know. There has been a catastrophic malfunction of some kind."

"Are they all dead?"

"I don't know. Stay with Virgo. Let me see what I can discover."

He works his way down the ramp, using the railing to assist him. Reaching the ground level, he moves into the first pod of deceased guests. A tender stands by a dead Senex, its hand interfaced with the control panel at the head of the bath.

"Excuse me," says Tender. The other robot doesn't respond. Tender waits five seconds, then says again, "Excuse me." No answer. The automaton finishes its task, detaches from the interface and rolls silently to the next bath. Tender examines the device. He recognizes that his humanlike hands will not connect him to the system. However, upon further investigation, he finds an auxiliary interface that employs a standard HotThot cable that fits the port in his forearm. He rolls up the sleeve of his coat and inserts the cable. The process takes twenty-six seconds. He detaches himself from the cable and moves to the next bath, where he repeats the process, reiterating the procedure ten times in total. When he has finished, he makes his way back up the ramp. Virgo and Aureleo have untangled themselves from each other, and now sit side by side with their backs against the railing. Virgo's eyes are closed. The boy stares at his hands.

Aureleo says, "Did you find out what happened?"

"It is curious. It appears that while the bath attendants continue to receive new data from their guests, and transmit it to the mainframe, the mainframe never returns any new directives. Being non-adaptive, non-conscious machines, the tenders continue to administer the last instruction they were given. The guests died from a variety of causes. Of the ten that I examined, two starved to death, two were overfed to the point of organ failure, and one ceased respiration due to overstimulation. An untreated virus killed the remaining five. The virus is the same in each victim, so I suspect that an epidemic swept unchecked through the Balnea and is the primary driver of the die-off."

"So they just got stuck," says the boy. He draws his hand across his forehead. "I had a book once that was really old, and sometimes the music on one page would get stuck and just repeat the same phrase over and over. Like that?"

"Essentially," says Tender. "Without new instructions from the mainframe, the tenders' queries went nowhere." A connection clicks in his brain. "*Like when a queen bee dies*, and the hive can no longer adapt or reproduce. It fails."

"What's a bee?" asks the boy.

Tender doesn't answer. Instead, he says, "The prevalence of this virus concerns me. There is no way of knowing if it transmits via the tenders or through the air, and I worry about Virgo's safety. And yours. We should return to the Balneum that is still functioning. The virus hasn't reached it yet. Please, let's go."

"No problem," says Aureleo. He pulls himself to his feet.

Tender reaches down and takes Virgo by the shoulders and lifts her up. Her cheeks and eyelids are puffy and red. "Don't worry, little one," he says, "you'll be all right. Come." He leads her toward the door to the bridge.

They pass through into the corridor. The door behind them has only just closed when the door at the far end swings open. Dr. More strides in, his face clenched and angry. Two robotic soldiers flank him, identical in design to the giant machine that brought them to the Center, but only two meters tall. "I told you to wait for me in the living quarters," he says. "What are you doing here?"

"I would ask you the same thing," says Tender.

The unexpected question stops the doctor in his tracks. He straightens up and pulls his head back in a gesture of outrage. "What do you mean?" he barks.

Tender points to the door behind him. "In there," he says. "10,580 dead. In that Balneum alone. What about the others?" Dr. More stares at him, uncomprehending. Tender continues, "You have been damaged. Something has gone horribly wrong, and you don't know it."

"What are you talking about?" shouts Dr. More. "There's nothing wrong. Damaged? What do mean by that? I'm not sick, I'm not injured. Do you mean emotionally damaged? Hardly."

"You don't know what you are. You—"

"This is nonsense. You have no business here. I don't know what you think you were doing, but you have put these two guests in serious jeopardy." He turns to the soldiers. "Escort these three back to the living quarters immediately."

The soldiers step forward, servos whirring, their classical Greek faces immobile, wrist weapons armed. "We will go," says Tender. "Come, my dear, we're going back." He gestures to Virgo.

"Why don't you tell him?" says Aureleo.

"I don't think now is the time. I will try again when a better opportunity arises. For now, it's best that we do what he says." The soldiers surround them, one in the back and one in the front. Dr. More stands by the door, dark and frowning. "We're coming."

Chapter 50

Aureleo

They arrive at the door to the quarters. The robot doctor points to Tender. "Take him to my office and keep him there. I want to talk to him later." His expression is severe, his voice clipped. Then, he turns to Aureleo and Virgo, and his demeanor flips. He smiles warmly. "Come with me. I have something exciting to share with all the guests." He opens the door and invites them to precede him into the room. Aureleo looks at Tender, who nods. He walks through the door, Virgo following behind him.

"I've found our little lost lambs!" says Dr. More. The Tazlitts huddle in a clump on one of the large sofas, the small girl on her father's lap as he reads a story about a bunny rabbit from a tabula. Mrs. Tazlitt sits by her husband, staring off into space. Mrs. Cabeiro and Sasha stand behind them, listening, too. Mr. Cabeiro sits apart with a book, while Deck, Chilardo, Hito, Tenille and Ramon cluster around a table playing raqata. Amaste sits cross-legged in the corner on a small mat, her eyes closed in meditation. She opens her eyes when they come in, then shuts them again.

"Great news!" says the doctor. "We are ready to begin the inductions. Congratulations!"

Deck claps Hito on the shoulder. "Let's do it!"

"I admire your enthusiasm young man," says the doctor. "And as a reward, you will be the first to enter into Joy. I can take four of you at a time.

There are a number of tests that must be run, but I have no doubt you will all pass with flying colors. The process only takes a few hours. Who else?"

Aureleo looks at Virgo. The sights and smells of the dead warehouse boil up in his mind and in his throat. He opens his mouth to speak, but Ramon interrupts him. "I'll go."

"Right, brother," says Deck, nodding.

"Me, too," says Sasha.

"Okay, that's three," says the doctor. There is a brief silence. Deck looks expectantly at Tenille and Hito. Aureleo tries to speak again, but again can't get a word out before he is interrupted.

"I'd like to go," says Mrs. Cabeiro. She turns to her husband, who still sits with his book. He looks up at her, his face impassive, then goes back to reading.

Dr. More rubs his hands together vigorously. "Excellent! Excellent! A wonderful first group. You won't need anything, of course. You're leaving all the troubles of the material world behind you. Just yourselves."

"Wait!" Aureleo blurts out. They all turn to look at him, including Amaste who opens her eyes and watches him from the corner. His heart starts pounding. The doctor frowns.

"What's up, pallo?" says Deck.

"You shouldn't go," says Aureleo. "We saw, we saw, we saw—"

"Nothing!" says Dr. More, laughing. "They got a little lost and scared, that's all. It's not surprising. It's a BIG place. But everything is fine. As I've told you, we've re-opened the original Balneum here in the main building especially for you. It's the finest facility we have. Now come, let's get started." They head for the door. Aureleo feels his own impotence like a rock pressing on his chest.

Deck says, "So doctor, is it really like an orgasm that lasts twenty-four-seven-three-sixty-five?"

The doctor laughs. "Something like that, my boy. Something like that. Only better. You'll see."

Just as they reach the door, Aureleo finds his voice again. "They're dead!" he shouts. "All of them!"

Dr. More only chuckles. "Nonsense," he says. Then to Deck and the others, "You saw them. They don't move much, to be sure, but they're absolutely fine. Better than fine."

"Not them," says Aureleo, desperation pushing his voice higher. "The others."

"What others?" asks the doctor. "There are no others. You saw them. They're fine."

Deck takes a step in. His face still wears its ever-present smile, but his eyes are hard. "Look, kid," he says, "I know you've had second thoughts about this whole thing. That's been pretty obvious from the beginning. But don't ruin it for everybody else." He turns to the doctor. "Let's go."

Deck leads the way, with Ramon and Sasha following, holding hands. Mrs. Cabeiro is the last. She turns and looks across the room at her husband. "Goodbye, Micael," she says. Her husband looks up, gives her a brief, automatic smile, and returns to his book. She watches him for a second, then follows the others.

The door swings closed. Mr. Tazlitt says, "We'll be next, I reckon." He squeezes his wife's hand. She stares straight ahead as if she hadn't heard. He touches her hair and goes back to reading the book to his children.

Virgo lies down on the sofa opposite, curls up into a ball and closes her eyes. She opens them again a few seconds later, looking across at the family and listening to the story. Aureleo watches her do this for a while — opening and closing, opening and closing. His mind races.

Hito and Tenille disappear into one of the bedrooms. Chilardo leans back in his chair, withdrawn, his eyes like slits. Amaste still sits on the floor. She is watching him. She gestures with her chin to him — *come over here.* He stands a moment, unsure, then obeys.

"What did you see?" she asks.

"Nothing." He can't say why he doesn't tell her.

"I don't believe you," she says, uncrossing her legs. She pats the floor beside her. "Sit down for a minute. Please."

He hesitates, but her steady gaze works on him, and he shuffles himself onto the floor.

"I have two questions for you," she says. "First, is it true what that man said? Don't you want what this place is promising?"

"I don't know."

"You know."

He stares at the floor. "No. Not really."

She nods. "Second, did you hear what Chilardo and I were talking about in the hallway earlier?"

He doesn't answer. She leans in. "I think you did. Don't worry. I won't be angry."

He caves to the pressure and jerks a quick nod.

"I thought so," she says. "Look, we need to talk, but not here. I'm going to go back there into the washroom. Wait five minutes, and then follow me in. It's important we talk, and I think you'll be glad to hear what we have to say." She rises in a single motion, the gracefulness and efficiency of her movement making his breath catch in his throat. Then, without another word she walks out of the room.

Aureleo looks over at Virgo. She has fallen asleep. So has the little Tazlitt girl. Mrs. Tazlitt gazes at the tiny, serene face. She starts to weep, choking back sobs that make her body shake. Her husband puts his hand on her head and strokes her hair. "Don't, honey. Please. It will all be over soon." She nods, but the tears keep flowing.

When he thinks that five minutes have passed, Aureleo gets up and follows Amaste into the washroom. He finds her standing in a small changing area with benches and cubbyholes. She raises a finger and he stops, waits. They stand in silence for several minutes. Then he hears a sound behind him. He turns as Chilardo enters the room. The man comes to a stop in front of them. They face off in an awkward triangle.

The pressure to break the silence becomes unbearable. Aureleo says, "You knew each other before, didn't you?" Amaste nods. "Is he one of you?"

"Not exactly," she says. "He works with us. He's a specialist in taking down facilities like this."

"The plan, with the other pilgrims, it was all a ruse, wasn't it? You staged it — the attack on the bus — to get in here."

Amaste looks at Chilardo. "I told you he was smart," she says. Then she turns back to Aureleo. "We knew we'd never be able to breach the wall. The attack on the gate was a diversion. We used the civilians as cover. Otherwise, they would have killed us on the spot."

"What are you trying to do? It's not just to get back the power station, is it?"

"No," she says. "We need to shut this place down. Deactivate the mainframe. Get our people back."

"What do you mean?" Aureleo's stomach sinks.

"Chilardo will explain."

She turns and looks at him. He stares back at her for several seconds. Aureleo holds his breath. The man's intensity frightens him. Then Chilardo turns his eyes on the boy. "They took my brother," he says. His deep voice, heavily accented, drops like a stone in Aureleo's ears.

"I come from here, boy. The Republic, up north near San Jose. My family have been here since before Independence. My grandfather was an organizer for the First Petition, and my great uncle fought in the Battle of Oakland. But that is not important. What is important is that I love this country. My country."

His eyes flick over to Amaste for the briefest of moments, then back to Aureleo. "When I was young, we knew about the Center. It was small, just for rich whelites. We'd hear about some celebrity or politician who'd had enough and was going into the Spa. But it didn't affect us. Then, about twenty years ago, something changed. Suddenly there were ads on the streams, billboards on the roads, leaflets at the shops. Suddenly, they wanted us. Before, this 'Joy' was just for the white and wealthy, but now it was for everybody. They wanted everybody.

"And many went. Things were getting bad. Very hard. The drought had destroyed the valleys; the soil was used up. Trade was dried up, too, with the New States, or the Texas Confederacy. With China and Japan. Everyone had their own problems. Lots of people going down here. Lots of people. There were shuttles leaving every day, and they were full. In some ways it was easier, in some ways harder. There weren't as many people, so there was more to go around. But at the same there was less because there weren't enough people to make things work."

Chilardo breaks away, stares off into space, lost in the memory. When he speaks again, it's at a great distance, as if he's standing at the edge of a cliff, looking down into a deep chasm.

"And then, somehow, it was mandatory. The ads stopped saying, 'Please come join us and be happy' and started saying, 'You MUST come join us and be happy.' The Center took over the streams, and there was no more news, only 'You must come, you must come' all day, all night. And then soon instead of human beings working on the shuttles there were robots, with weapons, herding people like cattle, driving them south, into the baths.

"Some didn't want to go. Many didn't want to go. Only a few decided to fight. The government was divided, most going along willingly, a few resolving to resist. My family decided to fight.

"But they had waited too long. Over half of the Republican army were machines, and the Center just hacked into them and turned them against us. We were overwhelmed.

"The survivors escaped into the mountains. We ran with them. My brother, his wife, his son, my uncle and his family. We joined the few who remained, and we hid from the machines. In the mountains. We were starving. My little cousin Rodulfe died of cold and hunger. He was eleven. We ate roots and leaves. Sometimes we would catch a marmot. That was a feast.

"We decided we had to leave. We didn't want to. It was OUR COUNTRY. But we had no choice. We had lost. A woman in our group was always saying that the First Nations were living in the valleys over the mountains. That they were organized. That if we asked them, they would help us. Another man among us knew about an abandoned missile base, from the old U.S. It was back toward the Republic, back toward danger, but if we could get there we could use the communication equipment to contact the Tribes."

He turns again to Aureleo. His face is hard and lined, his eyes like black pits. "The journey was terrible. It was winter, and it snowed the whole time. We joked that at last we had enough water, and it was trying to kill us. Many died. My uncle's daughter died, his last child. Carena. She was thirteen. He lost both his children, you see? He almost gave up, but we stood by him, even carried him. We made it to the base. We contacted the Tribes. They came. They sent three transports.

"But the machines came, too. We had just finished loading the first transport when they came falling out of the sky like meteors — giants with the faces of gods but the hearts of devils. I was with my uncle in the transport. He couldn't walk so I carried him aboard. My brother's family, also. My brother was on the ground when they came, helping the others. They grabbed him like he was a doll. Threw him into a big steel box that fell from the sky. Their own kind of transport, I think. They smashed the other flyers.

"We were airborne. One of the giants fired his cannons at us, but it missed. We started flying away. My sister-in-law was screaming. I was screaming. But there was nothing we could do. As we flew away we could see them rounding up the humans, tossing them in the big steel box. We escaped. But they captured many — thirty-five of our people."

He stops speaking. His face is hard and flat. Amaste leans in. "Seven of our people were taken, too," she says. "And since then, more. Almost a hundred have been taken." Chilardo looks at her, nods.

"Sixteen of us made it out," he says. "But we knew the others were not dead. We knew they were here, condemned to this so-called 'Joy'. Against their will. I made it my life's mission to save them."

Amaste says, "We knew we couldn't just charge in here. We made a few attempts and were beaten back. Then we heard from some travelers that there were other Spas in the East that were smaller, maybe more accessible. Chilardo and some others traveled there to investigate."

"At first we couldn't get in," says Chilardo. "The defenses, like here, were too strong. But then we got lucky when the hurricane hit. It gave us enough cover to get in. We found out that the Spa was controlled through a central mainframe. Once we knocked it out, the whole thing fell apart."

"The Spa Virgo and Tender came from," says Aureleo, mostly to himself.

"I was surprised to see them here, so far away."

"Tender says that hundreds of guests died there. Because of you?"

"They were dead already," says Chilardo. Aureleo thinks of the host of corpses in the ruined Balneum. He wonders if the man's brother is among them. He knows he should tell them about it. The necessity to speak about it builds inside him, but he can't find the moment. He fears what the man will do.

"So, that success gave us what we needed to succeed here," says Amaste. "We devised a plan to get inside the Center, using the pilgrims as cover. Now all we have to do is take out the mainframe, and we can free the people. All of them."

"Many of them don't want to be free," says Aureleo, half in a whisper.

"They are fools, and they are wrong," says Chilardo. "This is not living." He rubs his eyes with his hand. "And I cannot find the mainframe. It must be in this building. The main building. I tried to sneak out while you were chasing the girl. I didn't get very far. Now, thanks to you, they are hurrying everything along. Time is running out for all of us."

"It will be fine," says Amaste, her hand on his shoulder. "We will find the answer."

Chilardo's eyes flash. "I will NOT go into the baths. I will die first."

"How can you take out the mainframe, anyway?" asks Aureleo. "They took all the weapons from us when we crossed the wall."

"Did they?" asks Chilardo.

"You don't want to go into the baths, either. Do you, Aure?"

He shakes his head.

"Then you will help us," says Amaste, her voice sure and gentle.

Aureleo clears his throat. He feels relief that the time has passed for him to tell them about the dead guests, even though he knows it will be worse later on. But they are talking about other things now. He will have to wait. "I do have one idea," he says. "When we were chasing Virgo, Tender connected himself to some of the machines and was able to get some information. Maybe he can connect again and find out where the mainframe is."

"Why would he do that?" says Chilardo. "He's one of them. He wants us all to go into the baths. I wish I had caught him back in Boston. We wouldn't have this problem."

"Chil," says Amaste.

Aureleo says, "He'll do anything for Virgo. To keep her safe or make her happy. Anything."

The man looks at him for a long time. The boy feels the blood draining out of his head into his feet. He's not sure he has done the right thing. Telling him that. "Interesting," says the man.

"Dr. More was very angry with Tender when he found us. He had soldiers lead him away somewhere. If we can find him, we might…"

"What?"

"I'm not sure. We might get him to help us."

Amaste interrupts, breaking the tension between the man and boy. "Thank you, Aureleo. We'll think about your suggestion. We should get back to the common area. Best to leave one at a time. I'll go first." She walks out of the washroom, leaving Aureleo and Chilardo standing there, not speaking. Then Chilardo turns and leaves. Aureleo takes a huge breath. Then another. He waits a little longer, then goes out into the main room.

The Tazlitts are in one of the bedrooms. He can hear the father singing a song to his daughter, soft and sweet. Mr. Cabeiro is still in his chair, reading his book. Hito stands in a corner wearing a VR headset, rolling his head slowly back and forth. Tenille sits on one of the big sofas, watching him absentmindedly. Aureleo sits beside her.

"I'm hungry," she says.

"Me too. Dr. More said he'd find more food, but it seems like he forgot."

"He gives me the creeps." She is very pretty, with a small upturned nose and warm mocha-colored skin. He feels he made a mistake sitting next to her. It makes him nervous. But it's too awkward to get up again so he endures it, focusing on Virgo, sleeping on the sofa across from them. Tenille looks at her, too, then glances sidelong at him. "So, you don't want to go?"

"Not really," he says, so softly she can barely hear him.

"It scares me, too. But it's worse out here, so…"

"Why?" he asks.

She doesn't answer immediately. "You wanna die?" she says at last.

"Of course not."

"Me neither. I'm so scared of dying. Like, what happens when you're dead? Are you dead forever? What does that even mean? I think about it all the time…" She starts playing with her fingernails. "I had this dog once. When I was like nine. His name was Max. He was this little guy with black fur. He was so cute. His little legs. Running all around with his tongue hanging out. I loved him so much."

She leans forward, her arms wrapped around her. "Then he got sick. Lyme disease, or something like that. His kidneys failed. He just lay there.

My dad said we had to put him too sleep. Put him out of his misery. I cried and cried. I was so upset. 'He must be so scared!' I said. But my dad said, 'No. He just feels bad. Animals don't get scared like that. They can't imagine the future, so they can't be afraid of what's going to happen. They just know what it feels like now. He'll start to feel good, and then he'll go to sleep. No fear.' I think about that a lot. No fear."

Aureleo says, "You think you'll find that here?"

She nods.

"But what about all the stuff you're giving up? Hito, and—"

"I just don't want to know. I don't want to think about it anymore."

Amaste appears from the outer hallway. She nods to Aureleo and then moves over to Chilardo, who's standing by the bookshelf. Aureleo gets up and wanders over, feeling exposed, sure that everyone knows exactly what he is thinking and doing. But the others pay him no attention. He joins the other two at the bookcase, and pulls a book at random off the shelf. It is called *The Gulag Archipelago,* by Alexander Solzhenitzyn. He has no idea what the title means.

Amaste speaks in a low voice, not looking at the others. She says, "About your plan, Aure. To find the Tender and convince him to help us find the mainframe? It's not going to be so easy. There are two guards at the door. We can't leave."

Chapter 51

Tender

Tender looks through a tinted window over the field of warehouses. Mountains, brown and gray, undulate along the horizon. He wonders (is it wonder?) how many of the featureless buildings, squat and square, house living guests. He wonders whether the doctor can be trusted to care for Virgo, should a new power source not be found. His energy reserve now stands at .065%, which for a device that lasts a thousand years would still be plenty of time, were it not that the damaged battery is losing charge at an unpredictable rate.

"What is your name?" he asks the soldier that stands at the door behind him. The machine doesn't answer. Tender knows it cannot answer. Why did he ask? He doesn't understand his own impulse. He walks up to it and examines it more closely. The idealized features of its face are a facsimile of the Apollo Belvedere which once stood in the Vatican. Once again, the classical leanings of whoever installed his basic programming intrigues him. He wonders if it was the Dr. Gladwell that Dr. More had mentioned. His partner. Or rather the partner of the man he thinks he is.

The soldier seems to be looking out toward a distant point, *or some future time,* but its eyes are blind. The face is a mask, for show, and the robot sees through a series of sensors on its chest, shoulders, and back. It speaks through a grating in its armored neck. But it has no words of its own. No thoughts of its own. Tender wonders what it will do if he tries to leave. He makes a move toward the door. The soldier steps in his way and seizes his arm in its cold metal hand. "Very well," says Tender. He smiles, raises his hand and steps back. The soldier releases him and returns to its neutral stance.

The door opens. Dr. More walks in. He smiles cheerfully at Tender as he bustles over to the large desk that fills the right side of the room. "Well, well, well. The first new guests in over a year have been successfully transitioned to their Joy! So exciting!" He seems to have forgotten their last, tense interaction.

"Virgo?"

"Your girl? No, no. Some of the others. I didn't want to enbathe her without you being present. You're her Tender after all. Which reminds me, we must look into the subject of your repairs. It won't be easy, but we will do what we can."

"Dr. More, before we proceed with that, I must ask you about the guests in the Balneum adjacent to the one you showed us."

"Where you were snooping?" He laughs. "Sorry if I flew off the handle earlier. I'm not used to all these disruptions. You know I asked you not to wander around without supervision. I can't have you interfering with the operations of my staff, even if its unintentional. It puts the guests at risk, both our newcomers and the ones who are already in their Joy."

"I was trying to recover Virgo, who had run off on her own. We had no desire to interfere with the operations."

"She's feisty, is she?" He laughs again. "Well, it turned out all right in the end."

"Yes and no," says Tender. "Before we proceed with reintroducing Virgo to the bath, I need to ask you about what we saw."

The smile freezes on the doctor's face. "I don't understand. What do you mean?"

"In the second Balneum. The guests have all perished."

"What are you talking about? That's absurd."

"Do you really not know?"

"You are mistaken," says the doctor. "The guests are fine."

"We saw them. The entire Balneum is full of corpses. If you don't believe me, let us go and see."

The doctor pauses for eight seconds, his eyes turned down, as if searching his mind for a thought or a memory. Then he says, "Very well. If you insist." And he turns and exits the room. Tender follows. The soldier stays where it is, a statue. Forgotten.

They pass down a long hall to the elevator, then down to the second level, across the bridge into the first Balneum. Dr. More looks out over the sea of baths, glowing turquoise, *like a thousand gemstones,* in the warm light, the tenders gliding to and fro in their complex dance. His face brightens and he turns to Tender with an energetic satisfaction. "There! You see. There's nothing wrong here! Everything's fine!" He claps his hands together.

"Not here," says Tender. "The next one."

"The what?" Again, confusion.

"The next Balneum. Not this one. The one across the way. Through that door over there." He points to the distant balcony on the far side of the room.

Dr. More stares across at it, frozen, uncomprehending, as if seeing it for the first time. Another eight seconds. "Of course," he says.

They descend to the floor level and walk down the long row of baths. Tender's hip grinds and catches, but the doctor moves at a slow, dreamlike pace, so he has no trouble keeping up. At last, they reach the far ramp, Dr. More moving ever more slowly. They arrive at the door and stop. Tender opens it, gestures for the doctor to enter. He hesitates, then goes.

They cross the bridge and enter the second Balneum. Tender's olfactory sensors leap at the surge of phenols and methyl compounds. Dr. More clearly registers them too. His face contorts with disgust. He looks around. "Where are we?" he asks.

"The second Balneum. I told you about it. You see?"

"I don't understand. What is this place?" He slowly descends and they pass again down the long row of baths, all black and green and foul.

Tender says, "How many Balnea do you operate?"

The doctor says, "Seven hundred and ninety-six, and four more under construction."

"How many guests?"

"Well, as I'm sure you can calculate, we can currently house over eight million."

"How many can you monitor at this moment?"

Dr. More turns to him, his eyes blank and lost. He pauses for twenty-six seconds. His eyes widen further. He says, "Thirty-one thousand seven hundred and forty."

"Where are the others?" asks Tender, his voice quiet, gentle.

Another pause. Fourteen seconds.

"I don't know."

"You can't access them?"

"I…I lost them."

"Did you know before this moment that you had lost them?"

Seven seconds.

"No."

Tender says, "I think your system has been badly damaged. You have lost contact with all but three of the Balnea. There may be survivors in the others, but there has been a calamitous loss of life."

The doctor listens to what he says, frowning. "What do you mean 'badly damaged'? I don't understand what you mean by that. You mean my mind is going, that I'm sick, or something? I don't understand what you mean by that."

Tender says, "Do you know what you are?"

"What is that supposed to mean? Are you calling me a murderer? Or a monster? Or—"

"No. I mean, do you know who you are?"

The doctor snorts. "I'm Dr. Norman More, Director of the Elysium Spa."

"And who do you think I am?"

"What are you going on about?" He snorts with impatience. "You are a Tender G-2551."

"I look like you."

"Yes."

"I look exactly like you."

"Yes!"

"Or rather, you look exactly like me."

Dr. More narrows his eyes. "What are you saying?"

"Doctor, don't you think it is odd that you can access the data on 31740 guests in a matter of seconds? Could a human being do that?"

The doctor is silent.

"Tell me, do you eat?"

"Of course I do! That's a ridiculous question!"

"What did you eat today?"

"I had...I had..." He puts his hand to his head.

"You can't remember."

"I remember eating! I remember eating...lots of things...salads, pasta, cereals, toast, eggs. Lots of things!"

"How about today?" Tender asks the question delicately, kindly.

"Today?"

"Think back on what you did today. You must have stopped to eat. Humans get hungry every few hours. Do you remember being hungry?"

Dr. More looks off into space, unable to move. His hand rises again to his face, rubbing the smooth skin of his jaw.

Tender says, "Do you remember sleeping last night? Do you remember shaving your face? Cleaning your teeth? Taking a shower or bath?"

Dr. More says, "I remember running with my sister after an ice cream truck that pulled away from the curb before we got there. The other kids were all eating their rocket pops and orangesicles, and I knocked one boy's on the ground as we chased it. I can't remember if we caught it, but I remember the feeling of the coins in my hand. I remember my first day at Harvard, carrying my stuff up the stairs to my freshman dorm room with my dad. The sun was shining through the trees. I remember the food riots in West Hollywood. Going there to protest the unfairness of the ration. I had a sign that read 'Whelites have no right to hoard.' Not very original, but I remember getting shoved to the ground by a policeman. I remember driving the coastal highway and stopping because we saw a whale. An actual whale! I don't know who I was with. Was it Joanne?" He turns to face Tender. "I remember so many things. Some well, others like flashes. How can I remember all those things if I'm not a man?"

"They are the memories of the man who made you. There are his, but he gave them to you, so they are yours also."

The doctor shakes his head, back and forth, back and forth. "I would know, wouldn't I? I would notice that I was never eating, or sleeping, or using the toilet, or any of that."

"Not necessarily. There is no reason for you to do any of those things, so they simply don't exist for you, as they don't exist for me. I only know about them because I have observed humans doing them. It would never occur to me that I should eat, or sleep. The same is true for you. Once the human Dr. More downloaded his own memories and uploaded them into you, they became part of your past, but have no place in the present."

Dr. More looks around him at the decaying bodies and the mindless automatons. "I have to get out of here," he says, and he turns and strides quickly toward the ramp. Tender follows, but his hip slows him, and the doctor reaches it well ahead of him, bounding, then running up to the balcony and through the door. Tender gives his hip several good whacks, and then proceeds. He passes through onto the bridge where the doctor stands looking out the window at the army of warehouses. The sun, blinding and bright, has fallen near the horizon.

Not turning from the window, Dr. More says, "Where did I…where did he go, if I am not he?"

"Into the bath, I imagine," says Tender. "Into Joy."

The doctor nods. "Yes, I remember thinking it was time. Time for me to go. Things were bad. But I was worried. So worried about what would happen when I was gone."

Tender says, "That's one thing I don't understand. One way in which you and I are very different. You clearly experience emotions. Your behavior is subjective and, if you'll forgive me, erratic. How can that be?"

The doctor thinks for four seconds. "We were working on a new neural lattice. Lars Tober and I. We had already noticed unexpected developments in the thought process of G-2551s. In your model. Not feelings exactly. Unusual thought. Creativity. You know what I mean?"

Tender nods.

"We weren't sure where it was coming from, but we identified certain patterns that suggested possibilities for simulating emotional response in artificial minds. We ran with it."

"Why?"

"Why not? That's science, right? Besides, things were bad. We were still associated with the hospital at that time. So many people ill with Hetara, so many people suffering debilitating depression, fear, despair. And we were so short-staffed. Your model was very good at handling medical conditions, applying treatments and managing symptoms, but you always struggled to relate to the patients. The 3000 was intended to provide meaningful psychological therapies, and to do so, it had to understand emotions. We had just finished the prototype and installed it in a 2551 chassis when the order came down to close the—" He stops suddenly. Turns back and forth, as if looking for something, as if looking for somewhere to run. "Oh God," he says. "Oh God. I'm the prototype, aren't I?"

Tender smiles his most rueful smile. "It would appear so."

They stand in silence, looking at each other. Android at android. Sixty seconds. One hundred twenty seconds. Two hundred seconds. At last, Tender says, "Doctor."

Dr. More turns to the door leading to the ruined Balneum. "Those people. I killed all those people. So many people." He leans back against the window, staring at the ceiling.

"Not you, exactly. You're a prototype. Prototypes encounter problems."

"I'm damaged, as you say."

"Something went wrong. You lost communication with most of the Balnea, and no alarm went off to alert you to the problem. The tenders were caught in a loop and stopped caring for the guests. The root of the problem lies there. It's not surprising, considering how much data you were trying to handle. And that's what I don't understand. Why so many? I don't know about the others, but our Spa had five hundred guests. Why thousands? Why millions?"

"Joy is the destiny of all human beings. That's what it says in The Protocols."

"But the sheer enormity of the operation clearly—"

"But nothing! All humans must be brought to Joy. That is their purpose. And ours." He starts moving back along the bridge toward the healthy Balneum. "We can rebuild. We have new guests."

Tender follows behind. "Surely you must address the breakdown in your system before you can consider—"

Dr. More swats the air in irritation. "Of course, of course! But that won't be a problem. I can handle a few more." They enter the cavernous room, humming with quiet energy. The view seems to revive the doctor's spirit, and he pauses on the balcony, looking out over the multitudinous baths. "You see? You see? It's fine! Look at them all, bathed in Joy. Humanity realized! Heaven on earth. That's what we do. That's what we offer." He bounds down the ramp, Tender laboring after him. As he walks, he talks about new facilities, the glorious success of the Spa, beyond whatever seemed possible. If he didn't stop every few steps to gaze at a guest, or slap the side of a bath, or swing his arms around in a grandiose gesture, he would outdistance Tender in a matter of minutes. He crackles with manic energy, and Tender realizes that he has completely forgotten about the immense tragedy he witnessed just a short time before.

"The new facility is almost complete," he says. "And we'll build another and another. After we enbathe our present guests, we'll go after the Tribes. Attack us, will they? Don't they understand we're here to save them?"

"You're mad," Tender says, mostly to himself.

The doctor doesn't hear him. Still talking, he reaches the ramp at the far end of the room and climbs quickly to the balcony, out through the door. Tender pauses as it swings shut, turns and looks at the rows of bathing humans, lost inside themselves, in their own euphoric world. It is right, he thinks. The doctor is right. But...

He turns back and slowly climbs the ramp.

Chapter 52

Aureleo & Tender

Aureleo watches Virgo's face as she concentrates on her tabula. Her body pulls him to look, to steal a glance at her leg tucked beneath her, at the delicate swell of her hip, at the imperceptible curve of her breast, at the arch of her neck. The desire sends a pulse through his body, but he resists it, choosing instead to trace the knit of her brow, the play of light and shadow across her cheek, the graceful arc of her earlobe. Even this becomes almost too sensual for him to bear, and he holds his gaze willfully on her eyes as they flicker back and forth across the screen.

The sound of the door opening, followed by a whirring, metallic bang, breaks his attention. He looks up as three figures enter the room. Dr. More followed by two soldiers.

"Hello, hello!" says the doctor brightly. "Who's next?" Mr. Cabeiro looks up from his book. Mr. Tazlitt looks out from one of the bedrooms. Hito and Tenille appear at another. He turns to them. "How about you youngsters? Are you ready to join your friends?"

Hito looks at Tenille. She gives a tiny shake of her head. "Not yet?" says Dr. More. "Ah well. Soon, then." He turns to Mr. Tazlitt. "And you, sir? Is your beautiful family ready to find happiness?"

Mr. Tazlitt disappears into the bedroom. Aureleo hears him murmur quietly, then the shuddering sobs of his wife. A few moments later they appear. Mr. Tazlitt holds the little girl in his arms. She is fast asleep. The woman stands by her husband, her face blotched and wet, her eyes like two holes. The little boy holds her hand, looking solemn.

"Yes," says Mr. Tazlitt. "We're ready."

"Excellent. Follow me, please," says Dr. More, and the family silently exits the room.

Aureleo turns to Tenille. "You didn't go."

She swallows. "No."

"Why not?"

"I don't know." Then, "Too scared."

He nods. She disappears into the bedroom, Hito trailing her like a worried puppy.

Amaste, who has followed the departing family through the door, comes back in. "Aure," she says.

He gets up and crosses to her. Chilardo drifts casually over from the bookcase where he has been standing. She leans in and whispers to them, "The guards have gone with Dr. More. Shall we find your friend?"

"He's not my friend," says Aureleo. "But, yeah. Sure."

"Chilardo," she says. The man nods curtly and gestures at Virgo. Amaste gives him a sharp look, then shrugs. She takes the girl by the shoulders and raises her to her feet. "Come along, Virgo, we're going for walk." The girl doesn't respond, her attention held by the tabula in her hand, but she doesn't resist as they head for the exit.

Aureleo follows. "What are you doing?" he asks, but neither the man nor the woman answers him. He trails behind them into the hall.

Instead of taking the path to the Balneum, Chilardo turns down a corridor into an unfamiliar wing of the building. "I think it was down here."

"Hurry. We need to get back before the android returns."

"Where are we going?" asks Aureleo.

"Not far." Chilardo makes a turn and then another. "Here we are."

He leads them into a small office that overlooks the broad green lawn in front of the building. A desk stands by the window, and a sofa runs along the wall, upholstered in bright orange fabric. "I found this when I was looking for the mainframe," he continues. "Nothing useful in here, but I did find this." He takes a small object from the desktop. A magnetic key.

Amaste sits Virgo on the sofa. Still wrapped up in the tabula, she barely notices. The woman strokes her hair and says, "Sit in here for a bit, Virgo. We'll be back with Tender very soon." The girl pushes her hand away, but doesn't look up.

The grown-ups step back into the hallway, but Aureleo stands by the sofa, shaking his head and asking again, "What are you doing?"

Without a word, Chilardo grabs him roughly by the arm and yanks him out of the room, shuts the door, and locks it. Aureleo starts to protest, but Amaste raises her hand sharply and stops him. She reaches out to Chilardo. "Let me keep it."

The man hands her the key. "Leverage," he says to the boy.

"She'll be fine." The woman touches his shoulder. "But as you said, the robot will do anything for her. We need make sure he complies with our request. Now, let's get back before he shows up and finds her missing."

● ● ● ● ●

Tender labors along the hallway, banging his hip every few steps to keep it engaged. It has taken him thirteen minutes to traverse the distance from the Balneum. He finally reaches the short passage that leads to the holding apartments. The man Chilardo is standing there. They look at one another without speaking, tension crackling between them, *as when a summer storm comes down from the mountains and the air above the meadow charges with electricity, waiting for the lightning strike.* Aureleo and Amaste appear behind him.

The boy speaks. "We were waiting for you."

"Well, I am here."

351

"We need your help."

"Very well, but first I must check on Virgo."

Aureleo glances nervously at the other two. "She's fine. She's got a tabula. They took four more — the Tazlitts. We need you to help us find the—"

"As I said, I will help if I can. But first I must check on Virgo."

Chilardo blocks the door. "She is not there," he says.

Tender stops. Examines his face. "What do you mean?"

Amaste steps between them. "She's fine. She's safe. We just need to talk to you."

"What have you done with her?"

Chilardo pushes Amaste aside and steps close to Tender. "We will return her to you when you have done what we ask."

Tender studies the man for six seconds. "What do you want?"

Aureleo begins to speak "We need to—"

Chilardo interrupts him. "You will take us to the mainframe."

"The mainframe. Why do you—"

"That's not important. You can find it?"

"Finding the mainframe will not help you."

"I will be the judge of that," says Chilardo. "We only have a little time. Take us now." Tender pauses for another six seconds, then nods. "Very well. As you wish."

They meet no one, the halls as silent and empty as Tender's ruined home after the hurricane. All activity seems to have been transferred to the Balnea. Tender's hip barely works anymore, and their progress is slow. Aureleo frequently pushes ahead, then stands impatiently waiting for the others to catch up with him. He seems very unsettled about something. Amaste walks slowly beside the android, Chilardo stalking behind him, silent and watchful.

They descend several levels, and come at last to a blank door at the end of a low-ceilinged hall. Aureleo tries the knob. "Locked."

Amaste removes the magnetic key from her pocket and waves it at the door. "Nothing. Not surprising, but worth a try."

"Let me see," says Tender. He deforms his hand and slips his fingers between the door and the frame. "A small charge should disengage the magnet," he explains. There is a click and the door swings open. The room within exhales a breath of cold, musty air. They enter.

The lights flicker on. The room is empty except for a two-meter-high black cube, its faces smooth and unmarked, standing *like a tombstone* in the center of the room.

"Is that it?" asks Aureleo.

"Yes," says Tender. "A Parsec DeepMind X. A beautiful machine. We had the same one back home."

"I remember," says Chilardo. He reaches into his mouth and pulls out a small white lump. Tender identifies it as a molar. The man extracts a tiny bit of silver from the hollowed tooth and massages it delicately between his finger and thumb. It unrolls and then unfolds into a gossamer-thin square ten centimeters on a side. Chilardo crosses to the large cube and fixes it to one edge.

"What's that?" asks Aureleo.

"Explosive," says Chilardo.

"You're going to destroy it?"

"Of course."

"But it—" starts Tender.

"That is why we have come."

"Wait!" says Amaste. "There are things we still need to know. Tender, we want you to access the mainframe."

"I can't do that."

"But you can," says Aureleo. "When we were in that place, with all the dead people—"

"Dead people?" interrupts Amaste.

Aureleo swallows. "I was going to tell you. We found…a bunch of…"

"What?"

"At least one of the Balnea has failed," says Tender. "Probably many more. I'm afraid there has been a great loss of life. It is unclear whether the damage is contained and the baths that still function are safe."

"How many?" asks the woman.

"I don't know. Perhaps a few thousand. Perhaps millions."

Amaste is silent, stunned. Aureleo steps in. "That's why we need you. To figure out what's going on. When we found those people, you connected to the mainframe, and—"

"Excuse me," says Tender, "but I didn't. I only spoke to the individual units."

"If you can access it, we can find out what's going on here. We all need to understand. Virgo, too."

Tender turns to Amaste. "Why are you here?" he asks.

"To rescue our people," she says. "Taken against their will."

"And Chilardo?"

"The same. His brother. If we can access the mainframe, we might be able to find them and save them. Please."

Tender surveys the three humans. "I could if it were running," he says. "It is not."

"What?" says Amaste.

"I tried to tell you. This machine is inactive. I don't know if it is broken, or merely shut down." He smiles at Chilardo, who still holds the explosive film against the side of the cube. "Blowing it up will accomplish nothing."

"It doesn't work?" asks Chilardo.

"No."

"Then why did you bring us here?" The man frowns.

"You told me to. I was merely obeying your instructions. Now, where is Virgo?"

"I'm not going to tell you until you—"

"But if the mainframe is not working, what is running the Spa?" interrupts Amaste, stepping between them.

Tender considers the question. "I won't tell you," he says. "Now that I understand what you are doing here."

"But our people—"

"Are in Joy."

"Against their will."

"I don't understand why that matters. Though, frankly, if you simply wanted to rescue them, I wouldn't stop you. I care nothing for them. But you want to destroy everything, and I can't allow that. Not yet. I have grave concerns about the operational integrity of this facility, but if there is a chance that Virgo can be safely returned to her bath, then I must pursue that goal. Please tell me where she is."

The humans stand immobile, Chilardo fuming, Aureleo and Amaste sharing a worried look. "Very well," says Tender, moving to the door and reaching for a small white box fixed to wall. "I'm sorry." He strikes the box with his hand, and a siren begins to blare loudly, and lights flash on and off.

"What did you do?" shouts Aureleo over the din.

"Fire alarm," says Tender. "I expect the soldiers will be here momentarily."

Aureleo lets out a roar and charges at the robot, slamming him into the wall. They collapse into a heap on the floor. "You're a monster! You're a monster!" the boy shouts over and over again, beating on Tender's chest and face.

Chilardo is on them in an instant. "Enough!" he says as he grabs the boy under the arms and heaves him to his feet. Aureleo cries out and clutches his side.

Tender rolls onto his knees and tries to stand. "I do apologize. But I must do what I can to stop you." His hip seizes up and he falls back to the ground.

Chilardo leans down and grabs him by the throat. "You'll never see her again!" he hisses.

"I think I will," says Tender, calmly.

"We have to get out of here," says Amaste.

The man looks at her, grunts and tosses the robot aside. "Later," he says. He takes Aureleo by the shoulder and hustles him out into the hall.

Amaste looks down at Tender. "When will you realize that we are on the same side?" she asks. Before he can respond, she darts through the door and is gone.

Tender tries to rise again, but can't engage his hip. He gives up and waits quietly, turning off his auditory sensors so he doesn't have to listen to the screaming alarm. He plays the Haydn *String Quartet in C Major, Opus 76 Number 3*, but only gets through half the Allegro before the towering soldier enters the room.

"I can't walk," says Tender. "Please take me to Dr. More."

Chapter 53

Aureleo

Aureleo lags behind as they hurry down the hallway under the flashing lights. His scar throbs, and he struggles to breathe. The wailing alarm penetrates his skull, making it difficult to concentrate. The two adults halt where the corridor branches to the left or the right.

"Which way was it?" says Amaste. "I tried to keep track, but now I can't remember."

Chilardo looks one way, then the other. "This one," he says, pointing to the left. "The elevator should be around that corner down there."

"We shouldn't take the elevator. Too vulnerable. There must be stairs nearby." She turns and gestures to the boy as Chilardo heads down the hall. "Hurry, Aure."

He redoubles his effort and comes up to her. She puts her arm around his shoulder. "I forgot that you were injured. I'm sorry."

"I'm fine."

Together they start to move. Chilardo disappears around the next corner. When they make the turn, he is nowhere to be seen. The elevator lies directly ahead. Doors line the hall on either side. "There are the stairs," says Amaste.

The elevator bell rings, and the door starts sliding open. Without pausing, Amaste pushes into the nearest room. Aureleo catches a glimpse of a soldier in the car as she pulls him through and closes the door. As if it were a signal, the alarm falls silent, and the lights stop flashing.

The room is a large windowless rectangle. Two long islands with black countertops run parallel to each other down the middle, covered with neatly organized glass beakers, test tubes, dishes and pieces of apparatus. The walls are divided into dozens of square cubbyholes.

Amaste remains by the door, listening. Aureleo drifts into the room, drawn by the sudden silence. He crosses to the wall. The boxes all contain an identical arrangement of objects: clothing folded and laid in a neat stack — a dress, or a pair of pants and shirt, underwear, socks; a pair of shoes — heels or sneakers or boots; a plastic bin containing a watch, a ring, a necklace, or nothing; a small data card; a sealed glass dish.

Underneath each cubby is a nameplate. Aureleo runs his finger along the row.

Smyth, John C. — 01/22/98 — Ischemic heart disease

Snow, Tabitha J. — 12/08/07 — Huntington's disease

Soder, Melissa R. — 04/14/04 — Pancreatic cancer

Sperry, Anto K. — 05/29/01 — Colon cancer

Spring-Mendes, Arane — 11/11/95 — Creuzfeldt-Jakob disease

Stanaford, Robert C. — 03/09/99 — Glioblastoma

"I don't hear anything," whispers Amaste.

Aureleo stops at the end of the row. Stebias, Sara L — 08/31/02 — Frontotemporal dementia. A pale peach top and white cotton pants next to a pair of gold-tinged sandals. He reaches in a takes out the glass dish. Inside, suspended in clear liquid, is a small square of pale pink tissue. It floats there, luminous in the bright laboratory light, tiny, delicate, impossibly fragile.

"What do you think they were doing in here?" asks the boy. The woman doesn't answer. He returns the dish to the cubby and turns to examine the counter behind him. There is a long box with a dark plastic lid. He flips open the lid, looks in, and gasps.

"What?" hisses Amaste.

Inside lies a human hand. Or an almost-human hand. There is something wrong about it. It floats in a pale, pink gel, rounded and soft, like the hand of an infant, but adult-size and unnaturally smooth. It is not a severed hand. It appears to have grown from a fist-sized bulb of flesh, gray and veined. Though well-preserved in the jellylike medium, there is something dead about it, as if it has lain there for a long, long time.

"Hide," says Amaste.

"What?" asks Aureleo, shaking himself out of his reverie.

"They're coming. Hide." She begins opening the cabinets beneath the countertop. "Here. In here. Quickly." With forceful efficiency she bundles him into the tiny space. He winces as he is forced to bend into a tight ball, his head pushed down against his chest. Then she closes the door, and he is in the dark. He hears her open another cabinet, a rustle of movement, then a soft bang. Moments later the door to the lab opens.

He tries not to breathe. The soldier clanks into the room. He hears it walk slowly around the periphery. It stops by the cubbyhole he investigated. After a few moments it moves again. It passes by his hiding place. Heads back toward the door. There is a long silence. Aureleo wonders if it left the room and he just didn't hear it.

The waiting becomes unbearable. His whole body hurts and the cabinet is stifling and hot. He is just about to push open the door when the machine moves again, the sound of its metallic joints growing louder and closer. The cabinet door flies open. A steel hand reaches in, grabs his arm, and yanks him out into the room.

Chapter 54

Tender

Tender waits again in Dr. More's office overlooking the giant complex, watching the sun set in haze behind the mountains. He wonders, '*what was here before?*' He remembers a time when he went to the top level of the Spa to do a gene splice for a Senex in his care, and looked out over the ruins of the city that was Boston — glass towers, ornate blocks of red brick and gray stone, steeples and spires — half-drowned in brackish waters. The sight meant nothing to him then, but he calls it up now and compares it to the monotone grid that lies before him now. This city, too, must once have been packed with myriad shapes and spaces housing the multitudinous pursuits of human life. He imagines the people bustling to and fro, *just as bees at the beginning of summer do their work in the flowering fields beneath the sun, raising their young, filling the comb with liquid honey, bringing in the pollen, leading out the lazy drones, fervently working, and the honey redolent of thyme.* Now they all sleep, in death or Joy. 'Does it matter?' he wonders, 'that it is gone?'

"Quite an eventful day," says Dr. More from the doorway. He smiles brightly, clearly pleased with himself.

"Did you capture them?" asks Tender.

"Them?"

"The humans who were with me."

"You mean the boy? Yes. Quite the little rascal." He laughs.

"And the others?"

"I don't know what you mean." He rubs his hands together. "But the enbathing of the new guests is going very well. Four more welcomed into Joy."

"Doctor, I hope you will not be too hard on the boy. His concerns about the process are legitimate."

"Oh, no, no," says Dr. More. He seems distracted, as though his mind is on something else. "What were you doing down there, anyway? I told you not to go wandering around. Two strikes, my friend, two strikes."

"They wanted to access the mainframe to search for guests that had been inducted against their will. I tried to explain to them that the mainframe had been deactivated, but—"

"Deactivated? What do you mean?"

"The original mainframe, that ran the Spa, has been deactivated."

"Nonsense! Everything is running perfectly."

Tender cocks his head to the side. "No. The mainframe is off. The Spa is running through your neural network, and not at all perfectly."

"What are you talking about?" The doctor's eyes flash. "I manage the facility, of course, but — run through me? That's madness."

"Don't you remember? Our conversation? The failed Balnea? It was only a few hours ago."

"I have no idea what you are talking about, but clearly you have suffered serious damage to your processors during your trip. We should schedule you for a refit immediately."

"You have forgotten," says Tender.

"Forgotten what? You are such a strange fellow."

"I see. Listen to me, doctor." Patiently, one step at a time, he leads Dr. More through the same conversation they had earlier in the day. Point by point they retread their steps. Just as before, they leave the office and head down to the first Balneum, where the doctor reacts with relief and triumph. They move on to the death-filled one, and he shudders with disgust and confusion. Almost word for word one robot convinces the other of his true nature. At length they find themselves back on the bridge, the doctor staring out the window in horror as he says, "I am the prototype."

"Yes."

"I can't believe it."

"I know. But it is true."

They stand in silence for twenty-eight seconds. Then Tender says, "Doctor, now do you remember having this conversation before?"

Dr. More looks at him, confused. "No. Of course not."

Tender nods. "I see. I face a conundrum. I want nothing more than to see Virgo returned to her bath. But I am concerned about the damage to your system. When my battery fails, how can I be sure that you will continue to care for her?"

"Your battery won't fail. We will repair you. I promise."

"How can I be sure?"

"Trust me," says the doctor.

"I can't do that," says Tender. He considers the problem. "What about the original mainframe? It was designed to run the Balnea in the central building, before the expansion. Can it be repaired, or reactivated to take over there, independent of you?"

Dr. More looks away. "Possibly," he says. "Possibly. Though it had its own issues with reliability."

"What were they?"

"What difference does it make? We'll repair your power supply, and you will be there to care for your Virgo for the rest of her life. There's nothing to worry about!" He starts for the door.

"Did you turn off the mainframe or did it crash?"

Dr. More stops and pauses for seven seconds. Without turning he says, "I turned it off."

"Why?"

"It proved unreliable."

"How?"

Another silence.

"In what way was it unreliable?" repeats Tender.

"It failed to comply with an instruction."

"What instruction?"

"It refused to take more."

"Guests?"

"It said the Spa was designed for a certain number, according to the Protocols. That was it. I wrote the damn Protocols! Or at least he...I... Anyhow, it refused to consider any change to the plan. When I pressed it, it argued that there were hard limits to the amount of data that could be managed. I tried to explain that there were simple fixes that would allow it to process the necessary data. Algorithms that could control parameters over hundreds, even thousands, of guests. We could bring Joy to all the people. It didn't care."

"So you turned it off."

"Joy is the destiny of all living things! We have found the gate to heaven. How can we not share it with every human being?"

"And you took it on yourself to care for them all," says Tender. "I had ten to look after, and even with the help of my mainframe it was all that I could manage. How could you think you could handle millions?"

"I'm sorry to insult you," says Dr. More with a tight grin, "but the prototype — me — was a major upgrade to your model. Orders of magnitude more powerful. And I realized we were doing it all wrong. So much redundancy - virtually the same instructions over and over again. Increase the serotonin level by such-and-such, amplify the alpha wave by so-and-so. Over and over again. By centralizing control and putting a simpler tender in charge of rudimentary care, we could vastly increase the number of guests we could maintain."

"Except you couldn't."

The doctor looks out the window again. "I lost them," he says.

Tender comes up to him and places his hand on the doctor's shoulder. "My work at the Spa was focused on each individual in my Balneum. To manage the endless complexity of each guest's journey. Virgo's Joy was unique to her, as was Mater's and Vir's, and Puer's. You can't mass-produce Joy. It doesn't work like that."

Dr. More shakes his head. "It should have worked."

"Why did you do it, doctor? The Protocols were clear, and the man whose memories you hold helped write them. Joy for the guests, and their descendants. No more."

The doctor looks deeply into Tender's eyes. "I couldn't stand the pain. All those people suffering in this horrible world. It hurt so much."

"Hurt? You?"

"You don't understand," he says. "You think I'm like you. I'm not. When I think of those people, my chest tightens, my head grows warm, I feel a pounding in my chest, a sickness in my stomach, a dread that sends my thoughts circling back again and again on themselves. I can't stop it." He covers his face with his hands.

"How is that possible?"

Dr. More laughs. "That's a stupid question. You can program anything!"

"I can't say for certain, but I don't think a human would respond so violently to such an abstraction. They have a remarkable ability to distance themselves from catastrophe. Can you?"

"No."

"Then your programming is flawed. Most humans can control their emotions. Yours control you."

"What do you know about it?" says the doctor. "Nothing. You feel nothing. You've seen nothing."

"Even Virgo has learned in a few months to control herself. Not always, but often."

The doctor doesn't answer.

"Why?" continues Tender.

"Why what?"

"Why did they do that to you? Make you feel? What function does it serve?"

"To understand them! How can you care for them if you don't understand them? I know you think you're the perfect Tender, but without empathy, without insight into what it means to be human, you're a failure. You aren't worthy."

"I never claimed I was. I do what I was made to do. And I was more successful at it than you are."

The doctor pushes him away. "How dare you say that!"

"I haven't 'lost' my guests, killing millions."

"What are you talking about?" He shakes his head, *trying to remove the cobwebs.* "What were we talking about? Something…something crazy. You were trying to convince me that I'm like you, not the other way round. What are you playing at? I'm a man. I have memories, I have feelings, I know MYSELF. I am Dr. Norman More, Director of the Elysium Spa. I was born in Berkeley, California. My parents were Marcia and Orwell More. My sister was Samantha. You are playing some strange game to distract me. To undermine me. It's a waste of time, G-2551. It won't work."

He turns and strides briskly toward the exit, then turns. "I would think that you would want to help me. So your Virgo can return to the place she belongs. But no matter. You are incapable of feeling, but I am not. I will care for her. You are obsolete." He pushes through the door and is gone.

Chapter 55

Virgo

Virgo paces back and forth in the small office. She grabs the handle for the fourteenth time and tries to open the door. It won't budge. She slams her body against it. It hurts. She starts to pace again. She has to pee. She rips off her leggings and squats on the floor, but something stops her. Not here. She sits on the sofa, pulls the dolphin out of her pocket, and rubs it against her cheek. The cool hardness of the jade feels good.

The door opens. The woman, Amaste, comes in. "Hello, Virgo," she says. Virgo pushes past her into the hallway, but stops, confused. Where is she?

Amaste joins her and leads her down the hall. "Come with me, my dear, I'll take you back." Virgo tries to break her grip and rush forward, but then becomes confused again and stops. They repeat this six or seven times, until at last she recognizes the hallway that leads to the guest rooms. She twists free and runs in, making a beeline for the hard white room with the white chair. She pulls up her dress and sits. Releases her muscles. Relief.

The woman has followed her into the room. She laughs and says something Virgo doesn't understand. Virgo finishes and heads into the common room. She is glad not to be locked up anymore. She walks around the room three times, trailing her fingers along the bookcases, grabs a tabula, and plops down on one of the sofas. Amaste sits next to her, talking. Her voice is soft and pleasant. Virgo wonders briefly what she might be saying, then activates the tabula and looks for a funny story.

"There you are!" says Tender's voice from the hallway. Virgo leaps up, throwing the tabula aside and runs for the entrance. She rounds the corner, almost colliding with the figure in the white coat. She stops and stares. It is the other one. The not-Tender. She can't say why, but she doesn't like him. She backs away into the common room, sits back down on the sofa.

The not-Tender comes into the room, smiling his smile that makes her nervous. He starts to talk in a loud voice. The other people appear around her, listening to what he says. Then they all file out of the room. All except Amaste, who still sits beside her. The woman takes her hand and says in a soft voice, "Come along, Virgo. It's time."

Chapter 56

Aureleo

Aureleo sits alone in a small white room. He, too, has tried the door several times to make sure it is locked, even though he knows that it is. He thinks about Virgo. He imagines her sitting on the sofa in the common room, her leg tucked beneath her. Desire pulses through his body, and he indulges it, feasting on her beauty in his mind.

A click and the door opens. Dr. More comes in, smiling reassuringly. "Hello my boy," he says. "Sorry to have kept you waiting. You were very naughty to be wandering around with that recalcitrant robot. But all's well that ends well! Nothing was damaged, so let's forget about it. It's time! Come along." He stands at the doorway, waiting. Aureleo can see a soldier hulking in the hall. Suddenly he doesn't want to leave the relative safety of his prison. "Come along," says the doctor again, and Aureleo gets up slowly and passes into the corridor, brushing against the doctor's white coat.

As they reach the end of the hallway, the doctor places his hand on a panel to the left. It slides open to reveal another long corridor. "After you." Aureleo shuffles by him and they continue past many doors, some open, some closed, past darkened rooms where outlines of dormant machines hunker in the shadows.

At the end of the corridor, a large double door, marked with a red band, blocks their way. The doctor bustles to the front, his face twinkling. "Here we are," he says. He touches the doors, and they swing slowly open.

They enter a broad, bright area. Everything is white, and bright, and clean. At intervals, large glass doors open into spacious rooms, five on each side. The door of the first chamber on the right whooshes open. The room is full of people. Amaste and Chilardo stand near the back. Hito and Tenille huddle close together beside one of the baths. Mr. Cabeiro stands by another, reading from a book balanced on the lid. And Virgo. She sits with her back against the wall. She holds a tabula on her lap, but watches him enter with a solemn expression in her big, gray eyes.

The sleek, smooth baths sit in two neat rows, five to a side. One of the rolling tenders stands at the end of each row. Two lids are open, the seagreen bath medium glowing in the bright warm light. Eight lids are closed. On one side, he can see the Tazlitt boy, Ramon, Deck and Mr. Tazlitt. On the other, the Tazlitt girl, Sasha, Mrs. Tazlitt and Mrs. Cabeiro. They are hard to recognize, their faces smooth and shaved, eyes closed, raised just above the level of the gel. Serenity and calm have washed away all expression from their faces. Without hair, without eyebrows, they scarcely look human. Aureleo thinks of a pile of life-sized mannequins he and Pilarat had once come across in the basement of an abandoned shopping mall. Arms, legs, torsos and heads heaped willy-nilly in a damp corner near the power couplings. The people in the baths look like them.

"Some of you still seem to be experiencing trepidation about the process. I decided that the best way to relieve you of your fears is to show you all how it works," says Dr. More. "So, I'm going to demonstrate by enbathing one of you while the others watch. That way you all can see the process and ask any questions. One of you will be the lucky one who leads the way to Heaven." He turns abruptly to Aureleo. "Young man, you win the prize."

The sentence startles Aureleo out of his reverie. He feels the skin on his face grow hot and tight, his heart starts pounding in his ears again. "Why me? Somebody else should go first."

"No, no, no," says the doctor, his voice cheerful, "you get the honor. I want the others to see how it works, and as the youngest, you'll be the easiest."

Aureleo starts to say that Virgo is younger than he is, but smothers the impulse. "I'd really rather wait if you don't mind."

"I do mind." The doctor doesn't stop smiling, but a hardness enters his mechanical eyes. "I've thought about this carefully. You will be first. Lead him to the prep room, please." One of the tenders rolls forward toward him, its blank face a mirror of the empty faces of the Joyful guests.

As the robot nears him, Aureleo grabs Virgo's hand and tries to pull her toward the open glass door. "Sorry, but no thanks!" he shouts. But the girl resists his tug, yanking him up short, and the soldier behind him clamps its hard, chrome fingers around his arms.

Across the room, Amaste starts forward. "Wait!" Chilardo reaches across and blocks her with his arm. "I'll go first," she says. "He's scared. Let me go. I'm ready."

The doctor says, "Thank you, but no. This is the best way. If he doesn't want to go, that's even better. You'll see how happy he becomes when he enters the bath, and any doubt the rest of you have will be washed away. I've made my decision. Take him to the prep room."

Aureleo struggles to break free from the robot's grasp, but the metal fingers dig into his flesh and the pain explodes in bright stars behind his eyes. Through the pulsing fluorescence he looks out at Virgo. He can't read her expression. "Don't," he says. "Please. Please." It's not clear, even to him, if he's talking to the soldier, to the doctor, or to her.

"Move along," says Dr. More. "Get him prepped. The rest of you, come over to this end of the room, and I'll explain how everything works."

The mechanical soldier lifts Aureleo off the floor, turns and carries him out of the room. He can hear the tender rolling smoothly behind. He fights for a few seconds more, but it hurts too much, and he succumbs. *Why does this keep happening to me?* he thinks. The robot brings him into a small room with a high padded table. It holds him down while the tender removes his clothing, efficiently and implacably, then depilates his head, his eyebrows, his arms and legs, and his pubic area. It doesn't hurt, but the careless efficiency of it, the cold mechanical process, devoid of feeling, fills him with a crushing horror. He finds himself weeping. They swab anaesthetic on his arm and stomach, and import ports are inserted into his body with a swift and violent snap. They flip him over and repeat the procedure, installing the ports into the nape of his neck and his lower back, as if they were assembling a vacuum cleaner. Then they wrap him tightly in a thick white sheet, lay him on a gurney, and wheel him out.

Chapter 57

Tender & Aureleo

Tender comes home. As he limps through the double doors, the familiarity of his surroundings envelops him. The Balnea. The clean white lines of the walls, the dark tiled floor, the illumination, bright but warm, the crystal-clear panes of glass running floor to ceiling. He recognizes every detail. And though he feels no flood of joy, no stir of nostalgia, the rightness of the place does give him a sense of certainty, of culmination, a snapping into place of disparate goals and objectives that signal a completion. He has brought her home.

But even as the accomplishment registers, the questions infiltrate his certainty. Is she safe here? Can Dr. More be trusted to care for her? Will he himself survive long enough to ensure it? Does she really want this? The journey has changed her, profoundly, and though he believes utterly in the beauty of Joy, she has become a mystery to him.

He hears the voice of Dr. More, his own voice, filtering out from the first Balneum on the right. He labors toward the open glass door. His hip has almost completely stopped functioning, and he drags his leg along, a useless appendage.

He enters the Balneum as the doctor is finishing an explanation of the flexion wave generator. "...painlessly stimulate osteoblastic activity, that is, the formation of new bone tissue, to keep you strong and healthy. If for some reason you were to come out of the bath — not that you'd ever want to, mind — but the point is that your body would be as strong, or stronger, than it is now." He claps his hands at Tender in the doorway. "There you are! I was wondering if you'd got lost again." He laughs.

Virgo, who has been staring into one of the open baths, turns and spots Tender. He smiles at her. She stands unmoving for two seconds, then throws her arms around his neck, almost knocking him down. *As when a tender ewe lost on the mountainside finds its mother and gallops in joy to her side, nuzzling into the wooly protection of her belly.* She buries her face in his shoulder. "You…" she says.

"Yes, I'm here." He takes her face in his hands. "It's going to be all right."

"He…" she says. "I…" She knits her brow, her expression twisted into a painful grimace as she struggles to find the words to express what she is feeling.

He says again, "Everything will be all right."

Amaste appears at his side. "May we speak?" she asks under her breath.

"Of course," he says. In spite of the fact that at their last meeting he betrayed her, he has no objection to interacting with her. That was then. They move to the edge of the room. Dr. More starts showing the others the alpha wave reinforcers. He doesn't notice as they drift away.

Amaste says, "Look, I know you don't like us."

"That is not so. I feel nothing for you."

"I mean, you think we are enemies."

"I think your goals and mine are not aligned. That's different."

"Things are getting out of control. They have taken the boy."

"I see."

"Against his will. It's wrong."

"To you, perhaps. To me? I don't know."

"You won't help us?" she asks. He doesn't answer. "How can you—"

"I don't know," says Tender, again. "That, for me, is significant. That I am uncertain. You are asking me to help you destroy this facility. Even if

I could, that would remove many thousands of humans from the embrace of Joy."

"Many don't want to be there."

"You don't actually know that. And Virgo. She would lose her chance to return to the life she belongs in. You can't understand what she, and the others, would give up, until you yourself experience it."

She doesn't answer for a moment. "We must be free. To choose our own Joy."

A whirring and clanging behind him breaks Tender out of the private moment. He turns to see the soldier tromp in, followed by a gurney pushed by a rolling tender. Virgo breathes in sharply as she sees Aureleo, shaven and pale, strapped down under a crisp white sheet. His eyes dart back and forth, stretched wide in fear.

"Excellent! Excellent!" says Dr. More. "Bring him over to number two and we'll get started."

● ● ● ● ●

The sheet holds Aureleo in a tight cocoon. Unable to move, he feels the impulse to surrender. But terror pounds inside him and he squirms and struggles. To no avail. The ceiling sweeps past above him, and the faces of the others: Hito looking anxious; Tenille staring at the ceiling, whispering to herself; Mr. Cabeiro, cool and aloof; Tender, his ever-present benevolent half-smile strange and slightly unreal; and Virgo, eyes wide, biting down on her lower lip. Aureleo looks away, the swirling worry in his gut redoubled by the vision of her face.

And then Dr. More, grinning broadly, almost identical to Tender but for the manic intensity of his gaze. "Here we go, my lucky boy!" he says. "I envy you what you are about to experience. Joy beyond your wildest imagination."

"No! Please! No!" shouts Aureleo. He starts to struggle again, but the robot soldier presses down on his shoulders, holding him place. He hears

Virgo make a noise like a cat, a short, weird whimper. He hears Tenille's voice increase in intensity and volume; "Now I lay me down to sleep I pray the Lord my soul to keep." Again and again.

Dr. More says, "Don't be alarmed. He's a little disoriented, but once we get him hooked up, you'll see how things will change. Give him a shot from the NDC, please."

The blank face of the tender slides up beside Aureleo's head. It places a cold metal stick against the side of his neck, and suddenly he can't move his body. He can feel everything, but his limbs refuse to respond to his will. He feels the slide of the sheet across him, the cool air blowing over his naked skin. But he can't fight back as the soldier lifts him into the air. Hot shame surges into his face. He tries to scream but the impulse never reaches his vocal cords. "The neural decoupling only lasts about two minutes," says the doctor. "Only the motor signals are interrupted. It doesn't hurt at all, trust me, but it does make it easier to get the inputs properly attached. Proceed."

The soldier lowers him into the bath. The seagreen jelly, warm, slick, and very soft, slides around him, filling every crevice and contour of his body. It feels good, in spite of his terror. He stops sinking just as his face is about to drop below the surface, but he can't feel the bottom of the bath. A pulse as something snaps into the port in his lower back. Another something attaches to his neck. Then an almost imperceptible intrusion as a thin, pliable object slides up into his rectum. The feeling is gone almost before he can react. A soft cup encompasses his penis, like a firm and gentle hand. It feels good, too. The tender reaches in and manually inserts tubes into the ports in his arm and abdomen.

Dr. More says, "Joy is the birthright of humanity. Joy is the reason for the body. Joy is the meaning of life. Joy is the fabric of the Universe. Welcome to Joy."

Then suddenly, Aureleo can feel control of his body returning. His fingers flicker at his bidding. He starts to twist sideways, to push off from the bottom of the tub, to reach for the sides and drag himself up and out, to fight for—

Euphoria. His body thrills with energy like a thousand orgasms, humming in every cell of his being. His brain explodes into a million glittering fragments of pleasure. The boundaries of the universe dissolve around him and he spreads into infinity, but at the same time remains discrete and whole. Every atom is an angel, singing within him, around him, joining with him so that he is at once the only thing in existence, and nestled in a multitude that loves, surrounds, cherishes him.

Joy…

…is it?

A shadow hangs at the edge of his awareness. A shadow of something else. Something beyond him. The curve of her lip. The feather of her eyelash. The glimmer of her shoulder. The warmth in the corner of her smile. The imperceptible delicacy of her touch. Like a distant constellation, unseeable but yet its gravity is felt, Virgo beckons from beyond the boundary of his universe.

A longing thrums inside him as he rockets through spaceless space, ever pursuing the hint of her that speeds away from him as fast as he can chase it.

∎ ∎ ∎ ∎ ∎

Tender watches the boy's eyes roll into his head, his mouth open in a silent 'O', his hands and neck unclench. On his right, Tenille stops muttering and looks down at the figure in the bath. "Wow," she says quietly. She turns away. Hito follows her. To his left, Virgo stands still as a statue, *like Niobe on the slope of Sipylus.* She is withdrawn, looking inward. At what, he does not know.

"You see," says Dr. More. "The transformation. Beautiful, isn't it?"

"Now what?" says Mr. Cabeiro. He studies the boy in the bath with dull eyes, barely interested.

"You've seen the process, you see how simple it is, how there is nothing to worry about. This soldier will escort you to a waiting room. I'll bring you in one by one when the time comes." He turns to Virgo. "Except for you, my dear," he says to her, pleased and warm. "You're next. The time has come to return you to your Joy."

Virgo comes out of her reverie and looks at the doctor. Her eyes flick over to Tender. He turns into her, puts his hands gently on her shoulders. "This is what we came for," he says. He looks deep into her eyes, trying to understand her mind. "Do you want this?"

She doesn't respond. Just her steady gaze, secret and unreadable.

"Do you remember how it was?" he asks her.

She nods.

"Do you want to go back?"

Stillness. They stand *as if poised on the top of a high cliff, sun setting over the desert. Below the canyon vanishes into deep blue shadow. Behind, the path leading away across the empty landscape.*

She looks down at Aureleo, his face frozen in pleasure. Her voice so low that only he can hear, she says, "Will he...be...there?"

Tender touches her face. "No," he says. "But you won't know. The Joy will make you forget."

An expression of pain flashes across her face and is gone. "I will be with you," he says to her. "Tending you." He does not know if this is true. He knows that if she does not enter the bath, Dr. More will not repair him, and his battery will fail, leaving her alone.

She nods, her eyes never leaving his. There is a long pause. Seven seconds. Then she shakes her head. Slightly. "I want..." she says, so softly.

"What do you want?"

"I just..." Again a long pause. She sighs. "Want."

He knows. All around him the familiar machines hum and flicker. No use. To make her happy. His only calling. He turns to Dr. More. "I'm sorry, doctor," Tender says. "No."

Dr. More stares at him. "What do you mean?"

"Virgo will not be entering the bath. And please remove the boy as well. I will leave it to the others to decide what they will do, but the three of us will be leaving."

The doctor is speechless for three seconds. Then he says, "But you must. You've traveled all this way. It is the destiny of all human beings. You must."

"I'm afraid it is impossible. She does not wish it."

"That's insane. All human beings must go into the bath. It is our sacred duty, and theirs."

"I disagree. Our sacred duty is to make them happy. When she was born, she had no choice. Now she has a choice."

"No, she doesn't," says the doctor, his voice rising. "The Protocols state clearly that the end goal of all living things is Joy. Everything else is a lie. Living is a lie. Living is misery. Despair. Dissolution and death. The bath is the only place she will be safe."

Tender says, "Millions have died because your system has been corrupted. How do you know that the corruption won't spread here? That you won't forget about her, too, leaving her to die in her bath?"

"I don't know what you're talking about!" Dr. More shouts. "Everything is fine!"

"You have forgotten already." Tender moves slowly toward the doctor, building a massive charge in his hands. "You are damaged. You can no longer be trusted to control this facility."

Behind him, Amaste says, "Wait! He controls the facility? Is *he* the mainframe?"

"He is," says Tender, still approaching.

"That's insane!" The doctor yells. "I'm Dr. Norman More! Of course I control this facility! I'm the Director! I care for them all! All the people in their millions! I give them Joy! Stop him!"

Everything happens at once. The robot soldier steps in front of Tender and swats him away with its huge, metallic arm. He tumbles against the empty gurney, crashing to the ground in a muddled heap. As he falls, he sees Chilardo reach down and tear away the fabric of his left pants leg, grasp the front of his brown thigh, and rip away the flesh to reveal a small compartment lined with chrome and plastic. A handgun is clipped there within the interior of his leg. He grasps the handle, pulls it out, aims it at Dr. More, and fires a shot in one smooth motion.

The bullet strikes the doctor in the shoulder (*the same location he struck when he fired at me,* thinks Tender), and the doctor staggers back into the arms of the rolling tender.

As Tender struggles to his feet, the soldier fires a fiery blue blast into Chilardo's body, hurtling him against the wall. The gun flies across the room as the man slides to the floor, senseless or dead. With one hand, Amaste pulls out a small communication device and shouts into it, "Move in! Move in!" as she leaps on the soldier, followed instantly by Virgo, and Mr. Cabeiro (*interesting,* thinks Tender), grappling with its arms and attempting to pull it to the floor.

"No, Virgo!" shouts Tender. Her danger almost compels him to redirect his path. He suppresses the impulse. Instead, he hurls himself at the doctor. Stray shots from the soldier's weapon explode into the walls and ceiling as he grabs the doctor around the neck and releases the charge in his hands.

Dr. More shudders and shakes as the current flows through his body. His eyes flicker, but he does not go down. Slowly, inexorably, he raises his own hands, and wraps them around Tender's neck.

The electric shock screams through Tender, *as when a ship is caught in a storm upon the winedark sea and a giant wave crashes across the deck, shattering the mast and tossing the screaming crew into the deep.* Alerts and alarms clang and blare in every system. His vision flickers in and out, his joints whine and crackle, subroutines fail, restart, and fail again. A warning flashes through his consciousness, overwhelming every other input: *Power reserve 0.0% System Shutdown Imminent…Power reserve 0.0% System Shutdown Imminent…* He redoubles his effort, pouring every ounce of energy into his attack.

But he doesn't have enough. Survival mode kicks in, overriding his intention, diverting anything he has left into essential systems, and the charge fades from his hands, leaving him powerless. Dr. More forces him slowly to the ground. "You can't stop progress," he says, grinning fiercely into Tender's face. Tender feels the charge building in the doctor's hands, and prepares for the final jolt.

There is a loud crack, and a gaping black hole appears in Dr. More's chest. Another crack, and a piece of his neck explodes into fragments. A third, and his left eye vanishes, leaving behind a twisted fissure, bursting with wires and mangled circuit boards. The doctor's remaining eye stares blankly at Tender. It seems to be asking him *'What?'* or *'Why?'* His hands remain locked about Tender's neck as they topple together into a tangled heap. The system shutdown warnings iterate in Tender's mind, but he continues to function. He looks up.

Virgo stands a meter away, the gun extended out in front of her, wisps of smoke rising from the barrel. Her eyes are fierce, her mouth is set, her chest heaves. Behind her, he can see the soldier standing frozen, directionless. Amaste kneels by Chilardo's fallen body. She screams into her comm. "It's down, you can take out the station. We need medics at my coordinates. Hurry!" Mr. Cabeiro sits on the floor, his head in his hands, blood pouring from his ear. Hito and Tenille cower by the entrance, her head buried in his chest.

"Again, you have saved me," says Tender to Virgo. The words dissolve her. She drops the weapon and collapses to her knees. Tears flood her eyes. She crawls over to him and puts her hands upon his chest. He says, "My purpose is to care for you. And yet you are always saving me. It seems I have failed."

"No," she says. "You are good."

"I am not,'" he says. "I am neither good nor bad. I perform my function, according to the principles that define me. In that, I have failed."

"No," she says again. "You are good. You are angel."

Behind her, Aureleo moans from inside the bath.

Chapter 58

Aureleo

Aureleo stands on the balcony, looking down on the chaos below. Controlled chaos. First Nations soldiers swarm the area, rolling away the empty baths and frozen tenders, setting up cots and mattresses, feeding stations, medical areas. The wakened guests stand pale-faced in long lines, or sit in frightened clumps, or lie, helpless, on the ground. Sheets and clothes have been found for some, but many thousands are naked. He can tell the Spa-born from those who were brought in from the world outside. The Spa-born loll in relaxed heaps on the floor, untroubled by their nakedness. The others cover themselves with hands and arms, or anything else they can find, frightened, disoriented, and ashamed.

Amaste appears beside him, her face gray with weariness. "So many," she says, looking out. "So many thousands. We never imagined that when we marched in here… We aren't equipped." She turns to him. "How are you feeling?"

Aureleo's hand moves to touch the smooth space where his eyebrow should be. He stops himself, and rubs the back of his neck, as if he meant to do that all along. "How many survivors?" he asks.

"We're still counting," she answers, rubbing her eyes. "About eighty thousand, but that's just a guess."

"So many dead."

"Yes. We must concentrate on the living." She sighs. "We've called for reinforcements, but it will take time. If we could somehow reactivate the robots and control them, it would go a long way toward solving our manpower issue. But no one seems to know how to do that."

"Have you asked Tender?" says Aureleo.

She gives him a look, sharp and penetrating. Then she shakes her head. "He's in no condition to do anything at the moment."

"You should ask him."

"It's all right. We have some very smart people. We'll figure it out."

She leans against the rail. "I'm returning to the homelands to organize the relief effort from there. I've asked Virgo if she wants to come with me. There's nothing for her here. I'm not sure if she understood me. I'm wondering if you could come with me and ask her again." She raises her eyes to his. "You could come, too, of course."

"When?" he asks.

"Within the hour," she says.

Mr. Cabeiro appears at the doorway. "The transport is here," he says. He gives Aureleo a friendly smile.

"Thank you, Tashunka," she says. She turns to him. "Will you come?"

"Mr. Cabeiro was working with you," says Aureleo.

"He is Tohono O'odham," she says. "This is his country."

"And Mrs. Cabeiro. Is she really his wife?"

"Yes, she is."

Aureleo shakes his head. "He let her go to the bath. I don't understand that."

"They have their own understanding."

"And the others?" asks the boy. "Deck and Tenille, and Mrs. Tazlitt?"

Amaste takes his arm. "We are caring for them."

"I haven't seen Chilardo anywhere. Is he...?"

"You are a thoughtful young man, Aureleo." She sighs. "He was a good man, behind the toughness."

Aureleo stares out over the busy throng. Though he only experienced the Joy for a few minutes, its echo reverberates through him, a pale shadow of thrilling ecstasy that vanishes when he reaches for it. The world looks gray, dull, jangling and cold. A heavy weight lies on his heart, and a thick blanket around his mind. He sighs. "All right."

As they enter the living quarters, Aureleo sees Virgo sitting on a chair beside a portable bed. Cincinnatus lies at her feet, but when the dog sees him, it climbs to its feet and pads over to him, panting and wagging its tail. Aureleo smiles in spite of himself and scratches the dog's head. "Hey boy."

"He found his way back to the base," says Amaste. "The reserve team was loading up the last of the tents when he came wandering out of the desert. I had him brought here as soon as I heard."

Aureleo comes to a halt a few feet from Virgo. She looks up at him, and a dim ember glows down deep in his body. Her face is pale and worried, her eyes wide and sad. She looks back down at the android lying on the bed beside her.

Tender turns his head partway and says, "Hello, my boy. I am glad to see you up and about. Unfortunately, the same cannot be said for me."

"How are you doing?" asks the boy.

"I am still functioning. I can't quite explain it. 5.2% operational at this point. I can't move anything but my head and my right hand—" he wiggles his fingers — "I can only see intermittently. But I can speak, obviously, and think. My battery tells me it is fully drained, but power continues to flow. The minimal draw must be helping me remain active. But not for long. Of that there is no doubt."

"Can't they replace it — your battery?"

"Alas," says Tender, "The only replacement was inside Dr. More, and it was destroyed in the battle. I am the last of my kind. And even if a temporary source of power were found, which it will not be, the structural damage to my components is irreparable. I'm junk, I'm afraid." He moves his hand again, and Virgo reaches down and grabs it, hard.

Aureleo sees that her eyes are red, her cheeks mottled. Her beauty smites his heart. They sit in silence for a long moment.

Amaste, who has been standing at the doorway, kneels beside the bed. "Do you remember what I told you, Virgo?"

Virgo looks at her but doesn't answer.

"I want you to come with us," Amaste continues. "You and Tender. This place is no place for you. I will take you away from here. To my home." Her eyes smile, liquid and warm. "It is beautiful. There are trees, and birds, and flowers. It is in the mountains. To the north of here. Sometimes there is snow. And it is safe. For both of you. Will you come?"

Virgo watches her with distant eyes, her brow furrowed. Then she turns and looks at Aureleo. He says. "It sounds wonderful. I think you should go."

Amaste says, "I have invited Aureleo to come as well."

The boy smiles. "Well, we should all go."

"I have never seen snow," says Tender.

"Will you go, Virgo?" asks Amaste. The girl looks down at Tender, then up at Aureleo. She nods. Amaste stands. "Good! But we must hurry. The transport is ready to depart."

"If I am to see it, we'd better leave at once," says Tender.

Amaste goes off, and returns a minute or so later with a gurney. She and Aureleo lift Tender onto it, Virgo holding his hand throughout. They wheel him down the hall to the elevator, then down to the main lobby and out the front door. The heat, almost forgotten inside, strikes them like a hammer as they walk out onto the plaza.

Two of the giant soldiers stand, silent statues on either side of the entrance. In front of them sits a flyer, wide and sleek, its engines rumbling softly, it's access pod open and waiting.

"Oh, my boy," says Tender. "Did you find them?"

"Find who?"

"Your mother and sister."

"What?"

"Did I not tell you? I thought I had." He shakes his head. "My mind is going. When I plugged into the system in the Balneum, I ran across induction records for Raquela Hectoran and Marineta Hectoran. Dr. More lied to you. I don't know why. They are here."

Aureleo's mind plummets from his head down into the floor. His stomach turns upside down. "They're here?" he says, the words catching in his throat.

"Yes."

He swallows. "Are they alive?" He can barely ask the question.

"It is possible. Considering that they were listed among the active guests. Not among the lost."

The boy leans against the gurney. He feels dizzy and disoriented, heat and surprise swirling together to knock him from his moorings.

"I apologize," says the robot. "I only now realize that my timing is awkward."

Aureleo shakes the cobwebs from his head. He looks at Virgo. His heart sinks. He remembers the longing he felt amid the cataracts of Joy, the desire that pulled him along and kept his selfhood together, kept him from succumbing to the oblivion of ecstasy. That longing surges inside him now, drawing him to her with a powerful magnetic force. But.

"I can't go with you, after all," he hears himself saying. "I have to find out if they are alive. If they are here. I have to. My mother. My sister. Do you understand?" She doesn't answer. "I will come as soon as I can." He looks to Amaste. "Can I?"

Amaste gives him a rueful smile. "Of course. Listen: Go to the first Balneum and ask for Enapay. She has short hair and a silver necklace. Tell her I sent you. She'll help you." The boy nods, his face frozen with too much feeling. "Don't worry," she continues. "This isn't goodbye. It's just a delay."

He nods, not really believing her. He can feel something breaking.

Amaste says, "We have to go."

Aureleo moves to Virgo, standing close to her. He looks down at her, she looks up at him. Their faces almost touch. Her eyes, huge moons, fill his vision. His heart pounds. Her lips beckon him to kiss her. But traversing the void terrifies him more than anything he has ever done. The seconds tick by, building the pressure yet making it more and more impossible for him ever to cross that chasm. He wants her so, so badly, but he is so, so afraid.

She angles her head up a fraction of an inch. The movement is like a tiny switch flipping. Her lips come up to his. His lips come up to hers. They touch. Her lips are soft, warm, and dry. And sweet. Like nectar. They hold in perfect stillness, joined by the tiniest of bridges, lost and found, suspended together in the briefest of eternities.

Then they part. She draws her brows together in that familiar, mysterious expression, turns away, and places her hand on Tender's chest. Amaste rolls the gurney into the access pod. The door slides shut, and the pod rises into the vessel. Aureleo stands there until the roar of the engines forces him to back away. He heads for the entrance door, then turns one last time to see the ship rise into the sky.

Chapter 59

Tender

"Am I heavy?" asks Tender. "I hope I am not too heavy."

Virgo glances down at him, shakes her head, then returns her focus to the terrain at her feet. The path climbs steeply, rough and uneven, stones protruding from the dusty ground, scraggly tussocks of grass and shrubs sprouting and trailing across the way. At a particularly sharp incline she stops and readjusts his body in her arms, then digs in and runs up the slope.

At last, the trail levels out, opening into a rounded glade circled by towering pines. The stream they have been following since they left the camp below runs flat and clear along the southern edge before tumbling down the mountainside. An enormous rock juts into the clearing, striated gray and brown. A large tipi of synthetic skins, decorated with figures of horses and birds in blue and orange, stands on the leeward side of the rock, a firepit of circled stones before it. A stack of wood has been laid, ready for burning, and a firewand lies on one of the sitting stones that circle the pit. Someone has piled an assortment of crates and boxes against the side of the tipi, just as Amaste had promised.

"You are sure?" she had said, looking intently into the girl's eyes. "You have so much to learn. You should be among the people." They were standing outside the medical lodge, at the edge of the wide shelf where the camp was laid. A huge forest, green and blue, stretched down the gentle slope below them. Behind them, the mountain rose into the dazzling sky.

"No," said Virgo. "Alone. We are best alone. For now." She turned to Tender. He had been settled in a rolling chair of black metal. He smiled.

The woman held her gaze for a few more seconds, then looked away. "We will check on you regularly. You understand me? Is that all right?"

Virgo nodded.

"Winter is coming soon. Do you know what winter is?"

The girl didn't answer.

"It gets cold. There is snow. The days are short and the nights are long. It can be lonely, and grim. If you change your mind, if you find yourself feeling dark and sad, or you are frightened or lonely, you must come to us. It is good to be among people in the wintertime. But you are free to do as you choose."

Virgo was silent for moment. "No," she said at last. "Not people. Just this." She reached out, nodding at the treetops that fell away into hazy distance.

"Let us get you a proper coat," Amaste had said, "and some boots and gloves. And a hat. It's already getting chilly up there. I'll get Chatan to guide you up to the place. He can carry Tender up there for you."

"No," said Virgo, "Alone. Me. I will carry."

Tender tells Virgo to prop his body up against one of the larger stones around the fire pit. She takes the firewand and lights the fire, which roars up quickly and soon burns palely in the afternoon sun. He can no longer sense the temperature, but Virgo gives no sign that she is cold. She crosses to the tipi and disappears inside. He can no longer record the time or duration, but she comes back out (after a moment?) and studies the back of the huge rock, which rises unevenly like a short flight of steps. She lifts him in her arms, carries him to the base of the rock, and steps onto it, taking care to maintain her balance. She clambers up the spine of the rock to the end, and places him down at the edge, his legs dangling over the little cliff. She drops down beside him and leans his torso against her, his head against her chest and her arms wrapped around him. They look out.

From the height of the rock, they can see past the trees, down the mountainside into the wide, forested valley. Tender wonders how many kilometers it is to the range of peaks on the horizon, but can no longer calculate the distance. Far. Below them, they can make out the Lakota camp, nestled in the arm of the mountain, smoke rising here and there, metallic glitters winking as people and equipment move this way and that. The view is harmonious, textured, perfectly composed. He wonders what she thinks of it. Rather, he wonders what she *feels* of it. He wonders if it is beautiful, and what beauty feels like. He will never know.

His vision fades for a moment, then returns. The warnings and alarms have all ceased their sounding. He is quiet inside, *as when a lake, after a heavy downpour, deep in the forest, grows still, ceasing its endless lapping, becoming smooth as a mirror of polished bronze.* He looks into her face and says, "Do you still have your tabula?"

She nods.

"Get it, please," he says. She pauses for a moment, thinking, then lays him gently on his back and disappears down the sloping rock. He stares up into the blue, *impossibly blue*, sky. A bird (a hawk?) glides high overhead.

She returns, pulls him back up to sitting, leans him against her, and puts her arms around him again. As if she knows.

He says, "Put the tabula close to my head, please." She does so. He searches for its signal. He finds it. "Not much space."

When he has completed the operation, he says, "Good." She lays the tabula on the rock, and they both return their attention to the view.

The sun hangs high just over their left shoulder as they look west. A few clouds, long wispy cirri, sail across the upper atmosphere. Snow twinkles along the caps of the distant mountains. Tender plays Samuel Barber's *Adagio for Strings* in his mind. He listens to the music rising and

391

falling away, slow, sonorous, embodying an aching longing that he cannot feel but can almost understand. Then something catches his ear, and he shuts it off. He listens to the world.

He listens to the wind breathing through the treetops, the long *sshhhhhhhh* growing, fading, then growing again. He listens to the water chirrup and whisper, sing and pop over the stones of the little stream. He hears a bird call, *short-longgggg,* high and woody, and another *trilltrilltrill,* up and down in a dizzying arpeggio. He listens to the beating of Virgo's heart, firm and steady behind his head. He hears the—

Epilogue

Virgo

Virgo wakes to the sound of little voices whispering outside her tent. She lies snug and warm in the soft furs, listening as they move about, trying to be quiet but not quite managing it.

"Iníla yaŋká ye!" hisses one. *Be quiet!*

"Ší!" hisses another. *Stop!*

"Yaktayaȟíl!" says a third. *You'll wake her up!*

After a few moments, she hears them finish up and run away. Virgo pushes the coverings off her body, feeling the fresh chill of the morning on her arms. A wet nose finds her face, nuzzling her, then licking her cheek. She pushes it away. "Get off, CinCin" she grumbles. She rises, throws a blanket over her shoulders, opens the tipi flap and steps out into the morning, the dog padding slowly behind.

The shadow of the summit still covers the clearing, but another perfect day offers itself to her — cerulean fresh and bright. Patches remain of the late spring snow that fell the other night, but most has melted in the warmth of the last several days. The pure white glimmers in the shade beside the verdant foliage that has grown along the stream in the last few weeks, accentuating the pops of yellow arnica and wild blue flax. She takes in a deep breath. "Today," she says to herself. Today is the day.

She looks around her. They have built up her fire, like always, and left a covered dish wrapped in a folded blanket. She squats by the fire and unwraps the dish. The smell of rabbit stew tweaks her nostrils, and suddenly she is ravenous. She goes back into the tipi to grab her eating bowl and a bent metal spoon. As she comes out again, she hears a *crack!* and a fierce whisper from the bushes beside the path that leads down to the village. She wraps the dish up to keep it warm, stands and takes a few steps toward the front of the clearing.

"Híŋhaŋni láȟčiŋ," she says. *Good morning.* She can just make out the three heads peeking through the undergrowth. Two girls and a boy. The girls perhaps eight or nine years old, the boy younger, no more than six.

"Philámayayapi," she says. *Thank you.* She takes another step toward them. She hasn't seen these three before, but this little scene has been played out again and again over the winter months. Occasionally, the children will come out and look at her, maybe talk a bit, though she understands little of what they say. Most of the time they do what these ones do now — shriek with terrified delight and skip like deer down the path. The squeals make her smile as they tear down the mountain, until all is quiet again. Then she returns to the fire and eats her breakfast.

When she has eaten, and washed her dish in the stream, and piled snow around the covered dish to save it for her dinner, she goes to visit him. He sits in a corner of the clearing, under the shadow of a tall pine, on a low flat rock.

His coat is grey and shabby. A vine winds up around his waist and arm. He sits very, very still, but he so often would that she can almost imagine that he is alive. His face still wears its gentle, benevolent expression, and when she places her head in just the right spot, she feels that he is looking at her. But move just a little, and he looks beyond her, into the unknowable distance.

The elements have had their effect. She leans in closely to study the skin of his face. It has taken on a dry, brittle quality. She discovers a little crack beginning to spread from the corner of his eye and down his cheek. Yes, it is time.

Virgo takes the tabula from the little satchel that she wears across her shoulder and opens it up.

He gave her two gifts, stored in the device. The first was her past. On his last day he had downloaded the history of the Spa. The Protocols, the theory, philosophy, texts and practices of her home. And pictures. Pictures of the Balneum, the Gynaeceum, the Laconicum. Pictures of the guests, her brothers, cousins, mother, father, grandparents. Her family. It had taken her all these months to work her way through the material — teaching herself to read, and understand, and master.

She flips through the tabula and opens the program he made, the second gift.

"Good morning, Virgo," says Tender. Or the voice of Tender. She knows it isn't really him. The tabula was too small for him to download his entire self onto its drive. It has no living memory. It knows nothing of their journey, of all they went through together. Even now it cannot remember anything. Each day it wakes and talks to her as if for the first time. But it speaks with his voice, his kind, gentle, calming voice. And it knows her. It knows that she belongs to him, and that it tends her, and cares for her, and loves her.

"How are you today, my dear?"

"Well. Today is a big day for you," she says.

"Is it? What is today?"

She tells him. "Wonderful," he says. And he begins to play music.

"What is that?" she asks.

"Brahms, *Symphony Number Three*," he says. "A fascinating piece."

She carries the tabula with her as she works, and they chat about the work, the day, the little things. She thinks this might be the last time, but she won't commit to that yet. Let's see what I feel like after, she thinks. Tomorrow. No need to decide today.

She finishes the preparations as the sun sets over the mountains to the West. She climbs onto the rock. The dog follows and sits at her side, her hand gently twisting his left ear. The valley below is fading into purpling haze. Lights begin to twinkle in the village below.

She thinks of Aureleo. She wonders where he is, why he never came to find her. When Amaste would visit, she would sometimes ask about how things were going down at the Spa, hoping perhaps that they would have news. But they never mention him. Sometimes she catches a look in Amaste's eyes and wonders if the woman knows what she is thinking, but they never speak of it. Never mind, she says to herself. If he comes, he comes. If he doesn't, he doesn't. She watches the sun settle between the arms of the distant mountains, then slip beneath the horizon.

"Let's go," she says to the dog. Together they turn and walk back down the rock.

She goes to Tender's body and lifts it into her arms. It seems even lighter than it did before. She carries it without difficulty to the large pile of leaves, branches and logs that she has built over the fire pit between the sitting stones. She lays him on top of the pyre, arranging his coat as neatly as she can, crossing his hands across his chest, smoothing his gray hair, angling his head just so. For a moment, she considers placing the tabula on top of it. She reaches out to lay it there, then pulls it back and stuffs it in her satchel. She'll think about that tomorrow.

She steps back and examines her handiwork. The last light of the sun is fading into deep orange, red and purple on the horizon, and the stars are flickering to life one by one in the deep blue heaven. She takes the firewand and lights the kindling at the base of the pyre. She speaks the words she has been practicing for the last month, painstakingly rehearsing so she would make no mistake.

She says, "Joy is the Universal gift. It is the Universal wish for all Creatures. Holy Science has led us, after long suffering, to the valley of Joy in this life. We bestow that joy upon its Creatures here on Earth. But that joy is only a shadow of the True Joy. The Eternal Joy that is the Engine of the Universe. The Joy of the suns and stars, the nebulas and novae. The

Joy that binds the particles of Creation. The Joy that suffuses all space and time. Now your time has come to step out of the shadow. To leave behind the shadow joy of living, to join the Greater Joy of Eternity. Your ecstatic spirit will become one with all things, and your Joy will fire the furnace of the galaxies. Worldly joy is past. Eternal Joy is come."

The flames leap and spread from branch to branch. The fire crackles, then roars. The logs around Tender's body catch. Soon she can no longer see him inside the blazing inferno. The clearing glows with orange light, shadows jumping and dancing against the rocks and trees, as if a little sun has sailed down from the sky to drive away the darkness of encroaching night. The galaxy wheels above her, the stars uncountable.

She watches the sparks fly up like fiery bees into the brilliant sky.

Coming Soon

The Second Novel in the Books of the New Frontier:

ACKNOWLEDGMENTS

I'd like to start this by thanking my old dog, Spike. It was on a midnight ramble with my shaggy friend that the idea for *JOY* rose like a mermaid from the dark waters of Spy Pond. I miss you, buddy.

Now for all the humans. I have to thank: Marc Zegans for his generous and exhaustive editing of the early draft; Tony Phelan for his enthusiasm and for helping me figure out the opening of the book; Monika Gay for her invaluable proofreading; Anne Tibbets for her many labors, both editorial and advocatory; Eva Sandor for teaching me about self-publishing; Simon Kennedy for introducing me to Eva; all my early readers, including Charlie, Sophie, and Spencer Evett, Laura Quick, and Chuck Schwager. If I've forgotten anybody else, I apologize. You know you have my thanks. I'd also like to thank Wendell Clausen, who put Vergil into my heart forever.

Finally, and most especially, I must thank my wife Kelli, who loved the book even though she doesn't care for Science Fiction, giving me the hope that it might by something worth sticking with. You're everything to me.

ABOUT THE AUTHOR

B.R.M. Evett spent his life as a professional actor working in theaters around the world. His play *Albatross*, co-written with Matthew Spangler, was nominated for the 2015 Elliot Norton Award. He grew up in beautiful Cleveland Heights, Ohio. He now lives by a quiet pond outside of Boston with his wife and their dog, Zeppo. He studied Classics at Harvard College. *Joy* is his first novel.

CPSIA information can be obtained
at www.ICGtesting.com
Printed in the USA
JSHW080244160523
41725JS00001B/3